Knight in Paper Armor
Red Adept Publishing, LLC
104 Bugenfield Court
Garner, NC 27529
http://RedAdeptPublishing.com/

---

1.   http://StreetlightGraphics.com

To Veronica, whose constant love and energy is the battery that charges my dreams.

"The opposite of love is not hate, it's indifference. The opposite of art is not ugliness, it's indifference. The opposite of faith is not heresy, it's indifference. And the opposite of life is not death, it's indifference. Because of indifference, one dies before one actually dies. To be in the window and watch people being sent to concentration camps or being attacked in the street and do nothing, that's being dead." Elie Wiesel

Part I:

Malkuth

1: Roseanna Peterson

The dark-eyed boy in the photograph looked normal, but he wasn't. Dr. Roseanna Peterson had studied his charts for days, but it still amazed her that such an ordinary-looking child—a third grader with curly black hair, freckled cheeks, and an awkward half smile pointed away from the camera—could hide such an other-worldly secret.

"This one is Billy Jakobek, correct?" she asked Mr. Linus, the ruddy-faced man in the driver's seat.

Linus fiddled with the AC settings. "That's his name, yeah." He loosened his tie. "This'll be the first of these weirdo kids you meet, right?"

Roseanna smiled. "Yes. It's *so* crazy." A giggle escaped her lips, but she muffled it. *Stop it, Roseanna. Act more professional.* "Sorry, sir. I'm too excited for my own good. No one believed in my line of work un-til now. It's wonderful to be here—you know—really doing it."

"Hey, it's cool. Dreams come true at this company." Mr. Linus kept working at his tie. "Mr. Thorne is real impressed with you, Dr. Peterson. Says you're gonna do great work for us."

"Thanks, sir." *Wow, Mr. Thorne said that? About me?*

Linus peered at the photograph in her hand. "Christ," he scoffed. "Forgot how goddamn Jewish that kid looks. Big nose, hair, all of it. Glad they passed that anti-corruption law so kids like him and every-body else in this place can't grow up to be greedy lawyers anymore."

Roseanna slid the photo back into her folder. She didn't respond, partly from shock but also because Linus was the right-hand man of Mr. Thorne, her new boss, the powerful heir of Thorne Century, In-corporated. *Don't blow this.* Wearing heels and a blazer made her self-conscious enough, but she felt especially guilty sitting in the air-conditioned luxury of a brand-new Thorne Hurricane two-seater, listening to such comments while looking out the window at the dozens of struggling Jewish families walking across dust-reddened sidewalks in 109-degree heat. *I guess I'm part of corporate America now. It's for a good cause, at least.* Hebrew symbols marked the apartment numbers of the brick building to Roseanna's right. She couldn't read them, but Linus had parked directly in front of what was, allegedly, the Jakobek family's door.

Linus chuckled uneasily. "Sorry, should be more 'politically correct,' I guess." He made hand symbols. "Truth is, a Jew lawyer bankrupted my parents." He shrugged. "I grew up dirt-poor. Dunno where I'd be today if Mr. Thorne hadn't hired me on."

Roseanna fidgeted. "Oh."

"Glad about the law, though," he said.

"Hmm." Roseanna sighed.

This business trip marked her first visit to Beth Shalom, the tiny ninety-third state of the 179 United States of America. The state had been created a little more than one year before, back in the year 2028, after Congress passed the so-called American Independence from Jewish Corruption bill, inspired by wildly falsified conspiracy theories, which restricted Jews from voting, working in legal, financial, or governmental positions, immigrating from the country, or even earning income. External pressure from Israel had forced the US to create a state where Jews could work freely, and thus, Beth Shalom had been established, forcing the entire American Jewish population—secular, Reform, Conservative, ultra-Orthodox, and all—into areas smaller than most metropolitan cities. From newborn infants to the few remaining Holocaust survivors, they all lived here. Though Beth Shalom was known for producing beautiful artwork, films, and synagogues, the state's economic outlook for the 2030s was looking dire, and the exhausted faces outside Roseanna's window told many stories.

She changed the subject. "I'm probably not the right person to talk to this boy's family. I tend to do better in labs than with people."

"Mr. Thorne believes in you." Linus repositioned his shades. "Huge compliment. Don't let him down."

"Right." Roseanna had barely met Mr. Thorne, but his emails were always surprisingly kind, with many questions about her home life. "Well, wish me luck."

"Sure."

Roseanna stepped out into breathless humidity, gasoline smells, and roaring construction noises. Across the street, bulldozers and cranes flattened houses, poured concrete, and erected the skeleton of Thorne Century's newest pharmaceutical factory. Roseanna coughed out dust, straightened her skirt, and rang the Jakobek family's doorbell.

"I got it!" squeaked a high-pitched voice from the other side.

Roseanna tensed with excitement. *It's happening!* The next hour would define her career. *I just need one patient signed up, and I'm set for life.* The years of mockery she'd endured would be redeemed, thanks to Thorne Century. She would earn enough money to support her family forever. *Don't blow it.*

The door opened, catching on the chain lock. A small face peeked out, far below, with a cute mop of black hair bouncing over an equally cute smile. At first, she thought it was Billy Jakobek, but she reconsidered. *Too young. The files said Billy has a sibling named...*

"I'm Eli!" the boy cried. "Who are you?"

Roseanna kneeled down—at six feet, four inches, she was always conscious of how her height intimidated people—and smiled at the little kid, whose cheerfulness reminded her of her son, Jamie. "Hi, Eli. I'm from Thorne Century, representing a new project that—"

Little Eli's eyes glazed over.

"Listen, are there any grown-ups I could speak with?"

Eli groaned. "Lame. Nobody ever talks to me. Whatever! I'll get my bubbe. Be careful." He lowered his voice. "She doesn't like when I answer the door for strangers!"

The door slammed shut. Inside, the squeaky boy shouted for this bubbe person—*That means grandmother, right?*—followed by grumbling whispers. The door reopened, revealing a tiny elderly woman draped from head to toe in beautiful brightly colored patterns, hunched over a walker. She looked too old to be the boy's grandmother. *Great-grandmother, maybe?* Though her movements were comically rickety, her gaze whipped up at Roseanna with astonishing fierceness.

"Feh." The woman's fingers tightened around her walker handles as if she were getting ready to use it use as a weapon.

Roseanna blushed. "Miss... Jakobek?"

"Tzeitel Shulz," the woman answered in a faded Eastern European accent. "You want something?"

Tzeitel. I remember that name from Billy's file too. So, she is the grandmother. Confusing as this was, Roseanna had a knack for memorizing numbers and quickly realized how the birthdates of Billy's mother and grandmother, and of Billy himself, had been spaced further apart than most families. *Huh. Those dates mean that both the grandmother and mother didn't have children until their forties. Strange dynamic.*

"Uh." Roseanna sputtered. "Sorry for the intrusion. I work for Thorne Century." She proudly flashed her gold employee badge. "Perhaps you've heard of us?"

The old woman snorted. "I have, yes. You are everywhere. Every product! Whenever a restaurant closes, a drugstore, theater, anything, Thorne Century takes over. I don't like it."

"Yes, well..." Roseanna wiped sweat from her brow. She was badly overdressed for the heat. "Do the Jakobeks live here, or—"

"They work very hard." Tzeitel's scarf slipped off her bony shoulder. "You outsiders might read about these meshuga laws we deal with, but the impact? You don't understand. My daughter and her husband work all day, like other families here. They make very little money. Me, I take care of the two boys. I do this, even though I have lived nearly one hundred years. You think I have the energy to schlep these boys around every day? No! But it is how it is."

"I'm sorry." Roseanna cringed at herself. "Ms. Shulz, Thorne Century can help. I'm offering a lucrative opportunity, enough money for your entire family to retire on, I believe."

Tzeitel arched an eyebrow. "You are not an experienced salesperson."

Across the street, the construction equipment buzzed loudly. Roseanna covered her ears. When the noise stopped, she continued. "No, I didn't study marketing. I'm a new researcher hired on for this one-of-a-kind project in a brand-new field of science—"

"Have I heard of it?"

"It's classified."

"Wonderful." Tzeitel groaned, rubbing her head. "Stop talking for a moment. Horrible headache today." She reached into her walker basket and popped an ibuprofen. "Medicine barely helps. You have a name?"

"That's—" She eyed Linus, who was hiding in the Hurricane behind the tinted windows and sunglasses. "Classified too. Officially, I have no name. Company policy."

"Bullshit policy, I say." Tzeitel rewrapped her colorful patterns around her head. "I've been alive for almost a century. Do you see these wrinkles? I'm too old to be tricked by the likes of you."

"Wrinkles?" Roseanna bit her lip. *Remember what your grandmother liked hearing?* "Tzeitel, you don't look a day over thirty-five."

Tzeitel flashed one of the most beautifully genuine grins Roseanna had ever seen. The skin around her eyes crinkled like aluminum foil. "Ah. Raised well, I see. Good for your parents, even if they forgot to give you a name!" She laughed, playing with the wooden beads of her necklace. "Hurry up, more specifics. My legs are splinters. I need to sit. I have many books to read, letters to write. Why are you here?"

Sweat poured down Roseanna's sides. "Billy Jakobek."

"My grandson?" Tzeitel's jaw hardened. Terror lit up her eyes. "He is not for sale. Do not come back here." Tzeitel started to shut the door.

"Wait!" Roseanna stopped the door with her foot. The construction equipment buzzed again, so she waited—staring into Tzeitel's petrified glare—until the noise ceased. "Tzeitel, I know Billy's secret."

Tzeitel's eyes narrowed. "You know." She seemed torn. "You can help him?"

"I think so."

Tzeitel unlatched the door. Roseanna's heart pounded. The old lady stood in the open doorway, wielding a stun gun. "No games, yes? Come inside."

2

The kitchen smelled of fresh-baked bread, and the table was blanketed with bills, notebooks, and medical papers. In lieu of AC, fans spun from the windows. Roseanna waited for Tzeitel to bring her grandson out of his room, sipping on a tea that the old woman had handed her.

The apartment was cramped, no doubt. Chipped paint and broken tiles stood in sharp contrast to a loving array of family photos, glass ornaments, paintings, candles, board games, and stacked novels written in English, Polish, Yiddish, Russian, and Hebrew. A Kabbalah-themed book had been left open on the table, and an intricate iron menorah, stored atop the shelf for the season, caught Roseanna's eye. Something about the apartment's busyness, though, perfectly embodied the warm, affectionate family environment that Roseanna had always wished for in her own life. *They obviously came here from a bigger place and never quite downsized.*

She thumbed through the paper piles before her. The parents, Jake and Ruth Jakobek, were listed as a registered nurse and a paramedic. The family's medical debt looked daunting. Roseanna reached for a charming photo of Tzeitel, accidentally knocking over an unlit candle and spilling a stack of crayon drawings to the floor.

"Hell." She gathered the drawings and flipped through them. Something about the art style creeped her out—it was somehow, bizarrely, both childlike and adult, possessing warped proportions and uneven skill. Lazy stick figure bodies held up hyperdetailed faces. Each drawing depicted a tiny boy with sad black eyes and a rainbow of colors that leaked from his body, touching the other stick figures.

Tzeitel's walker tapped around the corner. Roseanna hid the drawings. "Ah." Tzeitel emerged. "So, the tall mystery woman with the beautiful blue eyes has not left us?"

Roseanna smiled. "Thank you."

"Now, this is my oldest grandson—" Tzeitel looked around her then beckoned down the hall. "Come out, little one."

The boy from the photograph stepped into the light. His scrawny little body was lost in an oversized black T-shirt. Dark curls hung over his freckled face like a mask. He crept up to the table, head bowed, shivering as if the sauna surrounding him were an icebox. Roseanna's motherly instincts made her want to wrap around him like a blanket, but she knew better.

"Hi, Billy," Roseanna said.

The boy's upward gaze—pupils blacker than obsidian—sliced Roseanna like a blade. Her stomach jolted. His timid demeanor had briefly disguised the scarred eyes of an adult war veteran. *A kid shouldn't have those eyes.* Roseanna tried to speak again, but Billy's intense stare carved out her lungs. Her head pounded like a hammer, and electrical tingles ran down her spine. *Oh my god, he's really one of them. They're real. And he has no idea how powerful he is.*

Billy lowered his gaze. The bizarre physical sensations disappeared. She reconsidered. *Or perhaps he knows...*

Roseanna swallowed. "Billy, how are you feeling today?"

The boy touched his forehead and winced. As he did this, the jackhammer slammed into Roseanna's skull again—so fast, so sudden, she almost cried out—then receded. As the fog lifted, Roseanna noticed Tzeitel sneaking herself another ibuprofen from her purse. *I get it. Tzeitel has a headache, and...* Roseanna jotted down notes. *Billy absorbs his grandmother's headache because that's what he does, and he's trying to avoid sending those pain signals to me... but when he looks at me, it happens.* She repressed a smile. *This is so crazy!*

"Your head hurts, Billy?" Roseanna put her pen down.

Billy looked at his bubbe for support. Tzeitel protectively hovered over him. It was clear, instantly, that the old woman would throw herself over a bomb for that boy.

"Billy does not talk," Tzeitel said. "Sorry."

"I see." Roseanna bit the end of her pen. "Never?"

"Never."

"Got it." She noted this. "Does he ever touch anyone? Holding hands, hugging, anything?"

"He does not care for such things." She winked at her grandson, and he stared at her with a raw, loving expression that melted Roseanna's heart. Tzeitel rubbed her sore head. "Touching people, it... makes him hurt badly. Skin contact is the worst. So I've never hugged him, not even when he was a baby. It is what it is."

Roseanna sipped her lukewarm tea. *And maybe you have secrets inside your mind that you don't want him to unlock by touching you. Hmm.* "So," Roseanna said, "according to my superiors, young Billy came to the attention of Thorne Century due to his long medical history." She opened her folder and riffled through. "Dozens of child therapists, doctors, prescriptions, treatments... a wide range of disease symptoms and ailments as well as wild mood swings but no evidence of any physical illness or precise mental disorder. The word *psychosomatic* is bleeding from these papers. I don't buy it." Roseanna leaned forward. "I think it all fits a certain pattern."

"The doctors don't understand." Tzeitel bit her lip, paused, then spoke again. "Neither do his parents, though I love them. No. They merely say that he imagines things. Hallucinations, they claim." She glanced at her frail grandson still shivering in the humidity. "I disagree. He often gets sick, but the sickness comes not from him."

"Can you explain?" *I think she gets it.*

"As a baby, he constantly changed personalities, like this"—Tzeitel snapped her fingers—"depending on who held him. Smiling or shrieking, it flipped constantly, and whenever he cried, all of us cried with him for no reason. Not like a normal baby. His brother was not like this either."

"I see."

"It was not so extreme when he got older. But when others are sick..." She knotted her fingers. "He goes to them, touches the place it hurts, and the pain goes away. It goes inside him, instead, until it fades. Very strange." She frowned. "When people are sad? He walks into a room, makes himself smile—poof, no one is sad anymore, except he becomes sad. Sometimes, I catch him sneaking out across town to help people who are troubled." She eyed him. "I don't like it when he does that, though it is very nice of him."

"He senses things?"

"Doctor, my grandson has a gift. Yes, he senses things. He feels things. He does things to people... things that, perhaps, the world is not ready for."

Despite the heat, Roseanna felt chills. "I believe you." She redirected her attention to the relieved-looking Billy. "Is it okay if I ask you some questions, dear? You can just nod or shake your head. I know I'm some weird crazy lady in your house, but I'd appreciate it."

The boy smiled. Roseanna felt like she'd won the lottery.

"So, Billy..." She checked her notes. "When people experience emotions around you, do you feel like you... shall we say, absorb these feelings?"

Billy nodded.

"Can you change how they feel?"

His cheeks went red, but again, he nodded.

"Do you read thoughts?" she asked. When the boy looked confused, Roseanna realized her terminology was overly simplistic. *People don't always think in words.* "Let me rephrase. If you try hard enough, can you tell what's going on in a person's mind? For example, can you see another person's favorite memories play out in your head, like a movie...?"

Slowly, with pinched lips, he nodded.

Roseanna finished her tea. "Billy, I saw some unusual drawings on the table." She removed the crayon portraits from their hiding place. "Are these yours?"

Billy's eyes widened, and Roseanna's vision blurred. Pressure squeezed her forehead. *Stay calm.* She breathed in, breathed out, and when she came to, she realized that Tzeitel had been talking to her somewhere in the fog.

"—are not something he likes doing," Tzeitel finished with a stern expression. "He only draws as a favor to me, to show me what he sees deep inside, since he does not speak."

Roseanna held up the drawings. "Mind if I look?"

In a feeble manner, Billy gestured for her to go ahead. Tzeitel seemed less accepting, but Roseanna didn't wait. She quickly leafed through, and—despite the bizarre art style—she was delighted to see that each crayon portrait depicted the sad-eyed boy helping others with the rainbow colors that came from his hands. In one picture, it was a fireman, in another, a group of homeless people. A third showed his little brother. Then she noticed a black-smudged human figure darkening the corner of the page, with long black claws for fingers.

Her stomach twisted. *Something about that figure...* She flipped through the drawings again, finding this jagged black-inked man with his awful talons hidden in the background of every page. The shadow man had mean, slanted eyes shaded with blue crayon but no other features. He was tall and thin. Sometimes he hid in windows, sometimes behind trees, but he always—always—pointed his sinister blue gaze at the colorful boy. In certain drawings, he held a bleeding red object, symbolized by dripping red crayon marks. Upon reaching the final page, Roseanna shuddered. Here, the boy of many colors lay curled up in a ball, teardrops running down his cheeks. His eyes were blue—just like the dark man's—and the evil figure stood over his body, one arm extended unnaturally far down, pushing the bleeding red object toward the boy's open mouth.

"Billy," Roseanna said as the crayoned-blue eyes glared at her, "who is this man?" She handed the paper to the boy. He shivered, looked away, and refused to take it. "Is he someone you know?"

Tears filled Billy's eyes. He frenetically shook his head. Roseanna noticed her own eyes welling up as she imagined her son, Jamie, sitting in Billy's place.

She shoved the drawings back under the other papers. "Sorry, kiddo."

Billy wiped away his tears.

"Getting back to business..." She shut her notebook. "I think this confirms the speculations of Thorne Century's prior research. Billy has a unique condition, and"—she put on her best professional smile—"we'd like to study him in our lab so we can use his abilities to create the future of medicine. I'll need to talk to his parents first and have them sign the contract, but don't worry—he'll be totally safe. Mr. Thorne pays handsomely, and Billy would have guaranteed income for life, thanks to a special contract provision. We would just need to keep him in our lab for at least six months out of the year, with occasional periods of isolation, through adolescence, until..." She stopped.

Tzeitel was pointing the stun gun at her.

"Tzeitel?"

"You want to put him in a lab." The old woman's voice lowered. "Never."

"It's not like that." *Christ, never send a scientist to do marketing.* "Listen, I'm not some crazy doctor, and I know it's a big corporation, but we can do a lot of good for the world by using Billy's blood and tissue samples, his energy output—"

"You want to sell pieces of him for profit after you cut him open," Tzeitel growled.

Billy stumbled from his chair. He looked fearfully between the two women. Eli crept into the room, sneaking behind his brother, and the two boys watched from a distance.

Roseanna raised her hands into the air. "I'm sorry this came off the wrong way. No harm will befall your grandson. Just because he's different—"

"I was not born yesterday. I saw what happens!" Tears flashed in Tzeitel's eyes as she jutted the stun gun toward Roseanna like a dagger. "Children in labs. Cages. Camps. Just for being different. I know what happens to those who are different when they have independence taken away!" Tzeitel rolled up her sleeve, revealing an unmistakable string of numbers tattooed on her forearm.

Roseanna gasped. "Sorry, Tzeitel, I didn't realize—"

"You didn't *think*. Because you're not the one who has been different!" Tzeitel roared. "This country, when I came here? It was supposed to be something special. What happened over there"—Tzeitel waved the stun gun behind her then back at Roseanna—"was not supposed to come here. But I was always afraid. While the others married and had children as soon as they could to replenish the millions lost, I tried not to, for so many years, because I was afraid that I would bring an innocent baby into this world, and they would only get hurt by people like you. And now it's the same story again and again. I can't change it, but I can ensure that as long as I live, my Billy will never get put in a lab. He will never be held captive or have to go... through... what... whaa..."

Tzeitel stumbled backward. She looked around in a daze. "Why are there two of you?" The old woman blinked. "Not... won't... meshh..." The old woman collapsed to the floor. Her hip cracked so loudly that Roseanna fell back.

Oh no. Roseanna rushed to cradle Tzeitel's fallen body.

Tzeitel's eyes rolled back. One half of her face slumped downward. "Spllthh..." Drool ran down her chin.

As Roseanna held Tzeitel, Billy rushed forward and reached for the broken hip.

"Don't!" Roseanna threw her hand up in a stop sign.

The little boy fell back in terror. The younger brother, Eli, appeared around the corner.

"She needs medical attention, not pain relief. Call 911!"

3: Billy Jakobek

The hospital ICU was chaotic. Call bells rang. Nurses rushed between rooms. Fluorescent lights cast a horrible glow upon the linoleum floor. Equipment beeped. Patients screamed. Billy quivered in the hallway, his sweaty back glued to Bubbe's door, trying not to burst into tears.

People were everywhere, but Billy was alone in the fog. Every patient in every room pumped cold, toxic energy into his veins. *They all hurt. I hurt. I don't wanna hurt.* Nausea swirled through him. His skin dampened and dried. Each new patient sent different symptoms tingling through him—physical and emotional. Glossy eyes. Swampy stomach. Itching. Murky vision. He sensed dying parents, sick husbands and wives, repressed grudges, car accidents, heart attacks. Whenever the symptoms subsided, he remembered why he was there—and a lightning bolt struck his heart.

Please don't die, Bubbe. He fought back tears. *I need you. You're the only one who gets me.*

In the room behind him, his parents privately discussed her condition with the doctor. Up ahead, Eli kept bouncing up to the nursing station with new questions. To Billy, these voices were a mumbled daze compared to the sharp panic gripping him like a blood-pressure cuff.

"Hey, bro." Eli kicked him. "You okay?"

Billy shook himself from the nightmare. He blinked. Blurry shapes regained firm outlines. Nurses' chatting hummed into his ears. Focusing on the spark of his little brother's light, he gave Eli a forced nod. *I'm fine.*

Eli didn't buy it. "You're sick, dude." Then he leaned over to Billy conspiratorially and whispered, "It's your powers again, huh?"

Billy couldn't help but smile. *Powers, right.* That was what Eli always called the weird sensations Billy felt. Most people thought he was either a delusional kid or an alien freak, but Eli considered his big brother a superhero. *Yeah, I wish.* Billy rubbed his aching belly. *They'd call me the Horrible Hurt-Man, who makes people happier by sucking away everything that hurts them, like some lame human sponge.*

"Just go into the room." Eli excitedly tapped Bubbe's glass door. "Touch her brain, dude, and heal it back to normal! She'll be all good again. That's what you do, right?"

Billy shook his head. *Doesn't work that way.* Though the little electrical sparks of hope and admiration that Eli was unconsciously sending into Billy's body felt nice, Billy knew that his sponge of a body couldn't heal physical wounds—just feelings and thoughts. *Worst powers ever.* On top of that, Bubbe had, many times, made him promise never to touch her. She'd said it was for his own good, and she was a smart lady, so Billy listened. Tears welled up again. *Please don't die.*

The glass door slid open. Dad's eyes crinkled at the fluorescent lights. "Hmm." He scratched his beard. "Hey, boys. It doesn't look good."

Bubbe's doctor walked to the next room, and Mom poked her head out the door. Her reddened gaze shot right toward Billy. "Hey." Her dark hair was frizzed out. Black streaks ran down her cheeks. "Can you guys come in here?"

The two boys walked in slowly, their heads hung low. Eli glanced at Billy for support. Billy looked back, pushing out confidence from somewhere deep inside and sending that electricity into his little brother. They entered the death-scented room, where the oxygen machine blared its harsh chorus. The heart rate monitors beeped steadily, but Billy already felt Bubbe's heart beating in his chest. *Boom... boom... boom.* The shriveled-up old woman in the bed stared blankly at the ceiling, body unmoving, mouth gaping, lips dry and flaky. She looked dead, not asleep.

"Take a seat," Mom said, and they did so.

Mom started talking, but to Billy, her words fogged out into nothingness. He hated the pale shells that had replaced Bubbe's eyes. They just stared upward, occasionally blinking but otherwise vacuous. *Bubbe, please come back. Please, please.* Her yellowed scalp was stretched so tight that veins popped out. The plastic plugs in her nostrils reminded Billy of a cyborg. *She's not asleep. She's not resting. She's just... trapped.*

"Billy," Dad said. "Were you listening?"

Billy shook his head. *I don't wanna hear how bad things are.* Eli sobbed beside him, having listened.

"Okay." Dad crouched before them. Billy had never felt such sadness in him. "She's very sick, son. It's called a hemorrhagic stroke. The ambulance took too long to arrive, and it caused severe brain damage. Coma. Her vitals are fading. The doctor says she might've had ministrokes in the weeks before, and apparently, we were working too much this month to even notice that... yeah." He pinched his eyes closed. "Not good."

Dad's compassion radiated outward. *He wants to hug me. It makes him so sad that he can't.* Billy craved his father's warm embrace, but the last time his parents had touched him, he'd blacked out—apparently, he'd screamed and cried so uncontrollably that they'd brought him to the emergency room—so they hadn't tried again since.

Mom crouched beside Dad, and since the two couldn't hold Billy, they clutched each other.

"Your bubbe is dying, Billy," Mom said, and her grief hit him like an espresso shot.

He shook his head. *No. Don't say that.*

"She's got a few days at most. We're already making arrangements for shiva. I know this is scary, but—" Mom reached for Billy's hand on instinct then recoiled.

Now we're both even sadder.

"Sorry, I... just know that we're here for you. We love you. I know how close you are to her, so spend as much time as you can."

Tears formed rivers down Billy's cheeks. *She's not allowed to die.* He felt helpless. Lost. Isolated and unable to touch anyone.

Eli lunged into Mom's arms, still crying, and Dad stood up. "We're going to run home and grab some things," Dad said, "to spend the night here. Your mother thought you might prefer staying here while we're gone to—"

"Spend time," Mom said.

"Yes," Dad said. "We'll be a couple of hours, at most. If you need any help, you can ask the nurses. Do you want to stay here?"

Billy nodded glumly. *Mom's right, as usual.*

Dad dug into his pocket, and he handed Billy his battered old cellphone. "If you need to reach us, use this. Feel free to listen to the music on there too. It's got some good old eighties tunes." He winked, smiled, and kissed Billy's forehead.

Dad and Mom stopped by Bubbe's bed, and each took one of the old woman's hands. Together, they whispered a *mi shebeirach* for healing, closed their eyes for a moment, then left the room.

Eli raced out behind them—then he ducked back in, met Billy's gaze, and mouthed, "Powers?" before racing off again, closing the door behind him.

The heart rate monitor beeped. The clock ticked. Billy was alone with his grandmother, staring at her shell eyes. *I have to do something.* Once his family's footsteps were far enough away, he approached her bed. *I should help her.* He pondered breaking her one big rule. *Hey, well, she can't tell me not to anymore...* He immediately felt guilty.

She blinked, but she did not see him. *She never knew this would happen.* He stiffened. *I have to help you, Bubbe.*

He unrolled the blanket. Her pale arm spilled out, revealing the tattooed string of digits that she never talked about. Billy had figured out, long ago, that the tattoo contained her darkest secrets, having something to do with the evil monsters she and the other grown-ups called "Not-Sees," which they always talked about late at night, in hushed whispers, after he and Eli had gone to bed. Billy took a deep breath. *I'm coming to help you.* He touched the tattoo.

His arm went numb, as if he'd touched a live wire. Black spots burned his vision. Darkness swallowed the fluorescent light. The oxygen machine was drowned out by a crackle that grew louder, louder, and—

The dark figure rose over the bed. Its shadowy, human-shaped body writhed with his grandmother's heartbeat, and its claws pinned her down. The dark figure's insides were empty, blacker than black—like a cutout in the fabric of the universe, revealing desolate nothingness outside the reality he knew—and its fiery blue eyes burned like the sun, gazing upon Billy with something between cold calculation and ravishing hunger. Billy screamed, but no sound emerged, and the dark figure's smoky tendrils rushed down his throat.

He gagged. The crackling amplified. Billy seized Bubbe's hand, squeezing her for dear life. Her hand disappeared. He disappeared. Red-hot pain coursed through his lips before they vanished as well. Everything faded into colorless murk.

And then Billy was somewhere else.

4

Billy is somewhere else. Somewhere cold.

It feels like a dream, but it's not. Everything is hazy. His body is so weak and hungry that it hurts. His bones—he's never felt his bones before, not like this—ache as if they are ice-laden twigs. His skin is dry. Itchy. The wooden floor rumbles. Someone coughs. A dim light pierces the darkness, and Billy sees that he is inside a train car filled with hundreds of people crammed so tightly together that no one can move. It smells so awful that he nearly vomits. Some people have vomited already. Others sleep on the floor—no, not sleeping, they are corpses, dead for weeks—and the train just rumbles down the track. No food. No water. No bathroom. Billy can't scream, he finds, because his lips are sewn together with a metal thread.

Everything flashes white. The rumbling stops. "I told you never to come here," says the Eastern European–accented voice of a young girl.

Then he is somewhere else again.

The whiteness fades into a frosted gray landscape of dark hills and mist. His bare feet stick to icy rocks. The young girl holds his hand. She's so bony and bruised that it hurts him to even look at her. Broken nose. Chapped lips. Cheeks so gaunt that the imprint of her teeth poke through the skin. Her head is shaved. She wears giant moldy clothes that hang from her tiny form like striped blankets.

"It's me," the girl says in a creaky old voice.

Billy is so scared that he tries to pull away. He can't. His hand is sewed to her hand with the same horrible metal thread that stitches his lips. He looks into the girl's eyes, which are tiny white sparks in cavernous black holes, and realizes who she is.

"Yes, little one," says the young girl, who is his grandmother. "I warned you so many times. All those years. And yet here you are."

Billy ashamedly lowers his gaze to the ground.

"It is okay." She lifts his chin with her free hand. "You did what was right. You tried to help me. I wanted to protect you, but perhaps you had to come here someday."

Billy rushes forward and hugs her the way he's always wanted to in real life. She hugs him back, finally, and it feels so good, so right, so safe. When she pulls back, though, her expression is weary and sad.

"We don't have much time," she whispers. "A darkness is coming, and I feel it now like I never did before. It craves the light inside you." She looks fearfully over the horizon at plumes of black smoke. "This light?" She taps his chest. "I recognize it, for my mother had the same gift back in the old village. Perhaps you inherited it from her. Come, we must walk quickly, for everything changes every ten seconds. The only escape from here is through the Shadow Place... the very place I wanted to hide from you all these years."

Somewhere in the mist, parades of angry voices holler in a foreign language. Bubbe yanks Billy across the rocky earth by their stitched hands. The voices become men in uniforms following them with murderous glares.

"Listen, little one. When the evil people came to my village"—Bubbe gestures behind her—"my mother committed suicide because the gift gave her too much pain. She felt the suffering that was coming, and it was too much for her. I never met anyone with the same gift, all these years, until you were born. I was afraid that the darkness in my past might bring you to the Shadow Place. Now I see that I was a fool."

Billy shakes his head. He doesn't understand.

"I see now there is no hiding from the Shadow Place." Bubbe pulls him forward faster and faster. "But if you see it now, perhaps you can fight back when it comes for you. Don't slow down!"

She tugs Billy harder, and he has no idea what she is saying, what happened in her past, or what this Shadow Place is, much less who the evil people are. *Not-Sees?* The landscape shifts. Barbed wire fences sprout from the ground and reach upward like claws digging their way out of hell. Gunshots crack the air. Foreign voices shout. Small, dirty houses appear. Hundreds of people with shaved heads—all of them as thin as Bubbe, all wearing moldy striped garments and mismatched shoes—begin digging holes in the ground at the orders of the evil men.

The innocent people's pale hands bleed into the crusted earth. They toil beneath an increasingly dark sky as a colossal factory pumps flesh-smelling smoke—so black, so thick—up, up, up into the air. Bubbe nods her bruised chin toward a fresh plume of smoke. "That is my father in there. My aunt. My cousins..." She has tears in her eyes. "This is where I come from, little one."

Billy cries with her. He gets it now. He wishes he didn't. Snow falls from the sky, but it is not truly snow or rain but ashes of the family members he will never know. Gunshots ring through the air. Blood rains from the clouds. The sky turns red. Billy fearfully glances back at the fences, looking for answers, but the fences are gone, replaced by a cloud of black smoke. It twists and churns into the outline of the dark figure. Flaming blue eyes erupt on its shadowy face.

Bubbe tears Billy away. "Don't stare at it that way." Her voice is shaky. "Walk faster. Don't force me to schlep you through this entire thing!"

Bubbe drags Billy along like a dog on a leash, cutting up his unshod soles. The dark figure, immersed in the smoke, closes in on them. Blackness swallows the factory, the ground, the people. The crackling noise bursts through the ground, tearing everything to pieces, shredding Billy's eardrums.

Bubbe looks back. Ashy flecks of skin peel off her face, revealing patches of bone underneath. "My mother saw that same terrible dybbuk you see!" she yells over the noise. "She wrote in her journals. I read this years ago. She said that human evil, everywhere it was... that a dark figure stood behind it... like a man, but not a man. She called this thing the Shape!"

The sky is still bloodred. A cackling screech bursts from the clouds, burning with the lightning. The Shape chews through the ground, killing all plants and life, burning it into volcanic charcoal.

Bubbe turns to face Billy. "When I saw it in your drawings, I was too afraid to tell you that I recognized it. I don't want you to have an ugly life, little one. But here, between life and death, I sense that it has been coming for you... biding its time, waiting for a time when I can't protect you. You must get out of here, Billy. Go through the Shadow Place. See what is coming for you, then leave quickly!"

Billy frenetically shakes his head, trying to tell Bubbe no, no, no, he doesn't want to see this evil thing or where it comes from, but it's too late. The darkness surrounds them. Billy falls into the nothingness, disappearing...

He is nothing.

He is...

The darkness swirls away. He walks dazedly through a blighted landscape beneath a bloodied sky. Bubbe's voice echoes from between the ground's cracks. "You are in the Shadow Place. Look, see, but do not stay."

The ground thumps like a heavy heartbeat. Billy approaches more barbed wire fences. Beyond them, he sees a bigger factory. Colossal machinery pounds away, creating the Shadow Place's rhythm, reverberating with his own pulse. *Boom, boom, boom.* The machinery has pipes and pistons but is also built of muscles, organs, living parts that are sewn together with the same metal thread as his lips.

Billy closes his eyes in horror. His heart pounds faster. So does the machinery. *Boom-boom-boom-boom.*

When he opens his eyes, he sees a different version of himself—an older version—on the other side of the fence. The older Billy is surrounded by hundreds of people. They are cheering for him, shouting his name. He looks back at his younger self, winks, and goes into the factory. In moments, an explosion of flames erupts from the doors and windows. Smoke billows out. All the people are ripped to shreds, becoming skeletons, and collapse into bony heaps on the ground.

Billy screams through his threaded mouth before he is whisked away in a fog of darkness. When the smoke clears, he stumbles back into the desert. The moving smoke snakes upward—carrying the electricity of his fears, his own horrified face highlighted inside it—and feeds these fears into the clouds. The clouds flash with lightning, showing the silhouette of monstrous wormlike creatures crawling inside them, with mouths full of circular teeth.

"My mother's journals called them the Feeders," Bubbe's voice says from the ground. "Humanity feeds them, but they are weak, dependent upon the Shape... don't stay in the Shadow Place, Billy. Leave soon."

Billy doesn't know how to leave. He weaves away from the smoke, gagging on the taste of flesh. He turns around. It's too late. The Shape looms before him.

"Get out of the Shadow Place now!" Bubbe cries.

The dark figure towers over Billy's head, its incandescent-blue eyes burning through the shadows. Its claws writhe like snakes. Billy can feel no love inside it. No life. No passion. Nothing but hunger.

Billy falls back, and the Shape catches him in its tendrils of smoke. It drags him forward and rips its own chest open to reveal a hot red beating heart that drips blood. The Shape takes the heart out and holds it before Billy's mouth. It smells of raw, spoiled meat. Billy gags. The thread unravels from his lips. He dares to return the monster's sapphire glare, and the blue light overwhelms him. He sees nothing, feels nothing, but hears the Shape's heart beating louder and louder.

In the darkness, the Feeders squeal, "The Shape! The Shape! The Shape!"

"This is the way, little one!" Somewhere in the shadows, Bubbe's hand seizes Billy's and rips him away from the blue lights, away from the Shadow Place, back into the colors, back into...

5

Billy gasped for air. He stood in his grandmother's hospital room, shuddering as if he'd stepped into a freezer. The oxygen machine rumbled. Nurses gossiped outside the door. His lips weren't sewn together anymore. He closed his eyes, counted to five, and re-opened them. Everything was normal. *I'm here. Oh god, I'm alive...*

Bubbe's fingers were locked around his hand so tightly that a puddle of sweat had formed between their palms. She couldn't see, couldn't move—but still, her fingers clung to him. Billy looked into her sightless eyes. His little heart shuddered. *Are you in there? Are you... in the Shadow Place?*

He steeled himself. *She needs me.* He squeezed her hand. *Okay, Bubbe, let me take whatever is hurting inside you.* He closed his eyes—slowly, out of fear that he might see the Shadow Place—and in the darkness, he located her deepest memories, happy thoughts of family, of joy, of all the times she'd been there for him, and of how much he cherished her for it. *If you're going to die, let me help you die in peace. I'll show you how much I love you. Please.* His fingers tingled. His skin became gooseflesh. His lungs dried up into sandpaper, and his chest compressed as if he were wearing an iron vest that tightened with every breath. *Feel better, Bubbe. I love you.*

Bubbe's heart rate slowed. Billy swallowed the bile in his throat, squeezed her hand, and—as her eyes regained life, if only for a mo-ment—grinned alongside the baby version of himself that still exist-ed in her dreams. *I'm here.* He choked back tears. *I'll never let you go.* The old woman's mouth stretched into a pained smile. Her heart pulsed into Billy's palm, fading and becoming softer.

Her hand went limp. Billy held on as the last burst of oxygen expelled itself from her lungs. The little boy placed his chest to hers, letting the tears run freely, and Tzeitel Shulz died peacefully in his arms.

6: Natalia Gonzalez

A thousand miles away, in the sixty-first US state of New Puebla, a nine-year-old girl named Natalia Gonzalez Rodriguez went to bed with a smile on her face. *So many good things happened today!* Not only had her third-grade teacher proudly announced that she had the highest grades in class, but her big crush, Kyle Lopes, had smiled at her, she'd done great at soccer practice, and Mamá had made *rellenitos de plátano* for dessert as well. It was such a good day that even her baby brothers, Juan and Carlos, hadn't managed to irritate her too much. The next day was Friday, so she expected to sleep in.

The dream ended when, in the middle of the night, Natalia's mother frantically shook her legs. "Wake up, baby. C'mon, get up!"

Natalia jolted upright, straightening her X-Men pajamas. "What?" She rubbed her eyes. The sky was still dark outside the window. The lights were out. Across the room, the baby boys were still asleep in the crib. *This is so weird.* "Why are you doing this, Mamá?" Natalia frowned. "It's nighttime."

"We have to go." A car drove by, headlights blasting through the window, and terror streaked across Mamá's face. In that brief flash of light, Natalia saw tears in her mother's eyes. "Right now," Mamá whispered.

Natalia leaned forward. "What about Papá? He's still at work." Papá always did overnight shifts. Natalia's favorite parts of the mornings, before school, was when he came home from work, swung her in a big circle, and said how much he loved her.

Mamá looked down, saying nothing.

"Papá's not home yet," Natalia insisted. "We need to wait for—"

Mamá squeezed Natalia's leg so hard that it hurt. "We need to *go*, baby. Get all your favorite things packed, and just—listen, go. Go to the car. Go!"

Natalia knew that when Mamá became this serious, she could get mean, so as soon as her mother moved to wake up the baby twins, Natalia hurried. She packed her favorite clothes and keepsakes into her torn-up little backpack. She didn't have much, so it didn't take long, and the only possession she truly cared about was her sketchbook. Drawing made her happier than anything else—except maybe Papá's hugs—and while the sketchbook didn't fit into her pack, it tucked in nicely beneath her arm.

Natalia, still wearing pajamas, hoisted her backpack over her shoulder and went outside. The car was already running. Her grandmother, a strong, proud woman with broad shoulders and big hands, waited by the car. Her long white hair was tied back in a hasty ponytail. She carefully scanned the horizon, as if expecting to see zombies or aliens.

"Abuelita?" Natalia leaned against her grandmother's leg. "What's going on? Where is Papá?"

Abuelita kissed her granddaughter's head then returned to scouting. "*Hablaremos después,*" she muttered.

Mamá burst through the front door, carrying one howling twin under each arm. She and Abuelita quickly strapped them into their car seats.

Natalia looked back at their little home, the apartment she'd always lived in, wishing she hadn't rushed out so fast. *What if I never see it again? I should draw a picture while they're packing up so I remember what it looks like.*

"Get in," Abuelita said.

Natalia climbed into the car. Mamá jumped into the driver's seat. Sweat ran down the back of her neck, and when Natalia caught her mother's eye in the rearview mirror, she noticed dark circles. Mamá put her foot to the gas, and the car rushed up the hill, out of the parking lot, and onto the highway.

"Wait!" Natalia jumped up, shouting over the crying babies. "We need to wait for Papá! If we go somewhere without him, he won't find us, and—"

"Your papá cannot come." Abuelita's voice cracked.

Mamá shot Abuelita a glance. She looked back at Natalia. "Natalia, baby, I promise we'll explain later. Maybe Papá can follow us later at some point, if things work out, but right now we need to—"

"Some point?" Natalia shrieked, lunging for the front seat. "We need to stop the car!"

Abuelita softly but firmly held Natalia down in the back seat. "*Escúchame.* Your papá cannot come."

Abuelita's fixed, absolute voice settled the panic in Natalia's mind—if not the sadness—and she sank back into her seat. Natalia's eyes welled up. She pressed the sketchbook against her chest like a shield. *Papá is my real shield. He's my...* She sniffled. "What's happening?"

"We're going to a new place," Abuelita said. "Finding new work with a bigger company. Much nicer than here. Safer. When you get there, you just need to remember one thing." She turned around and held Natalia's gaze. "Listen."

"I'm listening." Natalia sniffled again.

"If anyone asks, you tell them our family is originally from Mexico. You tell them your great-grandparents came here many years ago. You hear me?"

"But, Abuelita, that's not true. We're Guatemalan." Natalia pouted. "And you—"

"Not anymore." Mamá sighed. "Just do as we say, baby. Trust us on this. It will go better in this new place if we say Mexican instead of Guatemalan and if we say we have been here for generations. You'll understand when you're older."

Orange light cracked the night sky. The car rolled up a steep bridge. Natalia stared longingly out the back window as the hot skyline of her hometown disappeared behind them like a mirage. *Is Papá still back there?* She clung to Mamá's statement of him maybe coming later. The more she considered it, the faker this sounded—like a pretty little grown-up lie—but she tried not to think that way.

Please come, Papá. Natalia pressed her tiny fingers into the back of her sketchbook. "So where is this stupid new place, anyway?"

"Way up north," Mamá said. "It's a little town called Heaven's Hole."

"Cool." Natalia brushed the tears from her eyes. "Sounds like a dump."

Part II:

Yesod

7: Boy

The teenage boy had a name, but when the bad people put him in the dark tank, he never remembered it. He couldn't remember where he'd come from or what had led him there. All he knew was that whoever he was, *whatever* he was, he was sick and in the tank, and he was supposed to sleep.

Sleeping wasn't easy. For days and days, the nameless boy lay on his back, submerged in warm, viscous fluid. Needles plugged his veins. Liquid bubbled in his ears. His teeth bit down on a regulator shooting dry, mechanical air into his lungs. Sometimes, he remembered where he was, and panic seized him. He would fight against the restraints on his ankles and wrists. Then a needle would plunge into his neck, and the darkness would return.

Time moved in waves. Questions bobbed up and down like buoys—*Who am I? Why am I here?*—and floated away. Sometimes, when he slept deeply enough, nightmares sliced through the darkness—a dark figure with glowing blue eyes, trying to feed him its heart. Bullets. Fires. War-torn landscapes. Always, either at the end or the beginning of his nightmare, a factory exploded, shooting out plumes of smoke and fire, death and destruction—and melting the flesh off hundreds of innocent people. He was always the cause of it. *I'm the one*, he would think. *I am the new world.* He would push this thought away. It horrified him. But it always came back.

A blue light blinked over his eyes. The liquid in the tank rustled. *Oh god.* He turned his head, avoiding the light. *They're waking me up again.*

The blue bulb continued blinking. *Go away.* He hated that light. It reminded him of the incandescent eyes of the dark figure. It flickered faster and faster, casting a bluish glow on his plastic face mask. *Go away!* He kicked against his straps. Muffled voices taunted him outside the tank. Electrical pulses tingled his skin. He thrashed his head. *Get me out!* He hyperventilated into his regulator, blasting bubbles everywhere.

The lid of his metal coffin snapped open. Fluorescent tubes blasted his corneas. Liquid spilled off the sides of the tank.

A shadow stood over him. *No! Not...* He blinked, and the shadow brightened into an oddly familiar Caucasian woman with a white-speckled brown ponytail, a lab coat, and cheekbones resembling cut diamonds. *I know her... from somewhere...* Her small round lips spoke, but her sounds were indecipherable. The boy shook his head. *I don't understand you.* The woman's tiny eyes—like sky-blue pins fastening the heavy bags under her eyes to her cheeks—squinted, and she spoke in weird sounds again.

Fluid gurgled into the tank's drain. Goose bumps covered the boy's skin. *So, so, so cold.* The woman unplugged something behind his head, and queasy warmth emanated from her, like she was a broken space heater. The boy shifted away, popping his joints. The woman stretched on rubber gloves.

This strange woman won't touch... my skin? Why? Wait, yes, because I'm sick, contagious. She removed his needles, and he winced at each little prick. *Why is she torturing me?* Another prick. *Ouch! C'mon, memory. Please come back.*

The woman handed a row of rubber bags filled with dark-red liquid to someone behind her—*Hey, that's my blood!*—then changed into new gloves and removed the boy's mask and regulator. He spat water. *Yuck.*

She made confusing noises again. He shook his head, not comprehending.

Trying again, she slowly enunciated every word. "Hey, Billy." She flashed a wounded smile. "Time to get ready for school."

8: Billy

It took thirty minutes before Billy gained the strength to rise from the tank, dry off, and stumble over to the cushy twin-size bed across the room. His body felt waterlogged. His brain was muddy, and his skull seemed heavy enough to snap his neck. When he stretched, a violent shudder overcame him. *So damn cold.* He perched on the bed like an owl and wrapped the towel around his shoulders.

He focused inward as pieces of his memory snapped back into place. *She said my name was Billy... so that's cool.* He rolled this name around his mind like a stone, breaking down soggy cardboard walls. *Billy's short for William, and I'm... Billy Jakobek. That's right. That's me. I'm sixteen... no, seventeen years old. I think.* He smiled, noticed invisible electrical sparks singeing his fingers, then slumped down. *Oh yeah, and I'm a freak. Forgot that part.*

He examined the sterile, windowless laboratory surrounding him. *Is this place supposed to be my bedroom...? For real?* The bed was comfy enough compared to the awful metal tank he'd come from, but the steel walls and big machinery weren't particularly homey. He scratched his chin and was happily surprised to feel stubble. *Nice. I can grow facial hair now.*

The white-coat woman approached him again, and his smile faded. "How are you, Billy?"

He shrugged. The woman was surprisingly tall—taller than him by a long shot—and her body emitted a sickly, damaged heat that made him nauseated. The man standing behind her, a pale, blocky blond guy with oversized glasses, was even worse. His mouth was like a pinched dot between two doughy cheeks, and whenever Billy focused on him—doing that thing he did—his fingertips went icy, as if he were reading a corpse. *Repressed as hell, that guy. Gives me the creeps.*

Billy glared at the man. The scientist ducked down, as if Billy had thrown something at him, then slowly stood back up. *Oops.* Billy opened his mouth to apologize, and both doctors threw their hands up in terror.

"Don't!" they cried in unison.

Billy's jaw snapped shut. *Oh yeah. It hurts people when I talk.*

"It's okay," the woman said, shaking as if she'd avoided a car crash. "I'll get you some clothes."

From the dresser, she brought Billy a black T-shirt and jeans. "You and your black shirts," she said humorously.

Billy tried to figure out why—or if—he liked black T-shirts so much, and he stared at her for answers. This made her wince, almost as if he'd punched her, so he quickly broke eye contact. *Why do I feel like I'm supposed to call her Mother? She's not my mom.*

Acting unhurt, the woman said, "You got terribly skinny in the tank this time, Billy."

Billy poked his ribs, not liking how visible they were, and quickly stretched on the black shirt he apparently loved. The cotton was wonderfully warm but carried residual traces of the woman's touch—feelings of itchy nervousness, a pitter-pattering heart—that she'd passed on to it before handing it to him.

Mother. He glanced at her again. *She cares about me, I think.* He looked at the man. *I guess I'm supposed to call him Father.* This man's energies were so prickly and guarded that it was almost as if he'd taken a class to block out Billy's probing. *An anti-Billy class, probably.* Billy smirked at this, noting that Mother wasn't as talented at blocking her sadness. *She probably got a C in the anti-Billy class. Mr. Stick-in-the-Ass got an A+, I'll bet.*

"Hey," Mother said, "I'm sorry you were in the tank so long. It's been three months."

Billy tightened his lips. *Three months?*

She moved closer. "Billy, please understand." She sighed. "I care about you. You know that we wouldn't keep you in the tank so long if we didn't have to, right? I promise, we gained a huge amount of blood and energy samples that will be fantastic for the project. It was worth it, but I'm sorry it took so long." Her eyes pleaded, and her heart pleaded even more strongly, its tense energies sending ripples of nausea into Billy's stomach.

Billy shook his head. *Three months. No wonder my memory is shot.* Anger boiled inside him. *Who the hell are you people?* He tried to remember. *My real mom and dad, they must be... oh no.* He closed his eyes. *No.* The gory memories flooded back to him. *Gunshots. Blood. Screams.*

A sensor in the laboratory beeped loudly. The doctors looked at each other in a panic.

"Calm down, young man," Father demanded.

Billy glared at the two doctors. *Liars. Butchers.* A hot coal lit up in his chest, spreading inner flames down to his fingertips. *They're afraid of me.*

The woman stumbled into the man's arms. The sensor beeped faster. Their eyes bugged out with fear.

"Billy, please," the woman begged.

Billy clenched his fists. *Never. I won't...*

He stopped as a voice inside him—his grandmother—said, *Stop it, little one.*

He exhaled, unclenching his hands. *These fake parents didn't hurt my family. Those people aren't around anymore.* His cheeks flushed with embarrassment. Once he cooled, the sensor stopped beeping, and the fake parents cautiously approached him again.

Father cleared his throat. "Well, some good news. This is the last move. The project is nearing completion, thanks to all those samples you supplied for us in the tank. You won't need to go back in when you sleep anymore because this place has reinforced walls." He knocked on the steel. "See? This is your new home, new school, all that. A regular bed, to boot."

"We can stay here, Billy," Mother said in a cloying voice, "until the end of the project. No more moving from place to place. You can even graduate from high school here. You'll get to be a normal kid again."

Billy flinched. *That's the first time you've lied.*

"Hey, Father." Mother turned away. "Let's give him some space. He has forty minutes until the bus comes." Her smile was unconvincing. "I'll make breakfast, Billy. Maybe even coffee, just the way you like it?"

Billy nodded. *Whatever.* The white coats left the room, leaving the bank-vault door open behind them. He considered poking around the laboratory, but the machines creeped him out too much. *Three months in a fish tank. Wow.* He stepped into his jeans. His feet were so wrinkled by water that they looked like they belonged on an old man. *Gross. I need some socks.* He opened the top drawer of the dresser and, instead of socks, found rows of identical black T-shirts. *Why do I like these things? What the hell?*

The photographs in the second drawer punched him in the gut. The happy family in the pictures seemed foreign to him. He easily recognized his true mother, father, grandmother, and little brother, but the little boy with them, the young Billy, was a total stranger. He touched the photos—heard the muted laughter of his lost family ring through his ears—and a tear ran down his cheek. *They're all dead.* Now that he remembered, he wished his memory could be lost again. *I hate my life.*

The other side of the drawer held a silver Star of David pendant attached to a broken necklace chain. *Oh yeah. Bubbe gave this to me.* Underneath a yellowed stack of comics was a chintzy old phone, with headphones coiled around it, that he recalled coming from his dad. It didn't make calls anymore, but it contained old photos, texts, and his dad's playlists. *I pretty much just listen to music on this, I think.*

"Hey, Billy!" Mother called into the room.

Billy quaked. *I hate this.*

"Breakfast is ready." She leaned in. "Don't take too long, or you'll miss the bus."

When she left, Billy slammed the drawer. *This sucks. Everything sucks.* He opened the third drawer, finally finding socks. He stuffed the old phone and necklace into his pocket, left the room, and got ready to pretend to be a regular kid again.

9: Natalia

For Natalia Gonzalez, seventeen years old, mornings were always a rush, and this one was no different. She got out of the shower to find her two little brothers standing outside the bathroom door, staring up at her with mischievous grins. Neither was dressed for school. *God damn it*, she thought, shaking her head. *This day is going to blow.*

"What are you guys *doing*?" She threw her arms up. "You're supposed to be eating breakfast by now. The bus is coming in less than thirty minutes!"

Both twin boys gazed fixedly at her, their expressions locked in such perfect unison that Natalia wondered—as she often did—if they were secretly robots. Then Carlos, the louder boy, clapped Juan's back. They both screamed with laughter.

"You lost the staring contest!" Carlos snorted.

"Awesome." Natalia rolled her eyes. She started for her bedroom, and the twins went roaring, giggling, and swinging across the couches. *Man, they'll never be ready in time.* She raced back, holding her towel, just in time to see Carlos pinning Juan to the floor, dangling drool from his tongue. "Carlos!" she cried.

Carlos looked up. "But I'm Venom!" He swished his mouth around loudly. "Venom always does crazy stuff with his tongue!"

"And I'm Spidey!" Juan joined in. "I'm going to win this fight, anyway, so it's all cool."

Natalia physically separated the boys then pointed at the section of the living room, blocked off by dividers, that served as their bedroom. "Get ready for school, heroes. Time to eat breakfast and put some real clothes on." As they ran back to their bunk bed, still midgame, she noticed permanent marker stains on the back of Juan's neck. *Okay, he can explain that crap to his teachers.* Natalia rushed to the kitchen, poured the boys each a bowl of cereal, and called out, "Breakfast is at the table when you guys are ready!"

The twins rushed over—they dressed pretty quickly, once they'd started—and inhaled the cereal like vacuums. Through the windows, dreary gray sunlight oozed into the kitchen. The mist outside was thicker than a wool blanket.

Natalia sighed. *Yep, another freeze-your-ass-off day in Heaven's Hole. It's only October, and the snow's already coming tonight. Great.*

Natalia, who by this point had mostly dried off, raced back to her bedroom—a converted closet in the hallway, with her artwork tacked up on every available surface—and since her tiny bed took up all the floor space in her tiny room, she stood atop it while stretching on torn skinny jeans, fingerless gloves, and her papá's rumpled old giant black hoodie. The sleeves had burn holes, which she rolled up so no one would see them.

Her phone's should-be-out-the-door alarm clock went off. *Yeah, I'm definitely late again. Fuck.* She popped in her phone's earbuds so she could blare music without waking up Mamá in the bedroom, and she cranked up the volume. As electric guitars blasted in her ears, she perched in front of her mirror, buzzed her undercut, and styled the black wave of her hair to fall perfectly down her forehead. She adjusted her nose ring, checked her many earrings, and decided to ditch makeup for the day. She didn't have time. While she didn't care if she was late for school—*that place can go to hell*—she cared about getting out the door in a timely manner so as not to set a bad example for the twins. *They're good kids. Not like me.*

Down the hall, Carlos and Juan shrieked, laughed, and pounded with an insane level of energy for such an early hour. Natalia put a finger gun to her head and pulled the trigger. *C'mon, little dudes. This is why Mamá never gets enough sleep. You guys know how late she works.* She finished her hair, squeezed her sketchbook into her backpack, then reentered the hallway with her personal soundtrack blaring.

It wasn't much of a hallway, really, or much of an apartment. Like so many of the low-income housing projects in Heaven's Hole, the Gonzalez Rodriguez apartment comprised two adjoined hotel rooms, middle door removed, with a miniature kitchen added. The town had a lot of hotels that had been turned into cheap apartments since the place had apparently been a thriving ski-vacation spot back before what Mamá called "the tanked economy." Natalia didn't understand much about this whole economy business but assumed it was pretty bad if they'd turned these dumpy hotels into even dumpier apartments.

Natalia passed by Mamá and Abuelita's bedroom, and the horrible sound of Mamá's oxygen machine blasted through her music. She drew out her earbuds, listened to her mother's stuffy, gasping breaths, and cracked the door open.

The two women's beds paralleled each other. A colorful handmade wooden cross—the one item Abuelita had carried with her from Guatemala—was centered on the wall between them. Mamá's bed was a jumble of blankets, and an oxygen tube snaked between the folds. The sound of her congested inhalations—like a vacuum sucking up wet rocks—made Natalia grimace. *One day I'll look in here, and she'll be dead.* She closed the door. *Man, it's so unfair that her lungs are all messed up.* Mamá had never smoked, and she'd tried to exercise, but coming to Heaven's Hole had destroyed her health. Natalia blamed the giant Thorne Century factory where Mamá worked every night, earning pennies. That factory had ruined Mamá's lungs, cut off three of her fingers, and never paid her medical bills. Most of Natalia's friends at school had parents working for Thorne Century who had similar health issues. Nobody spoke up. People who protested always disappeared. *Just like Papá disappeared.*

Natalia rushed down the hall, knowing that if she listened to Mamá's harsh breathing much longer, she would burst into tears. The boys continued to rampage through the living room, but at least they were ready for school. What Natalia didn't like was the sound of the tap running in the kitchen.

"Carlos." She seized her little brother's arm. "Why didn't you turn off the sink?"

He frowned. "We didn't do that."

Natalia peered around the corner and sighed. "Damn it. Abuelita!" She hurried to the kitchen, which now smelled of fresh-brewed coffee. Natalia's grandmother stood at the sink, washing the boy's cereal bowls, wavering upon rickety thin legs that stuck out from her nightgown like sticks. Her wheelchair sat uselessly behind her.

"Abuelita!" Natalia hurried to her grandmother.

Abuelita's heavy dark cheeks were always pulled downward, the sign of a hard life. When her loving gaze flashed up at Natalia, though, she resembled the sun peeking through the clouds. "*Estoy bien*, Natalia," she grumbled.

"No, you aren't fine." Natalia tried to nudge Abuelita back into the chair.

Abuelita grumbled again. "It's fine. You are always so good at getting the boys up in the morning." Her short, calloused fingers pushed hard against the sponge. "I just need to help, at least a little—"

"You're not helping anybody by killing your knees," Natalia said.

"Knees?" The old woman snorted. "My back—that's what's killing me."

"Sit down. Please." Natalia gently but firmly lowered her grandmother back into the wheelchair. It wasn't even locked in place, much to Natalia's annoyance. "You know you shouldn't be exerting yourself, Abuelita. Doctor's orders."

"*Esos médicos son unos idiotas.*" Abuelita shook her head. "You know those stupid Thorne Century doctors know nothing. They just talk and talk and ask for cash." She mockingly flapped her hand like a butterfly.

Natalia smiled. *Hey, she's not wrong.* When the family first came to Heaven's Hole, Abuelita had worked alongside Mamá at the factory. Three years back, she'd tumbled off a ladder, and much like Mamá, the company hadn't paid any of her medical bills. The injury left Abuelita unable to stand for more than a few minutes, so her employment had been terminated, which Abuelita was still bitter about.

"I know, I know." Natalia kissed her grandmother's forehead. "Still, let me do the dishes, okay?"

"What am I supposed to do, then?" Abuelita scowled.

"Rest, Abuelita. That's what you do."

Abuelita scoffed. "Rest."

"Yes, rest. Rest like the delicate elderly grandmother you are," Natalia said.

Abuelita laughed, and Natalia laughed with her.

She pushed her grandmother's wheelchair to the table and locked it in place. "C'mon, old lady. Relax."

Abuelita groaned humorously. "Old lady!" Her craggy cheeks lifted back into a proud grin. "I'd tell you to watch your mouth, *young* lady, but I guess I'd have to watch my own as well."

"Not all of us can be as nice as Mamá. Here, I'll make you some coffee."

"*Sí, gracias.*" Abuelita pushed back in her chair, looking uncomfortable but pleased. "Servitude from the granddaughter. The only good thing about getting so old."

Natalia splashed a little fresh coffee with a lot of cream into a mug, as Abuelita liked it. She toasted some bread and poured a little cup full of Abuelita's expensive medications. Each pill was practically worth a meal, even with the reduced rates the Thorne Century pharmacy offered employees. She crushed the tabs, mixed them with applesauce, and set them before her grandmother. Hearing the boys frolicking in the living room, she called out, "Juan, Carlos! Get your bags and catch the bus." Natalia brought Abuelita some coffee and toast to wash down the nasty pills.

Before eating, Abuelita clutched the beads of her rosary and whispered a prayer. "*Dios te salve, María. Llena eres de gracia. El Señor es contigo...*"

Natalia wasn't a believer, but she closed her eyes out of respect and because she loved listening to the beautiful Spanish flowing so easily from her grandmother's lips. *I wish I could speak the language better.* Like many other Latino kids in Heaven's Hole, she only understood bits and pieces, and trying to improve her grasp of Español made her feel like a phony.

Abuelita looked up. "I have an appointment today. Can you bring me?"

"Yeah, of course."

"Maybe call the neighbor and have her watch the boys for an hour? That nice Catalina girl from your school?"

"Catalina's gone, Abuelita," Natalia whispered, checking that Juan or Carlos weren't walking in. "She disappeared last month, remember? Left her parents, school, everything behind. Everybody thinks she ran away to West California."

"Hmm." Abuelita frowned. "Is that what you think?"

Natalia frowned. *Not really. Catalina was always Ms. Responsible. She never would've run away.* Natalia suspected that something more sinister had happened. A handful of teen girls living in the building had vanished over the last six months with no trace. *I miss Catalina. I hope I'm wrong.* Before Natalia could dwell on this, the boys finally arrived in the kitchen, backpacks perched upright on their shoulders.

"Get to school, boys." Abuelita waved them toward the door, and they marched out like soldiers. After they'd left, the old woman raised her brow at Natalia. "You too. You need to stop skipping class."

Natalia smiled innocently. "Me?"

"Yes, you." Abuelita shooed her toward the door. Just as Natalia was about to put her boots on, her grandmother caught her leg. "Hold on." She pointed at Natalia's ankle. "This?"

Natalia looked down. *Aw, crap.* Her pant leg was hiked up just high enough to expose her inked handiwork from the night before. She pushed it down with her other foot. "It's just a tattoo, Abuelita."

"Of what?"

"An arrow. Shooting from the skies to, you know..." *Anywhere but this stupid town, hopefully. Someday.*

Abuelita crossed her arms. "Who is giving tattoos to underage teens?"

"Self-inflicted." Natalia beamed. "Sketched it on paper, got some ink, a needle. Homemade. Pretty cool, right?" *And it's not the first one, but luckily, you haven't noticed the others yet.*

Abuelita turned her wheelchair around. "Get to school. We'll talk later."

Natalia exited quickly. Frost crackled beneath her boots as she stepped onto the walkway just in time to see her little brothers catch the bus. Natalia pinched her nose, trying not to smell the chemicals pumping from the Thorne Century factory. Heavy fog blanketed the landscape, but high above it, Natalia could see the towering ridges of earth that encircled the town, the edges of the pit that gave Heaven's Hole its name. Atop the nearest ridge, at least a half day's hike through the woods, stood the town's famous fire tower, looming over everything like a watchful steel giant. Natalia often imagined climbing that fire tower, taking one last look at her putrid town, then running away forever. She hated the idea of spending her life slaving away for Thorne Century, like Mamá and Abuelita, but that seemed like a probable future since she could never leave her family behind. *At least I've got one more crappy school year left to figure out a solution.* This made her want to skip class, go to the woods, and draw in her sketchbook all day, but her grandmother's instructions to get to school stuck with her.

Natalia stepped down the icy concrete stairs, walked across the parking lot, and skipped down the sidewalk, passing by the other hotels-turned-apartments. Since the clock was ticking, she veered right onto the King Street shortcut.

This was risky. Most people avoided King Street because it was home to the oldest, craziest residents of Heaven's Hole—often called Heaven's Hooligans—and many of those white families, who had lived there for generations, blamed the influx of immigrants and refugees for "stealing" the penny-wage Thorne Century jobs. The true story, according to a now-deleted Wikipedia entry, was that recession and climate change had destroyed the former vacation town's economy years before, resulting in ninety-three percent of the original locals moving away. Evidently, Heaven's Hole's diverse demographics were a direct result of Thorne Century setting up shop, building the new factory, and openly hiring waves of new workers, all of them fitting the mold of Mamá and Abuelita—poor, desperate, and most importantly, foreign.

Natalia kept her head down as she passed through a neighborhood of once-nice houses, which now had broken windows and collapsed porches. She couldn't help but peek at the dilapidated shack of Darrell Jenkins, a former town councilman now known as Crazy Old Darrell. The property reeked of booze, and Darrell's patchy yard featured numerous homemade cardboard signs that changed every week. One sign said Aliens Go Home. Another sign depicted a cartoon Mexican in a sombrero dumping toxic waste into a hole that supposedly represented the town. Other signs said No More Illegals or Thorne Century Is a Dirty Shit Town. Natalia heard similar things every day, but the clear effort put into each sign bothered her. *This dude gets worse every time I pass by here.*

She stopped to snap a photo, and the front door opened. She jolted back, sneaking the phone into her pocket. Crazy Old Darrell stood in his doorway, beer in hand, wearing only a stained T-shirt and boxers. A tattered Nazi flag was pinned to the wall behind him. Beneath his ratty mane of sand-colored hair, Darrell squinted at her with unmasked hatred, and Natalia felt oddly sorry for him. She'd heard that he'd lost his fortune when the town had collapsed, then he'd lost his son in a car accident and drifted into an alcoholic haze he'd never recovered from.

Then Crazy Old Darrell pointed a shotgun right at her.

She shivered, barely resisting the urge to drop her bag and run, but she didn't look away. *Don't move, don't scream, don't freak out.*

Darrell lowered the gun and smiled. "Bang," he muttered.

"Fuck off," Natalia replied, covering her mouth right after speaking. *Whoa, that was stupid.*

Darrell's eyes flashed with rage. Natalia raced down the sidewalk, disappearing into the fog. She looked back once, but fortunately, Darrell hadn't followed her. She whipped into the woods, crossed the bridge, and hiked back to the main road.

Her heart raced. *So stupid. Me and my goddamn mouth.* With shaky hands, she took out a joint that her friend Felix had given her the night before. *Yeah, we were supposed to share it, but I need this ASAP.* She lit it and inhaled until her chest burned. She coughed. *It's okay. I'm okay.* She took one more hit, put it out, and walked to school.

10: Billy

The house surrounding Billy's so-called bedroom was eerily normal. As he wandered the corridors, the medical equipment and freezers of his sleepy-time laboratory gave way to tacky wallpaper and carpet. In the living room, ugly yellow walls were decorated with thrift-store paintings of boats and fields, while a leather sectional surrounded a glass coffee table and a fireplace. A flowery scent reminded him of home until he eyed the cheap air freshener plugged into the wall. *Cheesy, but it smells nice.*

Less pleasant were the foggy, polluted landscape outside the window and the security guards standing by the door. The men wore body armor and wielded guns. *Are those for me? Oy vey.* He tried to probe into the men, but they emitted the same cold, prickly sensations as Father. *Two more anti-Billy champions.*

In the kitchen, Mother stood over the stove as the mouthwatering aroma of scrambled eggs wafted around her. *If only she could add some bagels and lox, this would be a great breakfast.* Billy, noting the blinking red eye of a security camera over her head, quietly sat at the kitchen island. A clean, organized backpack waited beside him.

Mother turned around, saw him, and jumped. "Oh! Hey, you startled me."

Immediately, she gulped down some pills beside her. The bottle had no label, but Billy's slowly recovering memory told him that these pills were supposed to block his powers. *Something like that. They don't work that great, but they work a little.* Mother brought two plates of eggs to the island followed by two coffees, and she offered her best attempt at a smile. There was a softness to her that saddened Billy. *She's so lonely. She does care, but she's hiding big secrets from me.*

The pills let her do it. He dug deeper. *She gets anxiety attacks. Bowel disorders. Locks herself up in her room, crying for hours. Why can't I find her real name, though?*

"Poking around in my brain again?" She nudged the plate closer to him. "You're welcome, by the way."

Billy smiled weakly, feeling bad for making her uncomfortable. He dug into the scrambled eggs and nodded his approval. For him, food carried the feelings of however it had been prepared—factory-farmed chicken was inedible, and Mother's eggs felt warm and loving. *She was thinking of her son when she made them.* He peered upward. *So, she has a real son? Yeah, I feel it.*

"How are the eggs? Gross or okay?" she asked, and Billy gave her a thumbs-up, gulping down his coffee. Her fragile smile fluttered. "Thanks. Glad to know I can do something right." She pointed at the frigid neighborhood outside the window. "I printed out some info about this place, if you're curious." She pushed a small stack of papers toward him. "We're now in Olakhota, the one hundred forty-third state. This town is called Heaven's Hole—"

Billy scoffed, nearly spitting out his coffee.

"I know." Mother laughed. "Stupid name, right? The backstory is a bit intriguing, though. See, back in the late 1800s, a group of settlers found this huge hole in the ground. Biggest they'd ever seen, like a giant circular canyon. They were amazed by all the diamonds here and figured a hole so massive and beautiful could've only been carved by God, so the place must be blessed, sacred... hence the name. They built up a town here, and little did they know, this giant hole is actually a meteor crater. Biggest crater in the US by far."

Billy smiled. *Okay, that's kinda cool.*

"Anyway, it gets ludicrously cold here. We're only a little way into October, and there's supposed to be a freak snowstorm tonight, so you'll probably have a snow day tomorrow." She shook her head, clearly displeased. "That's probably why Heaven's Hole only has a population, of, umm..." She turned the pages around to read them. "In the last census, 3,530. Wow, small. Anyway, this place is beyond remote. It's not even on the map, and there's only one lousy road out of town. The nearest village is forty miles away through mountains."

Billy pointed at the papers then splayed his arms.

Mother frowned, confused. "Are you asking why we're here?"

Billy nodded.

"Oh." She gulped. "Well, because this is the location of Thorne Century's biggest factory. The project's endgame happens here."

Billy clenched his teeth. *Thorne.* The name sickened him.

"Listen, I know Thorne Century isn't perfect." Mother's hands twisted into knots. "But you know, we sacrificed a lot to get you here, in this house, instead of just the dark tank. Mr. Thorne, he..." She pinched her lips with distaste. "He's not always a nice man, but he's a *good* man. He's a businessman, but he cares. That's why Thorne Century has invested billions into this project—because we're going to use your blood, your tissue samples, your energies to save people all around the world."

Billy glanced at the security camera.

"For example"—Mother flipped midway through the stack of papers—"if it weren't for Mr. Thorne, this little town would've been wiped out. When the economy here collapsed, and everyone moved away, Thorne Century set up this huge factory, creating so many new jobs. We have to respect what Mr. Thorne does. You understand, right?"

Billy looked at the clock. *I'll bet the school bus is coming soon. I'm tired of hearing how great Mr. Thorne is.* He stood.

Mother handed him the backpack. "Sorry." She inhaled. "Can I see your ankle monitor before you go?"

He lifted his pants leg for her inspection, and the metal contraption blinked red like the cameras.

"Thanks." She turned away, downed another anti-Billy pill, and started washing the dishes. As the tap sprayed hot water, she kept talking in an increasingly nervous tone. "Listen, I understand that it's been horrible spending so much time in the tank, moving between so many labs all these years, being cooped up." She sighed, turned off the tap, and faced him. "But now that we're in Heaven's Hole, you deserve to have a normal life. Go out there. Make friends. Live a little. I *really* want that for you, Billy."

Billy maneuvered around her, shaking, until he could reach the door. Mother leaned in, making him feel sick. *She really does want me to be happy.* He backed away. *But there's some other motive too?*

"I know." She turned away. "I know what you're thinking. Yes, you having relationships with people helps the project too. More emotions give us more energies to work with, helps us generate new medicines, new treatments..."

She sighed, and Billy thought, *There it is.*

"I mean it, though. You deserve to be happy—not just for research purposes."

Billy pointed at the road ahead. *We're both going to vomit if I stay much longer.*

Mother nodded. "Yes, that's the bus stop, but before you head out, I need to ask you something." Her voice cracked. "I just need to document. Did you have nightmares about the shadow with the blue eyes again? In case—"

Billy launched into the cold outside, slammed the door closed behind him, and exhaled. *She knows I don't talk about that. Her fault.* He bypassed another set of emotionless security guards, and his feet crunched up the frosted-grass hill until he reached the end of the driveway, passing a sign labeled Kaiser House, then through a set of diseased-looking trees. The chemical-scented fog obscured the ridges of the crater, which disappointed him. Just as he reached the main road, the school bus cut through the mist and screeched to a halt in front of him.

The doors slid open with a mechanical shudder. "Getting on?" the bus driver asked.

Billy hesitated then climbed the stairs. As soon as he stepped aboard, his veins squelched. His heart sputtered. His spine tingled. *So many people.* The slew of new faces, new energies, and new personal traumas dumped into him in one monstrous burst. They all stared. *Gotta disappear, please just disappear.* His mind raced. *Don't look weird, don't panic—it just gets more attention.* He squeezed the railing. Dozens of heartbeats pounded his ribs. *Can't think. Can't breathe. Stay calm... calm... there's a* me *somewhere in this noise.* He inhaled deeply, exhaled the energies inside him, and stood tall.

The bus driver glared at him. "You all right, son?"

Billy smiled pitifully, gave the driver an okay sign, and wobbled to the back of the bus. *Damn it. They're all still looking at me.* None of the seats were empty. He frantically tried to find a place to sit.

From his left, a friendly voice called out. "Hey, new kid, got an open seat next to me."

Billy plopped down without even looking. *Whooo. That's a relief.* The bus jostled forward again, and everyone finally lost interest in him. Billy rubbed his eyes, trying to regain his composure.

"You okay, man?" The friendly-voiced boy laughed.

Billy jumped. *Oh yeah, I should probably figure out who I sat next to.* He turned to see a skinny black kid with a shaved head, an eyebrow ring, and a denim jacket. The kid's half-upturned smile was welcoming, and Billy found his energies deeply calming. *Nice guy. He's got a good heart. Seems to have parent issues... mother maybe? He speaks his mind. Extremely loyal to his friends. Makes friends easily.*

The nice kid suddenly flinched, muttering "Ow," so Billy softened his gaze.

Oops. I was focusing too hard on him. He hadn't been around normal people in a long time. He'd forgotten how much his powers impacted them.

"Sorry, sudden headache." The kid frowned. "Weird." He shook it off. "You don't talk much, huh?"

Billy smiled back, offering a casual shrug as his response.

"No problem by me, man. I'm probably gonna sleep the rest of this ride, anyway." The boy yawned. "But hey, the name's Felix. Welcome to Hellhole High."

Billy grinned at this. *Hellhole?* Then, as Felix leaned back to get some shut-eye, Billy rooted through his pocket, took out his Dad's old phone, and plugged in the earbuds. Scrolling through the ridiculously old-school playlists, Billy ended up selecting an album by Men at Work, a band he faintly remembered from childhood, and selected the song "Overkill."

With the music relaxing him, he stared out at the foggy town of Heaven's Hole, paying close attention as they passed the massive concrete pillars of the Thorne Century factory. It was going to be a long day.

11: Natalia

By the time Natalia got to school, everyone was already in their second-period classes. The empty hallways creaked and groaned. Natalia fearlessly strode through, her bootheels clapping the floor like a drumbeat. Every classroom she passed turned into a rubbernecking party. Everyone stared, but Natalia kept her shoulders back, smiling as if she didn't notice. *Let 'em look. Let 'em write me up.* Her bravado vanished when she reached her locker.

"Awesome," she muttered.

Her locker was busted open again and spray-painted, with obscenities scrawled on it in permanent marker. *GO HOME GONZO-LOS*, one message said, while another read, *SUK ME*. Her library books were ripped to pieces. A beloved childhood photo of her parents, taped to the door, was inked with mustaches and sombreros. Natalia slammed the locker. It bounced back open.

She walked down to her history class, where Mr. Abdul Nazari's baritone reverberated through the closed door. Not wanting to interrupt her favorite teacher's lesson, she entered the room as quietly as possible. This tactic didn't work. A classroom of heads flicked up, each student snickering. Natalia pretended not to see the disappointment on Mr. Nazari's bearded face.

"Salaam, Ms. Gonzalez," he said respectfully then raised his brow. "So nice of you to fit us into your schedule." His silver hair was tied back in a tight ponytail, and his sleeves were rolled up.

"No problem," she replied.

Mr. Nazari closed the door behind her, gestured toward the seats, and returned to his lecture. Natalia clenched her fists at the sight of

Chris Thompson's spiky red fauxhawk poking up from the desk she usually sat in near the bookshelf.

That douchebag totally took my place on purpose. Narrowing her eyes, not showing any softness, Natalia marched to the back of the room.

As she passed Chris, he wolf whistled at her. "Hey, chica." He flicked his hair, grinning. "Is being late to class a spicy Mexican tradition?"

Chris's friends burst out laughing, and though his pockmarked cheeks reddened under Natalia's furious glare, he still fist-bumped everyone sitting around him. Last Friday, Chris had asked her out in front of the whole class, and she'd said no.

Trying to save face in front of your little buddies, huh? She thought about her locker. *Ah, now I get it.*

She dropped her bag to the floor. It thudded loudly. Every kid in the room turned around.

"You want to say that again, asshole?" She slammed Chris's desk, and he shriveled into his seat like a spooked earthworm. "Go ahead, Chris. Can you repeat that?"

"Like, uh... uh..." Chis flinched.

Mr. Nazari cleared his throat. "Let's get back to our subject. Chris, no more bullying will be tolerated, understood?"

"Yeah." Chris gulped.

Natalia dragged her backpack over to the infamously cold desk by the window—ignoring the mean whispers of Chris's friends—and sat down. Chilly drafts cut through the cracked glass. *This seat blows. Literally.*

In the front, Mr. Nazari pinned up ancient photographs depicting a partially constructed Statue of Liberty. One picture showed Lady Liberty's face, not yet attached to a head, held up by wooden beams. In another picture, a man stood over the statue's giant toes, which were not connected to a foot.

Natalia marveled at these little snapshots of history. *I should seriously go to NYC someday. Post a selfie with that big statue and shock everybody who said I'd never go anywhere in life.* Natalia spread her sketchbook across her desk and tried to illustrate this future vision, but her hand had other ideas. Her sketch mutated into a depiction of the classroom, with blobs for students. One blob with piercings punched a spiky-haired blob's face.

"As many of you know"—Mr. Nazari tapped his ruler against the construction photos—"there's a poem mounted at the Statue of Liberty considered a definitive piece of American culture. First written in 1883, it's titled 'The New Colossus' and contains the iconic lines—"

Natalia raised her hand. "Got it." She smiled as the class turned to face her. "'Give me your tired, your poor, your huddled masses yearning to breathe free...'" She shrugged, leaving it there.

Mr. Nazari clapped approvingly. "Fantastic, Ms. Gonzalez. Consider your tardiness redeemed. Can you name the author, as well?"

She beamed. "Emma Lazarus."

"Perfect." He wrote this name on the board. "Write that in your notes, everyone. It's on the quiz."

The classroom groaned, but Natalia perked up. Guilt unloaded from her like a turtle ditching its shell. *Cool, he likes me again. This'll probably be the only class I score high grades in.* She returned to her sketchbook. Drawing always helped her focus, and Mr. Nazari was one of the few teachers who allowed her to do it during his lessons, which was probably the main reason she succeeded in his class.

Mr. Nazari continued, "We all know the cliché of this giant green lady over the water welcoming immigrants from around the world." He imitated the statue's famous pose, earning laughter from his students. "But frankly, for so many people running from genocide, persecution, and hatred throughout the generations... that statue has truly *meant* something. It certainly did when my family came here. And arguably, Lazarus's poem created this meaning."

Natalia examined Mr. Nazari, wondering what situation he'd come from and what had happened in his life to lead him to the Hellhole. She flipped to a blank page. *I'm done with these blobs.* She ran her pencil across the paper, back and forth, seeing if anything appeared in the lines.

Mr. Nazari kept speaking. "Ms. Lazarus, as it happens, was Jewish." He eyed the room. "During the 1880s, the Jewish population of Eastern Europe faced widespread persecution—"

Kara, in the front row, raised her hand. "I thought the Holocaust was just a hoax. That's what my mom says."

"No, it was very real. But it happened many years later." Mr. Nazari's brow furrowed, and he backed off, probably imagining a call from Kara's parents. "However, in the 1800s, the Jews of Eastern Europe faced such oppression that they fled to the United States... as refugees. Even here, Jewish people were not easily accepted, so these refugees hid their culture, changed their names, tried to blend in, all to avoid further persecution... to live in peace, even just to find work—"

"Buncha cheap Jews changing their names to make money," Chris whispered, punching his friend's shoulder. "Bet we coulda spotted their big noses anywhere."

Natalia kicked Chris's desk. He jolted in fright. If Mr. Nazari noticed this, he didn't show it.

"Emma Lazarus dedicated herself to helping these refugees, who struggled with the same plight of so many refugees today..." The teacher paused. "Of course, Jewish people are far from the only minority group who has faced systematic oppression, both here and abroad. People of so many nations, cultures, and ethnicities still face extreme prejudice. I know this firsthand, and many of you can say the same." Mr. Nazari started shaking and crossed his arms. "That's a discussion for another day. For now, the Statue of Liberty..."

Natalia wanted him to keep going, but she understood why he stopped. Talking about such subjects in Thorne Century's Hellhole was skating on thin ice, particularly for a Muslim teacher. *Man, I know how the poor guy feels.* She flipped to a blank sketchbook page. She pressed down her pencil too hard, and the tip broke.

Just then, somebody knocked on the classroom door.

Natalia jumped then felt like an idiot. *Whoa, Natalia, you're so tough that even a door scares you.* But as Mr. Nazari answered the knocking, a strange fluttering moved through her belly as if something big was about to happen, as if the perfect coinciding of the broken pencil and the knock meant something deeper.

"May I help you?" Mr. Nazari asked.

The stranger was hidden behind the door. Natalia craned her head to look, but she couldn't spot anyone. *Is there really someone there?* She could have sworn she saw orbs glowing from the hallway, like a magical fairy was outside. The fluorescent lights seemed to flicker. *I'm being stupid. If the lights were acting up, other people would notice.* Still, something about Mr. Nazari's expression as he faced the unseen stranger was bizarre. *Dude looks like he's seen a ghost.*

"Can you answer me, young man? Oh, wait." The teacher took a clipboard off the wall and read through a list of names. "You're the new student? My apologies, I forgot. Did you get lost in the hallway on your way from first period?"

The invisible stranger—male, apparently—didn't seem to answer.

Mr. Nazari hung the clipboard back up. "Is it William or Will?" He waited, as if the stranger was talking back to him, but Natalia didn't hear anything. "Billy, perhaps? Oh, okay." Mr. Nazari beckoned the ghost-fairy-ghoul inside. "Hi, class. Allow me to introduce Mr. Billy Jakobek."

Natalia pondered the unusual last name. *Juh-koe-bick?* The entire class leaned forward as the new student entered the room. Natalia's heart stopped at the first sight of him, though she couldn't figure out why since the oddly named Billy Jakobek looked less like a heart-throb and more like an extraterrestrial wearing human skin. His bony body was carved in sharp angles, and his slouched posture contrasted with a masculine jawline and deep-set cheekbones. His ridiculous-ly curly black hair had clearly never seen a comb. Something about him, though, yanked at Natalia like a fishhook. *I really like his face. His quirkiness too. It's unusual. Maybe I just want to draw him. That's probably all it is.*

The strange boy walked dazedly before the class, fingers splayed at his sides as if he'd never learned to relax them.

Mr. Nazari pointed him to the desks. "Please take a seat, Mr. Jakobek."

The boy smiled at this, like a complete fool, and for whatever rea-son, Natalia found herself smiling just as foolishly. She quickly cov-ered her mouth, embarrassed by her lapse in coolness. The boy con-tinued his confused wandering.

Mr. Nazari gestured more delicately. "Go ahead, young man." He pointed. "No assigned seats."

Billy jumped, somehow alarmed by this, then bizarrely twisted himself to the back of the room. Though he was certainly fidgety and klutzy, Natalia noted a lack of shyness. *He's not trying to impress any-body. It's more like he's just confused about how to assimilate with earth-lings.* There was a weird confidence to the way he sat down at a desk once everyone—except her—had looked away.

Natalia caught herself staring at him, noticed a strangely warm tingling in her belly, and looked back at her sketchbook. Instantly, the feeling vanished, replaced by the cold drafts of the window. *That's super weird.* She glanced back at the boy, and the temperature shift reoccurred. *Okay, what the hell did Felix put in my weed?*

Mr. Nazari went back to speaking, and Chris Thompson and his posse openly snickered about the weirdo new kid, but Natalia couldn't focus on anything but the boy's astonishingly clear dark eyes. *So sharp but so soft.* She stared deeper. *Almost like...*

The boy looked back at her.

Natalia jolted. *Awkward.* She looked away fast. The warm tingles from before became hot and electric. *Oh man, he's still staring at me.* For no explainable reason, strange memories popped in her head, like a strip of bubble wrap imprinted with photos of her past—Papá holding her in his arms, Abuelita singing her to sleep—and she shook off the unexpected nostalgia trip as if bringing circulation back to a sleeping limb. *That was trippy.*

Seizing the corners of her desk, breathing deeply, she bravely peered back into Billy's black eyes. Her heartbeat sped up, and to her befuddlement, a second heartbeat pounded inside her, slow and steady. *Boom-boom, boom-boom.* She looked deeper into Billy's eyes. Hundreds of unknown voices rang in her ears like radio stations. Old voices. Young voices. Happy voices. Sad voices.

The boy looked down. He pulled his hood over his head and sank into the desk.

The weird sensations vanished instantly. Natalia turned her back to him, her face hot. *Must be the weed. No, that doesn't make sense. Maybe it really is something more... otherworldly?* She grinned to herself as fairy tales played out in her mind until she realized that Mr. Nazari had been talking to her.

"What's so funny, Ms. Gonzalez?" Mr. Nazari asked.

Her eyes widened. "Nothing!" She covered her smiling mouth as the class chortled. *Thanks, Teach.* Once everyone looked away, Natalia flipped her sketchbook to the next blank page. She got out a new pencil and cut through the page with its graphite blade, carving cheekbones and curly hair. *Looks like I'm going to draw this crazy kid. That's just how it is.* Her gut told her that choosing to draw this person was going to change everything—her thoughts, her life, her future—but true to form, she didn't hesitate.

In permanent marker, she labeled the drawing Dark-Eyed Boy.

12

Natalia usually spent her lunch breaks either in the library, curled up in a nook with her sketchbook, or in the woods behind the school. She hated the cafeteria. Unfortunately, the library was closed for repairs, and the powers that be were patrolling the exits, so she allowed herself to be swept up by the crowd as every teenager in Heaven's Hole mobbed a single square room with nasty food, sticky floors, and not enough tables. The mass of students shoved Natalia through the double doors so hard that her sketchbook nearly bumped out from the crook of her arm.

Someone jumped her from behind. "Boo!"

"Who the hell—" Natalia swung around, fist raised, and almost punched Felix Kabongo in the face. "Oh." She punched his shoulder instead. "Don't *ever* do that!"

"Oh no!" Felix lifted his hands in a phony panic. "Geez, Nat. Can you stop being a badass for, like, three seconds?"

Felix's laughter was infectious enough that Natalia cracked a smile. The two friends broke from the crowd and hugged for the first time that day. Felix's trademark denim jacket was sopping wet.

She hit his shoulder again. "Asshole."

"Ow!" Felix grinned. "Okay, douchebag."

"Were you just outside?" She tugged on his drenched sleeve. "Making out with your boyfriend behind the gym again?"

"Shh! Yeah, but Paul skipped class after that, so keep it quiet. He already gets in enough trouble on his own." Felix made a zip-your-lips gesture. "What are you doing in here, punk? Aren't you supposed to spend your lunches in the library, being all moody and broody?"

"I heard some jerk named Felix Kabongo wasn't going to be in here, and I was so excited that I gave the cafeteria a chance." Natalia exaggeratedly rolled her eyes. "Imagine my disappointment."

Felix clapped hilariously at the insult. "Harsh!" His gaze softened. "Seriously, though, how's your grandma?"

Natalia shuffled her feet. "She's doing okay. Not bad. I'm more worried about Mamá really. What about you? Have you and your mom talked since that big argument?"

"Ehh..." He tilted his hand. "We're avoiding each other right now. Silent dinners all week. Been hanging with my dad, mostly, and hearing old war stories. Crazy stuff. He said whenever they finish this stupid huge project at Thorne Century, and he saves up enough cash, he wants to take me to meet all my cousins back home. So that's cool. My mom, though... eh."

Felix tried to keep things lighthearted, but Natalia saw right through him. She hugged him again. Then the two relaxed against the wall, watching the other kids buzz around the beehive that was the cafeteria.

"Mamá keeps complaining about this big factory project, too," Natalia said. "They're definitely working our parents to the ground in that dump." She sighed. "Okay, so the real reason I'm hanging out in cafeteria dumb land is because the library is still getting repaired from that one idiot bursting the pipes. Lots of moldy wet books."

"Really? That sucks."

"Yeah. Especially because all I want to do right now is work on this new drawing, and it's painful as hell to concentrate with thirteen gazillion people looking over my shoulder here." She eyed the room. "Not like a free table exists, anyway."

"New drawing?" Felix tugged her sketchbook. "Let me see."

"Hell no." Natalia pulled it away. "Barely even started it."

"Please?"

"Dude, it's private. Besides, it sucks right now. Something's off about it. I know you post your every little doodle on the internet, like, fifty times a day, but I try to make sure that my artwork is at least good before I—"

"Forget it." Felix crossed his arms sternly. "Just hide things from me like that. Whatever. We might as well not even be friends."

Natalia groaned. "Fine." She handed it over.

Felix snatched the sketchbook and flipped right to *Dark-Eyed Boy*. She cringed.

Felix grinned so widely his cheeks looked ready to pop. "So, Natalia Gonzalez has a crush on the new kid, huh?"

"I do not." She whipped the sketchbook back. "Shut up."

"Oh, 'I do not.' Please." He pointed at the drawing. "Look at those fine details. Look at the adoration in every line!"

Her face flushed. "*Do* I have a crush?"

"Obviously." Felix yawned. "Totally your type. Way cuter than your last boyfriend, though. Seems like a more interesting guy too."

Natalia leaned in. "You met him?"

"He rode my bus this morning. Quiet as hell, but he seems like good people. I think he lives in Kaiser House, though..."

Natalia twitched. *Crap, that's not a good sign.* According to the old-time Heaven's Hooligans, Kaiser House had once been a small orphanage, but nowadays, it was a mystery. Thorne Century owned the house, and every few years, a new kid moved in, hung around for a while, then disappeared—kind of the way Catalina and those other girls had vanished, actually, but those mysterious children had never before ventured off the property or appeared at the high school.

"Kaiser House." Natalia shook her head. "Oh man."

"That's probably why he's weird." Felix leaned back. "I like *his* kinda weird, though. You know what I mean? When he smiles at you, it's like you just instantly smile back and feel good, like he's got some X-Men power to make everybody happy or something. Hard to explain."

Natalia laughed. "Maybe you're the one with a crush."

"Not my type. Anyway, about your drawing... it's awesome so far, but..." Felix hesitated. "Okay if I critique?"

"Okay," she said warily.

Felix got more credit for his talent than Natalia did, so his comments sometimes cut deep and caused arguments. Still, his advice was usually good, and she occasionally critiqued his work just as harshly.

"You messed up his eyes, I think." Felix squinted at the drawing. "Yeah, that's it. You're making him look too normal, too doe-eyed, not freaky enough."

"Oh, stop—"

"No, really. These eyes here, that you drew? Way too soft, Nat. This Jakobek dude—his demeanor is gentle, but he's got eyes that burn like crazy. Intense, haunted, spooky eyes. Like he's seen crazy shit, and most of it ain't good." Felix laughed. "You hear what I'm saying?"

"You're so right." Natalia closed the sketchbook. *I need to erase those dumb eyes ASAP.* "I need to see him in person again to get them right, I think."

Felix leaned into her. "Don't waste time. Your boy's right there." He gestured ahead. "Two tables down, all alone, ready for the girl of his dreams to come say hello."

Natalia swallowed. "He's here?" *Duh, of course he's here.* She tried not to look, but once Felix pointed, she saw him—and couldn't unsee him. Between the packed tables, the dark-eyed boy sat by himself at an unusually empty bench. His head was lowered and hood raised, with tangled black spirals escaping from the top. His earbuds were plugged into an ancient little phone.

"How come nobody's sitting with him?" Natalia asked.

"Because people are scared of him." Felix bit his lip. "Just like they're afraid of you."

"Seriously—"

"I am serious. I've talked to a lot of people today, and they all feel butterflies around him, but nobody's sure if it's a good thing. He's either everybody's new favorite crush or the creepiest thing ever. No one knows yet." He clapped her back. "So find out. You like him. Talk to him. Beat the crowds."

Natalia stared at Billy's gangly legs crossed beneath the bench. "I'm nervous!" she whispered. *Is that a good thing?* Her heart was thumping hard and fast, which seemed ridiculous. "You really think I should talk to him?"

Felix stepped away. "Listen, buddy. I'm gonna go catch up with some other friends. Do whatever you want, but if I don't see you sitting there by the time lunch ends, I'll tell this kid that the cute artsy girl in the back wants his number."

"Felix!" she cried.

"I will." He waved, jumping into the crowd. "Follow your heart!"

Then Felix was gone, Natalia was alone, and the dark-eyed boy was still sitting there. *And I'm carrying a drawing of this kid under my arm, so maybe I'm the creepy one.* She only caught herself gawking at the boy when his eyes flicked up at her. She ducked behind a crowd. *He saw me. Oh god.* When she peeked out again, though, he was smiling to himself. *Okay, if he's smiling, that's a green light. What am I going to lose, anyway? Do it.* Natalia stuffed her sketchbook into her bag. She stood up, fixed her hair, and launched herself ahead.

The first step forward was heavy. The second was lighter. Momentum carried her ahead. *I've got this.* Her heart thumped louder than her boots. As she approached Billy's empty table, those same weird, warm little electrical tingles pulsed through her. *Have I ever felt that before with anyone?*

Billy looked up.

She sat across from him. "Hey. I'm Natalia."

Over the table, she flashed her biggest grin. Under the table, her legs tangled into nervous knots. The strange boy took out his headphones, and his alien eyes, the color of polished obsidian, sliced her like a blade. Then he smiled, and the unearthly confidence in his pupils didn't match the tender fragility of his mouth. *This kid is damaged, probably abused*, Natalia thought, not sure how she could tell but already wanting to punch whoever had hurt him. Billy suddenly broke eye contact, as if he'd done something wrong, and fidgeted with a silver chain wrapped around his wrist.

"So, like..." She flicked her hair from her eyes. "We're in the same history class. You seem cool." He still didn't respond. *Oh my god, dude, this is so awkward. Please say something, like, two words at least.* When he smiled again, though, Natalia found herself smiling back. "I think we're both outsiders," she said, leaning closer.

Under the table, the denim of her pants brushed against his, and he drew away sharply. *Shit, I blew it.* She cringed. *Kaiser House kid. Definitely abused. Probably an orphan. Something about me coming too close creeps him out.* Not willing to give up, Natalia leaned in more slowly. This time, he didn't recoil.

"It's okay," she said. "So, are you able to, like... talk? Physically, I mean?" *Whoa, way to be offensive.*

Instead of shrinking from her, though, the boy grinned as if her question was the funniest thing he'd ever heard.

Thank God.

He nodded, giving her a thumbs-up.

"That's cool." She laughed. "I'd like to hear your voice." Natalia reached over the table and clasped his hand. The boy's eyes widened. He tried to shake free, but she refused to let go.

Suddenly, the floor dropped beneath her. Gone. Empty. Void.

She toppled through space. Hot electricity shot up her wrist. The hairs on her neck shot upright. Her saliva went dry. The cafeteria, the kids, everything but her and the dark-eyed boy vanished into nothingness.

"Where... am... am...?" she gasped, and the boy disappeared.

Her heart jumped into her head, and then she couldn't see anything. *Help me!* Everything was cold, then it went hot like the sun, and she was... was...

13: Natalia... (Somewhere Else)

Natalia is somewhere else. She's a little girl again. Bare feet dig into white sand. Seagulls squawk in the distance. Golden ocean waves reflect a golden sky. She remembers this and says, "I remember," but her teenage voice is unattached to her child mouth. The cool ocean feels wonderful on her tiny feet. It smells of salt. A heavy hand claps her shoulder, and she looks up to see Papá, her papá, young and alive, teaching her to jump the waves. She remembers. He is a living mountain of broad shoulders and chest hair, with a laugh so powerful it scares away every wave. He is... he is...

"Papá's dead," she says.

Dead.

The beach twists and mutates into a cramped car on a busy highway. Papá is gone. She is in the back seat beside two screaming babies who will become Juan and Carlos. Mamá drives, Abuelita reads the map. Papá is dead. Gone forever.

"Please take me out of here, Billy," her disembodied voice cries.

But who is Billy? She sees him in the sky, trapped in a dark, floating splotch of ink. She leaps from the car, flies into the heavens, and follows the dark-eyed boy into his darkness... flowing, vanishing... and they crash-land inside a factory. Thorne Century's logo is emblazoned on giant machines, pistons, and pumps, but something red-hot burns at the center of the room. A giant battery.

The boy touches this heat. He doesn't want to, but he does. The battery explodes. Fire roars through the factory. The walls collapse. Screams fill the air. Everything goes red. Everything spins, whirls, changes...

Mamá dead, Abuelita dead, everyone dead dead dead DEAD...

14

Natalia gasped for air. Cafeteria stench rushed up her nostrils. In the darkness, her respirations boomed like bomb blasts. Dim voices popped up around her, and she faintly recognized the sounds of her fellow students giggling and chatting among themselves. The shadows became colorful blobs then blurry outlines, then they sharpened into people until she finally woke up in the cafeteria she knew.

Tears ran down her cheeks. *Whoa, am I seriously crying in front of the whole school?* Everyone at the next table stared, whispered, and pointed—except Billy, who still sat in front of her, holding her hand.

He blinked away his own tears and nodded at her knowingly, as if to say, *I was there. I felt it too.*

She whipped her hand away. "Billy." She exhaled. "What the hell just happened?"

The bell rang. Lunch was over. Billy wiped his eyes then darted between the tables, escaping through the double doors. Natalia sniffled, crossed her arms, and ignored the vicious snickers of the kids around her. *I don't know if I can handle this.* Her hand burned like she'd touched a stove top. "Dark-eyed boy," she whispered dazedly, "who are you?"

In his haste, the boy had accidentally left behind his thin silver chain, which she now saw to be a necklace. It had a triangular Jewish star as a pendant, which surprised her. *I thought Jewish people only lived in that little Beth Shalom state.* The clasp was broken. *I could easily fix that for him.*

She hesitated, eyed the room, and stuffed the necklace into her pocket.

Part III:

Hod

15: Billy

Heaven's Hole was a strange place, as foreign to Billy as he was to it. After school ended, he wandered through the frigid ghost town, where For Rent signs were spray-painted onto brick buildings, the only bar was a sketchy dump, and the few restaurants were generic fast-food joints with flashy Thorne Century logos. Wherever he went, listening to the eighties music on his dad's old phone, the high ridges of the crater poked up over the mist, encircling the town. A lone fire tower stood atop the cliffs, a tiny blinking light at its apex, watching down like a lighthouse.

Every street Billy traveled upon, every broken window or rusty car he touched, carried an undercurrent of despair. Thorne Century was everywhere, from the people's hardened hearts to the ever-present stench of the factory's noxious fumes. *I hate that my body is such a huge part of this whole shebang.* Billy avoided the toxic energies of King Street and cut into the forest surrounding Solitaire Lake, the town's meager body of water. As he walked along the pebbly shores, cold winds sliced his exposed cheeks like shards of glass.

Beneath the trees, he came across a gaunt, elderly white man in a muddy jacket, huddling close to a campfire. Billy took out his earbuds and approached the fire's crackling warmth, and the homeless old man's anxieties shuddered into him. *He's afraid of being cold tonight. Even now, near the fire, his bones are icy. Muscles crack when he moves.* Billy sat down beside the man, who regarded him with a feeble nod then repositioned the burning sticks.

"Thank goodness you're here, Tyler," the old man said, peeking up through cataract eyes. "Haven't seen ya since last Christmas."

Billy unzipped his backpack. Mother had packed up a scarf and gloves for him, which he now offered to the homeless man.

"You sure?" The old man's chapped lips smiled, and Billy pushed the bundle closer. "Thanks, Ty." The man wrapped the scarf around his neck appreciatively. "Gonna snow tonight. Big snow. Too early in the season. Folks ain't even got the plows ready yet."

Billy nodded. From the bushes, a bony male chocolate Labrador skittered up to the campfire and dropped his head into Billy's lap. The old man reached over and scratched the dog's back. "This here is Buddy. My buddy, Buddy. Get it?"

Buddy rolled onto his back, so Billy rubbed his furry chest. Dogs—and babies, for that matter—never recoiled at his touch the way adult humans did. He suspected they had nothing to hide, no pent-up negative emotions that his weird powers unlocked. *Easier to face the mirror if you don't care what reflects back.*

The old man cracked his knees. "Figure I'll camp out till the snow hits. Then me and Buddy'll curl up in one of them abandoned basements on the west side." The man's teeth chattered. "We'll bring us some wood for those fireplaces and hopefully won't freeze our dang butts off."

Billy stared into the man's blueish eyes, which hung bags over other bags. *He's so cold.* Billy pressed his palm against the homeless man's back—his powers dampened by the man's four layers of coat, jacket, sweater, and shirt—and he inhaled the man's quickening heartbeat. *His name is Eddy Walker.* Billy pushed deeper. *Navy veteran. Alzheimer's. Diabetes. Homeless for ten years but grew up in this town. Hates the thought of living anywhere else. No kids. Only surviving today because he loves Buddy so much.* Eddy Walker gasped, and Billy ran his hand up and down the man's crusty old spine, popping little energy bubbles. *Feel warm, Eddy,* Billy thought, raising his other hand to the fire, absorbing its rays, then channeling them across his shoulders and into Eddy. *Take my warmth, Eddy. Take it right into you. Doesn't have to be a cold night. Be warm, so warm...*

Billy let go, and Eddy Walker sucked in air through his missing teeth. "Warm," Eddy whispered. "So warm..." His eyes widened.

Billy smiled, gave the dog one last belly rub, and left. He walked quickly, not wanting Eddy to see him shivering—having absorbed the man's cold feelings into himself—but before he escaped, Eddy called out, "Thanks... Billy?"

The forest trail eventually led back to town, and Billy felt peculiarly drawn toward a large, pointed brick structure labeled Thorne Century Groceries, currently closed for the night. *I don't care about whatever crap Thorne sells here. But this place... there's something special here. It wasn't always a grocery store.* The wooden double doors bristled with history. *So many memories here.* He prodded the iron handle. *Love. Community. This was...*

A jolt of familiarity struck him, and he stepped back to reexamine. It was a synagogue. As he stared at the structure, with its arched roof and tall windows, it seemed obvious. Touching the handle again, he felt decades-old energies of a thirteen-year-old boy in a suit grasping that same handle on the way to his bar mitzvah. Billy's heart pined for more memories. *I remember going to a place like this every Friday night with Mom and Dad. We went to a Reform synagogue, just like this place once was. I always imagined what my own bar mitzvah would be like... but it never happened. Not for me or Eli.* He leaned close to the jamb, trying to absorb more energies.

The door popped open. Apparently, the manager had forgotten to lock it. Billy checked around, made sure he was alone, and stepped inside.

In lieu of a kippah, he pulled on his hood. He passed by cash registers then moved through another set of doors into the sanctuary—or what *had* been the sanctuary long ago—lined with aluminum shelves stocked with breads, canned veggies, and cereals. The tall windows were pasted over with hideous advertisements for Thorne Century produce, Thorne pharmaceuticals, and Thorne beauty products. The raised platform that had once lifted the Torah ark now held frozen meat products. The bizarre contrast clenched Billy's gut like a fist.

The aisles were overloaded with the frantic emotions of stressed shoppers, so he ran his hand along the brick wall, snatching up the fragmented memories of the building's older days. *Peace. Calm. Joy.* Deep in his ear, lost between the bricks, murmured the musical sounds of a congregation singing "Lekhah Dodi" every weekend, welcoming the Shabbat bride. Smiling to himself, he hummed the tune, proceeding forward until his fingers slipped into three holes in the wall.

Bullet holes. He frowned. The music stopped. Pressing deep into the holes, he heard the gunshots then turned back to the door. He gazed into the misty past and saw the small congregation who had sat there, in seats now replaced by grocery aisles, their faces lit by candles. *What happened?* He shut his eyes.

Friday night. The people are singing. The lights are dimmed. The back doors swing open, and an angry, bitter man bursts inside. He is not one of them. He lights up the darkness with a machine gun. Bullets rip through heads. Chests. Necks. Everyone is dead. Everyone. Bullets crash into the ark, cut into the wall—

The ghost bullets vibrated through his body. His eyes slammed open, and he again found himself in the unlit grocery store. He looked back at the double doors, squinting, trying to see the haunting visage of the shooter who had broken in all those years ago. The dark silhouette of a man had no face.

The man was gone. In the shooter's place stood the Shape. The air crackled. Black smoke flowed down the dark figure's sides. Billy ducked to the floor, tears in his eyes. *Take a deep breath. Long, deeeeep breath. It'll go away.* The grinding sound dissipated, and he shakily rose up, peering through splayed fingers. The Shape was gone.

He sighed with relief but no longer wanted to be inside the dark community turned commodity. He stumbled dizzily through the aisles of Thorne products, the hardwood floor creaking beneath his steps. *This place is just like me*, he thought, rubbing his eyes. *I'm just a human version of Thorne Century Groceries.* He rushed outside, raced back to the forest trail, and finally stopped at an oaken bench facing Solitaire Lake.

He sat down, teeth chattering, and gazed out at the lights of the factory across the water, its smokestacks penetrating the sky like needles. *Ruins the view.* Inside him, Eddy Walker's coldness was joined by the violent memories he'd absorbed from the synagogue. He knew that seeing the dark figure again, just one day out of the tank, was a bad sign regarding his mental health. He needed to go back to Kaiser House and be put to sleep, or further visions might appear. *I don't want to, though. I hate that place. Being treated like a lab animal. Guarded by guns. Locked in a tank.* Shaking his head in disgust, he traced the various carvings in the bench's wood surface, peeking into other lives. One set of initials, as fresh as spring, belonged to a young couple who had shared their first kiss on the same bench.

Heat flushed into his chest. *I'd like to kiss someone like that.* Suddenly, all he could think of was the girl who had touched him that day, with her short black hair buzzed at the side, her piercings, and those small brown eyes, which had cut through his defenses like a dagger. *Her name is Natalia Gonzalez.* He smiled, rolling every syllable over his tongue. *She's an amazing person.* He remembered the softness of her hand and the charged moment that their jeans had brushed against each other. *She's so sharp. Brave. Smart. Creative. Everything I admire, all wrapped up in that one girl.* Because she'd touched him, skin to skin, he'd seen inside her. He knew all her strengths, her insecurities, and even the qualities she didn't know about herself. *I shouldn't know these things, though. I don't have a right. She didn't realize what she was getting into when she grabbed my hand, and—*

Little bites of coldness nipped his nose and cheeks. The first snowflakes were falling. He pictured himself kissing Natalia on that bench while snow settled on their shoulders.

Stop daydreaming. He sighed. *I'm a freak. A corporate science experiment. Not a real person. It hurts people when I touch them. I can't let that girl get close to me.* His stomach knotted up. He'd never kissed a girl, never cuddled, and definitely never had sex. He sensed, in his gut, that when he'd accidentally left his grandmother's necklace in the cafeteria, she had retrieved it. While that was better than it being lost outright, he had no idea how he was going to get it back from her.

Billy tried to appreciate the beauty of the snowflakes, but a whiff of toxic chemicals filled his lungs, and the sky filled with a fresh plume of black smoke from the Thorne Century factory. Chills ran through him. *It feels like this is finally the one. The factory in my nightmares. The one that I'm supposed to blow up, killing a whole bunch of innocent people.* He trembled. *I don't want that.*

Grinding noises sputtered in his eardrums. *Oh no.* He jumped to his feet. Black smoke surrounded him. Blue eyes lit up the darkness. The sound amplified. *I need to get back to Kaiser House. Tranquilized. Put to sleep. Fast!* His heart pounded. The Shape's dark presence weaved through the trees, creeping between branches, watching him at every turn.

A childish giggle erupted behind him. Billy turned around to see the ghostly form of Eli. This wasn't the same little brother he remembered, however. The new Eli had tiny, sharp teeth. Blood dripped down his chin. One eye was replaced by a gaping bullet hole, while the other glowed a hot, smoldering blue with indigo steam rising from the socket.

"Hey, Billy!" Eli snickered. "You belong to the Shape... everyone you touch belongs to the Shape..."

Billy backed away, legs shaking, brushing tears from his eyes. *It's not the real Eli. Remember that. Don't fall into the trap again. Get to Kaiser House.* Smoky tendrils lifted from behind Eli's body, like a giant octopus made of dark mist. The streetlamp burned out. The snowflakes became ash. Billy kept backing away.

"Help me, Billy!" Eli shrieked as his tiny body was absorbed into the Shape. The dark figure sliced into reality. Its shadowy claws extended miles from its body, winding like snakes through the forest. Eli's tiny head sprouted from the Shape's ethereal form, gasping for air, then screamed, "You're so much better than all of them!"

The head of Billy's father flowered from the Shape's leg, then came Mom's head and the heads of everyone else Billy had ever cared about. "Rise above!" they shouted. "Embrace the power!" All of them possessed the same fiery blue glare.

Billy covered his eyes. *No, please, no!*

In the darkness of his mind, the wrinkled face of his grandmother stared back at him. Her eyes didn't glow blue. They never did. "Run, little one," she said, "and don't look behind you."

Billy took off down the trail, curved back into town, and raced back to Kaiser House as fast as his feet could carry him.

16

That night, the sky emptied itself. The crater of Heaven's Hole was baptized in white. Snow blanketed the town's sins, and its immorality flowed like sewage into one small drain—a tiny, thin-skinned Atlas named Billy Jakobek, who raced through the night, carrying the weight of every person on his aching back.

The Shape. The Shape. The Shape is inside me.

Billy's footsteps slammed through empty streets, racing from the shadows. He was panting. Sweating. Terrified. The lights blurred together into a hazy wet fog. Eli's giggle jittered in his ears. *Kaiser House. Tranquilizer. Sleep. Stay focused.* Clean sidewalks gave way to potholed asphalt, and Kaiser House appeared on the horizon like a bleary mirage. He tripped. He fell face-first into a pit of snow and gravel. He got up, spat out rocks, and plunged downhill to the front porch, where two armed security guards—wearing sunglasses at night, like in that song from his dad's playlist—waited for him with no expressions on their faces.

The blond guard on the right, wearing heavy gloves, patted Billy down. Billy desperately tried to feel some sense of humanity inside the men, but they were totally invisible to him. *How many of those anti-Billy pills do these guys eat a day? They're like robots.*

The guard spoke into his walkie-talkie. "The subject is back at Kaiser, over."

The other guard opened the door. "All clear. Proceed," he said, ushering Billy inside.

The scent of burning logs and crackling fire, emanating from the living room, reminded Billy of his first childhood home, before Beth Shalom, where his family had often played board games by the fireplace. As Billy walked toward the living room, the laughter of Mother and Father cut through the walls.

They're not happy. They pretend to be, they try, but they're not.

"I'm still flabbergasted that it's already snowing," Father's voice said. "Should we even put up Halloween decorations?"

Mother's laughter was of the alcohol-enhanced variety. "You were never planning on doing that in the first place."

"No." Father snorted. "Probably not."

"This weather is insane, though. Jesus." She gave a long sigh. "The climate these days... you hear about the snow in Northwest Nevada Two? All those years of drought, then—"

Billy entered the living room, and the conversation halted as if someone had pressed a mute button. Mother and Father—who were lounging in front of the fire, shoes kicked off, beers in hand—froze into grimacing human icicles, staring at the sweat-soaked human lab rat before them.

Billy looked down. *Oy vey.*

Mother lunged to Billy's side, carelessly dropping her beer to the floor. "What's wrong?" Her mouth tightened. "You're covered in perspiration."

Father shined a flashlight into Billy's eyes. "It's that dark-figure business again, isn't it?" He was stating a fact, not answering a question. "You're having more hallucinations about this ridiculous shadow monster, boy, now, aren't you?"

Billy frowned. *It's not a hallucination, asshole.* But he nodded.

Father pointed down the hall toward Billy's bedroom. "Sorry, son, but we need to put you back in the dark tank. Take more samples. Eradicate this nonsense from you."

Billy's jaw opened in horror. He frenetically shook his head. *No, no, no. The tank seems to be making it worse.* He shivered uncontrollably, almost as if he was having a seizure. Mother and Father towered over him, pushing him back into a corner. He kept shaking his head.

"We can just put him to sleep, Father." Mother touched the man's arm. "Knock him out for the night, and he'll be fine—"

"I don't think so." Father glared sternly. "I think today was too much stimulation for the subject. He needs to go back in the tank."

Billy shrank down farther and farther, still shaking his head, looking up at Mother with pleading eyes. *Please, Mother, feel what I'm feeling. Trust me, don't put me in the tank. No, no, no.* Shadows coiled around the walls like liquid black snakes. Billy fell to the floor, tears in his eyes. *Don't make me do something I regret. The Shape is trying to swallow me.* His negative energies radiated like a heater. Mother and Father winced, clutching their heads. As the shadows coalesced around Father, writhing up his legs—*He doesn't even notice!*—Billy slammed back against the wall, knocking loose a chintzy thrift-store painting. It crashed to the floor and shattered.

"Listen." Mother faced Father with a quivering jaw. "The poor boy—"

"The subject," Father corrected.

"He's traumatized, okay?" Mother said with anger that flushed into Billy. "That's not our goal, Father. All we need to do is get him through the night. Mr. Thorne trusts my judgment on these matters, and you know he'll take my side." Behind her, blood oozed between the wall's cracks. Bits of plaster fell loose. Billy cut his gaze away from it, stifling a scream. When he looked back, the crack was gone. No blood. Mother stepped closer. "Billy, calm down."

"Don't let the hallucinations get to you," Father said. "The dark figure is just a figment of your—"

"Stop," Mother commanded him.

The doors flew open. Dozens of security guards spilled in from corridors, from their dormitories, clad in body armor and pointing their guns. Laser sights lit up on Billy's chest. He swallowed. *I've got to calm down.* Shadows coiled around their weapons, dripped from the barrels, and formed black puddles on the carpet. The heartbeats of everyone in the room pounded harder and harder into Billy's veins.

Afraid. Afraid of me. All of them. Afraid. Of me. I have the power. I don't want the power. Don't. Want. Shape. Too much. Can't control.

"We need to get him into the lab fast," Father said in a rattled voice while he glanced at his wrist sensor. "His emotional energies are surging. We'll put him in the tank and—"

"No tank!" Mother pushed Father back. She snapped on gloves, reached into her pocket, and took out a clear bottle with a hypodermic needle inside the lid. She crouched in front of Billy, her eyes blazing. "Billy, stay still."

With shaky hands, Billy rolled up his jacket sleeve and exposed his bare arm to Mother.

"Thank you, Billy." She plunged the needle in. "C'mon, let's go to your room."

The guards dissipated, moving back to their corners, guns pocketed away. Father gruffly went to the kitchen and grabbed another beer. Billy stood up, already feeling woozy.

Sleep sounds good. Yeah. Yeaaah... He followed Mother back to his bedroom.

17: Mother

The subject, as all Thorne Century staff were commanded to call him, passed out seconds after collapsing into bed. Dr. Roseanna Peterson, the researcher only permitted to refer to herself as "Mother," pulled the covers over the shaky, terrified adolescent, fighting back tears. She was mandated to strap him down—that was the safety policy whenever the boy had an emotional outbreak—but she didn't have the heart to do so. *Those straps are childish. Billy isn't going to hurt anyone.* She attached a heart rate monitor to him, took a quick blood sample from his finger, then turned out the lights as she left the room.

Mother went back to the living room, where the lights were also off but the fireplace still burned. On the coffee table was the children's book *Goodnight Moon*, which she'd ordered a few days before after noticing it in the background of one of Billy's old childhood photos. *Did you notice it, kiddo?* She hadn't asked, but she knew that Mr. Thorne wouldn't approve. He always reprimanded her for not treating Billy clinically enough.

Mother considered sitting by the fire, but with the lights off, the blinking red security camera was too distracting. In times of stress, the only thing that relaxed her was work, so she proceeded to the secondary lab on the ground floor. On the way, she passed by Father's room, where the nameless middle-aged man pretending to be her husband hummed an Aerosmith song. She wondered, not for the first time, who Father really was or how Thorne might have blackmailed him into working on the project.

She opened the door to the lab, and the antiseptic-scented room clicked to life as automatic fluorescent lights revealed metal tables covered in notes, computers, and test tubes. The walls were lined with refrigeration units, each one stocked with Billy's hundreds of blood samples.

She covered her eyes. *So bright.* In the secondary lab, it always felt like morning. Back before the project, back when she'd still been Roseanna, she'd always been a dedicated morning person—tending to the gardens as the birds chirped, reading books as the sun rose, then waking up her husband—so Mother's night-owl tendencies were an awkward fit. She sat down at her empty, undecorated desk and collapsed her head into her hands, fatigued but not sleepy. Her reflection in the computer screen was puffy eyed, shriveled, and unlike the face she remembered.

Rousing herself, she rolled over to the microscope and studied Billy's latest blood sample. Back when she'd first started working for the project, the mutated properties of Billy's blood amazed her. His emotional energies had stretched her consciousness, fueling her like the world's greatest drug. Billy Jakobek could pierce through the minds of others and rewire entire psyches. Even now, he seemed magical.

The blood sample bubbled. Her computer beeped, recording the matching energy readings being taken from the boy's bedroom. Mother bit her lip. *If these test readings are correct, the subject had an intensely positive experience today followed by an equally intense negative one.* She charted this as Billy's heartbeat thumped through the overhead speakers.

Her phone rang. It was Caleb Thorne. *Jesus Christ, I don't want to talk to him right now.* Her hands trembled as she took the call. "What can I help you with, Mr. Thorne?" she asked then second-guessed her tone. "Sorry. It's the middle of the night."

"Well." Thorne chuckled. "Good evening to you as well." Mother cringed at his voice, picturing Thorne's boyish pasty cheeks crinkling up into that horrible fake smile. "I have to say, dear, your greetings to me have become increasingly rude lately."

"Prisoners don't tend to be kind," Mother said through closed teeth.

Thorne didn't respond. The silence was harsh and prolonged and made Mother nervous.

He always hates it when I point out the truth. Recovering her senses, Mother said, "Sorry, Caleb. I didn't mean to be so sharp. It's just been a long day. Billy was—"

"Billy?" Thorne interrupted, his thinly disguised Southern accent poking out a bit. "You mean the *subject,* yes?"

"Yes, the subject. Of course. The subject had a stressful night."

"I see." He cleared his throat. "I appreciate that you'll be sending me a report about it in the morning, yes?"

"Yes." Mother felt the corporate man's hands around her throat. "To summarize, his energy levels spiked today after he was released from the tank, followed by another outbreak tonight. He talked about his dark-figure hallucinations again."

"Hmm." Thorne was quiet, and Mother pictured the man in a lightless room, fidgeting with his mysterious rusty pocketknife. "I would suggest, perhaps, more time in the tank... but we're nearing the endgame now, yes? The subject needs to absorb the maximum emotional energies, and that only happens outside of the tank. Highs, lows, friends, enemies... we need more samples. There simply isn't time for another blackout period."

Mother wasn't sure how to respond to this.

"Would you agree?" Thorne asked. "I am basing this assumption on your research, you know."

"Ah..." Mother fumbled. "You're right."

"Thank you," Thorne said. "I always trust your opinion. Listen, I'll admit to being dubious when you first recommended sending the subject to school and allowing him to have proper socialization, much less freedom to explore these miserable little towns you've been stationed in... but the evidence speaks for itself. The project would never be so far along if it weren't for your brilliant notion of expanding the subject's emotional palate." He cleared his throat. "But of course, you're always quite intelligent about these things. That's why I like you, Roseanna."

Mother cringed. *Roseanna.* Thorne said her name with a sick sense of ownership, hoarding it, knowing he was the only person who ever called her that anymore. She shook with anger and finally said in a tiny voice, "You're welcome, Mr. Thorne."

"However, you will report to me if the subject ever becomes too dangerous, correct? You know, I'm always worried about your safety, Roseanna—"

"He's just a boy, Caleb," Roseanna spat out.

"Mother"—Thorne had deleted her name again—"that thing in Kaiser House is not a boy. Not to you. Never. Do not risk the fate of our magnificent country on such saccharine platitudes. Our project is too important."

Mother furiously glared at her reflection on the computer screen. "I understand."

"This *is* a very important project."

"Yes," she said, hot anger dripping down into a cool, tempered loathing. "I'm sure you can't wait to profit from all those pharmaceuticals you're developing over at that big factory down the road. Big money. You and your dad's company will earn billions."

"*And* we'll help billions of people." Thorne sounded annoyed.

There was a silence. Mother stared down into the microscope again. *Please just get off the phone, Thorne.* "I should get back to work," she said.

"That's a shame. I was hoping you could pay me a visit tonight."

Mother's heart threw itself at her ribs. "W-What?" She swallowed dryly. "Visit? You don't mean—"

"Sorry for not warning you." Thorne chuckled. "I arrived in Heaven's Hole this afternoon. With the project so close to completion, I want to stay close until it's done so I can go to the factory and cut the ribbon, as it were." His voice rose. He was nervous. "I'm staying in the honeymoon suite of the local hotel. Same place as last time I came to town. I would... really enjoy it if you we could spend some quality time together while I'm here. Like last time."

"I... uh... the work here, it's..."

"Roseanna," he pleaded. "It's lonely in this wretched town. If you come to the rooftop here, the views of the mountain range are simply dazzling. We could order some... maybe, you know, some hot chocolate. Watch this bizarre October snowstorm together. Just for a little bit, you know, and then you can go back home, and we'll catch up more thoroughly tomorrow, after we've had some rest."

Mother wanted to vomit at the tenseness in Thorne's voice. She did remember that hotel. She remembered having to take a shower after she went there. "How is my son, Caleb? My *real* son. My *real* husband. How are they?"

Thorne's tone stiffened. "You know I can't tell you anything about them until the project is complete. The contract is—"

"Didn't you say that was your father's contract?" Her tone spiked. "He's dead. You're in charge of the company now, Caleb. You're your own man. You *are* Thorne Century." She desperately tried to feed his ego. "You can change those rules, do whatever you want to. Tell me, please, how my family is doing."

"They are doing well," Thorne said, and the smirk in his voice filled Mother with such rage that she could have hurled the phone across the room. "The boy is fine, and... he is fine as well."

"Do they miss me?" she whispered. "Do they—"

"Perhaps I'll tell you a little bit... just a tiny bit... if you come visit me?"

Mother gritted her teeth. *You fucking asshole.* "The same hotel?"

"You know the one," he said, and Mother could hear him smile. "You're really coming, yes? Should I go ahead and order the hot chocolate? Or maybe some wine?"

"Hot chocolate is fine." She hung up.

Mother swiveled her chair around, resisting the urge to topple every freezer and break every machine. *He's not going to tell me much.* She knew that. But after years of hearing nothing—years of terror that her family might be killed or worse, due to Thorne Century's infamous secrecy procedures—even the tiniest glimmer of news was enough to keep her going. *Maybe he'll show me a picture of them. A video. Anything.*

She threw on her jacket and hurried out into the snowstorm. "I'll be back in an hour," she told the security guards. Then she brushed fresh snow off her car, started the engine, and drove to the hotel.

18: Natalia

It was two o'clock in the morning, but Natalia wasn't even remotely sleepy. She was wired. Electrified. Sitting with her legs crossed in the center of her tiny closet bedroom—which was also, as it happened, the center of her equally tiny bed—Natalia had spent the night unraveling the strangest mystery she'd ever experienced: *What the hell happened when I touched that kid?*

A eucalyptus-scented candle lit the room from atop its mountain of clothes. A configuration of tarot cards was spread out on the pillow next to a Carl Jung book where she'd highlighted the quote, "The meeting of two personalities is like the contact of two chemical substances: if there is any reaction, both are transformed." She'd worked tirelessly on *Dark-Eyed Boy* all afternoon, and anytime she tried to put her sketchbook down, it called to her.

As her pencil crosshatched Billy Jakobek's cheek shadows for the millionth time, she spoke quietly into her phone. "I'm telling you, Felix..." She stopped, frowned, and erased her work. "I can't even describe it. Touching his hand brought me into... like, another world."

On the other end of the line, Felix laughed. "Wow, that's what falling in love is like for Natalia Gonzalez, huh? So dreamy!"

"I'm serious," she whispered. "It was a like a drug almost, like—"

"Like falling in love?"

"Shut up, dude." Natalia tried sketching Billy's eyes again. "More like some whacked-out hallucination. Sort of. Or a dream, where all my deepest feelings just spilled out of me... oh shit. Hold on." Natalia erased everything she had redrawn. "Damn it."

"Erasing again, huh?"

"Yeah."

"So I'm the only person you've told about this?" Felix still sounded dubious. "Am I really that special? I mean, Juan and Carlos would probably be psyched to hear about a real-life superhero."

"Whatever." Natalia closed her sketchbook. *Duh, of course he doesn't believe me. Would I?* She picked at the tattoo scab on her ankle. "I wanted to talk to my abuelita about it, but she'll just think I'm a lunatic, like you do. Besides, the whole family was having so much fun tonight. The boys are all excited about the snow day... I didn't want to ruin it with my craziness." Natalia stared into the flickering candle, wondering if the tingles she still felt in her hand were real. *Did I just imagine it? I couldn't have. Billy was crying, too, and that was super weird.*

Felix sighed. "Okay, okay, maybe you're not one hundred percent crazy." Felix's voice got muffled then louder as he seemed to readjust his phone. "I heard some other Billy Jakobek rumors today too. You know Cody Deerfield?"

"Felix, this is the Hellhole. Everyone knows everybody."

"Cody and Jimmy Washington got into a fight today," Felix continued. "First-floor bathroom, because Cody kissed Jimmy's girlfriend. I can confirm that part! Saw hickeys on Cody's neck. Anyway, Maria tells me that her boyfriend, Rico, said that—"

"Can you tell a single story without namedropping fifty people?"

"Sorry that I'm so much better at socializing than you, jerk. So according to Rico, Cody and Jimmy got in this big fight in the men's room—"

"Why do I care, Felix?"

"Because your boy Billy Jakobek ran in there, that's why. All quiet and stuff, but he stepped between the two of them, stared at 'em both, and supposedly, the two knuckleheads just... stopped fighting. It was all mystical and stuff, the way Rico says it. Apparently, Cody and Jimmy were hanging out again later that day, all smiles and crap."

Natalia watched the candlelight shadows dance across the room. "See, there *is* something strange about this guy." She tried to remember what it had felt like when she'd touched his hand. *The floor dropped away—I remember that. Everything burned.* Shivers ran down her spine.

"You there, Nat?" Felix asked.

Oh yeah, I'm still on the phone. "Sorry, zoned out." She blinked, feeling tired. "Hey, dude, I think I'm gonna take a toke outside and maybe go to bed. That okay?"

"Sure. Hang out tomorrow?"

"Yeah, sounds good. Later."

Natalia threw on her hoodie and tiptoed out of her room, taking care not to wake up the rest of her family. She put on her boots and stepped outside into a cold rush of air, and though the walkway itself was shielded from most of the snow, six inches of white powder had already piled up on the railing. Snow collapsed from the sky in white buckets, covering the entire parking lot, the roads, and the trees. Natalia smiled to herself as she scooped up some snow in her bare hands. *I wonder if Billy likes snow*, she caught herself thinking. *It'd be fun to walk around with him right through the storm. We could make a snowman, even. Silly stuff like that.*

Natalia shook her head. *Get your head outta the clouds, goofball.* She reached into her pocket for her joint, and her fingers instead got tangled up in the silver Jewish-star necklace she'd recovered earlier. It was fixed now. All she'd had to do was replace the clasp. *Can't wait to see his face when I give it back to him.* She giggled and dug deeper, finding the joint. *Just a couple hits. Or maybe one.* She tucked the joint between her lips.

The icy floor cracked behind her. Footsteps.

Natalia flipped around. Crazy Old Darrell Jenkins stood behind her, sandy hair tumbling down his shoulders. Ropes hung from the pocket of his ratty winter coat. He was holding something behind his back. For a moment, Natalia found the sight so bizarre that she didn't even recognize him, much less react. It felt like a lifetime had passed since their tense morning standoff.

"Darrell?" she whispered.

He slammed a fire extinguisher into Natalia's head. She went down hard, instantly, crumpling to the floor. Everything went black except for the hot bump on her forehead.

As her senses slowly returned to her in a swirling mess of colors, she felt herself being cradled in a man's arms—*Papá, is that you?*—until the stench of hard liquor rushed into her nostrils. Darrell had carried her down the stairs and into the parking lot. *Oh fuck.* She tried to scream. Her mouth was taped shut. Her hands and legs were bound with rope. Her forehead felt scalding hot. *This is* not *happening!* Natalia wrestled herself out of Crazy Old Darrell's grasp, but it was too late. He dumped her into the trunk of his car, closed it, and drove away with her locked inside.

19: Billy

Billy jolted awake. No one had strapped him down, so he tumbled from the bed like a spinning Tetris block and somehow ended up on his feet. Cold sweat ran down his back. His creepy laboratory bedroom lay lightless except for the blinking machines. *Something's wrong.* He groggily stretched his limbs. The metal door to his room had been left ajar. *The dark figure. Danger. The girl... Natalia.*

His bedside clock said it was 2:13 a.m. He sat down, rubbing his temples. *I saw her in the snow. It felt real.* In his nightmare, the quirky artistic girl from school had stood on a snowy walkway. *Her family's apartment.* A shadow man had approached her with something heavy in his hand. *A fire extinguisher?* And...

Billy jumped upright again. *She's being taken somewhere.* The reality of it sank into his belly like a stone. It wasn't a nightmare. It wasn't a future vision. *It's happening right now. Somehow, I feel her. Locked in a trunk. Trapped. Scared.* Her tense, fragile heartbeat pounded in the veins of his wrists, thumping up his arms, beating on his chest. He anxiously paced the room. *How am I feeling this stuff from her? After that tranquilizer, I should still be unconscious.* His energy-blocking bedroom door being left open certainly helped, but he wondered if maybe it was something else—something stranger. *She held my hand for a long time. I left some emotional energies in her, or she left some in me, or...*

Billy dumped those thoughts. *She's going to die if I don't act fast.* He threw on warm clothes. *I feel her. She needs me.* He peered out into the dark hallway, taking note of the window at the end. He focused on the energies in the house to feel out who was awake. *Mother isn't home.* He frowned. *That's weird.* Unable to feel anything from the security guards, due to their high anti-Billy scores, he couldn't risk going to the main entrance. *I'm supposed to be tranquilized. They're probably more relaxed, thinking I was put out for the night, but...*

The window. It was the only way. He tiptoed out, cringing as a floorboard creaked, then darted for the window. The frame was heavy, ancient, and fortunately not equipped with an alarm. After a hard shove, it sprang open, and he was pelted by a bladed winter draft. *Yeesh! I'm going into that?* He heard footsteps back in the kitchen, so he moved fast. He climbed out the window, slipped, and collapsed into a freezing mountain of powdery snow.

He bit back a shout, brushed himself off, and checked for guards. He couldn't see any. *If they catch me, my freedom is over. Back in the dark tank for sure. I'm risking everything.* These fears were spiked and inescapable, but Natalia's heartbeat inside him was louder and faster, and he knew what he had to do.

He escaped to the forest and didn't look back. Tree branches stabbed through the fog. Sky and ground met in a dizzying white euphoria that eclipsed the horizon line. His bones shook. His hands went numb. His tennis shoes became soaked and icy.

He kept running deeper into the woods, kicking up clouds of snow behind him. He didn't know where Natalia was, but he knew how to find her. He followed her heart.

20: Mother

Mother parked in front of the Thorne Century Boutique Hotel, the tallest and most glittery building in town, but she didn't get out. She left the engine running. It had been easy to find the place, since it was the only hotel in Heaven's Hole that hadn't been converted into apartments. Being there, though, made her nauseous.

The attendant in the front lobby eyed her suspiciously through the window. He waved. She waved back and then gnawed on her fingernails. *I don't want to go in there.*

She started to open the door then stopped. *Anything more than hot chocolate, and I'm out of here pronto. He'd better start telling me about my family fast... if they're really still alive... or...* She eyed the top of the tower, which was all lit up, then traced the glowing highlights of the building itself. *Fancy as it is, I would imagine it's not up to the standards of a spoiled brat like Thorne.*

She pictured him standing up there, holding two cups of steaming cocoa. Her stomach lurched. *I can't do this. Can't. Just can't.* Mother rooted through her purse, bypassing the cheesy magazine cutouts she kept there—in lieu of the nonexistent family photos that her Thorne Century contract didn't permit her to have—and took out her phone.

She texted Thorne: *Sorry, Caleb, feeling sick... rough night. I can't make it. Will have to postpone. Sorry.*

Then, before Thorne could text back and persuade her otherwise, she revved her engine out of the parking lot. She covered her mouth, swallowing back vomit. *Thank Jesus.* Relief washed over her. *I don't have to go up there—don't have to see him.*

As she drove, the faces of her husband and son flashed through her mind and stung into her relief like little bees. "I'm sorry, guys," she whispered, wishing she had Billy's abilities more than ever. "I want to find out how you're doing, but not here. Not like this, at this same goddamn hotel. Please understand."

They didn't respond, of course, because they couldn't hear her. *If they're even alive.* As she drove through town, she noticed that the lights for the local bar—the scummiest dive she'd ever seen—were still glimmering. A drunk man was smoking outside. She'd overheard a security guard mentioning that the bar stayed open until five in the morning. *Is that even legal?*

Mother didn't care. Going back to Kaiser House seemed miserable, and alcohol had never sounded so heavenly. She parked behind the bar, ignored the inebriated catcalls of the locals, and drowned herself in a two-dollar beer.

21: Natalia

The car rumbled down unplowed gravelly roads. Every time the wheels slid, Natalia slammed back and forth in the trunk. It was pitch-black. Cold. Her mind was an exclamation point. *Fuck, fuck, fuck. This can't be happening.* Her forehead still throbbed in the place where Crazy Old Darrell had hit her. Blood ran down her wrists and ankles where prickly ropes were bound so tightly that they dug into raw flesh. She tried for nearly ten minutes to reach her cellphone before realizing that she'd left it back in her warm, comfy bed, sitting by that eucalyptus candle, abandoned.

She kicked. Banged. Thrashed uselessly. She'd tried so hard to scream through the duct tape that her jaw was sore. *Someone, help me!* In the front of the car, Darrell listened to the fizzling embers of a classic rock station drowned in white noise, occasionally clearing his throat. The car slammed over a bump. Natalia's head crashed into the trunk. *God damn it!* She prayed for a flat tire, but the car kept rolling along. The trunk smelled of spoiled meat. *Does he go hunting? Oh god, what if it's dead people? No! Have other girls been inside his trunk before? Oh shit. Shit!* The car's sputtering engine roared uphill. She kicked the trunk door hard. *Pop open, you stupid piece of junk!* It didn't open.

After driving for what felt like an eternity but might have only been thirty minutes, the car came to a screeching halt. Darrell shut off the ignition.

Natalia waited there, frozen and terrified. *I can't hear any other cars—no voices, nothing. I'm not liking this one bit.* Crazy Old Darrell's heavy footsteps mushed through the snow. The trunk's lid popped open. Darrell loomed above her, a longhaired silhouette against a forested backdrop of white-powdered evergreen trees. His eyes, though illuminated by the trunk's interior light, were deader than a corpse.

He cleared his throat again. "C'mere, little lady."

Natalia responded with a muffled shout. Crazy Old Darrell seemed totally unfazed. He lifted her out of the trunk. The cold rush of air worsened her headache. She kicked, twisted, and writhed in his arms.

"Stupid Mexican bitch," Darrell muttered. He dropped her.

She landed in the chipped snow face-first. Her ribs ached. Her eyesight was buried in whiteness. Ice cut up her cheeks. Natalia screamed through the tape. She tried to rip her hands free, spilling more blood down her wrists.

Darrell pulled hard on the roots of her hair, lifting her face from the snow. "Don't bother fighting. Nobody can hear you up here." He threw Natalia onto her knees.

She found herself perched on the edge of a towering cliff as the entire crater of Heaven's Hole glowed beneath her like a glistening bowl of little houses getting filled with snowflakes. *It's so pretty from up here*, she thought briefly, and then her eyes widened. *Wait. We're over the rim, miles out of town, deep in the woods.* She whimpered. *Oh my god, he's going to kill me.* She felt the most helpless she ever had in her life. She couldn't talk back. Couldn't fight. She blinked away tears.

Darrell's clammy fist grabbed tighter onto her roots, and he swiveled her head to the sides so she could see the mountains surrounding them. "Nobody ever comes up here 'cept me." He pointed her gaze toward a small, empty circle of log cabins behind them. "These little cabins, here, used to be for the tourists. Good, decent folk, like I was. When they came to ski, they wanted a taste of nature, so they stayed here. Nobody comes here now, not since you illegals trashed my town, took the jobs, ruined the beauty of it all." He stomped his boot down on the back of her bound ankles, and she cried out in pain. He chuckled. "That's why I like killing Mexicans up here. Feels like a tribute to the old Heaven's Hole before Thorne Century came around and ruined it with you fuckers."

Natalia tried not to sob. She didn't want the sociopath to see her cry.

"Nobody's coming to help you, bitch," Darrell's boozy breath whispered into her ear. "You're all mine."

Again, Natalia screamed beneath the duct tape. *I don't want to die like this. Please, somebody help me. Maybe he'll feel bad. Maybe he'll let me go. Something. Anything!* She jerked away from Darrell, and he yanked back hard on the roots of her hair. She whimpered. He pressed a cold metal barrel to the back of her head, and she heard the gun hammer click.

"Don't take this personally." Darrell exhaled. "Trust me, you ain't the first chick I've killed up here, and you ain't gonna be the last."

Natalia sobbed through the tape. *Catalina. The other girls who've been disappearing. I should've known it was this guy. I shouldn't have stopped in front of his house.* She wept ferociously, imagining her family finding her corpse. *Oh god, I don't want them to see that. Please no. No, no, no.* But it was too late, and she knew it. She stared into the beautiful little Christmas village nestled in its cavernous hole, wishing there was a way she could go back.

Darrell didn't waver as she sobbed. "Take one last look at this sweet town, little girl." He pushed the gun harder into her skull. "*My* town, not yours."

Something rustled in the woods. A lanky human figure emerged from the trees, tiny footsteps crunching on the ice. Natalia screamed through her tape, trying to alert her potential savior.

Darrell pushed her sideways into the snow. "Who the fuck are you?" he shrieked.

Natalia craned upward to see what was happening.

Darrell screamed at the intruder again. "You heard me, mother-fucker! Go away, or I'll shoot you too!"

Darrell fired his gun into the air. Natalia shuddered at the sound, knowing how easily it could have gone through her brain. He aimed his gun back at the skinny little person but then trembled—bizarrely terrified—as the stranger came closer until the lanky body of Billy Jakobek was illuminated in the golden lights of the town below.

Natalia's heart stopped. *God, we're so fucking dead.*

Darrell shot into the air again. "Go away! This is your last warning, dumbass. Put your hands up!"

Billy did so, but he didn't stop approaching Darrell. The dark-eyed boy was shivering. His head looked too heavy for his scrawny neck. Natalia's heart thudded with every step he took.

What the hell are you doing, Billy? She whimpered at the thought of him with bleeding holes in his body.

"You got three seconds!" Darrell roared. "Three!" Darrell aimed the gun.

Natalia knew he wasn't lying. *Run away, Billy!* She squirmed against her ropes.

"Two!" Darrell growled. "Okay, that's—"

And then Billy Jakobek spoke. "Stop."

The dark-eyed boy's voice was a million voices from a million different people, all colliding at once. His exhalation burst through the forest like a firework show. Darrell dropped the gun. Sound waves rippled through the trees, the snowflakes, and the air, each noise filled with emotions, thoughts, sensations—sadness, fear, pain, happiness, joy, sorrow, heartbreak, hope, terror, cold, hot, life, death, sick, healthy, everything, everything, everything—

Natalia erupted in tears. So did Billy. So did Darrell.

A slew of ghostly humanoid apparitions surrounded Billy, and other ones swarmed to Natalia—grayed-out visions of Papá, Mamá, her brothers, Felix, Mr. Nazari, and everyone at school, all of them fragmented, wispy, but real. When she looked at Darrell, the old man was surrounded not by loved ones but by the small battered blood-soaked bodies of the many people he'd murdered—teenage girls mostly but also teenage boys, an entire synagogue that Darrell had shot with a machine gun, countless victims that Natalia didn't recognize, each person marred by the old man's bullet holes.

Darrell fell to his knees, roaring in pain. "Make it go away!"

"I can't change what you did," Billy answered. His voice cracked. It was more human this time.

Ghostly gunshots streamed into Darrell's body. He jolted as if electrified. He thrashed madly at the ethereal visions that surrounded him—guns, flags, Nazi propaganda, bullet-riddled corpses, beer bottles, car crashes, and the disappointed face of his dead son—but none of it faded away. The terrified old man picked up his gun, wedged the barrel between his lips, and pulled the trigger.

Blood and brain matter exploded across the snow. The former town councilman slumped to the ground, and his ghostly nightmares vanished into the mist. Everything that was weird and unearthly had disappeared... except the dark-eyed boy.

Then Billy fell to his knees and vomited. After a minute of dry heaving, he crawled toward Natalia on all fours—shuddering, pale, clammy with sweat—and collapsed before her.

"Mmfffhhh!" she cried through the tape, awakening him.

He sat up drowsily and rolled his wet sleeves over his hands. Natalia understood immediately. *He's blocking his skin so that the weird thing doesn't happen if he touches me.* He dug around in the snow, located a sharp rock, and ran its edge against the ropes binding Natalia's hands, over and over, until they finally frayed open, releasing her.

She ripped the tape from her lips, and cried out, "Oh my god, Billy!" She flicked her wet hair out of her eyes. "Holy shit!"

Billy's eyelids were heavy, and he almost pitched forward. With a shuddering sleeve-covered hand, he made a shush motion. He pressed the cold, wet fabric to her forehead. Suddenly, his damp sleeve became a heating pad. Nourishing warmth flowed into her skull, healing the pain from where she'd been hit by the extinguisher. The headache vanished, running right into Billy's wrist—and into his head. *Did he just take out my headache and put it into himself?* Billy's face became so pale that it matched the snow.

"You saved me!" Natalia grabbed his shoulders. "Billy, you—"

He fainted.

"Aw, crap." Natalia shook him, but Billy was out, and his clothes were soggy and crackled with ice. His sneakers were sopping. His eyelashes carried icicles. *Whoa, he must have walked here.* She shook him again to no effect. *This dude is going to freeze to death. Okay, think fast.* She freed her ankles with the sharp rock, stood up, and examined her surroundings. The closest log cabin had a towering pile of brittle old firewood stacked on its porch, probably a decade old, and a stone chimney.

Natalia looped her arms beneath Billy's wet shoulders. "I hope you're not heavy, dude." She dragged the frozen boy to the cabin, busted down the door, and started gathering firewood.

22: Billy

Billy woke up to the oaky aroma of burning logs. *Hey, this isn't the dark tank.* He peeled open his eyes and found himself inside a beautiful log cabin. It was still nighttime, and the cabin was bizarrely empty, with no furniture or furnishings. Weirder still, his hoodie and shoes had been removed.

Snowy winds rattled the cabin's windows. The walls creaked. He sat upright, his jeans catching splinters from the dry hardwood floor, and scooted closer to the beautiful stone fireplace lighting up the room. *Where the hell am I?* The flames felt nice, at least, compared to the wintry ice monsters outside. *Monsters.* He rubbed his eyes. *Like the monster I just... oh. Oh man. Darrell Jenkins. The murderer. Did I just...?*

The cabin door flew open, releasing a draft so intense it almost blew out the fire. Billy jumped. Natalia Gonzalez, the girl he'd somehow just rescued, pushed in a rusty wheelbarrow of sticks and logs. She slammed the door shut, wiped the sweat from her brow, and unceremoniously dumped her wood near the fireplace.

"Hey." She smiled. "You're alive."

Billy swallowed. *I guess so.*

Natalia crouched next to him, emitting a soft, flowery scent that he hadn't noticed before. She shoved more sticks into the fireplace. "Can you pass me one of the heavy logs?"

Billy closed his mouth, feeling dumb. He handed one over to her.

"Thanks." She stuffed it into the fire. "Thanks for the *other* thing, too, by the way. I mean, holy crap. 'Thanks' doesn't cover it, but seriously..."

Billy stared at her quizzically.

"For saving my life, duh," she said. "You did that. Like, I'd be dead right now if you didn't hike up here in the snow, with goddamn sneakers on... seriously, I'd be dead. I have no idea what kinda insanity just happened back there or how you found me, but..." She shook her head. "I guess I know why you're so quiet now—'cause you've got one hell of a voice."

Billy grinned.

"So, yeah." She smiled again. "Thanks." She sat next to him, kicked off her boots, and extended her feet toward the fireplace.

Billy traced her firelit profile with his eyes, his mind whirling at the memory of what had transpired. *I can't believe I was so... brave. Me? I stepped in front of a guy with a gun and... wow.* He examined the cabin, piecing together the fact that she'd probably dragged him into it after he'd passed out. *So I saved her, and she saved me. That's cool.*

As he fidgeted with these thoughts, Natalia scooted closer to him. She bit her lip, and Billy caught himself staring at her mouth. "You're kinda amazing, you know," she said. "Seriously."

Billy looked down. *Oh boy.*

"So, what's with that crazy thing that happens when you talk?" she asked.

Billy tried not to stare at her too hard. *Don't even think about kissing her. You can't.* To answer her question, he pointed at his mouth then splayed his fingers from his chin like an explosion. *Wish I had a pen.*

Luckily, she giggled at his creative display. "Um, okay." She bit her lip again, driving Billy crazy. "So, from my perspective, I heard... like, a zillion voices just explode out of you, like they were all stored up. You absorb something from other people, don't you?"

Billy nodded.

"You *do* absorb something?" she asked.

He gave her an energetic thumbs-up. *Please understand.*

"Like, a psychic or something?"

Billy nodded again.

She jumped. "I knew it!" She clapped her hands. "That's so cool! Okay, okay, so you're a psychic... uh, person. It's telepathy. Empathy? Something like that?" She looked up with a nervous half smile. "Hey, how can I get you to talk out loud again?"

Billy shuddered. He shook his head. *She could probably make me do anything, though, if she tried hard enough.*

"Please?" she said. "That first time you spoke was crazy, but when you talked again, right after unloading all the super baggage... it sounded more normal, like it was your real voice. You have a nice voice, actually. C'mon, please?"

Again, he shook his head.

"Okay, fine." She tossed more sticks into the crackling flames. "So, Mr. Jakobek, let me get this straight. You're psychic in some way, so you're probably always absorbing people's thoughts or feelings or whatever as you go around during the day. But more intimate contact, say talking or touching... that kinda stuff releases everything you've stored up, like, to an insane degree." Her eyes sparkled as if she sensed she was on the right track. "You're like a sponge that suddenly turns into a goddamn fire hose. Am I getting close? Tell me if I'm being dumb or—"

Billy gave her a thumbs-up.

"Awesome. Yes! That is so cool."

Billy couldn't hide his grin. He was touched by this brave girl's acceptance of what he was. *She even likes the freaky parts of me. It's so amazing.*

She stared at him, fire reflecting from her pupils. "Billy, I... I've been thinking about you nonstop ever since we held hands." Her voice was uncharacteristically shaky. "God, that doesn't sound creepy, right?"

Billy smiled nervously and gestured for her to go on.

"It's just, well... is there some kind of... special connection, between us?" She backed away. "I'm sorry, that sounds so stupid when I say it aloud. Yikes. Never mind."

Billy resisted the urge to hug her. *It's not crazy at all, Natalia.* He couldn't touch her without hurting her, so instead, he pointed at his heart. Then he pointed at hers. He moved a few inches closer, closing the gap between their equally twitchy nerves.

"We are connected?" She beamed, and he bowed his head in response. She clapped again. "Oh, I knew it. Billy—"

Snowy winds slammed into the cabin. Natalia jumped up, fists clenched as if ready for a fight, and then relaxed. "Just the snow. Okay." She shook her head then looked up. "Oh! One sec. I have something for you. Didn't expect to give it you after nearly getting murdered by some nutcase, but..." She dug into her pocket and presented Billy with his grandmother's silver Star of David necklace. "I fixed it. Just replaced the clasp. No biggie. I figured it was probably meaningful to you."

Billy stared at her, feeling as vulnerable as he ever had in his life. *I want to say thank you. Should I just say it? See what happens?*

Natalia went behind him, and before he could protest, she clasped the necklace around his neck without ever touching his skin or hair. After lingering for a moment, she slunk back to the floor. "Looks good on you. You're Jewish?"

He gave her a thumbs-up.

"Awesome. Y'know, I really want to know more about you." She flicked her hair out of her eyes. "Listen, man, I'm going to say something crazy. Can you touch me again?"

He shrank from her, bringing his knees to his chest. *Dangerous. If she learns more about me...*

"Not through your dumb wet sleeve either. For real." Sensing his reservations, she leaned closer, brushing against his leg. "I know you've been through some shit. I'm no psychic empath, but I can feel it. Obviously, somebody hurt you. Maybe a lot of people did. But people have hurt me too. I mean, just look at that nutcase earlier tonight. This'll sound super crazy, but I think we need each other somehow." She looked away, laughing. "Okay, that does sound crazy, especially since I'm talking to a guy who doesn't talk back."

He smiled, but he didn't lower his shield. Natalia pushed forward, leaning so close that their noses almost bumped. "Seriously, Billy, I want to hold your hand again. To see the real you in whatever weirdo psychic place you transport people to." Her eyes sparkled. "I get that it's risky, but I don't care. Please show me."

Billy gazed down at Natalia's ink-splattered long-fingered hands. He hated that the first thought in his mind was Caleb Thorne. *Thorne will hurt me if I show her.* But the more Billy considered this, the less he cared. This girl, with her big grin and her beautiful heart, already knew he was a freak. *She even thinks it's cool.*

"C'mon." Her lips parted. "I want to know you, Billy Jakobek."

He took her hand. Electrical sparks bubbled and popped between them. Her eyes rolled back in her skull. She fainted, and Billy caught her. Her hand squeezed his. He squeezed back. Their veins pumped blood together. Their heartbeats aligned. The cabin disappeared. The fire vanished. Painting through the darkness with a mental brush, Billy recreated the golden ocean at sunset, an image he'd plucked from Natalia's fondest childhood memory.

"Where are we... where...?" Natalia mumbled.

Somewhere safe, he thought, knowing she could hear him.

"What's... happening...?"

We're becoming one.

23: Natalia... (Somewhere Else)

Sunset. Natalia walks through perfect white sand as cool golden waves lap at her feet, reflecting a golden sky. She remembers this beach. Papá took her here once, long ago, when she was a little girl—but now that little girl is off in the distance beyond the squawking seagulls, playing with a papá who'd never died. She's not that girl anymore, so she faces the ocean.

Out in the waves stands the dark-eyed boy. His windswept hair is even curlier than usual. He looks back at her with a grin so confident that it takes her aback.

"Where are we?" she calls out.

"Somewhere safe," Billy says.

She is shocked by his voice—so normal, so calm. *It's a nice voice,* she thinks. *Deep, a bit raspy, with an easy softness to it.* He walks toward her, marching barefoot through the waves with an easy comfort that he never has in the real world.

"What's happening?" she asks.

"We're becoming one." His voice vibrates a bit, briefly charged with the many souls locked inside him.

Natalia spins in the waves. It all feels so real, so vivid, so exciting. She turns to Billy. "You can talk to me here? And you're somehow creating all this around us? That's so awesome!"

He grins sheepishly. "Thanks."

She runs her hand through the real-feeling waves as wet sand sinks under her heels. "This is one of my happiest memories."

"Yeah. That's why I brought you here." He bashfully kicks at the mud. "You deserve to be happy. You're an incredible person."

She loves hearing his voice. It's so surreal to see him talking like anyone else. But his comment bothers her. "I'm not as great as you think," she says. "Some of the thoughts I have, the things I do—"

"Are what make you human." Billy faces her directly. "Seriously, I know people. Everywhere I go, I'm surrounded by pain, trauma, all of it. But you, Natalia?" He blushes, looks away, then smiles at her. "You have no idea how powerful you are. Strength, bravery—that's you. You're going to do huge things in your life. I feel it. And compassion... the way you've taken care of your grandma, your mom, your little brothers after losing your dad at such a young age—"

"Wait, you know about all that?"

He looks embarrassed. "Sorry."

"No, seriously. You learned my messed-up family history just by touching my hand? That's crazy."

"Yeah." He exhales. "I can't help it. So many thoughts, memories, and names come through whenever I get close to someone. It's hard to sort through sometimes."

He stops, so she takes his hand. As the sun dips lower into the sky, they smile at each other, and she gives him the strength to continue.

"To me, it feels unfair. So many things you never told me, I just know," he whispers. "Strengths, insecurities, favorite things..."

"Oh yeah? Then let's hear some secrets about me, bucko."

He grins from the side of his mouth. "Eucalyptus-scented candles are your favorite." She gasps humorously, and he continues. "You prefer soymilk in your coffee. You like the shape of your nose. But you really, really hate your belly button. I don't really get why. Once, you poked at it for hours..."

She covers her stomach. "Okay, maybe less of the insecurities."

"Okay." He chuckles. "Deeper stuff. You stand up to bullies no matter how powerful they are. You fight for people. You break rules. You're impulsive. Passionate. So creative. You don't rest easily. And when you love something, no matter what it is, you love it one hundred percent, no limits, and you'll throw your life on the line for it."

Natalia beams with excitement. "I've got to say, man, I like the person you're describing."

"Me too." His eyes flash—and then he looks embarrassed.

Natalia squeezes his hand, not looking away. He doesn't look away either.

"You're right about one thing, though," she says. "It's unfair that you know so much about me and I don't know anything about you. Show me some of your memories."

As Billy looks down, the entire sky darkens. "My memories aren't so wonderful."

"Show me."

The water becomes cold. Storm clouds rise. He looks at her with a sorrowful expression. "Okay." The white sands darken into charcoal, ash, and volcanic rock. The waves crash hard against the shoreline. Holding hands, they walk down the cold beach, and as the moon rises, a dazzling array of glowing white orbs appear in the water, hundreds upon thousands of them bobbing up and down like buoys. Some of them float to the black beach, and Natalia realizes that they are people—ghostly visages of everyone Billy has ever felt, touched, or experienced swimming in circles around his mind.

"I don't know who I am, honestly." Billy gestures toward the orbs. "I did once. But now, too many other people are inside me." He points at the black storm clouds poisoning the sky, spreading their inky tentacles over the clouds. "I see myself in that darkness. I hope it's not me. But I don't know."

Natalia shakes her head. She's afraid of these storm clouds. She doesn't want to believe that it's where her dark-eyed boy comes from. "I don't buy it. There's such a light inside you, you know?"

"You're not the first person to tell me that." Billy smiles. "My bubbe once said—"

"Uh, bubbe?"

"Grandmother." One of the orbs bobs to the shore, and Billy dips his fingers into the light, revealing the face of a fiery old woman who looks much like Billy but with a million stories carved into her wrinkles. The woman stands beside a little boy with curly black hair, protecting him. "When people are happy," Billy says, "I feel this light. The one that you and she describe. Other times..." He frowns. "Imagine getting sick everywhere you go. Knowing everyone's most horrible secrets. Prejudice everywhere. Hatred. Bigotry. All that pain, negativity, suffering—it's awful. I always try to help, and it feels so hopeless. And the vibes I give off because of it..." He sighs. "You can't imagine what it's like. Every time I walk into a room, people jerk away in fear—"

"Oh bullshit." She hits his arm. "You think I can't imagine what it's like to feel othered? You wanna see what it's like being a Latina in this country sometime?"

Billy slumps over, embarrassed. "You're right. I'm sorry."

"Anyway..." She leans on his shoulder and points at the little boy in the orb. "You were really close to your grandmother, weren't you?"

"Heh. Yeah." Billy smiles. "Guess me and you have that in common." The orb spins around them, and Natalia sees the little boy at his grandmother's deathbed, holding her hand. "Amazing woman. Holocaust survivor, though she never told me. I found out when I touched her hand." He sighs. "I absorbed her memories. Me doing that helped her die in peace, I guess. But her memories of the concentration camps..."

"Whoa." Natalia holds him. "That must've... changed you, right?"

"Sure." He nods. "Everything changed when she died. In her room, I once found a big book with our whole family tree in it. My mom's side were all Ashkenazic, of course. Eastern European..." He shakes his head. "Most of them became refugees or died in the Holocaust. But my dad's side, half of those were Sephardic Jews—"

"Huh?"

"They came from Spain and Portugal, I mean. Those ancestors were forced out during the Spanish Inquisition. Exiled."

"Whoa." Natalia looks down at his hands, which are clenched. "Do you—do you feel them inside you? With your powers, I mean?"

"Faintly. Like flickers of light." He taps his chest. "One ancestor especially. His name was Isaac, which is my middle name. Spanish knight in the fourteenth century—"

"Holy crap, your ancestor was a knight? You have records that far back?"

"Not anymore." He sighs. "They're lost now. Like I said, everything changed when my bubbe died. She always said my gift was meant to help people. I still try to believe that. But then..." He takes a deep breath, and points at the darkness again. "I always see this."

Boom.

An explosion rocks the horizon. Natalia jumps—then notices that Billy isn't running away, so she stands still even as her ears ring and the ground shakes. She stares out, trembling, and sees the shattered remains of a Thorne Century factory burning to the ground.

"Is that—"

"A factory, yeah. Maybe the one in Heaven's Hole, maybe a different one. All I know is that ever since I was young, I've had visions of it exploding, and..." He looks away from her, and his voice shrinks into his chest. "It's going to be my fault. However many people it kills, it'll be because of me. I'm the one responsible. Somehow. I see this damn explosion over and over, and it tells me that someday, the darkness will win."

"Or maybe it's just a nightmare," she offers, trying not to show how much what he's saying bothers her. "Or you're interpreting it wrong."

He looks weary. "Hope so."

"So..." She hesitates. "Can you tell me why you live in that Kaiser House dump?"

Billy sighs again. "You want the speech? I'm part of an important medical project. Thorne Century, of course. I'm pretty sure they own a copyright on me." He scoffs. "I've lived in various laboratories since elementary school. It's for a good cause at least. Thorne Century uses my body to create new pain relievers, cancer treatments, antipsychotic drugs... so they tell me, anyway."

Natalia reels at this. Whatever she expected to hear, this isn't it. "That is so goddamn weird."

"Yeah." He snorts. "Try sleeping in a chemical tank."

"Whoa." She touches his arm, and he leans into her. He suddenly seems even more damaged than before. "I'm so sorry, Billy. What about your parents?"

Billy freezes up, and the sky reddens. The orbs reflect it, casting scarlet on the water. Billy kicks the water, suddenly looking like a little boy. "I guess you really want to know." Tears well up in his eyes. "Okay." The blue flames on the horizon flicker into nothingness. The air cools. The scarlet orbs move faster and faster, spinning in circles, multiplying, and then...

Natalia finds herself in a hallway of doors resembling a hotel corridor. Sounds of the beach fade away. The smell of saltwater is replaced by dust. She spins around, paralyzed with confusion, and Billy's voice echoes through the walls.

"Choose what you want to see," he says and fades away.

She looks at the door immediately to her left. On the other side, she hears laughter. "Oh, I get it."

She cracks open the door, and on the other side is a messy living room lit by candles. The power is out, and a small family sits around a table, playing a board game. Natalia spots the little boy Billy right away—his curly hair and downward-cast black eyes are a dead give-away—and she laughs.

"You're a cute kid," she says.

She examines the other family members and quickly picks out Billy's mother—her name is Ruth, she senses—who looks just like him. The bearded man, Jake, is his father. The grandmother she's seen before, and the bouncy little boy—shrieking every time he wins a round—is Eli, the little brother. Satisfied by this memory, Natalia closes the door.

She opens the next door in line. In this room, the same two little boys, Billy and Eli, race around the apartment with flowing red capes tied around their necks. As these superheroes save the world, their grandmother reads a Russian novel. Natalia smiles, reminded of Juan and Carlos, and closes the door.

"I'm going to change this up." She goes farther down the hall, touches a doorknob—and it's scalding hot. "Ouch!" She waves her hand, cooling it off. "What the hell, Billy?"

Billy doesn't answer. She leans into the door. Machine-gun fire splatters the other side. A loud explosion shakes the frame. She smells smoke. "Shit." She reaches for the knob, grits her teeth at the burning metal, and flings it open. In this room, the apartment from before is on fire. She chokes on the thick black smoke. Cracks break through a wall, and it comes down. The family—Billy, Eli, Jake, and Ruth—are racing around, shouting out to each other.

"Jake!" Ruth cries. "We've got to go outside!"

Another explosion rocks the street. The sound of machine-gun fire breaks through the crushing inferno.

"Out there?" Jake coughs. "Do you hear those guns—"

"We sure as hell can't stay here!" Ruth screams, and there's not much arguing with that. The ceiling caves in, destroying the kitchen table. Billy races to Ruth's side. Jake grabs Eli and throws the boy over his shoulder. The family charges out the front door, breaks into the street, and—

"Oh my god." Natalia covers her mouth. "I saw this on the news."

The news, though, never captured the carnage. Every building on the block—except the factory, protected by distance—is burning to the ground. People race down the sidewalks, covered in dust and soot, only to be gunned down by a squadron of men in body armor. The gunmen don't have faces. Their helmets are opaque. They look more like beetles than men as they fire into the crowds, littering the sidewalks with bloodied corpses.

The Jakobek family looks around, and the horror in Jake and Ruth's eyes as they glance at their boys makes Natalia's heart sink. "We can go through the factory," Jake cries. "They haven't hit it yet. C'mon, Ruth, let's—"

The beetle-men unleash their guns upon Jacob Jakobek, ripping his body into bloody chunks. His faceless, gutted mass falls to the asphalt, sending a screaming Eli scuttling behind him. Eli crawls away, sobbing, alive—but one of the bullets has blown out his eye. A bloody black hole remains where the eyeball once was, and as the boy sobs, he can only form sputtering sounds rather than words.

Natalia almost closes the door, but she stands her ground. "No, no, no..."

Eli crawls, sobs and cries from his one eye, and crawls some more until Ruth and Billy race to his side. The little boy reaches for his older brother, and Billy takes him into his arms. Crouching down, releasing his own tears, little Billy puts his palm over his brother's bloodied eye.

Natalia knows what he's doing. "The same thing you did to me, with the headache..." She winces. "God."

As Billy tries to heal his brother's pain, though, at least fifteen of the armored beetle-men stomp up to the Jakobek family, surrounding them—and they point their guns right at Billy's tiny chest. The little boy's eyes widen.

Ruth puts herself in front of the guns, holding her hands up. "Leave us alone!" she roars.

One of the armored men steps forward. "Give us the boy," he says in a Boston accent. "He's our target. Move aside, lady, and you will not be harmed."

Ruth glances over at both her sons. Her eyes narrow as she examines Billy, realizing exactly which *boy* they want. She spits at the man's visor. "You can't have him."

The lead beetle-man steps forward and removes his helmet, revealing a dirty-blond military cut, a steel jaw, and blue eyes that look surprisingly apologetic. "Lady, don't make this harder than it already is. That boy you have—he's not human. Listen, I know this is difficult. I have a wife and son at home myself, and if you give us the boy peacefully, we'll get medical treatment for you and your other son." He points at the howling one-eyed Eli. "But that monster, Billy Jakobek? We have orders, and he's coming with us."

"The only monster is you," Ruth snarls.

The gunman frowns, seeming surprisingly bothered by this comment. Eli wails in horror. Billy freezes. Ruth and the blue-eyed soldier face off for a heated moment. The man sighs, looks down, then points his gun at Ruth's head. "Back off, Jew. I'm not a monster. Just a regular guy following orders."

"Keep telling yourself that."

"I said back off!" the man shouts then unloads his machine gun into Ruth's body while the other men shoot Eli.

Blood sprays everywhere. Natalia covers her eyes, and when she peeks back through splayed fingers, the little dark-eyed boy—so young, so innocent—is standing over the bloodied, broken corpses of his entire family.

The unmasked blond beetle-man looks at his handiwork, slack-jawed and horrified. He raises his gun at Billy again. "Come with us."

The beetle-men close in on Billy with their guns raised. For a moment, the boy seems ready to collapse in on himself—crying, horrified, broken. But then, as the men step closer...

His face darkens. His eyes slice upward. The boy stands upright, faces the men who killed his family—and suddenly, they all step back from him.

"I hate you," Billy says.

His voice vibrates through the air. The beetle-men freeze. They take off their helmets and drop them to the ground in unison as if following a dance. The blue-eyed man looks around at his team, shocked. He points the gun at Billy Jakobek and—

"Point those guns at yourselves." The boy cocks a finger under his own chin.

The blue-eyed man does what the boy orders—not with his finger but with his gun. His hands quiver. He doesn't want to. He's fighting it. The other men stick their guns inside their mouths, fingers on their triggers. They cry, gasp, and struggle to resist, but the child who controls them isn't a little boy anymore. His face is streaked with dark veins. His eyes are blue flames. Standing behind him is a tall dark shadow in the outline of a man—a towering hole cut in space, with the same fiery sapphire eyes. Wispy tendrils sprout from the dark figure's sides, wrapping around the boy's limbs. The dark figure raises its sinewy arms to the sky—arms that run the length of the entire street.

"What the hell is that?" Natalia screams.

From somewhere outside the hallway, outside of the vision, the Billy she knows finally answers. "It's called the Shape."

The Shape grows over Billy's shoulders, feeding its darkness into the flames. Tears run down each of the gunmen's cheeks. The shadow boy's rage is red-hot and palpable, and the blond man breaks down in tears. "I was just... following orders... I have... a family..."

"So did I," the boy says. "Bang."

The guns go off at once. The beetle-men shoot their own brains out, and their headless bodies drop to the street. The little boy stands there, surveying the bodies, walking through the smoke and flames... and then slowly, realization dawns on his face. The blackness streaks away from him. His eyes soften, and he drops to his knees, sobbing and confused. He crawls back to the corpses of his family and shakes them. "Please come back," he whimpers, clutching Eli's head. "Please be a nightmare..."

Natalia closes the door. "Okay." She shivers. "I get it."

The hallway disappears in a swirl of light, and everything fades away.

24

Everything was blurry and faded. Tingles ran down Natalia's spine. Burning logs crackled. The snowstorm whistled at the dusty cabin windows. She blinked, remembered where she was, and nestled down into the warmth of Billy's embrace. *He's been holding me this whole time?*

"Billy," she whispered. "Can you hear me?"

He squeezed her hand in affirmation but didn't speak, and Natalia already missed his voice. He tried to let her go, but she drew his arms back over her. "I like it when you hold me," she said, tucking into the dip of his chest.

He nodded.

"You *can* touch me, see?" She ran a finger down the protruding vein in his wrist, feeling the pumps of his heart—and the pumps of so many emotions inside it, little electrical charges that didn't belong to him or to her, emotions that created flickering, fuzzy images of other people in her mind. *So trippy.* "I think, actually, that you *can* touch people and even talk. I think it's just like a muscle that's all worn out because you never use it, and the more you do these things, maybe... you get what I mean?"

She faced him. Tears streaked down his cheeks, and he looked away in shame.

"Hey, you." She hugged him, and he melted into her. "I can't believe you went through that. You know it's not your fault, right?"

He shook his head. More tears rolled out.

"Listen to me, Billy." She gripped his chin, turning his face toward her. "What those assholes did to your family was not your fault. Got it?"

Billy nodded. He didn't seem convinced, but he squeezed her hand again, showing his appreciation. Natalia wiped his tears away. Each tear carried the sound of a gunshot, but she kept wiping until his cheeks were dry. "I can't imagine how alone you've felt," she whispered.

Billy nodded, blinking back more tears.

Natalia lifted their clasped palms. "I know we just met, but hear me out. You're not alone anymore, okay?" She kissed his hand. "Because I'll never let you go."

The dark-eyed boy smiled through his tears. Natalia snuggled into him and rested as his heartbeat thudded into her, spreading warmth down her belly, into her legs. *He knows me. And now I know him too. This is so crazy.* To her delight, Billy started playing with her hair. "That feels nice," she said, and fortunately, he kept going. "So hey, I guess we're snowed in for the night, huh?"

Billy nodded.

He's scared. I can feel that. Both of us are going to be in huge trouble tomorrow. In the meantime, Natalia didn't want to think about that, and neither did Billy. Not letting go of Billy's hand, Natalia stashed more wood into the fire.

They curled up together on the hardwood floor. As the snowstorm blasted the cabin, the fire kept them warm. They weren't safe, but as they gently drifted off to sleep, they *felt* safe, and that was the only thing that mattered.

Part IV:

Netzach

25: Billy

Billy awoke early the next morning. No birds chirped. Sunlight barely peeked through the cabin's yellowed windows. The snowstorm had stopped sometime during the night, and the fire was mostly burned out. He clung to the sleeping girl in his arms, still reeling from everything that had transpired. *Are you real, Natalia Gonzalez, or did I just dream you up?*

She yawned, stretched, and smiled up at him. "Hey, you."

He grinned back. *I guess you're real.* They stood up together, hands clasped—never letting go, not even for a second, for fear it might disrupt their connection—and awkwardly tumbled back into shoes and jackets. Their joints were creaky and their stomachs empty, but the energy shared between them was so vibrant that they needed nothing else. Once bundled up, they walked outside into the morning sun, which had frozen a thin, crunchy layer of ice over a foot of fresh snow. The body, presumably, was buried under the snow, but they didn't look for it.

Behind the cabin, a young deer stretched its neck into beams of sunlight. The animal peered into Billy's eyes and approached them like a familiar pet. "Is it just me, or is that deer staring right at you?" Natalia whispered, frost rising from her breath.

Billy nodded. *I guess animals don't do that for normal people.* He stroked the deer's white-speckled back, and Natalia followed his lead.

"So cool." She giggled.

Then the deer scampered off into the forest to begin its day, and the two teenagers trudged along the snowy crest of Heaven's Hole. Their clasped hands found a warm home in Billy's jacket pocket. Despite how cold it was, neither of them wanted to go back into town. Not yet.

After a half hour of aimless walking, Natalia pointed at the blinking light on the horizon. "Hey, let's climb up the fire tower." She beamed. "I've always wanted to do it."

Billy agreed. *Hell yeah. Sounds good.*

The goal made them walk faster. They scaled farther up the cliff-side, hiking through the rocks, stepping over fallen trees, almost slipping across icy trails. Finally, just as their calves were burning and their lungs drained, the steel colossus rose before them. The fire tower's light blinked down from heaven. Billy stared up in awe.

Natalia nudged him. "Looks way bigger up close, huh?"

He nodded. *Sure does.*

The rusty monolith rose into the sky like the hand of Adonai, grasping the clouds in a mighty palm. A rickety metal staircase spiraled up the tower's skeleton. Surrounding its base were sharp metal fences that unnervingly reminded him of the barbed wire fences he'd seen in his grandmother's memories long ago. Clearly, people weren't supposed to go up the fire tower.

Just as clear, though, was the fact that Natalia didn't care whatsoever. "Let's go!" She tugged on his hand, laughing. "C'mon, slow poke!"

Natalia pulled him to the fence, tucked her toe into one of the rungs, and yanked upward. "We've got this." She looked back. "Don't let go of me!" Billy followed her lead. They scampered to the top of the fence and leapt down, tumbling into the snow. "Almost there!" She laughed, brushing the snow off.

Together, they ascended the tower's first grated metal step. The railing shuddered. The foothold was icy. They looked at each other, smiled gleefully, and marched ahead. Each staircase reached a small landing, turned, then led to another staircase.

The railings had corroded into sharp safety hazards. Every set of steps rattled more than the last. The higher they went, though, the less Billy worried. *I can't remember the last time I felt so alive.* Heaven's Hole opened beneath them as if they were riding an escalator into space. He grinned so hard that his cheeks hurt. Natalia did the same. For the ten minutes it took them to dangerously progress up the fire tower, the two damaged adolescents became innocent kids, again, on a grand adventure.

Before Billy could realize it was happening, they'd risen to the tallest reaches of the sky-high platform that had seemed so impossible before. The blinking light waited right over their heads. The metal balcony spread before them like a welcome mat. Natalia enthusiastically shook his shoulder. "I've *always* wanted to come up here!"

Billy smiled. *Yeah, it's awesome. Especially with you here.* Together, they leaned over the railing and looked down from the top of the world. From so far above, the crater's ominous ridges were less like a barrier and more like comforting arms encircling a quaint village. *So many people down there.* Thousands of unique emotional energies whispered to him from below. *I bet if I closed my eyes up here, if I focused, I could feel the entire town at once. That'd be so amazing, but scary...*

"Hey, hero." Natalia bumped him. "I know what you're thinking."

Billy frowned.

"What? I do. We haven't been holding hands all day for nothing," she teased. "You've got a whole town down there, sending up crazy psychic signals and stuff, and you want to test your limits. You want to feel everybody down there at the same time. Am I right?"

Billy's mouth opened. It felt weird having someone read him the way he always read others. He nodded to her, refocused, and closed his eyes. From the town, thousands of soft little lights pricked through his darkness. Pockets of warmth just out of reach. *People.*

Feelings... they're there... but... He choked. *Too much.* He stepped back, so dizzy he almost fell.

Natalia caught him. "Didn't work, huh?" She held out a hand, catching new snowflakes. "Huh, it's snowing again."

Billy glumly stared down at the town. Embarrassment and irritation ran through him in equal measure. *Great. For the first time, I get an opportunity to show off to someone who actually thinks what I do is cool... and I'm not good enough.* He glanced up at the cascade of snowflakes. *Figures.*

Natalia hugged him. "Billy, I think I know what your problem is... you know, with these powers. You're afraid of them."

Billy wasn't sure how to respond.

"Hey, man, I don't blame you," she said. "You've survived some seriously heavy stuff, so it's normal that you get scared. But you know what? You're so sure that you can't touch people, but then here we are"—she lifted their clasped hands—"touching. Here we are, hanging out, even though we're probably not supposed to. And guess what? It's fine. I'd even say it's *good.* So yeah, you might think you're not strong enough to connect to that whole town at once since it breaks whatever limits you think you have... but last night, you heard me crying for help from all the way in Kaiser House, and you came. To be honest? I don't think you *have* limits."

Billy studied her hopeful glow and thought, *Maybe.* Snowflakes spiraled around them, nipping their faces, showering the countryside with an additional layer of crystallized cake frosting.

Natalia leaned closer. "Stop being scared that you're gonna cause explosions, dude. Don't be afraid of being true to yourself." Her voice softened. "And talk to me, for crying out loud."

Billy shut his eyes. *Do it*, his instincts screamed at him. His stomach fluttered. *Take the chance.* His legs wobbled. He took a deep breath, eyes still closed, and cleared his throat.

He said, "I'm not afraid."

Tingles danced down Billy's skin. He shivered, standing in place, terrified of what he'd just done. *She's going to have a panic attack. She's going to hate me. She's going to feel my negative energies and know how awful I am.* He pried open one eyelid then the other. Natalia hadn't moved. Bouncing electrical lights sparkled from her like fireflies.

Billy exhaled, and his exhalation became a laugh. "You, uh... you..." He got too excited, paused, and tried again. "You feel good?"

"Yeah." She bit her lip. A snow-speckled curl fell over her face. "I do."

Billy smiled, shaking his head. *This is insane!* He cleared his throat. "You're not scared of me."

"You're way too sweet to be scary," she murmured. "But I'm a little scared about what happens whenever we go back down there. I mean, do they put you back in that tank thing? I hate that thought. I like hanging out with you."

Her face softened. Suddenly, she looked ready to cry. They shivered together, embracing each other's gangly teenage bodies in the frosty winds. Billy inched closer to her—then even closer—and brushed his fingers along her cold cheek. *Oh boy. Am I really doing this? Yes. I'm doing it.* His heart pounded. *Here goes nothing.* Billy lifted her chin. "Even if they force us apart, Natalia, it won't last. I'll find my way back to you. No matter what it takes or how long."

"You promise?"

"Yeah." He smiled. "And when we meet again someday... I want to hold your hand as the world explodes around us."

He kissed her. Just a peck on the lips, a tiny kiss in the snow. *It's real. She's real.* He drew back. His heart leapt to his throat. The feelings inside her—inside them—glowed just as much as the fireplace had.

Natalia touched her lips in disbelief and gasped. "Whoa."

"I'm sorry," he said. *That was too bold. Too scary.* "Maybe I shouldn't have—"

"Shut up." She grabbed his shirt and pulled him in closer. "Kiss me again."

He did so. Sparks blasted between them. Their bodies melted together, and in the dark warmth between them, the tiny lights of the town pushed upward.

"Oh my god," Natalia said between kisses. "I feel it."

"Me too."

From the countryside below, the population of Heaven's Hole splashed into them like a tidal wave. Energy reverberated down the surface of their skins, making every hair stand on end. Their hearts thundered. Arteries, capillaries, and veins opened like balloons. Within the tiny town below, they became connected to every single person by thousands of shaky strings. *Together. One.* They felt the other high schoolers celebrating the snow day. Felix was watching a movie, bored, wondering why Natalia hadn't answered his calls. Mr. Nazari shoveled snow from his driveway, his bad knee acting up. The homeless man, Eddy Walker, snuggled in a damp basement with his dog, Buddy. Natalia's mother toiled away in a hot factory while two little boys, Juan and Carlos, played in the snow. *So much joy in those kids. It's beautiful.* Together, Billy and Natalia roamed through the crater like two flying ghosts, experiencing love, pain, sadness, frustration, anger, joy—and hope. All of it, good and bad, came from hope.

"So many emotions." Natalia teared up. "It's like... everyone is the same deep down. Everybody's just hoping for something more, something great, and trying to make it happen. I mean, I knew that, but to feel it..."

"Yeah. It's crazy." Billy's voice had become gravelly. He'd talked more in the last ten minutes than in his whole life leading up to that point.

Natalia wiped her eyes on Billy's sleeve. "I've never felt so close to so many people before. Totally surreal. And you... whoa, hold on." She cocked her head. "Billy, am I just imagining something, or was that your first kiss ever?" He blushed, and she quickly kissed him again. "Don't worry—you're good at it!"

He beamed, relieved. Then he pointed back down at the crater. "You know what it's like now." He cleared his throat. "To feel it all."

"I guess so." She huddled close to him.

"So many good people. Even the bad people have good in them. That's what kills me. So much pain. Like everyone is stuck in a dark room, trying to find a light. Maybe someday, we can..." His voice went dry, and he coughed. "Maybe someday, if you want to, when this corporation finishes experimenting on me... maybe we can do it then."

"Do what?"

"*Tikkun olam.*" He smiled.

"What does that mean?"

"Repair the world." He laughed—and laughing aloud felt so wonderful. "Seriously. We could go out there. Help people in a real way." He leaned in. "Together?"

Natalia's eyes glowed. "Definitely."

"It's a deal, then." He breathed in the wintry air and held his hand out over the railing, and a single snowflake landed on his chapped palm. A strong breeze captured the snowflake, carrying it into the sky, higher than the fire tower itself, until it disappeared in the clouds.

26: Natalia

To Natalia, every snowflake felt like a kiss from the sky. Even after they'd climbed down the fire tower and trekked for hours down the mountain road winding back into Heaven's Hole, she still jittered with excitement. Despite how cold it was, she felt warm. The air possessed an ethereal quality. The world was brighter, fuller, and more real than it had ever felt before.

They walked into town, icy gravel crunching beneath their heels. Slowly, the mountains disappeared behind the crater's growing ridge, and the familiar concrete and brick buildings came into view. Gravel became cracked pavement.

Natalia wanted to run away. *We could go together, forever, somewhere far.* But then she remembered her family and felt guilty for even entertaining the thought.

As they passed by the giant metal welcome sign—Heaven's Hole, Established 1896—Billy smiled at her. "Back to the Hellhole."

Despite the grim sign, she flushed and squeezed his hand, so energized by his smile that she could barely contain herself. They trudged through slushy roads, entering downtown. Though late morning was undergoing its painful transition into early afternoon, the town was barely awake. The roads were unplowed and unsalted.

"It's still early." She nudged Billy's shoulder. "Let's not go back yet."

He nodded and took the lead, bringing her to the forested trail by Solitaire Lake. They stopped at a little wooden bench overlooking the frozen water, which Natalia remembered from her freshman year. *Felix and I smoked pot for the first time right here. That's funny.* Then she sensed that Billy also had memories of the bench, and through their linked hands, she saw a flickering image of herself kissing him. *He totally pictured us here before everything happened.*

"You scoundrel." She kissed his cheek and draped herself over him, and they stared out at the beautiful white expanse of Solitaire Lake, which was marred only by the smokestacks of the factory. *This is so pretty, other than the nasty industrial crap across the water. I wish I had my sketchbook with me so I could just edit it out.*

Feeling warm, safe, and happy, she rested her head on Billy's shoulder—and out of nowhere, he tensed up. His mouth became a thin line.

"Are you okay?" she asked.

Footsteps crunched behind her. Metal clicked. Someone muttered into a walkie-talkie, "The subject has been located."

"Nobody move!" shouted a deep voice.

Natalia's heart stopped. Three men in long coats, hats, and sunglasses walked out, guns pointed at the two teenagers. More guns poked through the trees.

"Holy shit!" Natalia cried.

The men didn't react to her exclamation. Their guns were steady. Natalia squeezed Billy, terrified to let go. The dark-eyed boy's face paled. *It's like he knew this was going to happen... it's because he ran away last night, isn't it?*

Natalia inhaled deeply, tried not to hyperventilate, and stared at the men's faces, trying to pretend she didn't see their guns. "Hey, guys, it's my fault. This dude here, he didn't—"

"Don't talk," one of the men said.

Natalia didn't argue. *Okay, we're screwed.* From the trees, three more men emerged from the left and three from the right—more guns, all pointed at Billy. They were serious. Icy. Unfeeling. Natalia looked at Billy for guidance, but he had become a Popsicle.

An unarmed man and woman emerged from behind them. The man wore a goofily huge jacket, though his face—calloused, cracked like a chunk of old white rock—was exposed to the elements. The woman was bundled up in so many layers that Natalia barely saw a person underneath the clothes.

"I'm so sorry, Billy," the woman said, her achy voice muffled by her scarf. "I didn't want to do this—"

"Stop." The rough-faced man cut her off. "You're exposing too many emotions to the subject. Be professional."

The bundled woman lowered her head like a beaten dog. "Billy, you shouldn't have run off that way without telling me or Father."

She signaled toward the man, which confused Natalia. *These douchebags definitely aren't Billy's parents.*

The woman continued, "I understand that maybe you felt some intense energies, but we were so scared when we found that you weren't in your room—"

"Stop exposing your emotions, Mother," said the man.

Natalia frowned. *Oh, I'd like to kick that dude's ass.* Billy resembled a deflated balloon, so Natalia directed her attention to the stiff couple. "Okay, who the hell are you assholes?"

The man rocked back on the heels of his feet, stunned, which made Natalia smirk. *Didn't expect the little teenage girl to fight back, huh?* The odd adults looked at each other then at their armed guards, clearly befuddled about how to handle the unwelcome newcomer.

"We are the boy's parents, of course," Father said.

Natalia scoffed. "Bullshit."

Billy nodded. Natalia shook him, but he barely stirred. *What kinda control have these people got on you, man?* Natalia squeezed his hand, and he barely squeezed back. "Whatever," Natalia said, directing her attention back to the phony parents. "If we're going to play this game, then... hey there, Fake Mom and Fake Dad. I'm Billy's friend, Natal—"

"Natalia Gonzalez Rodriguez, age seventeen," Father said. "Daughter of Carlos Gonzalez de León and Maria Rodriguez Gonzalez. Yes, we know who you are."

Natalia's motormouth cooled. *Shit.*

"Mr. Jakobek," Father said, "this past night has been a complete violation of your contract. You've dragged this poor girl into some unfortunate circumstances. We don't want any more embarrassing scenes like this." He signaled toward the trail. "Son, you need to come home with me. We have a meeting with Mr. Linus to attend."

Billy stood up, his hand sliding out of Natalia's grasp. *You let go, Billy!* She jumped up beside him. "I'm going wherever Billy goes," she announced, facing down the array of gunmen. *Abuelita would kill me if she knew how crazy I'm acting.*

The fake parents looked at each other as snowflakes twisted between them.

"No," Father said. "You won't."

The armed men surrounded Natalia, blocking her off from Billy, and she crumbled beneath the tension. *Asshole called my bluff.* Fake Mother cut through and took Natalia's arm in a surprisingly loving manner. The woman, to Natalia's surprise, was very tall—taller than most men. "Sorry, young lady. You need to come with me."

"Oh, great." *Just shoot me at this point.*

"Our sensors, um..." The woman glanced at Father then looked back. Her eyes matched the snow. "Our sensors show that Bil—the *subject's* energy readings have been off the charts. He was with you all night, and it's easy to see that you know about Billy's condition, even though the contract clearly states that he is not allowed to divulge it to others—"

"Condition? *Energy* readings?"

"You know exactly what Mother is talking about," Father sneered as he carefully guided Billy away from the bench. "Don't try lying to us, little girl. You're interfering in a top-secret corporate medical project worth billions of dollars, so mind your place."

"He saved my life, though!" Natalia cried.

Nobody cared. Billy peered back at her apologetically before he and Father vanished into the forest with a troop of bodyguards surrounding them. Natalia thought about chasing them, but another group of gunmen were still targeting her.

Mother gripped Natalia's arm and lowered her scarf to reveal a long nose and tiny lips. "I understand—this must be a total whirlwind. Billy should not have told you what he's capable of."

Natalia stared longingly at where Billy had sat next to her mere moments before. *I already feel so much emptier without him here.* "He didn't say anything."

"Oh, nonsense. Trust me, I was a teenager once too." The woman shook her head, holding back a smile. "We can track those energy readings from miles away. He has an ankle monitor, and we have cameras all over town, so just... stop lying. Besides, if you just come with me, everything will be okay. My boss has requested a special briefing with you, and he's not the sort of man who takes no for an answer."

"Why should I care what your dumbass boss wants?"

The woman looked down. "Because he's Caleb Thorne."

27

The lobby of Heaven's Hole's only hotel looked straight out of a magazine and smelled of musk perfume. Natalia felt like an intruder as Mother and her bodyguards guided her past elegant wood-paneled walls, heated stone floors, and opulent furnishings that came from another universe than the town she knew. The more she looked around, the smaller she felt. The lobby seemed deliberately designed to exclude her—and anyone like her—by tantalizing her with beautiful things she would never have. A tired young janitor rushed past them, and it took Natalia a moment to recognize him as Miguel, a friendly classmate she'd briefly dated in sixth grade. She and Miguel silently nodded to each other. *So weird to see another normal person in this freaky one-percenter hotel.*

Finally, the guards seated her at a leather sectional in the back, beside a crackling fireplace. She looked closer. *It's electric. Totally fake. Not like the one that warmed us up last night.* She sighed, yearning for Billy to be next to her again. *I miss him.* She kicked off her boots and tucked her legs beneath her. The gunmen glared down at her like she was a stray dog, and she suddenly felt self-conscious about her ragged clothes, punky haircut, and facial piercings.

"Can you guys get a life?" she spat out.

The gunmen didn't look away, and after a prolonged silence, Mother ushered them down the hall. Natalia sighed with relief. *Finally, some space.* Before she could relax, Mother returned.

She touched Natalia's arm. "Would you like something to drink? Perhaps a coffee?"

Natalia shot Mother her best look that said, *Are you fucking kidding me?* "How about your name instead?"

The woman winced.

Bitch does that a lot.

"Mother."

"You're definitely not *my* mother. Who are you?"

"My name is Mother." Veins protruded from the woman's bony white neck. "Mr. Thorne will see you in a moment." With that, Mother walked away, and Natalia watched the electric flames, trying to figure out an escape from her current mess. *I just want to go back to that fire tower with Billy again.* She crossed her arms, hating everything about where she was and what had happened since they'd come back to town.

Heavy, slow, perfect footsteps tapped across the stone floor.

Natalia's body tensed like a rod. *Oh, here comes Mr. Boss Man.* When the tall white man in an all-black business suit emerged, he had the biggest grin—but his smile had too many teeth in it, and his eyes didn't crinkle. His receded hairline told Natalia that he was much older than the plastic surgery made him look.

"Ms. Gonzalez, welcome!" He extended a perfectly manicured hand. "My name is Caleb Thorne. Call me Caleb if you like. It's a pleasure to meet you. Or shall I say... *mucho gusto?*"

Natalia didn't stand, but she shook his hand, which was so huge that it made her feel like a toddler. *Too smooth, too, like this dude uses lotion every five minutes.* She tried to brush off his Spanish compliment, sickened by the possibility that Mr. White-and-Corporate might know her family's language better than she did.

"So, you're the big man," she said. "Mr. Thorne Century himself."

"Oh, that." He chuckled a bit too good-naturedly. "Yes, my father's company originally. I have expanded operations quite a bit since I inherited it, though, yes. Particularly in the areas of privatized urban development, as we did here in Heaven's Hole, which I'm quite proud of." He pointed at the leather seat next to her. "Mind if I sit down?"

She passively signaled yes, trying to hide how queasy—and terrified—she felt in his presence. Caleb Thorne sat uncomfortably close and reeked of expensive cologne. The businessman admired the fire, his creepy grin never budging. *I guess he's a handsome guy, if you're into that Ken-doll bullshit.*

"Well, now." Mr. Thorne Century Himself turned toward her, hands carefully positioned on his lap. "I suppose that you're wondering why I asked you to come here."

"Smart guy."

"I don't mean to frighten you in any way, I assure you." His eyes fixed on hers the way a snake regarded a mouse. "However, because you've become so acquainted with a very dear friend of mine, Mr. William Jakobek, we must discuss some things. First off, I apologize for the fact that Mr. Jakobek broke protocol. He should not have disclosed his condition—"

"It's not a condition. It's a gift."

"Hmm." Thorne's eyes narrowed. "I presume that Mr. Jakobek must enjoy your... spunk. Is that the right word? Yes." He smiled so tightly that his cheeks scrunched. "Now, of course, you are free to have any opinion on the young man's unique state, but the point is, you are not supposed to know about it. Now you do, unfortunately, and that means we need to set parameters going forward. So I'll need to... shall we say, peel the onion for you."

Thorne said the word *peel* in a way that sounded more like *pill*, revealing the slightest traces of a Southern accent. It was buried there but lightly punctuated every word, as if he'd spent his life trying to hide it only for it to sneak up every now and again.

Shame. The accent would make him more likable, at least. "Cut the goddamn onion in half," Natalia said. "Are there others like Billy?"

Thorne leaned his head from side to side, seemingly debating what he was willing to tell her. "There were a few," he said finally. "Some of the researchers call these children *psychos*... that's merely gallows humor, of course. Most of the psychic children we studied committed suicide, sadly enough, though a few made it to adolescence. It's an overwhelming condition to be born with. These risks are the reason that we have kept young Mr. Jakobek so closely watched. To protect him, you understand... and to protect others *from* him."

"That's why you're holding him hostage?"

"Oh?" Thorne cocked his head. "Is that what he says?"

Natalia pulled her legs up to her chest. "No. It's what I say." The leather squeaked beneath her shifting body.

"Heh, understood." Thorne finally broke eye contact, looking back at the fire. Natalia's relief at this was momentary, as the corporate man then removed a small, rusty little pocketknife from his jacket and twiddled it between his fingers. Thorne sighed heavily as he played with the knife, and Natalia realized that it was just a concentration tool rather than a threat. *The world's scariest fidget spinner, that's for sure.* "I am sorry you see it so cynically, Ms. Gonzalez. You must understand—Mr. Jakobek's unique body contains thousands of scientific breakthroughs. The stuff we're discovering about his condition, every day, funds the very factory that keeps this little town alive."

Natalia bit her lip. *I don't like this.* "Wait, mister. I know for a fact that nobody who works in that factory knows what they're actually working on. They just sit on their assembly line, follow directions, and stay quiet. Are you saying that all that stuff is based on..." She swallowed. "Billy's body?"

Thorne shrugged. "Much of it, yes."

"Whoa," she muttered. *I'm officially tripping out.* "Scientific, medical... what? Painkillers, psych drugs, that kinda thing?"

"Mr. Jakobek's body can change *everything* that a person feels, thinks, and experiences." Thorne closed the knife. "Can't you just imagine the possibilities inherent in his DNA? Understand, I do want to release him from our employment, someday, so he can live a normal life. When that happens, Thorne Century will reward him so handsomely that he'll never have to work another day in his life. First, though, my company needs to finish extracting all of the necessary... shall we say, ingredients." Natalia winced, and Thorne regarded her with an uncomfortably sympathetic expression. "Sorry," he said. "Poor wording."

"When will you let him free?" Natalia asked.

"We would have finished years ago, but unfortunately, we've been delayed by Billy's little..." He twitched. "Problem."

"Problem?"

"I'm going to level with you, Ms. Gonzalez. This young man you consider a friend is quite dangerous. I presume he had something to do with that former town councilman's death last night? We found the body some hours ago—"

"Crazy Old Darrell had a fucking gun to my head," Natalia blurted. "The dude was a serial killer and a Nazi. You'd better not leave that shit out if you're writing his obituary. Besides, Billy didn't try to kill him, he just—"

"Made him kill himself?" Thorne's face darkened. "Ms. Gonzalez, has the poor boy told you about something he calls the Shape?"

Natalia froze. She didn't know what to say.

"Ah." Thorne smirked. "So he has."

"What, um...?" She hesitated. "What is that creepy thing, anyway?"

"The Shape?" He fiddled with the knife again then gazed back around the lobby to make sure no one could hear him. "I'm no psychiatrist, I assure you, but our best counselors on staff believe that this Shape is an embodiment of repressed memories. Childhood trauma. Billy himself argues it is some sort of shadowy alien beast with big blue eyes, or what have you." Thorne leaned close to her. "He's wrong. The Shape *is* Billy Jakobek. It's a creation of his mind, locked inside him, and when that evil side of Mr. Jakobek emerges, he makes people act in ways they normally wouldn't. Innocent, God-fearing men suddenly turn against each other and... well, it's ugly business."

Natalia shivered. "Trauma from...?"

"His family was slaughtered in the Beth Shalom terrorist attack, Ms. Gonzalez. Perhaps you saw the damage on TV? They were executed by radical Islamic terrorists."

As Thorne spoke, Natalia sank downward, but this comment bugged her. *Those people in Billy's memory sure as hell weren't Muslim, Middle Eastern, or any of that. They were white American soldiers. Boston accent.* She didn't voice her disagreement aloud, but she paid close attention as Thorne continued.

"The young man saw this tragedy happen before his own eyes," Thorne said, "and he became the Shape."

"What do you mean he *became* the Shape?"

"He transformed into his darker half. One of my factories was across the street, and classified security footage shows the entire terrorist troop executing themselves on the command of that psychic little boy." Thorne made a pistol with his hand and tucked it under his neck. "Bang. You understand?" He lowered the finger gun. "The government then locked the poor boy in a vault, and it was only through a special medical loophole that my company was able to rescue him from a life of solitary confinement by placing him in our labs." Thorne stopped. "Are you okay?"

Natalia nodded, but she felt nauseous.

"Anyhow." Thorne flicked his knife again. "The incidents didn't stop there. Quite a few men have committed suicide after working with Mr. Jakobek. Some, well... they've murdered other people on Billy's orders."

Natalia couldn't look at Thorne anymore. *That's not the Billy I know.* She scrunched herself into a ball.

"Early on, there was an incident where one of our doctors was... regrettably, the doctor was abusing the boy." Thorne shook his head in disgust. "I won't make any excuses for that. We never should have hired that man. But what's important to understand, Ms. Gonzalez, is that Mr. Jakobek responded to this abuse by having one of his little Shape freak-outs. Later that day, when Thorne Century investigated the lab, all of the researchers had—quite literally—cannibalized one another. One man chewed on the other's leg like a chicken drumstick. I saw the footage, and personally, I've had nightmares ever since."

Natalia frenetically shook her head. *God, that's so awful. That's not the same Billy who kissed me on the fire tower.* Thorne reached out to comfort her, and she jittered away from him. "There has to be some way to help him," she said.

"We're trying," Thorne replied.

"I can help." Natalia sucked back tears. *Don't cry in front of this guy. No way.* "Maybe, if I—"

"Let's address your involvement, shall we?" Thorne popped the knife back into his pocket. Weirdly, without the knife, he seemed even more dangerous. "If you choose to stay involved—which, for the record, I don't think you should—we must establish strict parameters."

The flames sparked, rattling Natalia. "Okay."

"First of all, you will do nothing to endanger the project. Understood?" Thorne's voice became harder, stricter, and less Southern comfort than ever. "Secondly, no more overnights. Jakobek gets home by eleven o'clock every night. Third, no encouraging him to rebel against the project."

"Okay," she murmured.

"I trust that you will accommodate our demands." Thorne's grin resembled a jack-o'-lantern. "After all, Ms. Gonzalez, we wouldn't want anything terrible to happen to your sweet little old grandmother, now, would we?"

Natalia shot upright. *Did he just...?* Tears broke free from her eyes. "You—"

Thorne motioned for her to sit down. "Don't worry, young lady. Sure, my company and others make a big media circus on TV about how we supposedly want to close the borders, build walls, cancel immigrant protections, blah blah blah. In reality, though?" He winked. "It's all a show. We view illegal workers—pardon, *undocumented* workers—as something essential. With no offense intended, it's cheap labor. It cuts costs. US workers ask questions, demand higher wages, want benefits. Spoiled brats, the lot of them. Nice folks like your granny and your mom, Maria, play a key role in my company's success. Seriously, I'm a fan."

Natalia shriveled up inside. *He knows everything about me.*

"However..." Thorne leaned forward. "If you throw a wrench into my Billy Jakobek operation, your family's welfare ceases to be in my interest. There are entire government agencies dedicated to deporting your—not to be harsh—but your *criminal* family members. All it takes is one call. You wouldn't like that, would you?"

"N-No... no." Natalia's heart dropped. *Oh god, I should've never touched Billy's hand. Never talked to him, never kissed him.*

"I hate deportations myself. Ugly stuff." Thorne made a motion of washing his hands. "Especially when the poor criminals have health issues, like your sweet mother. However, I have a business to run. So if you break my rules, Grandma goes first. Mommy's next. As for those two cute little boys—Juan and Carlos, yes?" His stare sharpened. "They might *legally* be citizens, like you, but there are other things we can do to them."

Every word hit Natalia's skull like a hammer. *I hate this.* She wanted to run back into the inviting arms of yesterday. *It would have been better for them if I'd just died last night.* She broke down crying.

Thorne twirled his pocketknife. "I trust that things will proceed smoothly from now on, yes?"

28: Mother

Mother waited in her car outside the hotel, heater cranked on full blast. The snowfall had stopped, but the daylight was dying. She frantically tapped the steering wheel. She turned on the radio, heard static, then turned it off again.

She hated thinking about the mind games that Thorne was playing on Natalia Gonzalez. *I wish he would leave the poor girl alone.* For the first half of the conversation, she'd snooped from the corridor, up until the point when Caleb claimed that Billy had forced the doctors to cannibalize each other. *Such bullshit.* While such an incident certainly had happened, wherein an abused "psycho" kid had forced researchers to eat each other, it hadn't been Billy Jakobek. No, it was Hannah Michaels, an eleven-year-old from Missouri. *And Caleb knows damn well that Hannah went into solitary after that too. The poor child died in the dark tank.*

The hotel doors opened, and the little Latina walked out into the snow. The strong, demanding young woman that Mother had guided into the building had been reduced to a battered, quivering shell. Her spiky hair hung over a tear-soaked face.

Caleb is such a prick. Mother opened the door of her car, cupped her mouth, and shouted, "Hey, Gonzalez!"

The girl turned around, spotted her, and crossed her arms. "What do you want?" she called out.

"I was wondering..." Mother stopped. The wind was too loud to hear anything, so she ran out to meet the shivering adolescent. "Sorry, I know what my boss is like. He makes a severe case." Mother hunched forward, wishing she didn't tower quite so high over Gonzalez. "Not all of us have such a negative outlook on your friend."

"Is he really my friend?" The girl looked up with swollen eyes.

Mother took the girl's shoulder. "It's freezing. Would you like a ride home?"

Natalia shot her the viper eyes only teenage girls could pull off. "No, thanks, lady."

"Please?"

"Nah. It's cool." The girl held herself tightly.

"Well, if you change your mind..." Mother looked back at her car. "I think it's nice that you and Billy are friends. Really."

"Yeah, bye." The girl walked away.

Mother waited for a few minutes, hoping that Gonzalez would change her mind, but the teenager marched off by herself without looking back once. *That's one stubborn girl.*

Mother turned back to her car, nearly colliding with Caleb Thorne, who had just walked outside. "Oh!"

"Just me." He beamed, holding her. "I listened to that exchange. You have such a kind heart, Roseanna." Caleb ran his long fingers down Mother's arm, and her stomach churned. "I should, perhaps, learn more from you."

Mother squirreled out of his grasp. "You scared her. You didn't need to do that."

"She endangered the project." Caleb pocketed his invasive hands, probably fingering his creepy little knife. "I had to warn her. Now if she comes back, at least she knows the risk. She certainly won't be a problem going forward."

"Billy needs friends." Mother bit her tongue. *I need to cool it. He's going to threaten my son, my husband, everyone I love.*

Thorne's smile became a smirk. He wiped snow from his shoulders. "Yes, I understand. We need our subject to undergo a full palette of emotional experiences. A romantic partner would probably be quite useful. This Guatemalan girl, though?" He scratched his clean-shaven dimpled chin. "Her attitude worries me."

"I like her, actually."

"You would." He touched her hip. "Nonetheless, my dear, we have to be careful of the subject's well-being, because after the childhood trauma he endured—"

"You created that childhood trauma, you monster." Mother swiped his grabby hand away. "You're the one who ordered the hit on his family and then covered your tracks with a phony terrorist attack."

Thorne glared. "We don't talk about that, remember?"

"But it happened." Mother fumed. *Calm down, Roseanna.* "You didn't pull the trigger, but your little signature murdered an entire community of—"

"He needed to experience trauma. You know that." Caleb's jaw clenched. "This is the real world, horrible things happen, and those intense emotions awakened Jakobek's full potential, turning him into our most powerful psycho kid ever. Their deaths were necessary for the project's success—"

"No, they weren't." She glanced at the steam rising beneath her still-running car. "For Christ's sake, Caleb, every time I look into that poor boy's eyes, I have to swallow those psychic-resistant pills and try to pretend I don't work for the same company that ruined his life. You trained me on emotional suppression tactics, but dear lord, I'm sure he feels that something's wrong with me."

"I'm glad the medication helps your predicament." Thorne buttoned his coat. "I trust you have not let slip any—"

"Don't worry, he doesn't know it was you. But God, Caleb, let the kid have a happy moment with someone he likes. Show some compassion for once in your life."

Thorne's perfect cheeks flushed red. "Why are you treating me so unfairly?"

Mother stormed back to her car, slammed the door, and rumbled off into the wintry night. She watched Thorne become a tiny dot in her rearview mirror, and she wondered if there would ever be a day when that dot disappeared for good.

29: Natalia

Natalia hesitated at the door of her apartment. It was late. The lights were off. She felt dirty, cold, and hungover. *You know what? I should go somewhere else tonight so I don't infect my family with what a disappointing mess I am.* It was hard to remember how magical the world had felt that morning, before Mr. Thorne Century Himself had crushed her childish dreams into dust.

Despite her reservations, she turned the handle and tiptoed inside. Everything was quiet. The boys were sleeping. She draped her jacket over a chair, crept across the kitchen—and jumped at the sound of her grandmother's voice.

"Is that you, Natalia?"

"Hey," she whispered back. She found Abuelita and her wheelchair parked under a dim lamp, a knitting project spread over her knees.

The elderly woman's brow furrowed into a million creases. "Get over here."

Natalia approached. *I'm toxic. Don't touch me.*

"*Sí.* Lean in," Abuelita said.

Natalia expected a slap but instead found herself bundled inside her grandmother's thankful arms as kisses rained onto her cheeks. "*Gracias a Dios.*" The old lady squeezed her tightly. "We were so scared for you."

Relief flowed over Natalia in a cascading wave. "I'm sorry, Abuelita." *Hey, maybe I'm not so toxic.*

"Now, lean back."

Natalia did as she was asked, and her grandmother held out a stern finger. "Don't ever disappear that way again. We didn't know what to do. Your mother was so worried that she called out of work tonight, and she never does that. She's in bed now. Go see her."

"But if she's asleep—"

"Who cares? She can go back to sleep after she sees you. Go!"

Natalia smiled, seeing so much of herself in her grandmother, but her amusement vanished when she remembered Thorne's threat. *She could get deported, all because I have a stupid crush on some stupid psychic boy. My fault.*

Natalia knocked on her mother's bedroom door. Mamá didn't answer, but she went in anyway. Mamá's night-light was on, allowing the glorious Guatemalan cross on the wall behind her bed to drape long, Christly shadows across the room as her oxygen machine whooshed air into her sleeping lungs.

Natalia crouched beside her. *Mamá is so pretty when she sleeps. I love the wrinkles around her eyes.* The oxygen machine beeped. Suddenly overcome with sadness, she hugged her mother's sleeping body. *Don't ever die, Mamá. I won't let you.*

Mamá woke up. Her eyes brightened, and she gripped her daughter so tight that Natalia couldn't breathe. "Oh, my baby." She ran her fingers through Natalia's hair. "I was so afraid... I thought something happened to you."

"Stuff happens to everyone, Mamá." The back of her mother's nightgown was sweaty, but Natalia didn't care.

"It's the bad stuff I worry over. *Gracias, Dios, por todas tus bendiciones.*" Mamá kissed the crucifix around her neck. "I was so worried they'd taken you away from us or that you were dead, worried it had happened... happened—" She wheezed. "Again."

Mamá erupted in a fit of gargled coughs. Natalia brought over the trash can—in case it turned into vomit—but Mamá waved it away. Watching her mother cough, Natalia brooded on her COPD, wondering just how long she still had left. *Caleb Thorne is killing my mother. That's the truth.*

Mamá wiped her lip. "Where were you?"

"I... um..." She shook her head. *I don't want to worry her.* "It was nothing, I just—"

"We can talk more later, maybe. *Mañana.* I'm sure you weren't doing anything reckless. I trust you, baby. You're such a good person. A wonderful daughter."

Natalia tried not the flinch. *Actually, I'm a terrible daughter. I'm flunking my classes, and apparently, I'm into boys with major life issues. For real, Mamá, you wanna hear how much I suck?* Natalia sighed. "Hey, you should get some rest."

"You're probably right." Mamá smiled distantly, and she held out her hand for Natalia to grab.

Three fingers were missing, lopped off by a spinning blade in the factory six years before. Thorne Century—*Caleb Thorne, that asshole*—had never compensated her. Natalia took her hand, despising those three nubs like she never had before.

Mamá shivered. "Wow, static electricity. You're sparky tonight, huh?"

Natalia remembered the fire tower. The kiss. The feelings. *God, I'm going to start crying.* "Good night, Mamá."

Natalia kissed her mother's cheek then walked down to her little closet bedroom and shut the door. Sitting cross-legged, she stared at her rumpled sheets, her Carl Jung book, her tarot cards, her phone. *Should I call Felix?* She picked up the phone then dropped it. *Whoa, I can't. Thorne Century is probably tracking my phone. This blows.*

She lit a candle. *There's only one thing that always helps.* She drew out her sketchbook, which had slipped beside the bed, and opened it to her *Dark-Eyed Boy* drawing. Now that she knew Billy better, her old impressions seemed silly. She still wanted to draw him—*it's the only way I'll figure him out*—but the old drawing had to go.

She turned to the next page, sharpened her pencil, and started from scratch.

30

At 3:56 a.m., Natalia woke up with her face glued to her sketchbook. Every muscle in her body ached. *Man, I must've only been asleep for a couple hours.* She turned over, pulling the blankets over her, but it was too late. She was wide-awake.

"Awesome." She groaned. "So I'm just never allowed to sleep again?"

After a quick shower and a change of clothes, she illuminated her way to the kitchen with her cellphone light. Behind the room divider, the twins snored. *Those little guys sleep through anything. I'm totally jealous.* As quietly as possible, she started a pot of coffee. Black liquid gurgled into the yellowed glass. Then she plopped her sketchbook on the table, twisted the lamp to its dimmest setting, and looked over her two drawings from the night before. The first unfinished drawing, which she loved, depicted Billy. She'd finally captured his sweet little smile, if not the rest of his face. Her heart wanted to work on that one. She craved it just like she craved his touch. The second drawing—the one she hated—depicted the Shape. *Creepy goddamn thing.* Hallucination or not, its shadowy form and blue eyes seemed all too real.

The coffee maker sputtered its final puffs, filling the kitchen with its bittersweet aroma. Natalia poured herself a cup just as her grandmother rolled her wheelchair into the kitchen. The surprise entrance made Natalia's hairs stand on end, but she quickly relaxed. *It's not Darrell. Calm down.*

"Save me some coffee, girl," Abuelita said, still clad in her bathrobe. Her silver hair was frizzed out in every direction, and she had the ratty old broomstick laid across her lap.

"Seriously?" Natalia put her hands on her hips. "Don't you ever sleep?"

"Sleep." Abuelita scoffed.

"Yeah, isn't that what old people are supposed to do?"

"Pfft. Who the hell can sleep when little girls go poking around in the kitchen at four in the morning?" Abuelita lifted the old broomstick, wielding it like a baseball bat. "I thought someone had broken in, so I brought a weapon."

Natalia burst out laughing and quickly covered her mouth. "Yeah, real scary. You could crack some skulls with that thing."

Abuelita rolled her eyes exaggeratedly and wheeled up to the table. "*Un cafecito, por favor.*"

"It's so early though," Natalia said. "You must be crazy tired."

"Tired?" Abuelita tucked the broom to her side. "Granddaughter, you don't even know what tired means. I wake up at four every morning. Old habit. I like seeing the sun come up." She yawned. "Coffee?"

Natalia shot her grandmother a sly eye, but Abuelita shot her one right back. *Guess there's no arguing with old ladies. They get whatever they want.* Natalia closed her sketchbook and brought her grandmother a coffee, and they sat together in the dark, sipping on their hot mugs.

"Now," Abuelita said, "we talk."

"About Mamá?" Natalia asked, keeping her voice a whisper in case the twins woke up. "Do you think her COPD is—"

"No." Abuelita sipped her coffee. "*El patojo.*"

Natalia cringed. "There's no boy." *Except the one I can't stop thinking about. I wonder where he is. When that jerk led him away, he must've gone back to Kaiser House. Maybe he's...*

"I wasn't born yesterday." Abuelita arched an eyebrow. "Your mamá and I talked about this after you went to bed."

"Gossiping about me, huh?"

"*Sí.* You disappear, go out all night, then come back acting all weird and distracted. It's obvious. I told your mamá it was a boy. She agreed. Either that, or it's drugs. Now, tell me."

Awkward. "There's no boy. I don't like anyone in this stupid town."

Abuelita's eyes sparkled. "It's that friend of yours whose parents come from the Congo, isn't it? His name is Felix?"

"Felix is gay, Abuelita."

"Oh." The old woman shrugged. "Then who?"

Natalia stared into her coffee. *I can't tell her.* That was the part she hated most. Every time she looked at Abuelita, Mamá, or the twins, she envisioned them being arrested, deported, thrown into cages. *It would all be my fault. Thorne made that clear.* On the other hand, there was Billy, the guy who'd watched as his family was murdered in front of him. The child who'd helped his own grandmother die peacefully. The boy who'd kissed her on the fire tower, seen inside her, and appreciated her entire soul without any judgment.

Natalia swallowed more coffee. "Fine. There's a guy, okay?"

"Yes!" Abuelita smiled so widely that her cheeks wrinkled.

"But... um..." Natalia chewed her lip. *Be careful.* "I don't think I should see him anymore."

Abuelita frowned. "Why not?"

"He... comes from a bad background, Abuelita. Real bad. His, like... his family, yeah, they're dangerous, abusive, and I'm just... y'know, worried that they might come here and hurt all of you. They're awful people, and I don't want to risk you getting—"

"Yes, yes." The old lady waved her hand. "What about *him,* though?"

Natalia jerked. "What?"

"*El patojo.* You say his family is dangerous, but him? Is he bad too?"

"Er... no? I don't think so."

"What's he like?"

Natalia paused. Her grandmother clasped her hand. Natalia kissed it, suddenly feeling so thankful that she was alive, that her grandmother was alive, and that the universe had given them this moment. Natalia smiled downward. "He's a really kind, decent guy. He likes helping people. That's what makes him happy—when he finds people in trouble and makes them feel better—and the thing is..." She looked up excitedly. "He's *really* good at it. It seems like helping people is his main hobby, which is kinda weird, but—"

"He sounds wonderful." Abuelita patted her hand. "Your papá was that way too. No surprise you like someone like that."

Sometimes, the mere mention of Papá brought tears, but this time, it made Natalia happy. "What was Papá like when you first met him?"

"He enjoyed helping people. Too much, I thought. He'd spend hours digging random people's cars out of ditches." She sighed, expressing mock annoyance—but with a loving grin. "He came from a bad start, too, though. His family, they were all in violent gangs. They hurt people."

"Wait, did Papá...?"

"Never." She shook her head. "He was good. But I admit, I was worried when I first met him. Like you worry about this boy. Your mamá, though, she swore to me that he was good, and I came to find out he was. An amazing husband and an even better papá."

Natalia fought the urge to spill her guts, but before she could slip up, the old lady spun her wheelchair around. "Time to take a shower with whatever hot water you didn't use up." Abuelita looked over her shoulder with gleaming eyes. "Natalia, when it comes to this boy, life, whatever, if you have to listen to anything in this world—then put your hand on your chest, feel the beat, listen to that. *Corazón.* Always."

Abuelita wheeled away. Natalia reflected on her grandmother's words. Then she reopened her sketchbook and got back to work.

31: Billy

Dawn cracked the clouds, crept through the trees, and painted another cold day in warm colors. The October snowstorm was done, but it had left its sharp white corpses everywhere. Billy had missed the bus. That was okay with him. He needed more time to process the whirlwind of the past few days. So he plugged his earbuds in, swished through his dad's old playlists until he found a song titled "King of Pain," by a band called The Police, and walked the long way to school.

The night before, he'd been terrified of being forced back into the dark tank—but at Mother's pleading, Father had relented, and they'd allowed him to sleep in the normal bed, albeit strapped down. *It feels like that woman stuck her neck out for me somehow. I hate those Billy-blocking pills she takes. They make it so hard to figure her out.* The other individuals he encountered on his walk through downtown, from fast-food workers to homeless people, were far easier. All these strangers felt like old friends, thanks to his power explosion on the fire tower. *It's like I unlocked something—a potential I didn't know I had.*

He smiled to himself. *No, it was her. She unlocked something inside me.*

Billy's boots crunched through mushy white roads. He thought about the cabin. The fire. The softness of her cheeks. The kiss. *I kissed her in real life. My lips. Her lips. They touched!* He thought about the spark inside Natalia Gonzalez, the strength, the passion, how cute she looked when she flicked her hair out of her eyes, and the way she'd rested her head on his shoulder. When they were together, nothing else—nothing in the world—mattered.

His smile dropped. *She probably hates me now, though, after that embarrassing ambush at the lake.* She was tough but not crazy. All night long, he'd felt her thinking about him from the distance—and her thoughts had been sick, sad, and worried. *Definitely not happy.* Cold winds rustled the air, and Billy zipped up his jacket, hiding another one of his identical black T-shirts. He remembered why he liked them now. In a complicated world of so many mixed messages, basic fashion was an easy thing to control.

The foreboding gray bulk of the high school appeared over the horizon. Oddly enough, Billy felt comforted. *This place feels weirdly homey now. Maybe that's just a feeling I absorbed from Natalia?* He couldn't tell. The buses had arrived a while before, so swarms of kids chatted in front of the school. Others sneaked to the side to smoke vape pens and joints. As Billy approached, their emotions pricked into him—*bing, bing, bing, bing*—but didn't overpower his senses like they had the previous day. He recognized all of them, in a strange way, from the fire tower. He knew their names, their histories, their hopes and fears. He walked up to the front doors, where the crowd was smaller, and leaned against the wall.

A sharp jab hit him in the chest. It was so immediate, so hard, that he rocked backward. *Her.*

He looked up. Natalia and Felix—the nice guy from the bus, with the denim jacket—strolled around the corner. He grimaced, fully expecting her to dodge him altogether, avoiding eye contact.

Instead, she approached him directly—and smiled. "Hey."

Billy stared into her eyes, transfixed and frozen. Despite the hundreds of emotions surrounding him, Natalia seemed like the only color image in a black-and-white world. *She's not afraid?* He opened his mouth then snapped it shut.

Felix bumped her. "Staring contest, huh?" He laughed. "Hey, guys, I'm right here. Hello!"

Billy and Natalia looked down in unison—then peeked up again, trying to hold back their grins. Natalia flicked her hair out of her eyes. "So, um... Felix, this is my new... friend, Billy."

"We met on the bus," Felix said. "What's up, man?"

Billy waved.

"Billy's cool." Natalia kicked Felix's foot. "You know his ancestor was, like, a knight in the fourteenth century?"

Felix frowned. "For real? Dude, how do you even know that?"

The tension was shattered by the morning bell. Waves of students cascaded through the front doors. Billy, Natalia, and Felix stood back against the wall as the dam broke and every kid rushed past them.

Felix glanced back at Natalia then winked at Billy. "Seeya, guys!" he called out, disappearing into the frenzy of teenage bodies.

As student after student rushed before them in a mad blur, Billy and Natalia gazed into each other's eyes, their spirits jumping between fear and excitement.

Natalia slid a tiny folded-up paper note into Billy's palm. She whispered, "Write back soon. I'm impatient."

Then she launched into the crowd and disappeared from view, though her excited heartbeat continued lighting up the darkness in Billy's mind. He grinned. *Okay, I like this.* He unfolded the note:

Dear Billy,

So yeah, I've been thinking about what happened. The whole thing yesterday scared me, for real. But I definitely want to hang out with you after school today. Well, not just today. Every day. But definitely today, at least to start with. Okay? Good.

Sincerely,

Your new favorite person,

Natalia Gonzalez ☺ ♥

Part V:

Tiferet

32: Caleb Thorne

At midnight, Caleb Thorne stood on the balcony outside his hotel suite, alone, sipping a glass of the highest quality cognac in the world. The October snow had finally melted, but the November air still contrasted greatly with the warmer temperatures he enjoyed at home. Still, despite wearing nothing but slippers and a silk bathrobe, the chilliness fascinated him. He liked the sound of the ice clinking in his frosted glass. The redness of his fingers. The crispness of his breath. It felt real.

The hotel suite behind him—a luxurious room he owned, in a building he owned, in a town he owned—didn't feel real at all. Every inch of his living quarters was covered in decadent displays of wealth. Only the finest items. The best materials. He needed such things to feel comfortable, yet they often became suffocating. He was always surrounded by images of himself, ideas of himself, so much self-self-self that he wasn't always sure where the mythical Thorne Century leader ended and the real Caleb began.

Caleb took another drink. He beamed with pride at the smoke pumping from his factory. *That factory is there because of me,* he thought. *I single-handedly saved this shithole town from economic ruin. It was me who created the jobs here and who will save the world, for I'm three times the man my father ever was.* He finished the glass and stepped back inside. The lights were on—even when he slept, he never liked the dark—and he reseated himself at his executive desk, where three monitors blinked to life. As the live video streams refreshed, he twirled his trusty pocketknife between his fingers.

It was time to watch Billy Jakobek. The camera revealed that the psychic Jew boy slept like a baby. Almost every night, for years, Caleb had spent his evening hours watching livestreams of his human test subjects. He knew those gifted children were going to make a fortune and restore America to the top of the global hierarchy, so he wanted to see every minute of their lives. He hungered for their emotional outbreaks, their psychic energy breakthroughs, and their nightmares especially. Every time one of them committed suicide, suffered a complete mental breakdown, or went comatose, it felt like they'd personally betrayed him. *They were all brats except Billy Jakobek.* Billy never stopped chugging along. Billy was loyal to him, whether by choice or not, and now, the Jew boy had become his last chance at success.

The project was almost done. Billions of dollars were at stake. As Thorne Century's greatest project entered the homestretch, everything rested on Billy's psychic energies, and Caleb still simmered over the weeks-old memory of how that selfish Guatemalan girl had taken his prize subject off camera for a night. *That little bitch nearly stole my golden goose.* He closed the knife. *You're lucky that you're useful to me now, Gonzalez, as potential leverage.* He grinned. In the weeks since he'd spoken to the girl, she'd followed his protocols to the letter. He wasn't surprised. *People always listen to the strong man.*

On the live feed, Billy stirred. The computer's speakers beeped. The boy's energy readings spiked. He was having a nightmare. "There we go." Caleb poured another drink.

Caleb's factory was continually siphoning Billy's psychic energies, twenty-four, seven, so these energy spikes were like Christmas gifts. Whenever the boy's amygdala sparkled, it shaved days—sometimes weeks—off the completion date. That was why he'd finally moved the boy to Heaven's Hole—of all the project bases, it was the furthest along.

Caleb listened to the wonderful beeping sound of power being drawn, captured, and converted. *Keep it going, Billy. Have enough nightmares, and perhaps we can wrap this up before the quarter ends.*

The beeping slowed down then stopped. The boy slept peacefully again.

"Shit," Caleb muttered.

He pounded his drink on the table. He went to the bathroom. As he urinated, he admired the fresh stubble on his face. *It makes me look more manly, yes? I bet Roseanna will like it.* He grunted, flushed the toilet, and kissed a tiny photo of Roseanna tacked up next to the mirror. *She will be the greatest gift of all when this finally ends. When I bring her to Venice, when we go skiing in the Swiss Alps, she'll forget her boring husband and kids. Our life together will be perfect. Just you and me, baby, like two peas in a pod.*

Caleb grimaced. *Two peas.* The knife weighed down his pocket and reminded him of his first girlfriend, Kaley Somerfield, who'd once told him that "We're like two peas in a pod, baby." Sometimes he liked thinking about Kaley or remembering how much he'd loved her back when they used to break the rules, make out in the woods right before dawn, and talk about their future dreams. Usually, he preferred to forget it all. He flicked the knife open, remembering the rounded swell of Kaley's pregnant belly so long ago.

His daily alarm went off. *Oops. Time for my shot.*

Beneath the counter, Caleb opened a locked refrigerator lined with vials full of Billy's glistening red psycho blood. His mouth watered at the scarlet fluid, which uneasily reminded him of his father's alcoholism. *Once this project is done, I must kick this habit before I get hooked. It feels so good, though, once those ridiculous hallucinations wear off. So powerful.*

He uncapped a needle and flicked it. The blood bubbles floated to the top, where he expelled them. He plunged the needle into his neck. The injection whooshed. Veins swelled in his throat. He threw the needle into the sink. "Goddamn." He applied pressure to the stinging wound.

His vision blurred. Weird images flashed in his eyes, so he closed them. *Doctor said never to look in the mirror. Remember that.* He squeezed his fists, tightening his grip on the little bubbles of psychic energy popping through his bloodstream, revealing faces, thoughts, and memories from Billy's life. The world spun, making Caleb feel high. *Sit down.* Instead, he leaned against the counter, nearly toppling, as electricity tingled down his spine. "Don't forget why you do this," he muttered. *To keep that psycho out of your head, that's why. Let the scientists take their weak little psycho-resistant pills, but with these injections, I'm one hundred percent psycho-immune.* That mattered to him. He had important decisions to make, and if someone like the Jew boy ever mucked about in his head, it could compromise everything. He'd prescribed the same injection for his soldiers and guards as well as Mr. Linus, his right-hand man.

A garbled shout blasted from his computer speakers. Caleb stumbled back to the desk. On-screen, Billy wrestled against his straps, roaring those ethereal screams that used to make Caleb uneasy. The machines surrounding the boy's bed beeped and whirred, capturing energy that would be transferred to the factory's central battery. Billy's eyes flashed blue.

"That's my boy," Caleb said as he danced the pocketknife's blade along his fingertips. *Keep it coming, kid. Your psychic blowouts are funding my future yacht trips with Roseanna.*

The freak-out ended. Billy passed out, slumping down like a stone.

Caleb slammed his knife down, stomped across the room, then came back to pour himself more cognac. As he drank, the knife taunted him from the desk, reminding him once again of Kaley Somerfield. She'd given him that knife on his sixteenth birthday. "For my favorite li'l badass," she'd said. Since then, Caleb had never been separated from it.

The computer speakers screeched. A scratchy voice cut the air. "Hey, Caleb... explosion's coming soon... big boom..."

Caleb twitched. The speakers sputtered. The injection site on his neck burned. *Relax. That voice is simply a hallucination from the psycho blood.* Caleb hesitantly eyed the screen and was relieved to see Billy sleeping soundly, clearly not speaking to the camera. *Yes, good, I'm imagining the voice. No wonder these psycho kids go nuts, with this delusional nonsense.* Caleb walked back out onto the patio, and the hallucinatory voice rasped out again, "Big boom... bye-bye, Caleb... bye-bye, everyone..."

Caleb closed the glass door, left the hallucinations behind, and stared proudly at his factory again. This time, something bothered him. *It's too small.* In front of the natural grandeur of those mighty, snowcapped mountains, his smokestacks looked like wimpy needles. He didn't like it.

33: Natalia

For Natalia and Billy, the next few weeks flew by. The trees shook off their last leaves. Touches lasted longer. Kisses intensified. Daily hangouts became the norm. And suddenly, before Natalia knew what was happening, she and the strangest boy she'd ever met were an item. Natalia had been in relationships before but never anything like this. When she and Billy held hands, their souls intertwined, the air buzzed, and something distinctly weird—and special—was created. As they walked through the school hallways together, people looked. They murmured. They gossiped. To Natalia's delight, Billy didn't care.

The lunch bell rang. The stampede began. Natalia tugged Billy away from the cafeteria. "I have another idea. Come with me."

Billy shrugged his agreement. Their hands fused together, unbreakable, as they ruptured the mass of bodies, grinning at each other.

"C'mon, you!" she cried. "We can break through!" They reached the other side of the crowd.

Natalia led him around the corner, and they stopped at the art room. The lights were off inside since Ms. Stevens was on lunch duty. Natalia bumped the door open, slid inside, and dragged Billy with her. When the door was safely closed, she whispered, "Don't worry. Me and the teacher here are friends. She probably wouldn't be happy about me breaking in, but..."

Billy mockingly brushed this off his shoulder, which eased Natalia's silly concerns about corrupting him. *That's a stupid fear, anyway. This guy literally made a bunch of assholes shoot themselves when he was kid. Just because he's sweet doesn't mean he's naïve or innocent.*

She took his hand again—shuddering with electricity, feelings, and power, which she was familiar with now that they touched all the time—and brought him over to the walk-in closet behind Ms. Stevens's desk. She closed this door behind them, as well, then turned on the closet light, revealing shelves full of art supplies, paint buckets, canvasses, and so on.

What mattered to Natalia was the bottom shelf, which contained a pile of sketchbooks dating back to middle school. "Ms. Stevens lets me keep these here," she said, sitting cross-legged on the paint-splotched floor. Billy perched next to her as she pulled a book from the middle and blew dust off the cover. "These go back for years. I keep them here with Ms. Stevens because... I trust her, I guess. There's personal stuff in here"—she started opening the sketchbook then snapped it closed—"drawings I wouldn't want, like, my little brothers or Mamá to see, y'know? So whenever I fill up a sketchbook, I keep it here, and Ms. Stevens buys me another one. She's really nice." Natalia curled the sketchbook. *I can't believe I'm going to show him this stuff. Super embarrassing.* "Do you want to see this? I'd like to show you, but most of it is dumb fourteen-year-old stuff."

Billy chuckled. "Of course."

Natalia thrilled at the sound of his voice. He still rarely talked—and only when they were alone—so she savored every word. "Okay." She gulped. "Here goes."

She turned the book open to the middle, revealing a drawing of a tiny dark silhouette standing before the bloodied remains of another person, stomped to death by a giant boot. The silhouettes were drawn in sketchy lines, while the boot was made of firm, solid black ones. Natalia burst out laughing. "Oh god." She closed the book. "Maybe I shouldn't show you this. What a bunch of moody adolescent crap."

Billy reopened the book. "Hey. You're too hard on yourself." He nestled his chin into her shoulder. "That moody adolescent crap came from something real." He flipped through and somehow located the boot-stomp page immediately. He closed his eyes and ran his fingertips along every pen stroke.

"What are you doing?" she asked.

He double tapped the small silhouette. "This is you. When you drew this, you were in your bedroom. Crying about your dad. You'd just seen some news story on TV about immigrants being murdered. Reminded you of him."

Natalia jumped him. "Wait, you can *see* all that just by touching my drawing?"

He shrugged. "Yeah. Art is powerful."

"Whoa." Natalia shook her head. *New revelations all the time, huh?* "Hold on, you're telling me that we've been hanging out every day while I draw... and it took you this long to reveal your coolest superpower ever?"

"Well. I guess—" Billy leaned back and bumped the wall, almost knocking over the shelves of paint cans. "Oops." He smiled. "You're the one with the superpower here, Natalia. Not me. With a pen, you create something from nothing. Creativity. All I'm doing is reading what you already put there. Not so creative."

"That's charmingly romantic of you but annoyingly humble." Natalia laughed. She tapped the sketchbook. "Okay, wise guy, what else do you see?"

Closing his eyes again, he retraced every ink line with his fingers. "You were sad. Angry too. This part..." He stopped, pushing down on the giant black boot. "It's... society? Power structures? You weren't quite sure. You just knew something big and unstoppable killed your dad." Billy looked up. "You were a smart middle schooler."

Natalia exhaled. *I remember that day. I'd totally forgotten about it until now.* "Next drawing too?"

Billy turned the page—and did a startled jump. He showed it to Natalia, and her heart stopped. The drawing depicted the Thorne

Century factory exploding into a mushroom cloud. Billy shook his head. "This one... um."

"Yikes. We probably shouldn't read too much into it," Natalia said as much for herself as for him. *Okay, now I'm officially freaked out by my boyfriend's nightmares.* "Honestly, my mamá probably just came home tired that day. I might've just been pissed, wanted to blow things up... I dunno." *Right, pretend the coincidence doesn't freak you out.*

"Yeah, okay. Sorry. Can't do that one." Billy leafed through a few more pages. "These are just sketches from class. Distractions. But there's something intense coming up." He stopped. "Here."

Natalia shielded her eyes. "Oh no. That one?"

Billy grinned. "Yeah. It's cool." The drawing he'd stopped on was a self-portrait of Natalia looking in the mirror. But whereas most of her self-portraits tended to depict herself in rather monstrous form, this one showed her as an adult in some sort of apocalyptic getup. Her head was shaved. She wore a tank top. Her proportions were exaggerated. Blood and soot ran down her face, neck, and the walls behind her, and a crowd of tiny people cheered for her.

"So embarrassing," Natalia said. "Like I'm trying to portray myself as some kinda goofy-ass war superhero. Just skip it."

"Shh." Billy traced the pen work. "The day you drew this, you'd just smoked weed for the first time."

"Ah, that explains it."

"I see you standing in the rain." Billy's brow furrowed. "Watching the factory from a distance. An accident happened. Machinery collapse. People died, crushed beneath it, but names hadn't been released. You were scared your mom might be one of them."

"Oh crap, you're *right*. I was scared as hell." *I totally forgot about that day. Blocked it out.*

"You felt helpless," Billy said. "Everybody gathered around the block. You waited outside. Once you found out she was okay, you smoked for the first time. Drew this. You were angry at the factory. The company. The system. You imagined a version of yourself who could start a revolution." He grinned at her. "Honestly? Bet you could."

"Wow." Natalia exhaled. "You are so amazing."

She tackled him to the ground, and they made out on the floor, rolling in dust and pencil shavings. She yanked on his hair. He held her hips. She kissed his mouth, his cheeks, his neck. They crashed into the wall hard. Paint cans toppled to the floor, dumping vivid colors all over them.

"Oh!" she cried, but the cans had already fallen, and their bodies were covered in yellows and blues, so they kept kissing. She smeared the colors across his shirt. "That's for wearing the same black shirt every day!"

He laughed, and they painted each other's faces. Billy climbed on top of her. Heat rushed down to her midsection.

"Don't stop," she whispered, biting his lip.

The school bell rang. Natalia leapt upright, suddenly all too aware that they were at school, covered in evidence of their own disorderliness. "I've got this," she said, pushing Billy out of the closet. "Get outta here. Ms. Stevens knows me, and this'll be less awkward to explain if I'm the only one here."

"Uh…" He dabbed at his painted shirt. "People will ask questions."

"People think we're weird anyway. Don't worry. Get out of here!"

Billy frowned. "Your teacher isn't going to be okay with this?"

"No. I wouldn't be either." Natalia snorted. "But she'll accept it if I clean the mess, so just go. Go!" The hallway filled with laughing, shouting, clamoring students. Billy hesitated, not wanting to leave her behind. Natalia nudged him closer to the door. As he opened it, Natalia stopped him. "Oh, wait. I almost forgot—Felix invited us to a party tonight. It's at this abandoned lake house with no electricity. Really decrepit place, so I hear. You wanna go?"

"Um, party? As in, a bunch of kids getting together, with alcohol?" Billy's cautiousness eased, and he brightened up. "I've never... you know. Yeah, I'd like to." His eyes sparkled. "But wait, I'd have to be back to Kaiser House before—"

"Before eleven, yeah. Big Daddy Thorne's rules." Natalia made a thumbs-down. "I promise. So, we're going?"

Despite the dumb yellow paint speckling Billy's curly hair and eyelashes, the smile he gave her was the most handsome thing she'd ever seen. "I'll go anywhere as long as you're there."

He exited the room, and Natalia wistfully watched him race down the hall. Then she assembled the cleaning supplies and got to work on the closet, humming to herself—becoming totally oblivious—as Ms. Stevens marched through the door.

"Uh, Natalia?" the teacher said. "Mind explaining what happened here?"

Natalia threw her arms up. "To be honest, Ms. Stevens?" She held the mop like an exclamation point. "No clue."

34: Billy

A lukewarm sun hung low in the sky, pinned like a button, casting long shadows from the trees. Birds chirped, as if making funereal cries for autumn's death. Billy walked through the woods, staying close to the rocky shoreline of Solitaire Lake, following Natalia, who was following Felix.

To Billy, their destination felt dreamlike. *I can't believe I'm going to a real party.* He whirled with wonderment. *A freak like me gets to do normal teenager things. Wow. I hope something doesn't go wrong or nobody touches me and finds out—*

"Okay, Felix. Stop... *stop.*" Natalia panted, pausing halfway up an especially steep hill. "Do we seriously have to hike through the woods to get to this place?"

Felix, soaked in sweat, tied his trademark denim jacket around his waist. "You're hilarious."

"What's so funny? My legs are aching."

"Aww, poor legs." Felix drew a fake tear on his cheek. "It's an abandoned lake house, Nat. This is how we get there."

She sighed. "There are no roads whatsoever?"

"Yeah, there used to be." Felix snorted and pointed at what looked like a tree but was actually a dilapidated telephone pole. "Getting to the cool places in the Hellhole ain't always user-friendly. I told you, this place is abandoned as hell, and trust me, it's awesome. But we're gonna have to keep walking unless you've got a badass canoe you wanna use to paddle up Solitaire Lake. Hey, see"—Felix pointed at Billy—"your boyfriend thinks it's funny too."

Billy hadn't realized he'd been grinning at their exchange. Natalia frowned at him, and he felt that she was simultaneously amused and annoyed. Then she marched off into the woods. Billy understood—she was just tired.

But Felix called out. "Hey! Where are you going?"

"I have to pee!" she shouted back. "Wait for me!"

"Crazy ol' Nat," Felix muttered. He plopped down onto the boulders overlooking the water, and he stared out at the factory in the distance. "Hey, man, take a seat." He patted the rocks. "I've been wanting to talk to you one-on-one, anyway."

Billy joined him, secretly thrilled that they were getting a chance to connect. As Felix tossed stones over the lake, trying to figure out his words, Billy squirreled into his new friend's thoughts. *He wants to talk to me about Natalia. He wants to say how he always wanted a sibling, and Natalia is the sister he never had.* Billy focused deeper and felt that Felix was, in the back of his mind, also stressing over an argument he'd had with his mother that morning. *He feels like she doesn't like him. That she would've preferred for him to be a strong, silent type like his father instead of someone who is so fast-talking and extroverted.*

"Wow." Felix rubbed his temples. "That was weird. Sudden headache, and all I can think about is my mom. Out of nowhere, man. That was…" He looked at Billy with a frown. "Pretty weird."

Billy pretended to be confused. He removed a tiny pen and pad from his pocket and wrote, *Yeah, man, that's weird.*

"Totally." Felix focused on Billy with surprising intensity. "By the way, man? I know you're not mute. Nat told me."

Billy froze. *Be careful.*

"I'm not gonna push, 'cause that's your own thing." Felix seesawed his shoulders. "Just letting you know. But listen, me and Nat talk about everything. She's awesome. Definitely my best friend."

Billy nodded. *Why do I feel nervous?*

"To tell you the truth, though, that chick has never been happy in her life." Felix laughed. "She's always got an attitude, always got something to prove. But with you… man, for the first time ever, she's happy. Like, *really* happy. This'll sound corny, but I think you're giving her back the hope she lost when she was a kid. So, dude, I know we don't know each other that well, but I trust you. And I want you to know I've got your back. If your life ever goes south, I'm here, okay?"

Billy grinned and wrote down, *Got it, man. Ditto.*

"Cool." Felix looked up just as Natalia reappeared from the trees. "*¿Vamos?*"

"*¡Vamos!*" Natalia agreed.

They hiked through the woods again, and soon, the sounds of distant laughter and music flittered through the branches. Finally, a beautiful A-frame house jutted out over the horizon. The lake house's degradation became quite noticeable as they approached—from shattered windows to a hopelessly caved-in roof—but Billy felt positive energy booming from the soil. *This place has so many good memories. Lots of good parties... but before that, a happy family lived here once too.* They passed by a partially collapsed dock hidden by overgrown brush, which emitted cheerful memories of two little boys diving off and playing in the water. *I wonder where they went.*

"Let's go!" Felix cried, and the trio hurried toward the music.

On the shoreline in front of the house, more than a dozen kids from school were drinking beer, telling stories, and collecting sticks, which they deposited into an ashy hole. Many more teenagers were inside the house, in the trees, or playing in the water. To Billy's wonderment, the students were an eclectic mix—sophomores hung out with juniors, and teens of different ethnicities, genders, and languages all mingled together.

"Hey, Paul!" Felix said to his boyfriend, who emerged from the wooded hills carrying a bundle of dry wood.

Paul Vieux, a muscular white guy with a dirty-blond buzz cut, gave Felix a long, extended kiss then paused and caught sight of Billy and Natalia. He nodded at them as Felix grinned.

"Hey, folks." Paul adjusted the branches under his arms. "Cool to see you here. Welcome to the ghost house, Billy. Glad you could make it."

Billy beamed at this. *Me too.*

"Hiya, Paul," Natalia said. "You guys want help getting this fire ready?"

Paul shrugged. "Sure." He dumped his sticks beside the ashy pit. "First, though, y'all are looking awfully sober. C'mon, I'll get you some shots."

Billy thought of guns then realized that Paul meant alcohol. *Damn, it's a good thing I don't talk, or I'd be embarrassing myself every three seconds.* As he, Natalia, and Felix followed Paul through the growing crowd—past a portable speaker blaring music—everyone turned toward them. Billy started to hunch over then decided to straighten himself. *Look up. Be a real person.* He nearly crashed into Hassan, a boy he sat next to in Geometry. Hassan's eyes bugged out.

"Whoa! Billy Jakobek? Good to see you, bud."

The party cheered at this. Billy spun around, smiling and nodding at everyone like a buffoon. *This is so weird.* He rushed to catch up with his little group just as they were entering the house.

Natalia seized his hand. "Look at you, making friends," she excitedly whispered into his ear,

The house was dark other than morbid sunlight streaking in through the broken windows, and the music was loud, but Billy easily recognized the emotional-energy signatures of at least fifteen more classmates, who all smiled, waved, and greeted him from the shadows.

The trio of Jose, Mike, and Alejandro smoked a bowl in the corner and yelled out, "Whoa, Billy J. is here!"

Billy waved back awkwardly. *It's amazing. Here I am, a guy with psychic powers, and I was too much of a moron to realize all these people like me.*

Paul led everyone to a stack of sawdusty two-by-fours positioned as a makeshift table, and he placed down a handful of shot glasses. "Here we go," Paul said as he hoisted a big plastic bottle and filled the glasses with something that smelled like rubbing alcohol.

Billy pinched his lips. *They can't seriously expect me to drink that. Can they?*

"Hey, everybody!" Paul called to the room. "Another shot?"

A few other teenage masochists joined them.

Felix slapped his head. "Christ, man." He examined the glass with disgust. "Is this Crown Thorne vodka? How cheap can you get?"

"Hey, six bucks a bottle." Paul tapped the plastic. "And I'm not twenty-one, so..." He poured a few more glasses, including one for himself, and everybody raised their shots into the air. "Cheers to escaping this town someday," Paul proclaimed.

"If we don't poison ourselves with this cheap junk first," Felix added.

The group laughed. They clinked glasses and took their shots. As soon as the vodka went down Billy's throat, his chest erupted like a volcano. *Oh boy, this sucks.* He burst out coughing, sending ripples of laughter across the group. At first, he felt humiliated. *They're making fun of me. They're... wait.* He eased up. *No, they're laughing with me. Relating. Connecting.* He softened his gaze and saw that everyone else was coughing, too, sharing the misery—sharing the human experience. Billy ceremoniously slammed his glass down.

"Good man!" Paul said.

Billy felt dizzy but good. *I like this feeling.* He smiled for no good reason, closed his eyes, and sensed the emotional lights of everyone around him weaving together like a glowing quilt.

People laughed. Bonded. Connected on things both small and deep. He opened his eyes, smiling like a fool, and—

———◈———

HE'S GONE. EVERYTHING is dark.

"Billy, are you all right?" a human voice says from the real world, but he can't respond. His mouth is sewed shut with a steel thread.

He's in the Shadow Place.

The sky bleeds. The factory of organs and metal whirs and grinds. The earth ruptures. Beneath Billy's feet, inside the cracks, are millions of squirming pink earthworms with tiny human faces—the faces of his classmates and friends. The worms crawl up his legs, each one screaming at the pained emotions inside it—sadness, jealousy, anger, stress—and as they prick him, he kicks them away.

"We need you!" the worms squeal.

The Shape floats down before him. The dark figure stops. It examines him with its incandescent-blue glare. Then, never looking away, it extends its arms to the ground like elevators.

"Help us!" the human-faced worms scream upward.

Billy doesn't help. The Shape scoops up the worms in a messy, wriggling pile and brings them to the sky, where it feeds them to the cackling monsters in the clouds. Dark smoke surrounds Billy—until it is pierced by firelight. The factory is burning. The ground is covered in charcoal skeletons. The smoke puffs out from the ruins, blinding him. He can't see. He coughs. His chest burns, and...

"You okay, Billy?" the distant human voice asks.

He can't reply, but he's not okay. He's not...

Not...

———◈———

BILLY RUBBED HIS EYES. He was back in the lake house. People were laughing. Drunk. Natalia and Felix giggled over a joke he hadn't heard. Everything was normal. *Except me*, he thought. *I'm not normal.* His skull felt like an inflated balloon.

"Hey, dude?" Paul asked, "are you okay?"

Billy gave Paul a shaky thumbs-up and backed out of the spotlight. He sneaked away from the group, trying not to poison the others with his toxic thoughts. *I'm going to hurt them if I stay close.* He moved toward the exit. *I need to go.* He turned to leave, and—

The Shape waited for him in the doorway.

Billy crashed back against the wall. The Shape cocked its head, its fiery gaze fixated on him. Black smoke whirled around it. *You're weak*, he heard himself thinking. *Let the Shape make you strong. Feed the Feeders. Stop fighting what you can't change.* In a panic, he turned around, and everyone in the party—the kids he'd felt so connected to moments before—felt tiny. His powers cracked into their brains. He saw their fears and insecurities. *I could make them do anything.* He spun back, facing the Shape. *We could make them into our army. Take over this town. Go bigger. Change the world in our image.*

Be the Shape.

Billy shook his head. Tears stung his eyes. *No, no, I don't want that. Why are you telling me this?* When he looked up, Eli's smirking one-eyed little body was in the Shape's place. The little boy tapped his bloodstained sneaker on the dirt. "Big boom is coming!" Eli squealed. "Embrace the power. Be the Shape!"

No! Billy raced through the doorway, breaking through the illusion—turning Eli into misty fragmented voices behind him. *I don't want it. I want to be Billy. Not the Shape. Please, not the Shape.* The world spun around him, and he saw faces spiraling from every corner of his vision. *Everyone is watching.* Sweat beads rolled down his forehead. *Don't freak out. Don't...*

A voice stirred him. "Hey, baby. I'm here."

He shuddered, turned around, and found himself in Natalia's embrace. The dizziness faded. The world came back to life. The sun draped over the horizon, painting the sky in glorious watercolors. He closed his eyes and could hear his classmates partying, laughing, and playing music. When he looked up again, Natalia's eyes reflected the pink clouds, and her skin sparkled in the dimming light as if she were carved from crystals.

"Need to get away from a minute?" she whispered. "Maybe watch the sunset? It's definitely a gorgeous one."

He nodded. *Yeah. I think so.*

"Okay." She kissed him. "Where's our view?"

He took her hand and led her back to the dock in the woods. Holding her, walking beneath a watercolor sky, everything made sense again. *I feel safe now. Because of her.* As they reached the dock, Natalia opened her bag, revealing a handful of green glass bottles she had pocketed away. "So, maybe over these beers, you'll explain what just happened."

35

Sitting together at the end of the ramshackle dock, Billy and Natalia swung their legs over the cool waters of Solitaire Lake. They drank beer, listened to the party noises behind them, and watched as sunset bathed the forest in shades of pink, red, and orange. The beer tasted oddly pleasing. The temperature wasn't too cold. The crickets chirped their little song. Everything was perfect.

"Got a secret." Billy talked quietly so that his voice wouldn't bounce back to the party. He shook his empty bottle. "That was my first beer ever."

"Oh, great. And your first one is this cheap-ass Thorne Century lager? You're going to hate beer now." She handed him another bottle from her purse.

He popped off the cap, took a swig, and smiled. "I like it, actually." He hiccupped.

Natalia giggled. "Dork." She popped open a new bottle for herself and laid her legs over his lap. "There are beers you'll like better when you try them. More expensive though."

Billy drew circles around her ankles. "Yeah, if I were a rich man." He grinned and hummed. "Daidle deedle daidle dumb..."

He sensed that she didn't get the reference, but she laughed, and he laughed with her. They kissed, their heartbeats aligned, but just as Billy was about to wrap himself around her, she backed up. "One sec, mister. Tell me why you spazzed out back there."

Billy sighed and gulped down more beer. The more alcohol in him, the easier it was to talk. *Guess that's not just a grown-up myth.* "It happened fast." He drank again. "I felt good. Happy. Then I closed my eyes, and the Shape..." He stared down at his reflection in the water. "Darkness closed in around me. I think the explosion is getting closer. I feel it, Natalia. Which means the Shape is getting closer too."

"The Shape was *here*?" She squeezed his shoulder.

"It's everywhere, you know. Sometimes I notice it. Sometimes I don't."

"Okay, so that's scary as hell." She moved closer to Billy. "What is it, like... the devil? I mean, have you ever looked up similar stories online? Maybe there's a chat group on social media or something."

"Nah, never." He smiled weakly and took another drink. "Kidding. C'mon. Of course I've spent hours trying to find something on the internet. I dunno. I think that maybe people with my powers have seen this thing over the centuries, and all of the different religions interpreted it their own way."

"Makes sense." A breeze passed over the water, fluttering through Natalia's hair. "So yeah, it's the devil. Source of all evil. Right?"

"It's not really like that, though." Billy squinted at the sunset. "The Shape isn't the source of all evil or some sorta goofy evil overlord who wants to control the world. It's not even a person, honestly. It's just... an emptiness that feeds on negative emotions and empowers them."

"Creepy stuff." She crossed her arms.

"I hate to say this, but I think the Shape is just like me." *Or maybe it is me.* "As in, a psychic sponge. But it's not some clumsy schlemiel like I am. It knows what it's doing. It manipulates human insecurity and pushes people to do horrible, cruel things. It sucks up the pain and then gives that negative energy to those Feeder things in the clouds..."

"This is so crazy, man. I swear, if I hadn't seen that scary thing in your memories..." She shuddered. "So you're saying that it can't create evil from nothing, right?"

"Right. It can only work with whatever's already there—nudges people toward their worst impulses. Makes 'em go nuts, like it's done to me." He finished the rest of his beer and hiccupped. "That's what scares me—the thought that maybe I'm feeding it just by being me. Maybe I'm the problem."

"Shut up."

"Seriously." He stared into the water. "That's why I'm worried about you."

The sun disappeared over the crater's ridge. The sky darkened to a deep purple. The crickets grew louder. Natalia tried to skip a stone across the water, but it sank. "I can take care of myself."

"Being close to me isn't safe. I've got... issues." He brought his knees to his chest. *I hate admitting this.* "I've hurt people. Killed them, even. Why would you even want to be around someone like me?"

Natalia held the sides of his head. "Listen to me, Billy. That's not you."

Billy stared into her loving gaze. He wanted to believe her. *I still remember how I felt when I made those men shoot themselves. I liked it.* "I did what I did." Sickness crawled through his veins like fire ants. "How can you say that's not me?"

"Because I know you, and you're a good person." She didn't blink.

"Not—"

"Billy, your family was murdered in front of your eyes, okay? You've been boxed into a lab your whole life. Don't give me this bullshit about how you should've controlled yourself better, because that is some fucked-up stuff for a little boy to go through. You know who is responsible for any violence you've caused? Thorne fucking Century, that's who. You're just a tiny gear in a giant systemic nightmare, and Thorne Century is the one who pushed you into a corner. They want you to think it's your fault, man, to get the blame off their backs... but don't kid yourself. Those dead bodies are on them."

Billy considered this. *It makes sense.*

"You're a good person trying to do the best you can with the shitty platter that got handed to you. You know what makes you special? It's not your powers. It's the way that you've got your heart on your sleeve at all times—it's the fact that you care. The fact that even though the world craps all over you, your biggest goal is to help others." She squeezed him. "You're not the Shape. You're Billy, *my* Billy, and I'll never let go."

He smiled, watching the moon appear over the horizon. "Reminds me of Elie Wiesel. You know, the Holocaust survivor."

"Huh?" She put her legs over his.

"My bubbe had me read him when I was a kid." Billy smiled. "He said something once, something about... um..." He rubbed his eyes. "He said the opposite of love isn't hate but indifference. The opposite of art isn't ugliness but indifference—"

"And the opposite of life is not death but indifference, right? I remember it now." Natalia smiled. "You're right, man. That's definitely a message to live by."

He held her. Their lips met. An orange glow lit up the shoreline behind them. Flames crackled from the pit, sending roars of delight through the party. The strings of an acoustic guitar—played by Felix, Billy sensed—vibrated across the water. Looking back at the happy teenagers around the bonfire, Billy felt jealous. *I wish I could be part of that without endangering everyone.*

Natalia tugged him. "They got the fire started? Okay, let's go."

"But what if—"

"C'mon, you." She yanked him off the dock. "Be the human being you're meant to be!"

She's right. Billy and Natalia cut through the woods and approached the fire circle, where the joyous energies of the other teenagers wrapped around them like a blanket.

Felix plucked at the guitar. "The lovebirds return to the *fiiire...*" he sang, "after making out on the dock, filled with *desiiire...*"

"Hey!" Natalia yelled, but as they joined the circle, everyone laughed and applauded with no malice whatsoever. Natalia bowed, and Billy bowed with her, not sure what they were doing but realizing no one else knew either. *No one ever knows, really. We just make our best guesses.*

Felix launched into his next song. Billy barely noticed that Paul was next to him, talking into his ear.

"I said," Paul repeated, "you want another beer?"

Billy gave a thumbs-up, and a freshly opened beer was placed in his hand. Felix's voice bellowed over the trees, and soon, everyone else sang along with him. All around the circle, teens of different ages, orientations, religions, genders, and backgrounds—Latino, Middle Eastern, Congolese, European, and more—laughed, cheered, and sang with one another. Billy marveled at the scene around him. *Just being here, together, sharing this... it's like we're breaking from the terrible system around us.* He looked around and saw no hatred, no prejudice, nothing but unity. *We can do this. Just by singing together here... we're free.* Billy caught himself grinning. *I love this.*

With shaky hands, Billy pulled his Star of David necklace out of his collar, letting it hang openly over his chest. No one glared, condemned him, or whispered mean jokes about ovens, Nazis, or the size of his nose.

Hassan, his geometry classmate, nodded approvingly. "That's cool, bro. Be yourself. Listen, my family are refugees. Syria. If you don't mind me asking, do you have family who are still stuck in Beth Shalom?"

Billy shook his head. *No. All dead.*

"What about World War II? Any family members who were... you know?"

Billy wrote on his pad, and he displayed it to Hassan: *My grandmother.*

"Much respect, man," Hassan said. "Don't worry. We're all safe here with each other."

Billy clinked bottles with Hassan, took a drink, and silently thrilled at the flames, the guitar, and the company. Natalia started dancing, roped in Billy, and soon, the entire party twirled to the music. Their footsteps matched the beat, and Billy's heart thudded with the communion of positivity surrounding them.

Maybe this is the future, Billy thought. *Maybe, together, this could be the first step to a new world. A better world.*

The bonfire shot up into the dark sky, lighting up the lives of Heaven's Hole's teenagers, and everyone danced into the night.

36: Natalia

Natalia could have kept going all night long—and she sensed Billy wanted to—but by nine o'clock, she knew they had to get going in order to meet Mr. Thorne Century Himself's curfew. After making it through the woods, she and Billy drunkenly stumbled through the cold streets of Heaven's Hole. They swayed, cascaded, and at one point, slipped into a freezing puddle, but they never stopped laughing.

Finally, they reached the ominous concrete block that was Natalia's apartment building, and wistfulness overcame her. *I don't want this to end.* "This was such a wonderful night!" She swerved, and Billy caught her. "I just want to rewind and do it over again. And over and over..."

"Yeah, me too." Billy tripped over the cracked asphalt. "Heh."

"It's so funny to see you drunk!" Natalia fell into his arms. "And oh man, you heard my singing voice..." She shook her head.

"It's a beautiful voice." Billy kissed her.

She draped herself over his shoulders. *It's too early to say good night. I want longer. More. A lifetime! No, I shouldn't say that. It's too clingy...* "Y'know, Billy..." She sighed. "You still have nearly an hour before you have to get back to Kaiser House." She stepped onto his toes, elevating herself to his height. "What if you came in and met my family? I'd really like that."

Billy hiccupped. "Not sure tonight is the night. I'm drinda krunk. Drunk. Kinda drunk."

"I guess so." Closing her eyes, she longingly imagined him meeting Mamá, Abuelita, and her brothers then touched his temple, looking for answers in his mind. *It's more than that, isn't it?* She traced his jawline. *You're scared of meeting a close family, because you haven't been around one since yours died.* When she opened her eyes, Billy was shivering, so she hugged him. "I get it."

"Thanks."

"Hey, I had a lot of fun tonight."

"Me too."

They kissed good night, and Natalia pranced back to her apartment, spinning like a ballerina in the parking lot. "I feel so good!" she cried, and a grinning Billy waved from the distance. She twirled up the stairs. Once the door was in sight, she stopped, straightened up, and tried to seem less drunk. *If this was an audition for sober Natalia, I'd bomb.*

She popped gum into her mouth to hide her beer breath and walked inside. The lights were off. Everyone seemed asleep except Mamá, who was washing the dishes in her work uniform.

"Hey, baby," Mamá whispered, making a shush motion.

Natalia giggled. *Yeah, as if we need to be quiet to keep the twins from waking up. Please.* She leaned over her mother's shoulder and shut the faucet off, swaying more drunkenly than she would have liked. "I'll do the dishes, Mamá. You have to go to work."

"Thank you." Mamá dried her hands, started to speak, and broke into a cough. Once it subsided, she asked, "Out late tonight, huh?"

"Is it late?" Natalia mockingly faked panic.

Mamá cleared her throat. "How's this imaginary boyfriend that you keep seeing every night?"

"Oh, y'know, as good as any imaginary thing can be."

"Billy, right?" Mamá asked. "Your abuela told me that was his name."

Natalia crossed her arms. "She must be snooping through my things, then, because I haven't told her that."

"She's always been nosy like that." Mamá wheezed as she clipped on her Thorne Century badge. She opened the door. "Anyway, I'm happy for you. I hope we can meet him."

Natalia scoffed. "Yeah, right. Can you imagine how much Abuelita would embarrass me?" But she thought, *Hopefully soon.*

Mamá chuckled. "Good night, baby." She exited.

Natalia sadly watched through the window as her mother limped to work. *I wish she could get some good rest for once.* Natalia drank a few glasses of water then went to the living room, where Juan was passed out on the floor. She shook him. "Hey, kid. What are you doing here?"

Juan shifted irritably. "Carlos said."

"Carlos said what?"

"Carlos said I gotta sleep on the floor tonight 'cause I lost the game." Juan pulled himself into a ball. "That's what."

Natalia groaned. "That's stupid. Have you brushed your teeth yet?"

"No."

"C'mon, you." Natalia brought the boy to the bathroom, and she turned the sink on. "Go brush your teeth, and sleep on the bed like a normal human being. Carlos doesn't get to make decisions for you."

Juan begrudgingly wet his toothbrush. Natalia peered around the corner at Carlos, who was sleeping in bed peacefully, and reminded herself to lecture him later. *Just because he was born twenty minutes before Juan, he always bosses the poor guy around.* Hearing the tap still running, she returned to the bathroom and found Juan with a mouthful of toothpaste, toothbrush abandoned on the toilet lid, inspecting the faucet like a museum showcase.

"Dude." Natalia crouched next to him. "What are you doing?"

"I dunno." He climbed up and spat out his toothpaste. He stared at Natalia with big, circular eyes. "Big sister, can I ask you something?"

"Sure." She took out her gum and sat down on the toilet, landing there in a rather wobbly fashion that she hoped he didn't notice. She thought about putting him on her lap but realized that he was too big. *Man, when did that happen?*

Juan nudged her. "What was Papá like?"

Natalia's guts shriveled. *Crap.* "You don't remember him?"

"Only a li'l bit." He moved closer, and Natalia hugged him. His heartbeat boomed within his tiny chest.

"You remember the way he smiled?" she asked.

"Yeah."

"That's because he was always laughing." Natalia brushed Juan's hair from his eyes. "The guy always had a joke ready, even when things got bad. It was annoying sometimes but mostly just funny. He really liked playing games, having the family together, and... he liked bonfires with his friends, though he sometimes got too drunk. He also liked cooking, you know. He was an awesome chef. He was the one who decided that our family should start celebrating Thanksgiving, actually. When I was super young, one Thanksgiving night, he came home with a turkey, and he said that since we were Americans, he was going to start cooking turkey once a year." She whispered into Juan's ear, "Don't tell Mamá, but Papá's turkeys were always better."

Juan giggled. Then he ducked his head into Natalia's shoulder and mumbled, "If he was so great, why did people kill him?"

Natalia chewed on this. His heart was in her hands. Everything he'd ever know about his father was up to her. "Bad things happen to good people, sometimes."

"But why, Natalia?" Tears appeared in his eyes.

"Because... because..." She bit her lip, hesitated, then said what she wanted to say. "Because there's a lot of hatred out there, Juan. Sometimes, when people are hurting, they get scared, and they blame it on people who are... different from them. Then evil men come along with a lot of power and money and privilege, and these evil men manipulate the scared people by using their fears. They exploit the hatred, if that makes sense."

"Why, though?"

"Because if the little people all hate each other or are scared, the bad guys can pretend they're the only ones able to fix things by pretending the problems were caused by the people who are different. Hatred makes these bad men more powerful, I guess. But that's what happened to Papá. He didn't do anything wrong, but he got blamed. It's why the richest company in the whole world pays Mamá nothing but scraps while at the same time sending money to politicians who spout crap about people like her on TV, even though they're the ones who spilled so much blood in our home country that we had to run away for our lives. The rich get richer, the poor get poorer... the whole system is so messed up, Juan, and our papá got blamed for it just because we're different. It's not fair. But it happens."

"That sucks." Juan shook his little head. "What makes us so different?"

Natalia sighed. "Because we come from Central America."

"That shouldn't matter." He frowned.

"You're right," she said, and Juan clutched her like she was his seat belt in a car crash. *Don't let go of him. This could be a really important moment in his life, Natalia, so get this shit right.* "But I'll tell you something about Papá. If there's one thing you need to know, it's that he loved you guys. He loved you so much and would've done anything to be here if he could. And he's up there now, watching us all, proud as hell that you're such a strong, thoughtful little dude." Saying this felt like throwing off a heavy backpack. She and Juan rocked back and forth, his tiny hands holding on to her, and she kissed his forehead. "Time for bed."

He jumped from her arms, zipped around the corner, then stopped to look back. "Thanks, Natalia. I kinda remember him a little better now." He went to bed.

Natalia stood up, smiling to herself. *I think I did okay there.* Her shirt was smudged with Juan's toothpaste. "Blech, so gross," she muttered. She washed it off, brushed her own teeth, then retired back to her little closet bedroom.

She wasn't ready to sleep, though. Instead, she lit a candle, opened her sketchbook, and flipped it open to her never-ending *Dark-Eyed Boy* project. She'd worked on it every day, restarting multiple times, but it was finally progressing in a direction she liked. *Making it more abstract definitely helped. More about inner Billy instead of just outer Billy.* She hadn't told Billy about the drawing. She was scared to do so, especially after seeing the way he read artwork. *I need to finish it first, at least.* Her pen whisked across the page, creating fine, tight line work. *Dark-Eyed Boy* was quickly becoming the most detailed piece she'd ever worked on, and her perfectionist tendencies were at least half the reason it was taking so long. In the depths of her concentration, she pushed down too hard. The ink blotted. The line was ruined.

"Damn it." She threw the pen. It rolled into the thin crack between the wall and the bed. She groaned. *Don't be stupid. That's your best pen.* She reached between the crack, trying to fish the pen out, and—

Her hand went numb. Cold. Gone. She couldn't feel her fingers.

A humanoid shadow draped across the wall, flickering in the candlelight. She looked behind her. No one was there. Natalia tried to lift her hand, but it was submerged wrist-deep in the shadow's body—trapped in the wall itself—and wouldn't come loose.

"Holy fuck." She bit back on a scream. "Come free. Please, please, please come free." She yanked her arm. It was stuck. Tears filled her eyes. *Don't go crazy. Stay calm.* She pulled again and started hyperventilating. *How the hell do I stay calm?* The shadow emitted soft crackling noises.

A force pulled her arm into the wall hard, ripping her shoulder-deep into the void. "Let go!" she cried. She planted her feet on the nonshadowed wall, pushing hard against it. The force yanked her forward again. She wasn't strong enough. Her body tumbled forward into the darkness, falling away from the world she knew and into a state of dark, smoky emptiness.

She screamed, but her lungs produced no sound. Grinding pops filled her ears. She was drawn deeper into the void, toppling downward, until she landed face-to-face with a long-legged, pale, scorpion-like creature clutching her hand in its pincers.

The arachnid had Billy's face. His curly hair was matted down. His cheeks were scarred and swollen. Blood dripped from his mouth, and his eyes were blue flames. She tried to call out Billy's name but could only gag on the raw-flesh-smelling air.

"You're not supposed to be here," the Billy monster's inhuman voice groaned. The monster lunged at her.

Get away from me! She kicked the pincer, releasing her hand, and threw herself backward. She was flung out of the darkness—out of the void, out of the wall, and back into her ordinary bedroom, where she collapsed off the side of her bed. The crackling ceased.

She sat bolt upright. "What are you?" she shouted at the void. But it was gone, and the only shadow on the wall was hers. She cupped her mouth. *Don't scream. Don't wake everybody up.* After a moment of agonized repression, she breathed steadily again. *It's gone. It must have been something I absorbed from Billy. A vision or...*

Trembling, she pulled her bed away from the wall. The pen was gone. *Man, I really hope it's just under the bed somewhere.* Not willing to dig any further, she fled to the living room and curled up on the couch, clutching her sketchbook to her chest. "I hope you're okay, Billy," she whispered.

37: Mother

From the moment that Mother watched Billy stumble back into Kaiser House at 10:29 p.m., wobbling like a penguin, she knew something was off. The boy crashed through the door, slid into the wall, and shook his head. Mother leapt to her feet—abandoning the pasta leftovers she'd been picking at—and dug for the tranquilizer in her coat pocket. "What's wrong, Billy?"

The teenager grinned foolishly, as if she'd said something hilarious, and gave her the A-okay sign. He removed his earbuds—the chorus from "Sunglasses at Night" escaped from them—and stuffed the wires into his pockets, nearly falling over again.

She sniffed his breath. *Oh.* "Are you drunk, young man?"

Billy hiccupped.

She repressed the urge to laugh. "I see." She put her hands on her hips, trying to hide the odd feeling of pride bubbling up inside her. *That's terrific, Billy. Hanging out with Natalia Gonzalez has been so good for you.* She filled a glass of water from the tap and handed it to him. "Drink some of this," she said, and as he gleefully waved at her, she burst out laughing. *Cover blown.* Watching the boy try to lift the glass to his lips with jerky motions, she snorted again. "Natalia, huh?"

He nodded with a big grin.

"Well." She chuckled. "I shouldn't say this, Billy, but—"

Father appeared in the corridor. "No, you shouldn't. Time for bed."

Mother crossed her arms. Father regarded her with a lethal glance, snapped on a pair of medical gloves from the wall, and pointed the drunken teenager down the hall.

Once Billy had stumbled back to his room, Father looked back at Mother and whispered, "What the hell are you doing?"

"He's just a boy," Mother whispered back. "Can't you sympathize with him?"

"That's not protocol." Father eyed the camera.

"But it's true. Protocol or not. Please, let's be straight with each other. I'll tell you my story first, if it helps. In my real life, before this—"

"No." Father raised his palm in a stop sign. "Don't tell me anything. There is no real life before this, Mother. This is our life. And that subject..." He gestured down the hall. "That's our only concern. Good night."

Mother shrank beneath the hardness of Father's tone, but she noticed muted panic in the man's eyes. *Thorne is blackmailing him with something too. Perhaps his own family? Financial ruin?* Father escaped down the hall and slammed the vault door to Billy's room behind him.

Mother stood in place, shivering, unable to decide her next move. *Something about that interaction really bothers me.* Just as she was about to go down the hall and spend the night poring through Billy's latest blood samples, the door opened behind her.

She looked back, expecting a security guard, and was shocked to see Caleb Thorne in a long wool coat, holding a bouquet of roses. His mouth pulled into that giant loving grin that never touched his eyes. "Good evening, dearest."

Mother dug her fingernails into her palm. "Caleb."

Caleb handed the roses to her, and when she didn't take them, he delicately placed them on the table. His gaze flicked up at her as if trying to gauge her response, and he looked away with evident disappointment. "I came here to apologize." He hung up his coat. "I've done some... thinking. Our interactions have been rather cold lately.

You seem frustrated, and I believe my lack of transparency is the culprit."

Mother crossed her arms. "Oh?"

Caleb dug through the kitchen drawer. "I have been dishonest with you regarding certain key details of the project, and I believe that's the true cause of your frustration. I lied for your safety, of course, but in light of our recent arguments, it seems my opaqueness has weighed quite heavily on me and on *us*. So I'd like to make amends by—ah! Here it is." Caleb took out a wine corker from the drawer. Going back to his coat pocket, he removed a tall bottle of cabernet sauvignon. With swift, delicate motions, he began removing the cork. "Mind bringing me a few glasses, dear?"

"You're telling me... wait." Mother felt dizzy. She placed two glasses before him. "There's something I don't know about the project?"

"Again, I apologize." Caleb poured the wine. "I will rectify the matter, but this subject is rather heavy... so first, let's have a drink. Perhaps you know that Latin phrase, *in vino veritas*—"

"In wine there is truth." Mother shuddered.

"Exactly! Follow me." Caleb led her to the living room. They sat down, glasses in hand, and Mother took a big, expensive gulp.

38

For the first half hour, Mother was edgy and impatient. As they sat in the living room, beside the crackling fire, Caleb kept prattling about unrelated anecdotes, obnoxious political tangents, and even sports updates rather than the information he had come to divulge. It took her a few wineglasses to realize that he was nervous. *He's procrastinating—that's what it is.* This response to stress was uncomfortably human—Mother found it easier to pretend he was a demon than to acknowledge him as a man—but after the wine settled in, she relaxed. To her surprise, one of Caleb's old high school stories even made her laugh.

"Wait." She poured herself another glass. "You just made that up, right?"

"No, it absolutely happened." Caleb took a sip.

"You're saying you and your gang of sixteen-year-old 'good old boys'"—she snorted, making air quotes—"would sneak out of boarding school at midnight and drive through the wealthy neighborhoods, with a baseball bat out the window, just knocking over mailboxes? Is that right?"

Thorne laughed. His real smile was drastically different from the fake one. "Oh, you know how boys are."

"Hmm." She drank more wine. "The police must've apprehended you, right? You must've been charged with—"

"Please." Thorne waved his hand. "Our fathers were all rich executives. Sure, we'd get busted sometimes, but you think any police officer would risk his career by pressing charges against Mark Thorne's only son? Of course not." Caleb laughed, seemingly unaware that his Southern accent was slipping out more with every glass. "I was a bad kid. I appreciate having those experiences, however. Gives a man character when he grows up."

Mother laughed with him, but as she stared at the fake and perfect living room around her, she was struck by how little the Thorne Century heir understood his own life story or the world at large. She pictured a zit-faced teenage Caleb trying so hard to be tough and rebellious but shielded from any consequences. *You never had to suffer, Caleb, not like regular people do. You were always protected.* She didn't say this. Though wine made her bold, it didn't make her stupid.

"You as a good old boy, huh?" she said. "Odd image. I would've pictured you as a nerd."

"Perhaps I was." He ran his hands along his buzz cut. "I learned to be a different person. In this world, people like to complain about their lot in life, but we all have the freedom to be whoever we want. Self-determination. I chose my path. Nobody else chose it for me, not my father or—"

"What was he like?" Mother asked. "Your father, I mean."

"Daddy?" Caleb's genuine grin cracked open again, and his Southern accent peeked out. "He was cold. An absolute tyrant. He loved my mother, though, I must admit." Caleb plopped his trademark knife onto the table. "You should have seen his face the first time he found this knife on my dresser. That was the same day he found out about Kaley Somerfield, since she'd given me the knife as a birthday gift—"

"Kaley was your first girlfriend, right?"

Caleb stared into his empty glass. "That's correct."

"Do you still keep in touch with her?" *Like a regular human being, maybe?*

Caleb stiffened up, his demeanor shifting back into the corporate realm. He poured himself more wine, beckoned for Mother's glass, and refilled it. Finally, after swishing his wine for a moment, he said, "No."

"Why not? Even if she's not on social media, I'm sure your friend Mr. Linus could track her down. Frankly, considering that you still carry that knife everywhere, it seems that you—"

"I loved Kaley." He pocketed the knife. "But she's dead. Tragic accident many years ago."

Mother squirmed. "I'm sorry, Caleb."

"Don't be sorry, dear," he responded, giving her a piercing glare. "I like opening up to you."

There was a long silence. Caleb pounded his wine down like a shot and refilled his glass. He stared into the fireplace, no longer divulging his thoughts. Mother sat on the edge of her seat and listened to the sparking embers. "You know, Caleb," she said finally. "Billy, he—"

"You mean the subject." Any trace of a Southern accent had disappeared from Thorne's voice.

"I mean *Billy*." Mother smiled, forcing him to smile back. "I watch *Billy's* ankle monitor during the day, just like you ask. When he's not hanging out with his new friend, he visits all the homeless people in town. I know the hot spots by now because he always goes to them. I keep having to buy him new winter clothes, blankets, and food because he gives it all away."

Thorne stared at the fire. He said nothing.

"He goes to the hospital too," Mother said. "I got a report from them once, saying that he visits hospice patients. They don't know about his abilities or anything, but the hospice workers rave about how every time he visits a patient, they spend the rest of the day smiling, feeling less sick... you know what I mean. Then Billy comes home hurting. He makes himself sick so that other people can feel better."

"The hospital gave me that same report." Thorne's voice was listless. "Thankfully, the subject appears to be skilled at hiding his abilities when he does this—"

"Caleb, that boy is an idealist." Mother leaned back in her chair, threw her legs over the side, and took another drink. *Christ, I'm spilling my guts.* "Maybe it's the superhero comics, or maybe it's just his personality, but he believes in people's ability to be good. He wants to use his abilities to help make a better world."

"Shame about the miserable real world he lives in." Caleb put his glass on the table.

Mother lowered her gaze. "True." She drank again. "Caleb, let's stop beating around the bush, please. What did you come here to tell me tonight?"

Caleb squirmed. "Ah, yes."

"Is it about my son?" She winced. "Did you—"

"This has nothing to do with your family, Roseanna." Thorne shook his head. "However, what I am about to disclose to you is highly classified information. If you tell anyone—and I mean *any-one*—people will have to die as a direct repercussion. People you care about. Your son and husband, for example. Do you understand?"

Caleb spoke in a pleading tone that made Mother so nauseous that she had to sit upright. Hatred rushed into her cheeks, and she resisted the urge to break his stupid wine bottle against his skull. *What kind of child were you really, Caleb? Would that boy fear the man he has become?* Remembering her training—six months of brainwashing on emotional repression—she stuffed her anger back into her head.

"Roseanna?" Caleb asked.

"Yes." She exhaled. "You can trust me."

Caleb tried to pour her more wine, but she pulled the glass back. His mouth smiled, but his eyes looked hurt. "As you know, Thorne Century is one of the most powerful conglomerates in the world." He breathed heavily. "Not to brag, but the many companies under the Thorne Century umbrella are on the cutting edge of every big industry on the planet. One thing I've ensured since I took over is that every aspect is connected. We dominate in the realm of pharmaceuticals, of course, but we're also the world's biggest telecommunications company, and we make billions off the farming industry, private prisons, clothing manufacturing in developing countries. We run six of the ten highest-selling amusement parks in the world, candy companies—"

"Please cut to the chase." Sweat dampened her forehead.

"Yes." Caleb sighed. "See, when you first signed on to the so-called 'psycho' project, you did so under the belief that it was being done for our pharmaceutical wing." Caleb leaned forward. The fire cast an orange glow around his shadowy form. "I'm sorry for lying to you, Roseanna, but the pharmaceutical project was canceled six years ago. It was fruitless. Since then, your research has been redirected toward... well, something else."

Mother almost threw up. "Are you telling me that I've sunk years of life into this... thing, that's not even a medical project?" *My son. My husband. My career.* "Caleb, what the hell am I working on?"

"My apologies."

Mother dropped her glass. It shattered on the hardwood floor. She was about to wipe it up and to pick up the pieces but stopped. Her heart was racing. She thought about all the energy samples she'd collected over the years, all the time she could have spent with her family.

Caleb reached out to comfort her, and she pushed him away. "Stop. Please tell me the truth."

Caleb exhaled. "Roseanna, your work is being used for our weapons division. A contract with the Pentagon."

Mother gasped. *Fuck. This doesn't feel real.* She tried to figure out a way for her conscience to be okay, but no answers arose. "Christ." She blinked back tears. "This... this... how could it...?"

"Your ideas, Roseanna, have been invaluable to your country." Caleb emitted a fake laugh. "Your brilliant notion to let Mr. Jakobek live a regular life, to experience a normal range of emotions, has spiked his energy readings, fired up his amygdala, brought us so close to completion on the weapons project..." He grabbed her hand, and when she tried to jerk away, he wouldn't let go. "All thanks to you, Roseanna. Just imagine the emotional energies he'll emit if this relationship breaks up or he loses his virginity or—"

"Weapons development." She put her hands over her face and moaned. *I need to kill myself. To end this. Oh my god.* The pieces came together like Tetris blocks. "Those injections you have us give him when he's asleep—"

"They trigger a lucid dreaming state. See, Roseanna, Mr. Jakobek's less-than-friendly alternate personality is at its strongest when his conscious mind—"

"Jesus Christ, Caleb." Mother looked up sharply. "You're *trying* to turn him into the Shape. So you can weaponize it."

Thorne smiled—the real smile, not the fake one. "Precisely."

39: Billy... (Somewhere Else)

In Billy's dream, he is somewhere else. The streets of Heaven's Hole are charred, smoky ruins, blackened sidewalks, buildings reduced to steel skeletons. Ash flutters down like rain. Every house is cracked open and burning to the ground. Billy walks through what was once downtown, stepping over chunks of brick, oil spills, car parts, toilet seats... and piles of dead bodies.

It's all over. The explosion has happened. People have gone insane.

Anyone still alive is beating each other to death. Billy comes across Eddy Walker, his homeless friend, devouring the remains of Buddy, stuffing raw pieces of dog flesh into his mouth. Amid the remains of the high school, Billy's fellow students crack each other's skulls open with bricks until blood runs down their faces as they cry, "Hit me next! Hit me next!" and down the road, little children race into burning buildings, giggling, as the flesh melts off their bones. Machine guns are everywhere. Crowds of people shoot at other crowds, spraying bullets like hailstorms. Bones are broken, brains splattered. Blood runs into the city's gutters.

Helicopter blades chop the air. A drone opens fire on the remaining population, slaughtering everyone who is left. Billy looks behind him and sees Mother—dead eyed, disemboweled, with blood dripping down her chin—carrying two severed heads until she, too, is cut down by bullets.

He scuttles beneath a bridge. "This can't be happening. This can't be real. Please, no..." he says as if anyone can hear him.

It doesn't make sense—so many good people, normal people, turned into monsters. *How? Why?* But he knows. His reflection peers back at him from a puddle of gasoline, and blue fire puffs from his eyes. "Big boom," his reflection says. "Everything you touch belongs to the Shape."

Smoke blackens and thickens, and Billy chokes. The Shape swirls before him, accompanied by a chorus of grinding bones and hallucinogenic chants. As machine guns roar through the remainder of the blighted town, the Shape draws Billy into the darkness with its long tendril fingers.

"I'm not you!" Billy cries. "I don't want your world—I want mine!" But as the black smoke surrounds him, all he sees is chaos, murder, and bloodshed all over the world. His larynx is strangled by black smoke until... until...

40: Mother

Mother leapt from her chair. "Remove me from this project!" she shouted, surprising herself. "I want out right now, Caleb, before—"

"It's too late, dear Roseanna." Thorne tried to guide her back into her seat, and she pushed him away. He brushed off his blazer, clearly insulted. "We're in the final stages of development."

"Too late... weapons development..." she whimpered, totally deflated. She backed into the corner of the room, clutching her shivering body. *Dear God in heaven, please just strike me down. I can't live this way. I can't be the bad guy.* "I'm trapped... totally trapped..." She squeezed her abdomen, giving herself the support no one else could. Caleb inched up to her, reeking of musty cologne. Looking away from him, she muttered, "You're playing with fire, Caleb."

The businessman smiled. "I like the warmth." His wine-tinted exhalation landed on her face.

"Please let me resign." She sucked back tears. "Please, please..."

"It's too late."

Mother edged away from him. "Have you considered the possibility that the Shape isn't a delusion?" *I'm grasping at straws.* "What if the boy is right, and it truly is an extradimensional entity—"

"Horseshit," Caleb muttered. "You read the same psychiatric reports I did. The Shape is a delusion created by childhood trauma, and in that delusion, I believe, lies the true Billy Jakobek. The sensitive boy is just a tissue-paper skin masking the violent force of anger trapped within. Based on Father's studies—"

"Father knows?" She cringed.

"Yes. And he believes strongly that when the Shape is unleashed on rival nations, those mind-altering capabilities will be able to overtake entire towns, cities, perhaps even small countries. The subject's sudden energy explosion on the fire tower last month proved this case." Caleb snapped his fingers. "By controlling Jakobek's power, operating it with a digital switchboard, the Pentagon shall be able to make targeted attacks upon designated strike zones, making entire enemy squadrons go suicidal. Homicidal. Violent. Just imagine pushing a button"—he replicated this gesture as his voice rose with excitement—"and boom! An entire terrorist group, thousands of individuals, will slaughter each other in less than an hour... and the news media would never even know we were there. Your work will change the world, Roseanna. Psychic warfare will replace soldiers, drones, all of it. The new wars will be clean. Contained. Beautiful. We go in, we win, and it's over."

"The poor boy..." She shook her head, sputtering her words. "You know you can't control him, right? Once he's out there—"

"Indeed, which is why *he* won't be out there. Or, well, not his body, anyway." Caleb grinned. "We're harnessing his capabilities, his mind, not him. That's why this project exists—to absorb and amplify all those priceless emotional energies he puts out and to fuse them to a... shall we say, a piece of equipment. A battery built right in the center of this town... a fully controllable weapon, which I like to call my 'emotion bomb.' Catchy, yes?"

"Good lord." Mother shriveled up. "You're talking about the factory."

"Right you are." Thorne went back to his wineglass and held it up. "Another glass, my dear?" He took a drink. "To America reclaiming its place atop the global hierarchy!"

"An emotion bomb." Mother swallowed down bile. "So the energies we've absorbed from Billy's emotions are... ah..." She wobbled. "It all gets circulated to the machines in the factory?"

"Yes, exactly."

"All those poor, innocent people working there..." Her legs barely held her up. *This is so horrible.* "They don't know it's a bomb, do they?"

"Of course not." Thorne scoffed. "My technology is cutting edge, unrecognizable to the uneducated riffraff. All those illegals just work day in and day out on their tiny little pieces, having no idea what they're developing. Honestly, who could recognize a bomb that doesn't explode?"

"The repercussions of this... Caleb." Her voice cracked. "This thing you're making is going to cause millions of people all over the world to slaughter each other. How can you be okay with that?"

"Millions of *bad* people." Thorne grimaced. "Terrorists, criminals, rapists, enemies of the US, not normal Christian Americans like you or me. Don't be so weak, Roseanna, and—"

An earth-shattering scream pierced the room. Vibrations rattled through Mother's body. She collapsed to the floor as if an earthquake had struck.

Her head exploded in pain. She covered her ears as the shriek ripped through her, and she looked down the hall. Billy's door was open.

41

Mother crawled down the hallway. *Where is Caleb?* Caleb was gone. Billy screamed again, and his reverberating voice broke through the walls, pierced her eardrums, and cracked open her skull. She kept crawling forward as ghostly apparitions of Jamie, her husband, her parents, and everyone in her life flashed before her. *Keep moving.* She fell. Footsteps pounded. Voices shouted. *Die, die, die, hate, hate. Can't think. Straight. Scrambled.*

She crawled into Billy's room, fighting through the noise. Again, Caleb was nowhere to be seen, but two security guards—Mackenzie and Deerfield—stood right inside the vault door, holding it open. Mother looked up at them. Their faces were frozen in horror. *Billy made them open it. Through the door. Oh god... oh... oh...*

She peered between their legs, into the lab, and saw Billy levitating in the center of the room, his heels suspended nearly a foot off the floor. *Master.* She shook her head. *The Shape. Master. Let me kill myself, Lord.* The teenage boy's wrists were sliced open. Blood seeped down the cuts, dripping into tiny puddles beneath him. His eyes were closed.

Giant, bloody letters were painted onto the wall behind him: **TRUTH IS A LIE.**

"Oh my god." Mother covered her mouth. *Let me kill myself, Lord Shape. I'm a terrible person. Must die. Must. Die. Help me die.*

Billy's skinny, shirtless body twisted in the air like a paper-straw wrapper. Little throbs of negative energy pulsed through the air, buzzing like wasps, and every time one of them touched Mother, guilty feelings shot through her. *Jamie. So far away. Abandoned. I'm a bad mother. Weapons developer. I failed.* Blood drizzled from his wrists. *My wrists. Cut. Should be. Dead.* She pushed forward, creeping closer to the boy—and heard two clicks.

She looked back. Mackenzie and Deerfield pointed their guns at one another. "Don't shoot me," Deerfield said, tears in his eyes.

"I can't... help..." McKenzie groaned. "Please, kid... please..."

Billy opened his eyes. Smoky blue light blasted from his pupils. The boy's thin mouth smiled cruelly—looking right at Mother—and she screamed. Her body was frozen. *I must do as he asks. I am bad. Evil. Corporate weapons developer. Let me die. I want it.*

"Big boom is coming," the boy rasped. "Bow down to me."

Mother lowered herself to the floor. She felt her hands rising to her own throat. Her fingers gripped her neck. *I deserve to die. I want to. Please. Let me.* She couldn't stop herself. *I don't want to stop. I do. I don't. I... do.* Her ears filled with a harsh crackling. She clenched tighter. *No more pain.* She squeezed so hard that she couldn't breathe.

She fell to the floor. The noise stopped as if cut off by a mute button. The dizziness subsided. She sobbed for a moment. *I'm not dead.* Slowly, she peeled her hands off her bruised throat and sat upright. Billy's unconscious body lay on the floor before her, and Caleb stood above him, withdrawing a needle from the boy's spine.

"Subject is unconscious," Caleb muttered, facing the security guards.

Mother rubbed her eyes, shakily rising to her feet. *What happened? Did Caleb just... how did he resist?* The security guards looked at her, just as confused as she was. Caleb brushed past Mother, ignoring her, and only turned at the door to face the blinking, perturbed Mackenzie.

"Strap that disgusting creature back into its bed." Caleb winced, clearly having pulled his back. "Call Mr. Linus in the morning. Considering that both of you were affected by the subject tonight, it's clear that you require a higher dosage of your..." His eyes narrowed.

"Prescriptions." Finally, he turned to Mother. "Order steel bars to replace the straps ASAP. Reinforce the vault door. Understood?"

Mother nodded weakly, and Caleb left the room. Billy's unconscious face lay half-submerged in a puddle of vomit. Normally, Mother would have helped him out of it, but not after what had just occurred. She felt her throat. *He almost killed me. Good god, he is a weapon.* She shuddered. *If Caleb hadn't injected him, I was going to...*

The guards suited up to strap Billy back into bed, and Mother left the room. She locked herself in her bedroom and watched through the window as Caleb's car revved to life and he drove off into town.

She frowned. *How come Billy's powers have no effect on you, Caleb?*

Part VI:
Chesed

42: Maria Rodriguez

For years, Maria Rodriguez had spent every evening inside the hot, grimy interior of the Thorne Century factory, listening to the nightly chorus of rusty gears, the buzzing machinery, and the constant coughing of her coworkers. She punched in, put on her mask, and took her place on the assembly line. Every night, her scarred palms touched burning metal. She'd never been promoted and never had a raise. When she'd lost three fingers, she'd wanted to quit or at least complain, but she knew better. Compared to Paola—her sixty-year-old Honduran coworker who came in every night despite a severed hand, destroyed knees, and sciatica—Maria felt she had it easy.

As Maria stood at the conveyer belt, lined up alongside hundreds of mothers and fathers just like her, she often daydreamed about her childhood in Guatemala, playing with her friends in the sun. Then she remembered the trash littering those dirt roads and the fact that these friends were all dead, so her nostalgia instead turned to the birth of her first baby, Natalia. Maria had suffered two miscarriages before Natalia came into the world, and as much as she loved Juan and Carlos—and would never have admitted to having favorites—Natalia was the child of her heart. *She's the one that made this all worthwhile.*

A cloud of fiberglass dust wafted from the line, seeped behind Maria's mask, and cut open the raw tissue of her lungs. She coughed ferociously. *Slow down. Breathe.* She couldn't breathe. Phlegm gushed into her mask, so she ripped it off. *Oh my god, I can't stop.* She buckled forward, coughing harder, and Paola caught her.

With a stern glance, Paola gestured to the manager's office. "*Aguas con el jefe*," she whispered then signaled for Maria to take a break.

Maria backed away, still wheezing, as Paola quickly returned to the line. Maria glanced around to make sure the managers were elsewhere—bathroom breaks were so frowned upon that many workers brought jars to urinate in—and stumbled down the corridor. She lunged into the manager's bathroom and vomited into the toilet.

After she spent a minute dry heaving, air returned to her lungs. *The horribleness is now outside of me.* The puke filling the bowl was soot black. "*Púchica*," she muttered and flushed it down. She turned to exit the bathroom, but out of nowhere, tremors ran down her spine like she'd been touched by ice. *Something's wrong.*

She pressed her fingers to the bathroom wall. It softly vibrated. Maria drew her hand back. *That's not normal.* She touched the plaster again, and a high-pitched buzzing seeped through the cracks, as if a radio was trapped behind the drywall.

Maria ducked out of the bathroom. She glanced back at her spot on the line—*I have to move fast*—and then went in the opposite direction to investigate the central battery room. There, in the heart of the factory, a locked metal door stood ominously in her path. No one ever crossed through the door to the battery room except for Mr. Thorne's most trusted operatives. She never approached it normally.

Her suspicions were correct—something was buzzing behind the door, like a giant wasp. She approached, and the floor shuddered. She hugged herself—checking for managers again—then put her ear to the door's hot metal surface. The sound amplified.

She quivered away from it, examining the giant tubes, machinery, and wires that continually funneled energy into the battery. An odor of burned meat seeped beneath the door. Maria wrinkled her nose, touched the door again, and—

"What the hell are you doing in here?"

Maria flipped her badge, to hide her name, and turned around to see the red-splotched grimace of Mr. Linus, a man widely referred to as Mr. Thorne's chief enforcer. Linus walked toward her, stinking of sweat, his perfect suit utterly out of place in the moldy factory. Linus poked her chest. "I asked you a question, wetback. Answer."

Maria stiffened up. "I'm sorry, sir."

"You're off the line. Why?"

Maria sucked back another cough. *I must be very careful.* "Sir, this room is making a strange sound. Buzzing. It is very worrying, and since this job is my life, I want to protect everything we are doing here—"

"Yeah, yeah." Linus waved his hand. He put his ear to the door and shook his head. "Seems fine."

Maria checked. The sound had stopped. "Sorry, sir. I must've imagined it."

"Seems like it." Linus wiped perspiration from his bald head. "Fucking hot in here. Listen, get your ass back to work, or your job is kaput, all right?" Linus marched away.

Maria put her ear to the door one last time—and the buzzing returned. Her gut clenched. Her vision darkened. *You should kill yourself,* a voice whispered into her brain. *Your family would be better off without you.*

Maria rushed far away from the door as the voice subsided, and she returned to her place on the assembly line.

43: Mother

Mother woke up early, made coffee, and downed the entire pot by sunrise. She didn't want to be awake, but she didn't want to sleep either. She pored over a file of classified documentation that Caleb had faxed her—including, of course, an NDA—and sadly, the information he'd told her the night before was only the tip of the iceberg.

She rubbed her bruised, swollen neck as she flipped through page after page of atrocities. *Thanks for the sore throat, Billy.* The file went back for years. *Weapons development. Attack plans. Target populations.* She rubbed her eyes. *All those antinuclear protests I went to as a teenager. The money I sank into my education.* The thought of her careful research becoming dollars in the hands of capitalist warmongers nauseated her to the core. *I've become everything I ever hated.*

The hot coffee burned her tender throat, so she sucked on an ice cube. She rolled down the curtains to block out the sunlight and continued reading. The "emotion bomb," as Thorne casually called it, was going to be powered by a battery in Heaven's Hole—once enough energy could be captured within the factory, new emotion bombs would be transportable in cylinders small enough to fit in a briefcase. Heaven's Hole was the furthest along of the various factories scattered around the country. Others hadn't fared so well. In Jonestown, West Alaska, a "battery" had leaked for two hours, causing a hundred factory employees to go mental. Photos showed disemboweled workers beating each other to death with severed limbs.

Good god. This is my work. Mother quickly flipped past the photos and resumed reading. According to handwritten margin notes, it was estimated that any new emotion bombs, if siphoned from the

Heaven's Hole factory, were capable of causing an entire metropolitan city to erupt in targeted bloodshed, with low upfront costs and minimal property damage.

Mother heard footsteps. She slid the document under her place mat just as an unusually sweaty Father walked into the kitchen. He patted his face with paper towels. "I just unstrapped the subject from his bed," he said.

Mother pointed him to the newly refilled coffeepot, and he poured himself a cup. "Why so exhausted?" she asked.

"The subject is emitting horrendous energies today. Please document that." He turned to her, eyes hidden behind his glasses. "Mr. Thorne informed me that you're aware of the project's true nature now."

She lowered her head. "Yes."

"Glad to hear it." Father sighed, as if relieved of an immense burden. He gulped down his psychic-repression pills with coffee. His jittery demeanor was oddly endearing, if only because it made him seem less robotic.

Mother approached Father and whispered, "Tell me the truth. What sort of leverage does Thorne have on you?"

Sweat ran down the side of his head. He poured cream into his coffee, acting as if he hadn't heard her.

"Fine," Mother said, refilling her coffee. "I'll start. My real name is Roseanna, and Thorne has my—"

"Don't." Father's eyes widened as if she'd put a gun to his head. "Talking about what you love risks that he'll destroy it. For both our sakes, shut the fuck up." More loudly, he said, "You know who I am, woman. I'm Father."

Mother sank into her chest. "Yes, and I'm... Mother." *Because Roseanna is dead.*

"Good."

Billy timidly entered the kitchen, and Father barreled out. The teenager, whose face was pale and yellowed, didn't seem to notice or care. He maneuvered to the kitchen island as if he were stepping on coal, emanating queasiness from every pore, so Mother quickly swallowed another suppressant pill. "Good morning, Billy. Welcome to your first hangover."

Billy glanced at her bruised throat, and she turned away.

It wasn't him, not really. That's not fair. She handed him a coffee and a glass of water. "Water first. It'll help."

He nodded thankfully. Mother watched him, taking down notes. *He doesn't remember last night, does he?* She found it horrifying to look upon the oh-so-human boy before her and remember that he was the same "subject" discussed so clinically in Thorne Century's reports. Even after the nightmarish experience before, she still wanted to hold him, hug him, and protect him.

She opened the fridge. "I'll get you some breakfast. Would you like—" She looked back, and he was holding his hand up in a stop sign. His eyes hung dark circles, and he looked ready to vomit. "Oh. No food?"

He pointed at his belly, making a sick face. Then, reaching for her Sharpie, he wrote a note onto the nearest napkin and displayed it for her: *Something's wrong... something bad. Feel it in my guts.*

"Like what?" Mother sat close to him, ignoring the feeling as his nausea seeped into her. *This doesn't sound good.* "Should you stay home from school, maybe?"

Billy wrote a second note: *No, I have to go. I feel that too.*

Billy's dark eyes pleaded for help, but she didn't know what to offer. His wrists were scabbed over, and as she looked at them, he rolled up his sleeves.

"Okay." She sighed. "But if you start feeling any sicker, come home immediately, okay?"

44: Natalia

Natalia sat in Mr. Nazari's class, absorbed in her seemingly unfinishable *Dark-Eyed Boy* drawing. Ten minutes after the bell rang, the door cracked open, and she was startled by the sweaty, trembling skeleton that entered the room. She barely recognized it as a human being, much less her boyfriend. As Billy jittered his way across the room, Mr. Nazari backed away with noticeable concern, and the classroom murmured. Billy eyed everyone warily.

Natalia jumped from her desk. "Billy! Are you okay?"

The class laughed at her outburst, and Billy blushed. As Natalia sat back down, painfully embarrassed, Chris Thompson flashed her a kissy-face. "Taco Girl is worried about her creepy boyfriend, huh?" He snorted. "Maybe you just beat him up so bad that—"

Billy shot his eyes at Chris like a thrown knife. The bully choked on his spit, and his eyes widened into saucers. Billy walked toward Chris, glaring, and the class went dead silent.

"Billy!" Natalia said, horrified. "You can't..."

Billy looked away, and Chris erupted into a messy cough. Billy quickly realized his error. Luckily, everyone was too busy laughing at Chris to notice Billy, who had scuttled back to the seat beside Natalia. She snapped her sketchbook closed to hide *Dark-Eyed Boy*.

Mr. Nazari rubbed his head. "Anyway, back to the Great Depression..."

Natalia pushed her desk closer to Billy's, letting it screech across the floor. She leaned over and whispered, "What the hell was that? Powers in class, dude. Are you crazy?"

Billy didn't answer, but he desperately reached for her hand. His skin was cold and clammy, and nausea crept from it like a colony of spiders. *Something is seriously wrong with this guy today.*

She nudged him. "Tell me what's wrong."

As Mr. Nazari continued speaking, and Chris Thompson's posse whispered mean jokes, Billy dug into his pocket and took out his little pad. He ripped out a page, wrote a little note, and passed it to Natalia: *I'm scared.*

"Of what?" she murmured, handing the paper back.

Billy sighed. He tried to write a new sentence, but his pen ran out of ink, so she handed him a new one. The paper was too scratched up. She leaned closer to him, resting her chin on his shoulder. His hand motions were increasingly frenetic.

The lights went out. A total blackout enveloped the room. Everyone murmured.

Chris Thompson's whiny voice rose above the rest. "Yo, what the hell happened to the lights?"

Suddenly, a high-pitched alarm—the loudest, sharpest sound that Natalia had ever heard—pierced the air. The classroom erupted in screams of pain. The screech split open her skull. It broke down her eardrums and lit up her veins like fire. Natalia let out an agonized howl—but the alarm was so loud she couldn't hear herself. Her jaw ached. Her throat caught. She clenched her ears, but it did nothing to block out the sound.

In the darkness, classmates tumbled around the room. Chris Thompson collapsed before her. Mr. Nazari slammed into the wall. Natalia screamed until her throat hurt, unable to think, see, or feel as the alarm throbbed in and out of her head, beating like the heart of an enormous mechanical monster.

A chair was thrown into the window, shattering it. Students dropped to the floor, hiding beneath their desks—but others rushed outside. As an invisible claw tore through her jaw and daggers stabbed into every cavity in her teeth, Natalia looked outside. The ringing alarm was so loud, so powerful, that when a car rammed into the side of the school—spewing oil, glass, and scraps of metal across the sidewalk—the crash seemed silent.

That person must be dead! I can't, can't, can't—

More students flooded out the windows, shrieking, seemingly oblivious to the car accident. Natalia's heart pounded. She tried to scream out to them, but she couldn't even tell what she was saying—words barely made sense. *Scramble. Mad scramble. Can't think. Where's...*

Oh fuck. Billy.

She screamed Billy's name but couldn't see him. As pain rippled through her body, she pushed through the dark room and tripped over a desk. She slammed into the floor. The alarm throbbed harder and harder. *PAIN, PAIN, PAIN, hurt, PAIN.*

In a thin slice of light, she saw Billy. His body was sprawled out on the floor, gyrating and quivering. His limbs spasmed. Foam dribbled from his mouth. He was having a seizure. She clawed her way forward and shook him. *Wake up!* Electricity buzzed up her wrists. Numbness shot through her until she felt nothing. Her vision darkened. *No, no, no, not again, not now!*

It was too late. The floor dropped away. The siren vanished. The world around her disappeared, and she was...

45: Natalia (Somewhere Else)

Natalia walks up a hill of crusted white rocks—no, not rocks, bones—beneath a bloodred sky. Her bare feet scrape against femurs and rib cages, over the crest, until she finds herself face-to-face with a little boy...

"Billy." She shakes him. "Wake up!"

The boy nearly falls off the hill. She catches him, almost falling herself—and realizes that she is a little girl. Bones crumble beneath them. The boy hugs himself, and he looks away. "I don't know what's happening. So many voices... so much sadness... I can't... can't..."

"It's the factory, man! Your nightmare vision is coming true. You need to stop this."

Billy's eyes become so enormous that Natalia's tiny body is sucked into them until all her bones, muscles, and organs no longer exist—just blackness, emptiness, wind—and then they are floating through the streets of Heaven's Hole like flying spirits. They enter the factory's glass doors. They swoop inside, past crowds of terrified workers, as electricity sprays out like water... and in the very center of the factory, hidden inside a dark hallway, they find a locked metal door. The door glows red-hot.

"The central battery," Billy says from the ether. "This is where the sound comes from." Everything fades away into darkness. "I need to go there, don't I?"

"No shit," Natalia replies. "Because, hey, if that mountain of bones is any indication, you might be the only chance we've got."

46: Billy

Billy woke up, stumbling to his feet. The lights were off. The windows were broken. The classroom was empty, and an eerie quiet pervaded the air. *Wow. It's really happening. Everyone is following the siren call.*

A scream exploded beneath him. "Billlyyy!"

Natalia. She rolled across the floor, gripping her head.

"Natalia?" he asked.

She kept screaming, as tears rolled down her cheeks.

"Natalia!"

The siren from the factory—that blaring noise that everyone else heard—didn't sound off in his ears, but its vibrations surged through his bones. As he leapt down to Natalia's side, the siren call emanated through his ears as a tiny, fragile voice repeatedly whispering, "Help me. Help. Help me." As this creaking tone nestled in the pit of his stomach, he tried to ignore it—and the fact that it sounded like his own voice.

Natalia shrieked, tossing back and forth beneath the desks. Billy held her. He kissed her. Slowly, fearfully, she settled down. Her eyes blinked open, and she hugged Billy tightly. "That sound..."

"It's gone?" Billy held her in the dark.

"Yeah." She sniffled. "But I hear bits and pieces of it... it felt like it was going to rip my skull open—"

"Don't worry." He pressed his lips against her forehead. "It's going to be okay. I'm going to stop it." Billy stood up and helped Natalia to her feet. He tried not to listen to the siren's call for help, but it was growing louder. *It sounds as if it's in pain. As if it's alive.*

The classroom door was locked—in the power outage, the automatic magnet had been triggered—but the windows were smashed open, so he and Natalia climbed outside. The school grounds were empty. Desolate. Each empty wall rang with more reverberations of "Help me, help, help..." Outside the parking lots, cars were in ditches, smashed into telephone poles, and left behind—some of them still running. The convenience stores and gas stations that Billy and Natalia raced past were similarly abandoned.

"Holy shit, man!" Natalia exclaimed. "Where is everybody?"

Billy pointed ahead. "They followed the siren." He pulled her along with him. "Everyone's going to the factory. Remember that door in the vision?"

"Shit. We need to go inside that creepy-ass place, don't we?"

Billy nodded. "Let's go."

47: Caleb

Caleb Thorne had injected half a syringe of Billy blood into his neck when the loudest alarm on earth busted through his skull. The factory alarm sent him falling off the side of the toilet, and he got wedged between it and the wall. The needle slipped, tearing open the side of his throat. The tube shattered. Blood gushed down his neck as the remains of the injection stuck out like a porcupine's quill.

"God fucking damn it!" he yelled, but the alarm was so loud that his voice vanished inside the blaring, skull-shattering cacophony. He sank to the bathroom floor, gripping his ears, totally helpless to the auditory force. *That alarm. It's the factory. There must be an energy leakage from the central battery... it's...* As blood seeped into his shirt, he felt dizzy. He tried to get up, but it was too much effort, and he collapsed into the corner. *Need... medical...* He gasped. *Must go to the factory... must follow... must...*

He forced himself upright, fighting through the pain. *No. That's what the battery wants me to do, and if it weren't for this psycho blood coursing through my veins, I'd be there with all the idiots.* He forced himself onto his knees, teeth gritted. *What I really must do is get the hell out of town before the bomb... bomb...*

"The bomb!" He grunted, forcing himself upright. *Stay awake!* If the emotion bomb had gone off, everyone in town was dead. He blinked back drowsiness. The alarm swayed in and out, deepening and become scratchier, harsher, like knives to his ears. He clawed his way up the bathroom sink, facing the mirror—only to see the pock-marked white cheeks of Kaley Somerfield staring back at him.

"Heya, Caleb," she said in a voice that cut through the siren. She traced the swell of her pregnant belly. "Are we still two peas in a pod?"

Caleb blinked. *Go away. Fucking psycho-blood hallucinations. I need to leave town, not talk to a goddamn mirage.* He reached for the bathroom door handle, but his bloody fingers slipped right off it.

"Aww," Kaley purred as her eyes lit up into blue flames. "Don't believe in me?" Her teeth became sharp points.

"Get out of my head!" Caleb smashed the mirror, striking out against the alarm blaring in his skull, spewing shards of glass across the bathroom and cutting his hands.

Kaley's reflection looked back at him from each fragment, grinning, with his pocketknife—the one she'd given him—sticking out of her pregnant belly. The blade had cut her open from her throat to her navel. "It was always about control with you, wasn't it, honey?" Kaley sputtered blood. "You hated that I owned you with this. Hated it. But you also hated that your daddy was going to cut you off from your big ol' trust fund if we stayed together. So you took that little knife I gave ya, slid it right up inside me till you had my blood everywhere—"

"Shut up!" Caleb stomped on the shards. *I loved you, Kaley. Don't judge me for what I had to do.* He broke the glass down into increasingly small pieces then slipped on his own blood, falling back to the shard-covered floor. Kaley's sinister giggle rippled through him.

As Billy's blood swirled through his system—and as the rays of the emotion bomb exploded through his brain—Caleb's bloody fingers painted words on the bathroom wall that he didn't understand, against his will: Feed the Shape.

48: Billy

The streets of Heaven's Hole were horrifyingly quiet. Every house, apartment, and business had been emptied. No stray dogs walked the streets. No cars rumbled through the potholes. In every abandoned car, Billy glimpsed the future. *It's happening. Fuck. It's really happening.* His guts clenched, and he squeezed Natalia's hand even tighter.

As the factory came into view, the silence gave way to a circus of screaming, chanting, and thrashing bodies. Hundreds of people were pushing into the Thorne Century parking lot, screaming at the siren call in their ears—the same siren that had led them there. The mob crushed in upon the factory walls like spectators at a concert, crawling over one another to get a better look—but no one went inside.

"Help me," the siren whispered in one of Billy's ears while his other ear empathically ruptured at the roaring scream that everyone else heard. "I need you, Billy."

Billy and Natalia pushed into the loud, bustling crowd. Everyone's eyes were glazed over. They were crying. Hollering. Pushing and shoving each other to get a better view. Very few of them were injured—yet—but among the scraped elbows and bruised eyes, Billy felt the tension tightening around his neck like a noose. *If I don't stop this, it's going to get worse—more violent.* He bumped through the sea of bodies, pushing for the factory doors. Everyone pushed him back. They yelled into the gray sky, unable to hear themselves over the siren—but Billy and Natalia could hear them.

"The sound! Ahhh!"

"Help us!"

"No one go in that factory, no one!"

"It's the end of the world!"

An elbow collided with Billy's jaw, splitting open his lip. He fell backward, catching himself on the asphalt. A foot pounded on his ankle.

"Hey!" Natalia cried, but the person who'd crashed into him was gone.

They don't know.

Natalia helped him to his feet. "These people, man..."

Billy wiped the blood from his lip. *Ow.*

The crowd was growing as more siren zombies streamed in from the road. Factory workers collided with children. Wheelchairs pushed into crowds. Even among the faces he recognized, he barely saw the people underneath. Billy and Natalia tried to push through the sweaty, screaming bodies, but no one budged, and they were pulled apart from each other. Limbs became tangled. Heads bumped. He couldn't breathe. Bodies pushed in on him from all sides. Emotions battered his chest. *Fear. Hate. Terror. Anxiety.* He squeezed his fists. *Enough... enough...*

"Enough!" Billy shouted and lifted his hands above the mob. "Everything's going to be okay!"

In one wave, thousands of people... stopped. Their screams were cut off as Billy's voice echoed across the parking lot. The crowd filled in with ghostly apparitions—their loved ones, their regrets, their hopes—swirling through like liquid electric snakes. Every person stumbled back, shell-shocked, as swells of emotion rippled through them—energies they couldn't explain, feelings they couldn't process. *Enough... enough... enough...* Their eyes widened. They turned to stare at the boy who had been silent and was silent no more.

Billy stood before them, shivering from the realization of what he'd done. His secret was out. *Now they know I'm a freak.*

A factory worker who Billy sensed was named Jon approached him with a scared expression. "That kid over there, he just... just..." Jon gasped. "I feel so weird... the sound..."

"He turned off the sound!" a voice cried. "Are we safe now?"

"No, I hear it. It's just quieter..."

Felix spun on his feet, dizzily colliding with another student. "What's happening?"

Dozens of whispers were exchanged simultaneously. Ripples of awe passed through everyone.

Chris pushed through the crowd and faced Billy directly. "You can talk?" he whispered.

"I can't believe it." The homeless man, Eddie Walker, stumbled back. "This kid is... what is he?"

"He's awesome, is what he is," Hassan said.

Natalia burst through the crowd and took her place beside Billy. "Damn straight," she said. "And he's going to save us."

The crowd murmured. Thousands of eyes faced Billy, and he trembled beneath the immense pressure riding on his back. *Try to feel calm. Make them feel calm.* He thought about Eli, and he forced himself to smile the way Eli always did. Suddenly, the crowd followed his lead. Each of them beamed with joy. Billy's smile became bigger, broader, more real—and so did theirs. *So many people. So many emotions.* Billy fell back, flabbergasted by the power he held over so many people. *Maybe I could tell them to run far away in case I mess up, but...* He shook his head. *They wouldn't get far enough.*

Billy stared up at the menacing smokestacks before him. He'd imagined this moment his whole life. The factory. The explosion. *A metaphorical one, I guess? But I never pictured it like this.* As the crowd hummed with excitement, he cleared his throat. They went silent, to hear him out.

"Hey, guys," Billy said. "I need to go inside. Please let me through."

Billy walked forward, and the crowd—children, adults, the elderly, factory workers, and students—parted like the Red Sea. He walked down the narrow path with Natalia beside him. All along both sides, people whispered.

"Save us, Billy."

"Can we stop it?"

"Please, young man... please."

Every tense emotion pricked Billy like a pin. The closer he came to the factory, the harsher the battery's whispers became. He was running out of time.

"I'm a bomb," the siren said. "You're my power. My energy. You're the only one who can turn me off." Sweat ran down his back.

He passed by Mr. Nazari, who gave him a solemn nod. Felix did the same. A crowd of children gazed in awe. Factory workers waved.

As he and Natalia neared the doors, he whispered, "You don't have to come with me."

Natalia scoffed. "Yeah, I do." She took out her phone and started filming. She began talking to the camera—explaining the situation—but Billy couldn't hear her. The siren was growing too loud. *Big boom is coming. Unless I can stop it.*

The factory doors opened, and they walked inside.

49

The inside of the factory, lit only by thin strips of sunlight from the overhead windows, was like a mausoleum. In the darkness, with all the machinery shut down thanks to the power outage, the grime and soot on every surface glistened. Everything smelled of oil. The concrete floor was sticky. Thorne Century logos were everywhere, like a stamp of pride on a dumpster.

Billy had expected all of that. What he hadn't expected were the corpses. There weren't many of them. Most factory workers had fled into the parking lot as soon as the alarm had sounded, but a few had been crushed in the rush of panic. One bloodied body was trapped beneath a piece of machinery. Another man looked like he had bashed his head into a wall until it cracked open. Everyone who hadn't left the factory was dead.

He leaned into Natalia. "Your mom is outside." His voice echoed. "Don't worry." *Unless I fuck up, anyway.*

"Oh, I saw her. Trust me, she was the first one I looked for." Natalia's confident tone masked the panic he could feel circulating through her. Unable to stay calm, she went back to filming, aiming her phone's flashlight at a dead body. "Okay, see that?" she told the camera. "These were innocent people, workers for Thorne Century, and now they're dead..."

She continued narrating. *She wants to make sure there's a record before this all gets covered up.* Billy's instincts guided him through the dark halls of the factory, but as he got closer, the strange voice inside it—the battery—scraped against his eardrums.

"I'm hurting," it said. "Please help me."

Billy slipped on an oil slick and caught his balance on a rusted piece of dead machinery. When he touched the metal, a decade of agonized memories seeped into his fingers. *Long nights. Hard work. Unfair. So unfair.* He felt the buzz of activity, the power that had kept the machine running day after day, year after year until that morning. It reeked of despair. Everything in the factory did.

"You okay?" Natalia asked.

He nodded, and they pressed onward. Closer to the central battery room, wires hung from the ceiling, sparking with loose electricity. Even though the battery had knocked out all the power in town, it was still live.

"The battery knows we're coming," Billy whispered.

Natalia narrowed her eyes. "Why are you talking about a piece of machinery like it's alive?"

"I don't know." Billy couldn't explain, so he kept walking. After a long, lightless hallway, the metal door of the battery room appeared before them. The bodies of three dead scientists were sprawled out before it. *They tried to stop it.* "This is it," Bill said, shakily clasping Natalia's hand. "It's here... I... need to..."

"You've got this," she said, but Billy felt the mortal terror in her. Not one to dwell on her fears, Natalia again hit the record button on her phone and shined it in Billy's face and at the battery door. "As you can see, we've reached the—what is called again?"

"Central battery," Billy mumbled, shying away from the camera.

"Central battery." She examined her surroundings. "This is what powers the whole town. Everyone who works here has no idea what this thing is. It's supposed to be a medical project they're working on here—"

"It's not." Billy looked down. *Now that I'm here, I can feel what it really is. They've been lying to me. I hate to say it. Don't want to admit it. But...* As the camera's light returned to him, he said, "It's actually a bomb."

Natalia jolted back. "Huh?" She hovered over the pause button but didn't press it. "Did you say this is a fucking bomb?"

"That's what I feel here. An emotion bomb," Billy said. "The medical project was a cover."

The whispering siren intensified, screaming the word over and over to him. "Bomb, bomb, bomb."

Natalia started to ask questions, but he could barely hear her over the battery's scrambled tones, so he approached the steel door. *They lied to me. All of them. Mother lied. Father. Thorne.* Rage tightened his veins. *Maybe I should let it blow up.* Frightened by his own anger, he pushed that thought far away.

The steel door had no handles. The retinal scanner was broken. Billy touched the door's surface, and electricity sparked to his fingertips. Inside the battery room, a warm yellow sickness called out to him. It felt like a person. *But not quite.* He closed his eyes, pressed deeper, and saw his own face looking back at him. *I'm inside there. A part of me, anyway. My blood. My energies. I'm the bomb. Me.*

His jaw clenched. He pushed his mind through the door, tapping into the warm yellow behind it. "Who are you?" he whispered.

A thin voice tapped into his heart. "We're the battery. We're the emotion bomb. We are—"

"You're me," Billy said.

"Yes."

"But you're also something else."

"We are... something terrible... something we never wanted to be..."

Billy choked back tears. Everyone outside the factory—all those raging and hopeful emotions that had seemed so vivid before—vanished, and all he could focus on was the yellow. He and the yellow were in total blackness, looped together in a place where only the freaks could go. Natalia's voice tried to break through to him, but her words were indecipherable. He was somewhere else.

"We were like you once," the battery said. "Free... alive."

"Don't hurt all these people." Billy tightened his eyes. "Don't be the monster that you were turned into. The people out there are innocent. Don't—"

"So angry... so much rage..."

"The darkness isn't what defines you." Billy opened his eyes and faced Natalia. He turned back to the door. "Whatever you are, you're better than that."

The voice sputtered. Billy pressed his hand to the door and could have sworn—for a tiny, bizarre moment—that another hand was pressing the other side. Then he stepped away, took Natalia into his arms, and said, "Everything's going to be okay." As they waited, the hundreds of hearts outside the factory thumped back into his chest. *Fear. Tension. Hope.*

The lights came on. The machines spun back into motion. Computers blinked. Gears turned. The factory achingly groaned back to life, and relief washed over Billy in waves. *I did it!* He kissed Natalia, passionately drawing her into his arms. *The factory didn't explode. I broke the vision.* "I'm free." He shook his head in wonderment.

"You're free." She smiled, and they kissed again.

Outside, he felt the town's lights come back on, and excitement erupted through the populace. Everyone was released from the siren's control. The crowd muttered, blinked, and then cheered so loudly that their voices shook the walls. They chanted his name. "Bill-y! Bill-y!" He squeezed Natalia harder than he'd ever squeezed anyone in his life. *My name? Wow. The nightmare is finally over. Take that, Shape. Take that, Thorne—*

The metal door slid open. Putrid mist spilled from the dark room. Pain stung Billy's pores. *Oh no.* He stepped in front of Natalia, hiding her behind him, expecting something to crawl out. Nothing emerged. Behind the door, in the shadows, machinery beeped. Billy stepped toward it.

Natalia stopped him. "Dude, what the hell are you doing?"

"I have to." He pushed forward.

"Fine." She sighed and started recording again. "Okay, so we're going into this scary battery room now..."

They stepped inside. The energies were so toxic that Billy had to swallow his own puke. In the near-total darkness, he saw only reflections of light from outside bouncing off glass surfaces on the walls. *Tanks, they look like.* Billy tapped one of them and felt around. The tanks seemed to be elevated a few feet from the floor.

"I'll shine some light on it." Natalia turned her flashlight app back on and shined it through the battery room. Each of the dozen or so tanks was about eight feet tall and had a scattered array of tangled, sizzling wires snaking from its base, feeding into a cylindrical machine at the center of the room. Natalia directed her light into the nearest tank and fell back, almost dropping her phone. "Oh my god." She cupped her mouth. "Is that—"

She shined it again. A charred, blackened corpse of a preteen girl was trapped inside the tank. Her skin and hair were burned off. Hundreds of tubes were plugged into her pores, each one crackling with electricity and hooked up to the wires beneath, circulating energy into the cylinder at the room's center. "Fuck." Natalia held her mouth. "Do you see her chest?"

Billy shied away. Every vein inside him felt constricted. *Don't look.* He couldn't help it. The dead girl's heart was still beating, pumping electricity into the battery. He touched the glass, and the girl's living face flashed into his mind. *She was Hannah Michaels, eleven years old, from Missouri. She... feels me looking at her.* He ducked away as his own heart sped up—and the girl's heart did the same. *Her powers. She's dead, but her powers are alive, and this factory...*

Billy stumbled away. *Can't do this. Need to get out.* He crashed into another tank, this one holding a teenage boy. This boy, like Hannah, was burned to a crisp. His heart also pounded into the machinery. Billy stepped back, so dizzy he almost fell. Natalia's light shined around the room, revealing that every tank had a different burned corpse in it.

"They're like me." Billy was choked up, barely able to get the words out. "Psycho kids. Like me."

Rage boiled within him. His heart—and the other heartbeats in the room—pounded harder, faster, violently. He rushed forward and slammed his fists against the nearest tank. "This was the plan the whole time!" he shouted as fire swam from his lungs. "This!" He hit the tank again then slumped over it. *They tried to reach out for help. Whatever's left of them, anyway. That was the alarm. And I shut them down.*

"Billy..." Natalia touched his shoulder.

He jerked away—then reached for her. "Sorry," he mumbled. He looked up at the tank he had been beating on. The child in this one was collapsed at the bottom. *He tried to escape. Holy shit, he was alive in this thing.* The battery boy's fingers were nubs, but at some point before dying, he had painted bloody letters onto the interior glass: **I AM THE SHAPE.**

Billy shrank into Natalia's arms. "I have to get out of here."

"Yeah, let's go." Her voice was shaking.

They exited the battery room. The metal door closed behind them.

50: Natalia

Natalia felt like a shredded paper taped back together. As she guided her dazed and glassy-eyed boyfriend back through the factory—now lit by fluorescent lights but still reeking of a landfill—she was too overwhelmed by Billy's emotions to piece together her own. *That was fucking horrifying.* The more she thought about it, the worse she felt. *My mom and Abuelita work here. Everyone works here. They don't even know that it's all to create some bomb powered by dead children. Man, what the hell reality did I slip into?*

The closer they came to the exit, the weirder it all felt. Outside, the mood was triumphant. A chorus of approval pounded at the walls. Hundreds of factory workers cheered, hollered, and shouted Billy's name. "Bill-y! Bill-y! Bill-y!"

Natalia studied her boyfriend. He felt cold. His mouth was tight. *He's still in there with those locked-up dead kids.* As they approached the front doors, where the crowd waited for them with thunderous anticipation, he stopped her. "Don't come outside with me."

She frowned. "Huh?"

He grabbed her shoulders. "You trust me?"

"Yeah, I mean—"

"Stay put. Don't let them see you." He kissed her. "Trust me."

He walked toward the doors, flashing her one last mournful look, and Natalia tried to follow him—but her feet wouldn't budge. "Hey!" she cried. Billy turned away, and Natalia felt tingles run down her legs. She couldn't move. She was frozen. "Billy!" *You bastard!*

"Sorry," Billy said, and he stepped outside.

The crowd erupted in applause, and the doors closed behind him. Natalia stayed put, stuck, unable to follow him.

She yanked forward. Nothing happened. "Billy?" she whispered, torn by betrayal. *Why the hell would he do this to me?* She pitched forward, gasping for air—and fell onto her knees, released from his control. She panted. *God, that was scary.* She looked up, listening to the cheering outside the factory. Then she stood up, her legs weak from the psychic spell, and limped toward the door—

A gunshot broke the air.

"Oh no!" She rushed toward the door and peeked through the glass. Billy stumbled before the crowd, clawing at a red-flared needle in his neck. A tranquilizer. He collapsed onto the parking lot asphalt, spasmed, then passed out.

Natalia gasped. *Now I get it.* She started to push the door open then heard the rumble of an engine, and she stopped. The square black shape of a truck pushed through the crowd, forcing people to jump out of the way, heading right toward Billy. Soldiers in black uniforms, wielding enormous machine guns, shoved people away from the truck then surrounded Billy's sleeping body. One of them fired into the air.

Natalia ducked behind the door. "This is bad," she whispered. *I should be out there.* Natalia fought the urge to lunge out and tackle the soldiers. *No, they'll kill me. I'm not some billion-dollar psychic, just a poor daughter of immigrants. Bullets are cheaper than tranquilizers.* She heard pounding boots and the rattle of the back of the truck opening, and tears stung at her eyes. Her heart thudded harder and harder. The crowd erupted in shouts, boos, and dismayed noises. *Mamá's in that crowd. Everybody. If they open fire...*

One of the men spoke into a walkie-talkie. "Subject has been captured, over."

The back of the truck clanked closed. The engine revved. The loudspeaker in the factory crackled, and the smarmy voice of Caleb Thorne boomed through the air. "Dear townspeople, do not be alarmed..."

Natalia jerked upright. "Guess I'm no good at staying put."

She kicked through the doors of the factory, lunged into the crowd, and collided with a swarm of musty factory uniforms. The truck with Billy in it was driving away. She swung her fists through the crowd, trying to follow it, but felt herself yanked backward—and into the arms of her mother.

"Hey!" Natalia cried.

"Calm down!" Mamá whispered harshly. "You're going to get yourself killed."

"Where's that truck going?"

Mamá pointed forward with her mutilated hand. The truck had joined four other armored vehicles at the end of the parking lot, each one mounted with giant loudspeakers. A crew of armed gunmen surrounded the trucks, patrolling the area. The loudspeakers blared Mr. Thorne Century Himself's voice. "I understand that this was a scary, confusing morning for all of us." Thorne paused, and the crowd hollered. "But do not worry," Thorne continued. "I have answers!"

A hush passed over the parking lot as hundreds of would-be rioters went dead silent. Natalia squirmed out of her mother's grasp and started filming the scene before her. *Asshole knew exactly what to say and how to manipulate everyone here.*

"What you have witnessed here today, I fear, is a tragedy." Thorne's voice rang out. "It was an attempted act of sabotage by a foreign government. I am sorry to say, but it seems that the young man living in your midst—Billy Jakobek was his code name—was a sleeper agent sent by the terrorists. He infiltrated our American factories—"

Natalia shouted at the top of her lungs, "Explain his powers, then!"

The crowd turned, listened to her, then turned back to the loudspeakers. "Explain!" someone chanted, and others joined in. "Explain! Explain! Explain!"

"To..." Thorne went quiet as the speakers screeched. "To... ah... yes. As you have seen, dear townspeople, the terrorists have unearthed a way to manipulate human emotion by using agents such as this boy to conduct unprecedented psychological warfare. That is why he controlled you. It is why he used this alarm to brainwash you. He is not truly a boy but a living weapon of unimaginable power..."

A scared murmur passed through the crowd.

Natalia jumped forward. "Bull—"

Mamá's hand clapped over her mouth again. "They'll shoot you right here," she whispered.

Natalia pulled free and kept filming.

Thorne continued. "Thanks to you all, though, the terrorist has been apprehended. The US government has agreed to allow us to take him into indefinite detention so we can study his inhuman abilities and perhaps use them to strike back at the terrorists who attacked us today." He paused as if expecting applause. There was none. "For all of my loyal workers, I am giving you the rest of the day off. Go home. Hug your children. Tomorrow, Mr. Linus will discuss a workplace bonus with each of you for your valiant efforts today. God bless you all, and God bless America."

The speakers whined to a close. The soldiers climbed into the trucks and drove off. The parking lot went quiet. People looked at each other. No one knew what to do, and slowly, they dispersed. Friends whispered to each other. Workers went home. Natalia turned her camera off and slumped downward. *It's over.*

As Mamá turned to go home, Natalia went across the parking lot. Everyone around her was quiet, lost, and confused. Felix passed right by as if he didn't recognize her. Natalia was about to call out to him but stopped, remembering how weird she'd felt the first time she'd touched Billy. *They're feeling like that now. But while I got to talk to him after, they're just hearing BS answers from Thorne. He gave them an easy excuse. Blamed it on some invisible terrorists.*

She stormed to the end of the parking lot and watched the trucks departing down the road. The caravan took a right toward the dead-end road leading to Kaiser House, no doubt to lock Billy back into the dark tank that he'd told her about. *Thorne still needs him in Heaven's Hole to power up his little emotion bomb. He needs Billy. That's a weakness.* She remembered the caged kids. The battery.

Teeth gritted, Natalia looked through the video footage on her phone. Then she uploaded it onto each of her social media streams. She took a deep breath. *Here goes nothing.*

She hit Publish, and the evidence went live.

Part VII:

Gevurah

51: Boy

The teenage boy couldn't remember his name, but he knew that he was in the dark tank again. The water was cold. His neck hurt. Time passed, but he didn't know how much time.

I did something.

He didn't know what, but he knew it had caused the bad people to put him back in the tank. *I feel so sick.* He sucked in the harsh mechanical air and kept his eyes closed. *So cold.* He didn't remember much. One thing he did remember, though, was the name of a power—an energy—that kept him going through the darkness.

Natalia Gonzalez.

As the boy lay in the water tank—his veins plugged, his senses deprived—he comforted himself with the memory of her face. Her brown eyes. The gentle slope of her nose terminating in a silver ring on one nostril. Her oneness pumped through him, shining through the cracks.

This feels different than the other times.

The longer he spent in that tank, trapped and semiconscious, the more vividly he felt the psychic energies of the world outside beating against the tank. Something big was happening. Something unprecedented.

It's going to change everything.

52: Mother

Only ten days had passed since the factory had nearly melted down, but the landscape of Heaven's Hole had irrevocably changed. Mother drove through the streets, barely recognizing the place she'd lived in for months. Whereas every corner, business, and homeless person she'd passed had once been gray with despair, the town was now red with anger. Protestors shouted from street corners, raising homemade signs high above their heads. "Down with Thorne!" they chanted. The amps were turned up. Tension snapped in the air. Painted graffiti fists splattered the concrete walls.

At an intersection, Mother stopped her car to let a group of teenage protestors cross the street. One young girl held up a harsh caricature of Caleb's face and yelled, "Thorne kills kids!"

Mother parked at Thorne Century Groceries, turned off the ignition, and sighed. *Naïve kids. I wish they had a chance, but all these rallies are just... hopeless. They can't beat Caleb.* Brushing aside her guilt, she stepped out into the drizzly, cold air. She walked across the empty parking lot and tugged on the heavy wooden handles of the grocery store. They were locked. The lights were off.

"Hell," she muttered. "That's another one down."

For two hours, Mother had driven around town, trying to find a single place selling paper towels, dish soap, and toilet paper. Nothing was open. Even the gas stations were closed. Mother threw her hands in the air. *More workers going on strike? I give up. I'm certainly not going to drive six hours to the next town.*

She drove back in the direction of Kaiser House, noting far fewer protestors in the streets. More cardboard signs were hung up on streetlights, mailboxes, and benches. One said Free Billy. Another said Children Aren't Weapons.

Mother shook her head at all the drama. *How can they not see how pointless this whole thing is?* She tapped the steering wheel. *It's too late now. Caleb's already got everything he wants, and he's just going to deport them for this. Silly protests never change anything, no matter how well-intentioned they—*

Mother slammed on the brakes, coming within inches of a road-block. "Shit!" Her wipers swished across the windshield, and she breathed heavily. "What the hell?"

The road ahead of her was a dead end, so there was no alternate route. She made a U-turn, finding dozens of other vehicles parked on the grass and in the dirt the way she and her friends had done at the DIY concerts of her youth. Seeing nowhere else to go, Mother parked beside a broken-down old Thorne Hurricane and got out into the drizzling rain. The entire road was blockaded.

"Great," she muttered.

An electric megaphone squealed from the distance. "Never again!" shouted a female voice through the mountain air. Far away—in the direction of Kaiser House—a crowd roared in approval.

Mother squeezed her thumbs inside her hands. *Caleb's not going to be happy about this.* She took off down the road, leaving her car behind. Pounding her feet against the asphalt, gasping for air, she raced into the cul-de-sac that held Kaiser House. There, hundreds of tan-uniformed factory workers surrounded the house, joined by an even larger mass of high school students.

Their protests roared through the sky. Their signs went upward. Parents joined with their children. People of different ethnicities, ages, and orientations all stood together, arm in arm, shouting, "Down with Thorne! Down with Thorne! Down with Thorne!"

Mother felt dizzy. "Jesus Christ," she muttered.

Three men holding giant cameras, each emblazoned with popular news media logos, weaved through the mob, capturing live TV footage. Mother shoved her way to the front, relieved that no one recognized her. A station wagon was parked sideways in front of the house, leaving a muddied trail of torn grass behind it. A small group of students, factory workers, and teachers hovered alongside the vehicle's sides like bodyguards.

A teenage girl with a nose ring stood atop the car, clutching a bullhorn. Mother gasped. *Oh my god, it's her.* The adolescent, with her buzz cut, ripped jeans, and baggy hoodie, looked so small yet seemed enormous before the masses. Natalia Gonzalez, seventeen years old, faced the crowd with a confident smile. She was the icon of the protest, the one who'd put the footage online. *The girl who broke the rules.*

When she raised the bullhorn to her lips, Heaven's Hole cheered. "That's right!" Natalia shouted. "We're done being Caleb Thorne's slaves. Listen up, Kaiser House, Thorne, and any other corporate exploiters because we're not going to shut up—never again!"

"Never again!" the protestors thundered.

Mother glanced behind her as armored trucks rolled down the road. *This is going to get bad.*

53: Natalia

Hundreds of people stamped the ground. Their voices rose into the rainy sky. They waved signs over their heads. Natalia—who just two weeks earlier would have been nervous to speak in front of even twenty people—stood before her town. Her heart pounded. *This is so crazy.* Surrounding the car, her inner circle—Mr. Nazari, Felix, Paul, Felix's parents, and Mamá and three work friends—all stared up at her, beaming with pride.

"You got this, Nat!" Felix cheered, lifting his boyfriend's and his mother's hands at the same time.

"Gon-zal-ez!" The crowd boomed. "Gon-zal-ez! Gon-zal-ez!"

The rain came down harder. *Gotta keep going. Don't think.* She ran her hands across her shaved head, took a deep breath, and stomped on the car. "This is *our* time!" she shouted, to the audience's thunderous approval. "They claimed the footage I posted online was fake! They threatened my family, your families, all of you, to cover up the truth—that Caleb Thorne caged, tortured, and murdered psychic children and teenagers to create a weapon." The crowd booed, and she continued, "Innocent people like the boy in this house behind me!"

"Free Billy!" Felix cried.

The multitude responded. "Free Billy!"

"Thorne's cover-ups almost blew up this town." Natalia paused, eyeing the giant TV cameras. *Whoa, are those the big news networks? Hope there's nothing in my teeth.* She cleared her throat and announced, "But we're not going to believe Thorne's lies again, are we?"

"Never again!" the masses responded.

"That's right!" she said as the bullhorn sizzled. "And are we going to cover up his bullshit for him?"

"Never again!"

Natalia gazed proudly at the hundreds of people before her. Almost everyone she'd ever known was there. Old teachers. Neighbors. Students. She looked up into the clouds as rainwater streaked down her face, listening to the crowd chant her name. *This isn't about me, though, or about Billy. It's about something much bigger. Freedom.*

She looked down. Armored trucks were pulling into the crowd, trying to get people to disperse.

Talk fast, Natalia. "Thorne Century owns everything—*everything!*" she yelled, and her voice cracked a bit, an outward slip of her inward nervousness as well as a painful reminder that despite it all, she was still just a high schooler. "It's a monopoly that controls every part of our lives and one of only a few corporations that controls this entire country. They own the politicians. They own the banks. They own the food supply, the farms, the pharmaceuticals, the weapons industry—"

The trucks opened. Thorne's black-suited soldiers spilled out, waving their guns around. Smoke grenades burst into the crowd. People screamed. They darted away. Protestors were tased and handcuffed. Natalia gestured down to Felix, who quickly took out his phone—to livestream the carnage onto social media—as she returned to her megaphone. "Look at this, right here! As Thorne sits in that ivory tower he calls a hotel, sipping his million-dollar wine and turning children into weapons, he exploits our labor. He threatens us. Wants us to shut up. Will we put up with that anymore?"

Through the smoke, rain, and beatdowns, the crowd roared, "Never again!"

Police cars whizzed into the field. Protestors were beaten to the ground. The crowd broke apart. Natalia crouched, faced her inner circle, and whispered, "Everybody record everything, okay?" Mr. Nazari nodded, taking out his phone. Everyone else followed.

Natalia stood up again. "He's been using us!" she shouted over the chaos and into the rainstorm. "The system has been abusing us! We want transparency, we want answers—we want freedom—for us, for the psychic children, for everyone!"

Machine-gun fire exploded in the air. People screamed. The crowd panicked and ran. A man in black armor—the Thorne Century logo centered on his chest plate—broke through the wrestling masses, lunged to the front, and pointed his gun at Natalia. "Gonzalez!" the man shouted. "Turn yourself in, or I'll shoot!"

A shiver went down Natalia's spine.

She felt a tug on her pant leg, looked down, and saw her Mother's teary eyes. "Please run, baby," Mamá said.

Natalia shook her head. "Sorry, Mamá." She jumped down from the car and marched directly toward the man with the gun. As Thorne's other soldiers joined him, standing alongside him, her troops rallied to her sides, and hundreds of phones flashed into the sky, recording everything. In the light of the cameras, Natalia pushed forward—fighting through the pounding of her own heart—and stepped inches away from the gunman.

"Get back!" the gunman ordered.

"No." She took the man's gun—he was shaking as much as she was—and placed the barrel against her own forehead. *Okay, I'm officially one hundred percent crazy now.* She forced herself to smile. "Try me."

"Back off, little girl," the man said in a trembling cadence.

"You won't shoot me." Natalia thought back to the last time she'd had a gun to her head—*Crazy Old Darrell*—and her smile broadened as she realized how much had changed. "Look around you, asshole. You might not care about killing me, but see all those cameras? Social media's one thing, and there's at least three major news networks too. Are you really going to execute a teenage girl in the United States for the whole world to see? Go ahead, man. Destroy Thorne Century for me by making it the company that shoots teenage protestors. Put your face in the history books. I dare you."

She stared through the man's visor. He was Caucasian, young—a few years older than her, at most—and sweat ran down his brow. She glared into his fearful eyes, never blinking, as his finger twitched over the trigger. *If I'm going to die, this is the way to do it.* Her heart pounded so fast that she could barely breathe.

The man lowered his gun. "Fuck!" he gasped, turning away.

Natalia laughed—hiding her mortal terror with faux confidence—and shrugged for the cameras. "Didn't think so." Looking back at the lawn, she saw a police car rolling toward her. She turned to Felix, who was slack-jawed, and gestured for him to go. "Hey, man, get out of here."

"Holy crap, Nat!" Felix cried. "That was—"

"Talk later." She pointed at the soldier, who was now sitting on the ground, rocking back and forth. "You've got the fundraising campaign ready to launch? We're gonna need bail for everybody who got arrested today."

"I mean, yeah, but—"

"Go," she said.

Felix nodded, with tears in his eyes, then grabbed his mother's arm and joined with Mamá, Mr. Nazari, and the others, fleeing the scene. *It's good to see them getting along.* Satisfied that Felix and his mother had gotten away, Natalia turned to the police car with her hands up. She walked forward, not losing her cool, as an officer jumped out with his gun up.

"Freeze!" he shouted.

Natalia sighed. *So many damn guns.* "Yeah, yeah." She held her hands out. "Just went over this. Go ahead and cuff me."

The cop approached her, his gun still out, a confused expression on his face. He snapped on the cuffs, pinching the skin of her wrists.

"Ouch, man." She winced. "Be careful, huh?"

He guided her into the back of the car. "Watch your head."

"So considerate." She landed in the back seat with a plop. A mixture of fear and excitement swelled inside her. *Okay, I'm scared as hell. But on the other hand...* She stared out the window at the tattered remains of the Kaiser House lawn. People were still holding up signs and shouting her name.

"I don't know what the hell you were thinking," the cop said, his eyes sliding to the rearview mirror. "I mean, I agree with y'all, but what do you think all this shouting is going to accomplish?"

Natalia grinned. "Revolution."

54: Mother

When the black helicopter first chopped through the skies of Heaven's Hole, it looked so out of place that, to Mother, it might as well have been a fairy-tale dragon. Climbing into the back of it had been even weirder.

Due to motion sickness, Mother spent the first hour of the flight with her eyes closed, dreading their arrival. *I don't want to smell Caleb again. Or see his weird smile.* The other helicopter passengers—Father, Linus, and the bodyguards—didn't talk much during the flight, so Mother tried to nap. This only led to sad memories of her son, Jamie, who'd always loved helicopters, so she tried to distract herself by admiring the snowcapped-mountain views outside the window.

She nudged Father. "Pretty, isn't it?"

Father nodded. "Sure is."

"Did Caleb tell you anything about this meeting? I mean, why is he flying us all the way out here?"

Father glanced over at Linus, who was sitting ahead of them. *Linus probably creeps out Father, too, I suppose*, Mother thought.

Father started to say something, stopped, and simply shook his head.

Before Mother could push him, the pilot made an announcement. "Approaching Johnson City."

Mother squeezed her hands together, nauseated by the thought of dealing with Caleb's anger. *We're almost there.* Johnson City, the capital of the state of Olakhota, loomed over the horizon. The helicopter swerved downward, jolting her stomach. Mother looked down at the endless array of trailer parks, shacks, and broken-down roads surrounding the city. A flat white rooftop was painted with giant red letters: Gonzalez Is Right.

Mother blinked and nudged Father. "You see that?"

Father frowned. Mother looked closer and saw similar signs dotting the yards in front of people's trailers. *So weird to see that this craziness has spread all the way out here. That little girl has no idea what she's done.* The helicopter swerved deeper into Johnson City proper, which was primarily composed of gray office buildings, followed by the glittery streets of the financial center with its five-star hotels and glass condos. Johnson City's centerpiece, of course, was the jutting silver tower of the Thorne Century Unlimited Building, a stunning example of postmodern architecture in blunt defiance of the dull metropolis surrounding it. As the helicopter approached the landing pad on top, though, Mother spotted thousands of protestors surrounding the tower's base, spilling across the streets, holding up signs. *Caleb must be furious.*

The helicopter swerved toward the landing strip, its blades cutting the air like knives. Mother covered her ears and tried not to vomit. *Just land, please.* Finally, the aircraft thudded onto the rooftop, and everyone climbed out in a mad jumble. Mother stayed close to Father, and they followed the bodyguards through a series of glass-paneled halls, past a café, and down the glitziest elevator she'd ever ridden in her life. A television screen in the elevator aired live footage of the protest below, which everyone watched with the same sickened expression.

As the elevator doors opened, she nudged Father again. "What are our names again? Kennedy?"

"Keller," Linus answered for him. "You're Mr. and Mrs. Lewis Keller."

The guards led them down the hallway, through two sets of locked doors, and finally into the most magnificent conference room she'd ever seen. A giant window—overlooking the entirety of Johnson City—flooded the room with natural light. At a circular conference table sat a dozen businessmen with serious expressions. Caleb Thorne stood at the center, dressed in a blue suit. Mother was seated by the guards.

Caleb's eyes lit up at her, but he didn't smile. "Hello, Mrs. Keller. And Mr. Keller, of course. Gentlemen, I'd like to introduce my two most prized scientists on the emotion bomb project."

"Uh, hi." Mother waved shyly at the businessmen surrounding her then did a double take. *Oh my god, I know these people.*

To her right was the blotchy, sagging face of Jim Krauser, the billionaire CEO of the for-profit weapons development corporation Krauser-Kline. On the other side was Leonard "Lenny" Fax, the fresh-faced, smug twentysomething heir to a pharmaceutical fortune. The previous year, Lenny had made headlines for single-handedly raising the price of chemotherapy across the nation. And between Krauser and Fax were the Wilson Brothers, owners of a multinational petroleum corporation that was also responsible for massive deforestation in South America as well as for having obliterated the nearby Native American reservation with a leaky pipeline while also producing the world's best-selling sneakers. She didn't recognize the other suits, but all of them fit the same profile—white, male, and wealthy.

A waiter appeared at Mother's side. "Mrs. Keller, can I offer you coffee? Wine? Or—"

"Coffee," she managed to say, and the waiter poured her a cup. She held it to her lips with shaky hands. *All these men could destroy my life with one pen stroke.* She whispered in Father's ear, "This is so goddamn weird."

Rather than ignore her, he nodded. "Yes."

"Thank you for coming, doctors." Caleb clasped his hands. "Now, gentlemen, I think our conversation—"

"Was going badly," grumbled Jim Krauser through bulldog jowls. "All of your shareholders are thinking of pulling out, Thorne. Across the board. The media is on your ass like a thumbtack, and if these protests get any worse..." Krauser guzzled his coffee down loudly. "Unlike you, we care about profit."

"Ah." Caleb gave a smile, but Mother saw the simmering rage behind it. His face was unshaven. His neck was still bandaged.

I've never seen him so unsteady. Hell, I almost feel bad for him.

"That's a tad unfair, Mr. Krauser. The biased news media will certainly move on at some point, and the project is nearing its finish. Isn't that correct, Mrs. Keller?" He faced Mother.

She nodded yes, to his visible relief.

"We have the subject in solitary—"

"Oh, the *subject*," George Wilson, the elder Wilson brother, replied with a snort. "You mean the Jewish kid you've got locked up in a tank—the one that these idiots outside are protesting over?"

Caleb stiffened. "Indeed."

"Bad optics, Thorne." Krauser groaned. "Locking up kids never plays well on the news or on social media."

"Yeah." Wilson ordered a glass of something dark then turned back to Caleb. "Why didn't you knock out the town's internet service to start with before all your immigrant workers decided to go all digital Karl Marx on you? Hell, why not disconnect them today and give yourself time to finish the project without all this heat?"

Thorne sighed, clearly struggling to hide his annoyance. "We did a risk-assessment survey. Now that the world is watching that town, cutting the internet will only cause a bigger flood of negative media coverage. Human rights groups will get involved. Instead, I instructed my dear friend Mr. Linus"—he waved at Linus, who was standing across the room—"to cancel all passenger aircraft flying in or out of Johnson City Airport, thereby minimizing traffic." Caleb beamed then seemed disappointed that no one congratulated him.

"My point, gentlemen, is that our chief intent isn't to fight with the protests but to wrap up this project as soon as possible."

A small man with fuzzy white hair raised a feeble hand. "Sir, I must object to the human rights abuses you're perpetrating."

Mother leaned forward. *Wait, is that Senator Graham Klein?* She rubbed her eyes, astonished to recognize the US Senator of Olakhota sitting across from her, looking far meeker than he did on TV.

"Senator Klein," Caleb said, "do you have something to add?"

"I... it's just..." The senator shrank into his chair like a snail. "Nobody told me that you were experimenting on kids down there, much less killing 'em to make some kind of bomb battery. I'm really not okay with this."

"You're not?" Caleb's voice carried an undercurrent of gravel.

Klein flinched. "I'm certainly not."

"Well." Caleb cracked his knuckles. "Senator Klein, you would do well to remember who financed your reelection campaign." Caleb's smile widened, and Mother was sickened to see the blood returning to his face.

He loves winning against people.

"After all, Senator Klein, I'd hate to release those secret documents—"

"Please, don't." Klein's face went red.

"Or the recordings, or perhaps the settlement payments..."

"I won't interfere." The senator lowered his head. "I'm just saying, I don't like this."

"Noted." Thorne waved his hand. "Now, gentlemen, am I correct in assuming that, negative media aside, we're still proceeding forward with the contract?"

The businessmen looked at each other. Mother nervously fingered her coffee mug as Krauser's voice rose. "Of course. Lots of money to be made," the bulldog said. "But you sure as hell need to fix all these protesting illegals, not to mention that shitty Latina girl. She's making you look like a fool."

"Gonzalez." Caleb squeezed the end of the conference table as if he were about to flip it over, and Mother shrank away. "Don't worry about her. I had her put in jail last night."

Lenny Fax laughed aloud. "Not anymore, bud." Fax swished his perfect hair from his eyes, and he held out his phone. "Check the headlines. Your gal went free this morning."

Caleb's head jerked back. "Pardon?"

"Just what I said." Fax scrolled downward. "Seventy-nine thousand online fans donated to an online-fundraising account, posted by her crew, and paid her bail. Bailed out all the other protestors too. She knew she was going to get arrested, dude. She had a plan. She *played* your ass."

"God damn it," Caleb muttered.

Mother crossed her arms. *Holy shit. This girl is good.*

Lenny Fax whipped his hair back again. "*No bueno*, el Thorno. She also just posted a video saying she's going to hold another protest tomorrow night, demanding higher wages, benefits, amnesty..." He kept scrolling, and his eyes bugged out. "Oooh man, and she wants a democratically elected government in Heaven's Shithole? She just started a new hashtag calling you hashtag Dictator Thorne. Ouch."

"Stop talking about her," Caleb muttered.

"Whatever, man." Fax grinned like the Cheshire cat. "Just sayin', young folks eat this sorta thing up. If you're not careful, bud, she's gonna ruin your project, shit on your company, and before you know it, we'll have to start calling this chick *President* Gonzalez." Fax kicked his feet onto the conference table.

Krauser, the Wilson brothers, and Senator Klein all shifted uncomfortably. Mother tensely watched a vein bulge in Caleb's head. *No one has ever, ever gotten under his skin like this before.*

Caleb turned to the window. "I'll handle Gonzalez. Meeting dismissed. We'll regroup next week to negotiate contracts."

55: Thorne

After everyone filed from the room, Caleb glared at the dimming sky outside the window. The protests down at the base of his tower were growing louder. Larger. Longer. *Even here in Johnson City, I'm not safe anymore.* He squeezed the knife in his pocket. The wound in his neck throbbed, as it had ever since the incident, and he craved another injection of Billy's blood. Someone touched his shoulder, and he whipped out his knife.

Roseanna leapt back. "Caleb!"

He exhaled. "My apologies, dear." He returned the knife to his pocket, walked back to the conference table, and poured himself a glass of Scotch. "Can I be frank with you?"

"You can," Roseanna said as her long, slender neck bowed downward in a timid gesture that Caleb found almost irresistible.

Sensing her discomfort, he instead drowned his passion in a gulp of Scotch. "I want to kill this Gonzalez girl. I want to slice her open, tear out her heart, and paint this office in her blood. I'd like to gouge her eyes out. I feel such hatred for her." A weight lifted off his chest—then hoisted itself back on. "However, I don't think I can get away with it." He poured Roseanna a glass and handed it to her.

She took it hesitantly. "Even Caleb Thorne can't get away with everything, huh?"

"Correct." He leaned against his desk. "A powerful man who doesn't know his limits is a man who loses his power in a day." He stared into her beautiful blue eyes, losing himself in them, and turned away. "Lenny Fax is swine, but he's right. She played me. I can't deport her family anymore, or she'll post it online and get even more support from the riffraff and imbeciles. I can't have her killed, or she'll be a martyr to her cause. If this controversy gets any bigger, my shareholders will drop out within a day."

"And you can't deport the protesting factory workers either." Roseanna drank her Scotch.

She takes it like a man. I like that.

"Because then you'll have no workers left. Correct?"

"You see my dilemma." He sighed. "I'd have to rehire an entire new workforce. Linus ran the numbers. It would delay the project by a year, at minimum, and that's assuming we retained funding. Which is, well…"

"If that meeting was any indication?" She drank again. "Your outlook doesn't look bright."

"I always said you were smart." He smiled at her. She didn't smile back. *Why does she never smile back?* The sky outside darkened. "That spoiled little brat has no idea what sort of damage she's doing. She's ruining lives for a foolish little crusade. She… she…" He didn't know what else to say. Breathing deeply, holding the knife, Caleb stared down at the metropolitan lights, imagining Natalia Gonzalez's head on a spike.

"Caleb," Roseanna said. "I think I have an idea."

He flipped open the knife and spun the blade in his palm. "Yes?" A tiny spot of blood peeped out.

"Negotiate with the girl," Roseanna said. "She's the one leading the protests, so give her something she wants in exchange for standing down."

"You want me to negotiate with a fucking teenager." Caleb slammed his glass down on the table, splashing expensive Scotch onto his jacket. "Are you insane?"

"Listen—"

"You listen." He whipped his glass to the floor, shattering it. Roseanna jumped back, and Caleb advanced on her. "I'm Caleb goddamn Thorne, Roseanna. I'm the man behind Thorne Century, the engine that powers the United States. There's no chance in hell that I'm going to suck up to some little underage Hispanic bitch who—"

Roseanna shoved him away, angrier than he'd ever seen her. "Give her Billy."

Caleb slackened. "Pardon?"

"I'm telling you, Caleb, this is how you win." Her face paled. "As much as I despise your project, I know I'm stuck until it's done, so I want it done. And I've been watching the energy readings. If you want to finish your emotion bomb, we need at least one more big, booming explosion of emotional energy from Billy. He needs to experience something passionate, something big. You'll never get that in the dark tank."

"I'm listening."

"Now, the way I see it, you have two problems: a boy too dangerous to let out of solitary and a girl too powerful to kill. But their weakness..." She looked down, biting her lip. "Is each other. So if you take him out of the tank for a little bit, as part of a negotiation with Gonzalez—"

"Wait." Caleb's heart leapt in his chest. *I get it now.* "You're brilliant."

Roseanna frowned. "Wait, you're open to...?"

"Absolutely." He grinned. "I'll agree to give her a supervised visit with Billy on the condition that she tell her troops to stand down and stop protests until..." He slid next to Roseanna, feeling her heat. "How long do you need to wrap things up? Christmas? New Year's?"

"I guess... a month, at least. It depends on how much emotional energy he puts out while he's out of the tank—"

"New Year's, then." Caleb boomed with pride. "She'll get a Christmas visit from her little boyfriend. We'll get the energy splash from him being all happy about it, and then, right when she's about to protest again in the new year—" He clapped his hands. "The project will be done, we can plug him back into the tank, and we can deport all those ungrateful workers. And you..." He stepped up to the window, clasping his hands behind his back. "You'll be the one supervising this visit, Roseanna. Because I trust you, and so does the subject."

He stared at Roseanna's reflection in the blackened window.

She looked uneasy. "Me?"

"Yes." He admired the squareness of his jaw. *I feel like myself again.* "I'll discuss arrangements with the brat tonight."

56: Natalia

Natalia collapsed on the living room couch. Her legs felt so heavy that she half seriously entertained the thought of never moving again. *Seriously, man, nobody ever warns you that revolutions don't come with massages.* When she finally managed to kick off her boots, they thudded heavily to the floor like cartoon anvils. She needed a shower. Her clothes were ripped and dusty. *But I'm here.* She smiled to herself, drifting off. *I'm breaking the system.*

Two tumbling little bodies pounced on top of her, nearly pushing her from the couch. "Hey!" she cried, gripping the pillows for support as the giggling duo of Juan and Carlos rolled off her with a thud.

"Big sister!" Carlos lay on his stomach, his head perched in his palms. "What was the jail cell like, huh? Please tell me!"

"Sleeping on concrete is awesome." She messed up his hair. "C'mon, dude. It sucked. Duh."

"Did you get in prison fights?" Carlos asked, awestruck.

"Yeah, right. Fights." She curled up on the couch, closing her eyes. "Y'know what I didn't get? Sleep. So how about—"

"You were so cool that day!" Carlos shook her awake. "Me and my friends watched the videos of you standing on that car and giving that speech to all those people." The little boy stood atop Natalia's hips and replicated her pose from the footage.

Now I'm the car. Great.

"You're like a superhero, Natalia. Total badass!" Carlos continued.

"Carlos!" Abuelita yelled from the kitchen.

Carlos ducked away. "Total badass," he whispered.

Meanwhile, Juan tucked himself into her side, pushing her to the edge of the couch. "Yeah. It was awesome."

Natalia grinned and sat upright. "Come here, guys." She hugged them both at the same time. It felt good to have their approval, their smiles, and their support, but more than anything else, it felt good to hold them. Even though she'd expected to get arrested—prepared for it, even—the dark quiet of the cell the night before had scared her. *Not anymore. Not when my family is here. They make this worth it.*

Juan tugged on her sleeve. "Big sis, are you gonna make sure the bad people stop putting kids into bombs?"

Natalia kissed his forehead. "I hope so." She kissed Carlos's forehead, too—he squiggled out of her grasp, feigning disgust—and stood up. "I'm gonna say hi to the grown-ups. Be right back."

She groaned and dragged her way to the kitchen, feeling more like a ninety-year-old than the action hero her brothers thought she was. When she got there, Mamá and Abuelita were both perched behind a laptop, wearing glasses, frowning at the screen. Natalia sat down with a wince, and her mother snapped the laptop shut.

"Hey," Natalia said. "Hiding stuff from me?"

"It's nothing." Mamá went to the sink, filled a teakettle with water, then sighed in a way that said the exact opposite. "Just people online saying horrible things."

"Things about you, girl," Abuelita said, pointing a shaky finger in Natalia's direction. "Racism. Sexism. Death threats. When you break things, Natalia, some people aren't happy that they're broken."

"Good." Natalia crossed her arms. "Somebody had to do it."

Abuelita's brow furrowed. "Yes. Probably so."

Natalia sighed. *I feel bad. They shouldn't have to read that crap.* She thought about going to her room and working on the eternally procrastinated *Dark-Eyed Boy*, but the tension in the kitchen felt like it had to be addressed. *Weird how it's scarier to talk to Mamá and Abuelita than it is to face a gun.*

"Hey, guys," she said. "Be honest with me. When I posted all those videos online... did I do the right thing?" The two women turned to look at her, and her voice became a whisper. "Am I doing the right thing now?"

Mamá walked over, gave her a hug, and kissed her cheek. "Of course, baby. I'm scared, but I'm proud." She went back to her teakettle.

Abuelita looked sterner. "My brain wants me to tell you no. It says you're being dumb. Impulsive. Too risky. But..." She took Natalia's hand. "My heart?" She smiled, creasing up her cheeks. "That part of me, it says yes. You did the right thing. I admire the strength in you."

Natalia blushed. "Really?"

"Except this awful mess on your head." The old woman rubbed Natalia's buzz cut with a look of disgust. "No hair. So terrible. Why would you do such a thing to yourself, going almost bald like this? That I don't like."

Natalia laughed. *Okay, I can handle that.* "It's a statement, Abuelita. Like—"

There was a loud, authoritative knock at the door. Everybody went quiet. The boys crept forward, peered at each other, and hid behind the wall. The tension was thicker than molasses. Another knock followed.

"This is Thorne Century," came a voice from the other side. "We have business matters to discuss with Natalia Gonzalez."

A shudder passed through her.

Mamá peeked through the blinds. "There are lots of men. Mr. Linus is the one at the door."

There was another knock, and the man said, "The matter is urgent."

A quiet sob escaped from the living room—either Juan or Carlos, she couldn't tell—and the older women were silent. Natalia moved toward the door. "I'm going out. Mamá, keep your phone pointed out the window. Livestream every second to the website in case something—"

"Be safe," Abuelita said, squeezing Natalia's trembling body. Mamá did the same.

Natalia opened the door. A cold draft tumbled in. Standing in the door was the bulky figure of Mr. Linus, who smelled of onions and didn't look happy to see her. "Gonzalez," Linus said, frowning at Mamá—who, as asked, was filming the scene. "Come with me."

Linus stepped away, frost crunching beneath his heels. Natalia put on boots and a hoodie then followed him outside, where four trench coat–clad men with sunglasses waited. Linus guided her down the icy walkway, past the door of the next apartment—which was abandoned, as of the previous week—and there, at the corner of the walkway, stood Caleb Thorne.

"Good evening, Ms. Gonzalez," Thorne said, flashing a smile so plastic it looked like a button.

She did a startled jump. "Holy fuck." She glared at the vampiric figure before her, his cashmere coat flapping in the wind like a cape, and couldn't form words. *I totally wasn't prepared for this.*

"You're a lot less talkative than you were the other day." Thorne chuckled. "Listen, dear. We've been at odds with each other. But I'm a businessman, and good business comes from good deals, so I'd like to make you one."

Natalia kicked at the ice. "Yeah, because you can't shoot me, deport me, throw me in prison, or fuck with my family anymore without me putting it online. That's why you're here." *Great, there goes my mouth.*

Thorne's eyes flashed with rage. "Ah." A bodyguard reached for his gun, and Thorne gestured for him to lower it. "There's that charming spunk again."

"Thanks. So, big man, what're you offering?"

Thorne stepped so close to her that she felt suffocated. Leering at her, he said, "Billy Jakobek."

Her heart caught in her throat. Hearing Billy's name, spilled so casually from Thorne's lips, reopened the wounds. *The fire tower. The party. All those kisses, all those times we touched.* She shook her head. "Shut up."

"I presume you want him released, yes?" He towered over her. "I can't do that, of course, but I am willing to offer you supervised visitations with him. We'll release him from the tank and permit him to spend the evening with you on... shall we say, scheduled occasions. However, there's a stipulation."

"Of course." She shifted away, peering in the parking lot below.

"Indeed. If I allow you to have visits with Jakobek, I want a cease-fire agreement, in writing, where you will stop riling up my workers. I want these protests to end."

Natalia shook her head. "You know I can't do that. This is about more than just Billy. It's bigger than that." She stared up at the fire tower blinking from the ridge and pushed back her tears. *Sorry, Billy.*

"I had a feeling you'd say that." Thorne smiled, clapping her shoulder in a fatherly manner that repulsed her. "Good business is built on compromises, little girl, so here's one that suits both our ends. If you can agree to delay future protests until after the New Year, I will release Billy to your care for a Christmas dinner. This will give us both a month to relax, think, and come to a better future agreement for the long term." Caleb held out his hand. "May we shake on it?"

Natalia looked at his massive palm. *God, I want to see you, Billy.* Her whole body trembled at the thought of holding him, hearing him, and kissing him. *Christmas, huh? Whoa, I've got an idea.* Steadying herself, she flashed a mischievous smile at Thorne. "Billy's Jewish."

Thorne frowned. "So?"

"He doesn't care about Christmas. I want him for Thanksgiving instead. Do that, and I'll call down the protests until Turkey Day is over, *then* we can negotiate—or I'll start protesting again. How's that?"

Thorne bristled with rage. "Absolutely not. That's only three days from now."

"Three days of cease-fire. Isn't that what you want, big guy?"

"Shut up, Gonzalez." Linus stepped forward. "Mr. Thorne wants—"

"I know what he wants," Natalia said. "A full month of no protesting, no news, nada, so the fire can die down and the project can wrap up. Yeah, uh, no." Natalia smiled at the fury in Thorne's eyes. *I've got you, bastard.* She reached into her back pocket and unfolded a crumpled lined paper that she'd been keeping there for the past week. "I've got some other demands, too, if you want this deal." She read from the list. "For one, I want wage and benefit discussions, starting next Monday. Two? A televised town hall debate, me and you, broadcast on all the major networks. Three, we're going to talk about a pathway to citizenship for—"

"This is ludicrous." Thorne balled his fists, refusing eye contact. "You think a poor, uneducated child like you can demand these things from me?"

Natalia stepped up to him. "I think—" She poked him hard in the chest. "You don't have a choice. Thanksgiving dinner with Billy. Town hall debate. The works. Otherwise, I'm going to rally thirteen hundred people to crash Kaiser House tomorrow night, and the TV networks will be watching."

Thorne's expression shifted from anger to embarrassment to hurt, like a moving kaleidoscope image. He whispered in Linus's ear. After a pause, Linus snatched the crumpled paper from Natalia's hands and walked away.

Once Linus had vanished, Thorne narrowed his eyes at Natalia. "My lawyers will write up a contract, and they'll email it to you tonight. I'd better not see you doing any posts, speeches, or *anything* before Thanksgiving, or the deal is off. If you fulfill that obligation, the boy will be here that evening and back in the tank by eleven. On Friday, we'll meet again to negotiate this 'town hall' you so desire. I expect the contract to be signed by midnight."

"So Billy's coming over for Thanksgiving?" Natalia jumped for joy. "Yes!" *Oh my god, he's really coming!* She laughed, did a twirl, and said in a mocking voice, "Oh, thank you, Mr. Thorne. Such a generous man!"

Thorne sighed, touched the bandages on his neck, and looked up at her. "You're playing with fire, Gonzalez." Then, surrounded by his bodyguards, he whipped downstairs to the parking lot, got into the back of his limousine, and drove away into the night.

57: Boy

The boy in the dark tank woke up. Water swished around him. The blue light flickered. *Something is happening.*

His veins tightened. He breathed in short, rapid bursts, spewing bubbles everywhere. The lid of the tank opened, and the rush of light was so intense that even when he closed his eyes, it cut right through the lids. *Headache. Stress. Too much.* In the bleary fog, a salt-and-pepper-haired white woman stood over him. *I know her. She is... she... what's her name?* The woman made sounds with her mouth, but he couldn't understand.

She tried again. He shook his head.

Leaning down, breaking through the fog, she slowly spoke the words, "Hey, Billy. Can you hear me?"

He nodded feebly. *That's my name.*

"Happy Thanksgiving, kiddo." She smiled. "We have a dinner to attend."

58: Caleb

Caleb Thorne threw the covers off at ten in the morning. He hadn't slept. Hours of tossing through the sheets had produced only frustration. At one point, he'd woken up so frustrated that he'd tried to ease his mind by watching his favorite sitcoms from his youth, but he'd been unable to concentrate on anything but his present situation. *Can't do this anymore.* He stood up and opened the blinds to see the snowfall outside the window. The sunlight pierced his temples. *Hangover.* He stumbled back, rubbing his head. *Need aspirin. Coffee. Psycho blood.*

He reached for the hotel phone and dialed the lobby. "Breakfast." He paused. "And a Bloody Mary."

He hung up the phone, sat upright, and examined his hotel room. Despite the beautiful artwork, furnishings, and heated floors, it felt like a prison cell. *Thanks to that anchor-baby brat, I can't even show my face in my own town. I own this place, yet I'm an outcast. It's so unfair.* He scrolled through his cellphone. His email was plastered with turkey images.

"Fucking Thanksgiving." He tossed the phone aside.

He threw his robe on, stomped across the room, and chewed a handful of aspirin. His computer monitors, tablet, and smartwatch all blinked Thanksgiving Day reminders, as if taunting him with his failure. *This is supposed to a holiday for real Americans, like me. I'm in my fucking town, on my fucking holiday, trapped in a hotel room because of some lazy immigrant girl with a big mouth.* He reached for his phone, about to dial Roseanna and call off the whole visitation, then reconsidered. *I should've never tried to negotiate with Gonzalez. Huge mistake.*

Room service knocked on the door. A gangly Latino boy in an oversized uniform held out his tray. "Happy Thanksgiving, Mr. Thorne!"

Caleb eyed the tray suspiciously. "Place it on the table." He stepped aside. "I hope you're having a swell Thanksgiving as well."

The boy eagerly placed the tray on Caleb's table, poured the drinks, and waited in the doorway with a forced smile.

He wants a tip, doesn't he? Caleb closed the door in his face. Smiling to himself, Caleb sat down in front of his meal, placed a napkin over his lap, then lifted the lid. The food smelled delicious, but he had no appetite.

Sipping his Bloody Mary, he distracted himself by flipping through pictures of tropical beaches, imagining his future with Roseanna. *We can stay in the Azores for a few weeks. Sip cocktails in the sun.* He scrolled deeper. *Spend another week in this gorgeous castle.* His phone flashed with a text from Roseanna, and his heart sank. She was just letting him know that she'd gotten Billy out of the tank.

"Damn it," he mumbled. *Too late to change my mind, I suppose. It appears I traded three days of no protests so that a Jewish kid could eat Thanksgiving with some illegals. What is this country coming to?* The stab wound in his neck burned.

He winced. "When will this goddamn thing heal?"

Nobody heard him because he was alone. *I'm always alone.* This vulnerable realization fluttered through him, so he crushed it beneath his heel. *Such is the fate of brilliant men like me. Isolation. Little idiots like Natalia Gonzalez get love because they are feeblemind-ed sycophants. But not me. I'm brave enough to say things people don't want to hear.* Caleb picked at his breakfast. *I hate Gonzalez's smirking face. Her obnoxious high-pitched voice. She's such a condescending piece of shit. She doesn't know anything about how the world really works.*

Blood trickled down his neck. The bandage was saturated. He pressed the wound, sighed, and hurried to the bathroom to change the dressing.

When he removed the bandage, the wound was yellowed with infection and smelled disgusting. Covering his mouth, he wiped away the pus and sanitized the wound. He avoided looking at his reflection, bothered by what he saw there. *I don't like my face anymore. It's the face of a weak man. An idiot who gets outsmarted by a teenage girl.* He took the knife from his pocket and imagined running the blade along Natalia Gonzalez's neck. *That would feel so good. To have her hot blood spilling through my fingers...*

He dropped the knife. It lay on the floor, glancing up at him. Caleb ducked down and hesitated. Instead of picking it up, he unlocked the hidden fridge. He removed a fresh vial of Billy's blood. "Just to get through Thanksgiving," he told himself. "Then I'll cut this out."

He flicked the syringe, took a deep breath, and injected it into the uninjured side of his neck.

59: Billy

After getting ready, Billy walked through the halls of Kaiser House, mesmerized by the fact that he was alive. The fireplace crackled in the living room. The guards stood silently by the doors. Outside in the snow, the car revved up. Billy touched the walls, the windows, and the counters, piecing together what had happened. After getting shot at the factory, he'd thought he was dead—and during the weeks in the dark tank, he'd *wished* he were dead. He'd never expected to be revived in Kaiser House, much less getting ready to eat Thanksgiving dinner with the one person who somehow had kept him going through all those dark days.

Natalia. He grinned, seeing her face in the fire. *I can't wait to see you.*

Excitement sparkled within him like a firework. He sat down at the coffee table and leafed through the newspapers. Every headline was about her. Stories described her as everything from a "would-be revolutionary" to a "punk kid," but no one disputed the seriousness of what she'd done. Flipping through, he came across an article about Beth Shalom, his former home, and was saddened by a line at the beginning of the second paragraph: *The majority of Beth Shalom's residents, most of whom live beneath the poverty line, are employed at Thorne Century factories.*

He squeezed his necklace. *I need to go back there someday. Break my own people out of that prison somehow.*

Mother walked in from the kitchen and offered him a warm cup of coffee, which he took gratefully. "Are you about ready to go?"

He ran his finger down the mug's handle, feeling the energies that Mother left behind. *There's something different about her today.*

He closed his eyes, and in the darkness, he saw the face of a young boy. *A son. She has a son named Jamie.* He smiled at her, and she smiled back but with noticeable worry. *Somebody forgot their anti-Billy pills.*

Mother shuddered. "Stop poking around in me." She turned away, crossing her arms.

Billy didn't push, but now he understood. *That's why you're in this project.* He circled the coffee mug's handle. *And this dinner tonight...*

Billy ripped off the corner of a newspaper, wrote a little note on it, and handed it to Mother: *You made today happen somehow. I know it. Thank you.*

Mother blinked back tears. "You're welcome," she said in a tiny voice. She turned away, trying to look solemn, but he felt the hidden relief melting beneath her frown. A horn honked outside. "Let's go. No time for coffee, I guess."

Billy beamed as he stepped into boots and a coat. *I'm coming, Natalia.*

60: Natalia

Snow poured from the clouds, and by early afternoon, the sky was so dark that Natalia flicked on the lamps. She sighed with exhaustion. Not only had she and Abuelita spent all night prepping the turkey, using Papá's old "recipe book"—scraps of faded paper stapled together—but then she'd woken up early, had a quick splash of coffee, and spent hours in the kitchen with Mamá, their hands buried in flour. The apartment was a mess. The timing on every dish was badly misaligned. Despite her outer fatigue, though, Natalia was so excited she could explode. *He's coming!*

"Wow." Natalia laughed, elbow wiping the sweat from her forehead. "It's so hot in here I think we might melt all the snow."

Mamá chuckled. As they washed their hands in the sink, she bumped Natalia with her hip. "It's a special occasion. Would you like some wine to celebrate?"

"Not yet." She squealed, reminded of what was happening and how close it was. *I can't believe it!* "Just don't embarrass me when he gets here, okay?"

"Says the girl who stands up on cars." Mamá dried her hands. "I'm feeling a bit dizzy. Can you get my oxygen?"

"Sure." Natalia rushed through the living room and collided with a sheet that had been pinned between the couch and table. She spun away, tangled in the fabric, and swatted at the two little boys dancing around her.

"Hey, you ruined our fort!" Carlos yelled as Juan hummed melodramatically.

Natalia kicked the sheets away. "C'mon, guys! Get in the kitchen and help out!" She looked at Abuelita for support, but the old woman—sitting in her wheelchair, watching the scene with an amused grin—offered nothing but a playful shrug. Natalia dumped the fort onto the couch. "The table needs to be set—"

"Oh, whiny-big-sister alert!" Carlos held up a finger to the sky. "You're just sca-a-a-ared 'cause your boyfriend is gonna come over!"

"Yeah!" Juan backed him up.

"*Niños locos.*" Abuelita waved a hand.

"Forget it." Natalia ran to the bedroom and wheeled the oxygen concentrator out—swooping past the rampaging boys in the living room—to the kitchen, where Mamá was pouring two glasses of wine. "Have some." Mamá winked, handing one over. "You need it."

Natalia shook her head. "I'm okay," she said, helping her mother with the nasal cannula.

"Suit yourself." Mamá shrugged. "What do you think it's going to be like when you see him again?"

Natalia grinned. "I dunno. Those first moments?"

"Yes."

She squealed with excitement again. "Oh man. First, I imagine I'll hear the car pull up. I'll run outside into the snow and just—" She giggled. "I'll just jump at him. Like, seriously, you can't imagine how excited I'm gonna be when—"

The doorbell rang.

Natalia jumped back. *Oh no. I'm so, so not ready for this.*

Mamá beamed up at her and pointed at the door. "Better go make your moment happen, baby."

Natalia shivered, gave her mother a big squeeze, and went for the door. *Oh man, here it comes.* Before she could get there, Juan and Carlos came barreling through.

"I got it!" Carlos cried.

Natalia jumped to intervene, but the boys flung the door open. Snowflakes spiraled into the apartment. The fake mother stepped in first with a tense look on her face, carrying a tray wrapped in aluminum foil. Then, following right behind her...

Natalia nearly fainted. *It's him. My dark-eyed boy.* Billy looked thin and sickly, but the smile on his face lit up her heart like a bonfire. She squeezed her hands, coiled up like a spring, and bounced toward him. "Billy!"

She threw her arms around his neck. Electricity sizzled between them. Their mouths met in a kiss—at that moment, she didn't care who saw—and as their hearts collided, she felt all the sadness that he'd experienced since the factory incident. *Darkness. Coldness. Loneliness.* He ran his hands down her back, absorbing her anger, her passion, her memories of the protests. He kissed both sides of her shaved head then kissed her mouth again.

"God, I missed you." She beamed. "You. *You.*"

"Gross!" Carlos cried, reminding Natalia of her surroundings.

She winked at Billy, turned around, and introduced him to a room full of watching eyes. "Uh, hey. Everybody, meet Billy. He's... my one."

"Hello, one." Mamá smiled warmly. "I hear good things."

Billy nodded and gave a slanted little smile.

God, I missed this boy.

Mamá redirected her attention to the fake mother, who was standing awkwardly in the corner. "Hi there, Doctor. Thanks so much for coming to our Thanksgiving."

Fake Mother struggled to smile. "Hi. I brought, ah... some casserole. I have some wine too."

"Well," Mamá said, pointing at the open bottle on the table. "First, let's finish this, then we'll move on to yours. Deal?"

The fake mother visibly relaxed. "Sounds wonderful."

Mamá handed her the glass Natalia had refused and invited her to sit down, and the two quickly became embroiled in conversation. Natalia nestled herself into Billy's arms, loving the sparks that ran down their skin. *God, I missed this.* She stared into his black eyes. *I feel like myself again*, she thought and loved that she wasn't sure whether the thought came from him, her, or both. *We feel like ourselves.*

"Introduce yourself!" Carlos shouted as the boys lunged at Billy like two cannonballs.

Natalia tried to block them, but they broke through, wriggled past her, and climbed up Billy's legs like spiders. Natalia bit her nails, waiting for them to fall backward, to be transported to the somewhere else—but nothing happened. The boys didn't freeze. They didn't jump back. They frowned, looked up quizzically, then went back to climbing over her boyfriend like he was a jungle gym.

Natalia's jaw dropped. *Nothing happened. Just a little buzz. That's crazy.*

Then Billy crouched before the twins. He flashed them an earnest smile. "Hey, guys, what's up?"

Natalia fell back into a chair. *Holy crap. Did he just...?* She watched in dizzy amazement as Billy tickled the boys, laughing with them. No electricity touched the air. Ghosts didn't fly. *Nothing weird happened. That's... that's...* To Natalia's bewilderment, her little brothers pulled Billy into the living room, and they all disappeared.

Mamá slid a fresh glass of special-occasion wine in Natalia's direction. "Hmm. I thought you said this boy didn't talk."

"He, uh..." She blinked. "He doesn't." She took a deep gulp of wine. "I think I'm going to need a lot of this stuff."

61: Billy

Billy rolled across the living room floor, and the two little boys wrestled him against the couch and wrapped him up in a sheet. Their joyous laughter reverberated through him. He pried loose from the sheets, making zombie noises, and they fell back, giggling.

"It's alive!" Carlos yelled.

Billy grinned. *It feels so good to be human. To play. Wow, maybe I want to be a dad someday.* He rose up, making monstrous noises, as the boys fended him off with imaginary weapons. Their open delight was what had given him the strength—and the bold impulsivity—to talk to them. He hadn't planned it. Even two months ago, he definitely never would have done it. But he was glad he had.

He caught Juan in his arms, wrapped the sheet around him, and made gobbling noises. "Got you!" Juan laughed and tangled himself in the sheet, and Billy rolled outward, panting for air. "Now I'm free from the monster." Billy pointed at Carlos. "You have to eat him!" The boys resumed their game, and Billy crawled off, gasping, and plopped onto the couch.

Despite his psychic abilities, it was only then that he noticed Natalia's grandmother sitting in the hallway, surveying the scene with her hard brown eyes. Billy gulped. *Guess she saw the whole game.* He stood up to introduce himself, offering a bow that felt awkward.

The elderly woman nodded. "*Hola, patojo.*"

She and Billy regarded each other silently. He studied the lines in her face and the hardened stubbornness in her psyche. *Strength. Solemnness. Wisdom. But an inner joy, too—a realness about all things.* Her eyes, fearsome as they were, belied a powerful love for her granddaughter. Billy smiled at her, knowing he probably looked like a complete fool but unable not to.

"You're a strange one," the old woman said finally, with no malice.

Billy shrugged. *True story.*

"Sit down." She pointed at the couch, and Billy did exactly as she asked. The woman rolled her wheelchair to a position across from him and crossed her arms. "I should warn you not to hurt my granddaughter. But somehow, God bless you, I don't think I have to. I have a good feeling about you. I don't know why."

Billy nodded appreciatively. Something about the woman reminded him so much of his own grandmother. After a moment of hesitation, he whispered, "Thanks."

The old woman winced. "That." She shook as if she were standing in the snow outside. "That feeling. It comes from inside you. You see inside others, I hear?"

He nodded.

"I want to see this myself." She held out her calloused palm for him to take. "I have lived a hard life. My granddaughter says you can feel such things. But I want to know what sort of life you have lived as well. Then I may fully trust you." She waved a finger. "Maybe."

Billy glanced back at the kitchen, where the women were drinking wine and laughing. He looked at the boys, still embroiled in their game, then listened to the fizzling of a nearby candle. Finally, he sighed. "It's painful to touch me. Traumatic."

"I have seen too many things to be traumatized, boy."

Billy couldn't argue with this. "Okay." He took her hand, which felt like cracked leather, and electricity sizzled between them. Her eyes closed. She slumped forward in her wheelchair, and Billy caught her. *I'm here.* Holding her, closing his eyes, he fell into the darkness, where lights popped like balloons, and...

There was darkness.

62: Billy... (Somewhere Else)

Darkness.

Sun.

A blue sky. Green trees. Houses of many colors. A beautiful place, beautiful mountains, beautiful people... but the ground is red with blood. The woman before him—a young woman named Isabel, decades before she will become Abuelita—is holding the dead pieces of her husband after his body has been chopped apart by a machete.

Billy steps back in horror. "Oh my god."

Isabel sobs over the bloody chunks as the sky and mountains behind her continue to be beautiful, like they are pretending that nothing is wrong. Isabel's belly is round, so pregnant she looks ready to pop, and the father is nothing but pieces in her arms. The killer drops the bloody machete to the asphalt. "That's a warning," the man says—in the somewhere else, Billy can understand his Spanish—and as the man walks away, Isabel cries and cries.

Billy goes to comfort her, and she looks at him, holding the severed head. Her soft and teary young eyes transform into those of a hard older woman. "This is where I come from," Isabel says.

Billy flows into her eyes, and he moves through her memories. She lives through gang violence. Poverty. Rape. Drug wars. Houses being burned down. The conditions are fraught. It reminds him so much of what he saw in his grandmother's mind all those years ago. Decades of pain and hardship, and the cause... *the cause...*

"This violence, it doesn't come from you, your family, the locals. None of this is your fault," Billy says. "Someone else caused this in your home. Like what the Nazis did to my family or like..."

"Your government destroyed my country," Isabel says. "The United States did this to us."

Billy jolts back—almost shaking them out of the somewhere else—but grabs her hand again and finds himself back inside the violence. "What?" He doesn't want it to be true. No one has ever told him this. It was never taught in his classes. However, the fire in Isabel's eyes does not lie. "How?"

"Many, many years of turmoil paid for and ensured by the United States," Isabel says. "We fought back. We lost, always. The US government. United Fruit Company. We elected governments democratically, and your CIA toppled them, installing dictatorships. Violence... it grows from poverty, you see?" The older woman stands up beside him, looking down at the woman holding pieces of her husband. "When my daughter became a teenager, she had a boyfriend. His family was killed by gangs. My family was mostly dead too. Our house was burned to the ground, and I was taking care of my sister's children. So we left. All of us."

Billy looks down, "For safety."

"Yes." Isabel sighs. "Your country calls us illegals, but really, we are..."

"Refugees. Like my grandmother." Billy wipes away the scene before them, moving deeper into her mind. "Show me how you came."

A long field stretches out before them. Billy sees Isabel marching with a troop of children surrounding her, including those who will become Natalia's parents. All of them are sick, tired, and weary, but they keep marching through grass and mud, down highways, and across rushing rivers. Isabel's only bag is tattered, carrying nothing but food and a beautiful wooden cross.

"Not all of them made it," Isabel says. "But we kept going."

The sky darkens, and Billy finds himself walking through a dark, muddy river alongside a slightly older, slightly wearier Isabel with a hunched back. She holds his hand, guiding him through the river.

"My family is my life. Inside you, I see that you have known pain, but you are hiding it from me. I also see my granddaughter, my Natalia, smiling in your eyes." She stares intently at Billy. "I am old. I don't have long in this world. Show me why she matters to you so I can feel safe."

"Okay." Billy sweeps his hand across the water, remaking it into the fire tower overlooking Heaven's Hole. He shows Isabel another Billy, a few months younger, standing there, kissing her granddaughter in the snow.

Isabel rests her hand on Billy's shoulder. "I see."

Billy sweeps his hand again, moving to the cabin with the fireplace as the two of them hold each other through the night. He shows her the art-room closet, paint all over the floor. He dances through the party at the lake house. Then he focuses on Natalia's eyes—her passion, her strength, her hope—and he turns to Isabel with a shrug. "Natalia saved me. I might've saved her life, sure, but she saved my soul."

Isabel becomes Abuelita, takes Billy's hand, and smiles at him. "So you love her."

His mouth opens. He doesn't know what to say. The world whitens, disappearing into the mist. Everything fades. Everything is cloudy.

And then...

63

Billy exhaled.

They sat in the living room. The old woman's eyes fluttered open. She smiled at Billy, regarding him in a far more grandmotherly manner than before. She rolled her head in a circle, clearing away the strange vision, and squeezed Billy's hand. "You are a weird one. But I like you."

Billy touched the veins, scars, and calluses along her fingers. "I think you're right." Tears welled up in his eyes. "I do love her."

"Tell her. She deserves to know."

Billy looked at Isabel's knees, which had become skinny, knobby rails. *All those miles she walked. Then all those years in the factory. So much work, so much fatigue...* He wiped his eyes. "Your legs are tired. But the real pain is in your back."

She rubbed her lower lumbar area. "*Sí.*" She leaned back again. "Hurts like hell. What, you are a doctor too?"

"Let me help." He smiled. "It's kinda my schtick." He gestured for her to lean forward, and he touched her spine. *Feel better, Isabel.* He inhaled—breathing in the ache, pulling it into his own back, causing tingles of sharpness to pinch at his spine—and then exhaled soothing vibes, calmness. *Let the pain fade away. Let it go.* The old woman sat upright, shivering, and looked at Billy, flabbergasted. She tried to say words of gratitude—he could hear the amazement inside her—but merely sputtered out tears.

She breathed deeply. "I don't remember... this..." She rubbed her back. "It has never felt so normal... in all these years..."

"Hey, don't mention it." Billy winced. *Sure hurts my back, though.* He stood up, taking her hand, and they went to the kitchen to help with dinner.

64: Mother

Maybe it was all the wine. Maybe it was the holiday, or maybe it was being around normal people again. Whatever it was, Mother couldn't recall the last time she'd felt so much like Roseanna Peterson.

She spent hours laughing, joking, and trading stories with Maria, whom she now felt half tempted to trade phone numbers with. She developed an immense respect for Isabel, the matriarch. She played with the twin boys. And throughout it all, Billy came alive in a way she'd never seen. When he was with Natalia, he smiled constantly. Every time the food prep slowed down, the two teenagers would sneak away for a kiss. Instead of being quiet and innocent, he seemed energetic, wily, and fun. *I bet he and my Jamie would like each other if they could meet.*

When the turkey finally came out, crispy and mouthwatering as it was, Roseanna felt saddened by what it meant—at some point, the night was going to end. *When we're done eating, we'll need to go back outside, where all those men with guns will march us into the car, drive us to the house, and...*

Her phone buzzed, signaling another lonely text from Caleb. She'd been ignoring his messages all night, responding only when he seemed especially desperate. Her phone was nothing but a harsh reminder that outside of this happy circle, she was a scientist who experimented on children.

Roseanna silenced her phone, and Maria nudged her. "Doctor, are you there?"

She shuffled. "Oh, yeah, of course."

"Mind helping me bring this bird to the table? The platter is heavy."

"I'd be glad to." Roseanna smiled, so happy to have someone who felt like a friend, even if only for a night.

Together, they carried the turkey—a small, splintered thing, as far as turkeys went, but glorious all the same—and plopped it down in the center of the table. Roseanna also helped Maria bring over the rice, tortillas, beans, and corn while Natalia rallied up the boys and served drinks. Once everyone was assembled at the table, Roseanna sat down between Billy and Maria.

The grandmother cleared her throat, quieting Juan and Carlos. "Now we will do a blessing." With one hand on her cross, Isabel prayed in Spanish, and everyone in the family lowered their eyes.

Roseanna peeked up, surveying the loving faces around the table, only to find her gaze colliding with Billy's.

To her immense surprise, Billy smiled at her, leaned over, and whispered, "This night is so great."

Roseanna loved his smile. "It certainly is," she whispered back and closed her eyes for the rest of the blessing.

65: Caleb

Caleb was drunk, sweaty, and in his boxers. Each bottle in his cabinet was worth more than the average US citizen's salary, and he relished the power—the prestige—of so callously dumping liquid gold down his throat. *The miserable holiday dinner that spoiled immigrant family is eating costs less than a sip of this. Drinking this—that's true rebellion!*

Whenever his loneliness returned to him, he texted Roseanna. She barely responded. Meanwhile, as the liqueur in the bottle spiraled downward, the prison cell that was his hotel room constricted around him like a snake's throat. The room was a mess. The coffee table before him was lined with empty glass vials—formerly filled with Billy's blood—that he'd been shooting into his neck every hour. *Fuck the limits. It feels good. I can take it.*

He slumped onto the floor, cradling his dizzy head. "I hate this," he muttered to the empty room. "Does Roseanna truly love me the way I love her?"

The hazy hallucination of Kaley Somerfield giggled before him but didn't answer. As she crossed her legs, blood seeped from the gash running from her throat down her pregnant belly. The sight was gruesome, but over the past few hours, Caleb had gotten used to it. *Kaley isn't real, but at least she's here for me. Unlike everyone else.*

"Please tell me, Kaley."

Kaley's sharp teeth grinned. "It really bothers you, doesn't it?" She peeled back the sliced layers of her abdomen. "Control."

Caleb groggily shook his head. "Pardon?"

"You don't care if she loves you. You just care that you can't force her to love you." Kaley uncrossed her bloodstained legs. "A loss of control. Maybe she's actually enjoying her time with that poor family."

"Shut up." Caleb patted the reddened bandage on his neck. The wound stung. He closed his eyes, focused on the psychic feelings coursing through him, and felt a soft, rhythmic heartbeat tapping at his veins. *That's Roseanna.* He concentrated on it. *She feels happy. I wish she could feel that way with me...*

"Control," Kaley said, and her eyes flashed blue. "Isn't that what you really care about?"

"I don't need to seek power." He sat upright. "I have it."

"Power is fragile." She stroked her bleeding stomach. "When this happened, it bothered you so much that I wanted to get an abortion—"

"I forbade it. You listened."

"But when I forced you to choose between me and Daddy's trust fund? Heh. You cut us wide open without regret. Like I said, it's about control." She giggled. "And now you're jealous of that little Jewish boy's power, aren't you? Because it's *true* power. Sure, you get a taste of it with these injections. You feel what he feels... but you can't do the things he does. Doesn't that bother you?"

Caleb silently took a drink.

"That's why you sliced me open, after all." Kaley again reached into her cut and pulled it wide open—revealing her rib cage, digestive system, and the fetus inside her—then closed it. "You didn't like me taking your control away. You *loved* murdering me, didn't you?"

Caleb brought his knees to his chest. "Never. I just did what I had to do."

"You loved it."

His heartbeat sped up. The room spun. "I certainly did not." *But I did, actually.* He looked into her grinning mouth. "I carry your knife to remind me—"

"Of how you took control. You fucking loved it, Caleb. You know you did." Kaley crept toward him and wrapped her black-fingernailed hands around his throat. Her palms were ice-cold. Caleb tried to jerk back, and her grip tightened. "You've lost that power, Caleb." Kaley giggled. "You're weak now. That's why you're such a mess."

"Get off me." Caleb gasped.

She didn't budge. "No." Kaley Somerfield's mouth unhinged from her jaw. Darkness poured out of her throat. Her mouth opened wider, wider—and then drew back as the face of Natalia Gonzalez flowered from inside her blackened lungs.

"Pussy," Natalia whispered.

"Get off me!" he shouted, and he kicked her away.

The black-streaked feminine creature quickly found its footing and crawled around him like a wildcat. Natalia Gonzalez's eyes glowed like blue flames. Caleb jumped to his feet. *Just a hallucination. Don't be scared.*

The smoky black creature flicked a forked tongue and hissed at him. "I own you," it said in Natalia's voice. "You thought you were so big, so powerful, such a man... but I showed you. Mr. Thorne Century Himself, taking orders from a little girl." She laughed gutturally.

"Never." Thorne spun around, watching the creature prowl the room.

"Too late," Natalia rasped. "I'm going to tear you down. I'm going to destroy your company. Your wealth. Your power. Say buh-bye, Caleb, because this chick is going to ruin everything you—"

"Never!" Caleb picked up his coffee table and threw it at the creature. The table smashed against his bed. Its leg fell loose. The creature scuttled away into the smoke until all that remained were its fiery blue eyes, and then it was gone. Caleb stood there, panting, lost in the fog of his drunken rage. He was just a lonely man in a hotel room, playing with imaginary things, locked away from the outside world.

"You'll never own me," he whispered. "I won't allow it."

Caleb threw on his robe. He stepped onto the porch—out into the snowstorm, the soles of his feet pressing onto raw ice—and raised his arms to the sky. *None of that was real.* He stood in the snow, letting each snowflake cut through his skin. *I'm Caleb Thorne. I'm not some little girl's bitch. I'm not...*

His phone rang. It was Linus, so he answered. "Yes?"

"Happy Thanksgiving, Mr. Thorne."

Thorne's feet burned. Hearing the voice of another human being—a real one—made him realize how insane he was acting. *For fuck's sake, I need to go inside before I get frostbite. Drink some water. No more of this nonsense.* He stepped back inside, shivered, and asked, "What's going on?"

Linus cleared his throat. "I talked to the docs—"

"And?"

"They've got all the energy they need. Way ahead of schedule."

Caleb sucked in air. *Thanksgiving. The little Jewish psycho is so happy to be with his girlfriend's wetback family that he's pouring psychic energy from the gills. Maybe we can turn this shitshow around.* "That's fantastic," Caleb said.

"Tell me what you want to do, Mr. Thorne."

Caleb looked at the broken coffee table. He thought about Natalia's face. Her voice. *She tricked me.* "First of all, Linus, we need to remove the subject from Heaven's Hole ASAP."

"Got it."

"We can move him to solitary confinement in Johnson City, where we can drain his energy for future emotion bombs. Meanwhile, we can wrap up the emotion bomb work in the factory within a few weeks, maybe a month at most, at which point we can get rid of all those pesky workers..." His heart was racing so fast he had to stop. *The nightmare is almost over.*

"Boss?" Linus asked. "Do you want to arrange transport for the subject tomorrow morning, sir?"

Caleb pressed the greasy phone closer to his ear. "Tell you what, Linus. I have another idea."

66: Billy

After dinner was done, Billy whistled as he did the dishes. *Me, doing dishes. Enjoying it. Now, that's weird.* By doing the cleanup work, he could quietly treasure the energies of the boys playing, the older women chatting, and the overall communal warmth around him. Once the primary dishes were finished, he left a couple of pots to soak, remembering this practice from his own mother. *Heya, Mom. Miss you.* He dried his hands.

When he went to the living room, everyone was snoozing. The boys had crashed on the floor. Isabel snored from her wheelchair. Mother and Maria had passed out on the couch, still clutching their wineglasses, the latter wheezing in her sleep. Slowly, carefully, Billy touched Maria's sleeping shoulders and soaked in the damage from her lungs. *Breathe easily, Maria.* He coughed. His chest filled with fire. But as he withdrew, her breathing became steady and calm, so Billy felt good. Coughing, he met Isabel's eyes.

"You're a good boy," she whispered from across the room.

Billy smiled. "Thanks."

"My granddaughter is in her room." She pointed down the hall. "Go see her."

Billy approached the door to Natalia's room, and immediately, his heart dunked into a soggy mug of angst. Tears flooded his eyes. *She's crying. Lost. Oh no.* He opened the door, slipped inside the tiny room, and wrapped himself around her quivering, sobbing body.

She quickly hugged him back. "Oh god." She pushed her face into his chest. "It's so unfair. I wish this wasn't just one day. I hate this."

Billy kissed her. As her tears filled his eyes, he gazed in awe at the many drawings pinned up on her walls. *Her creativity is so beautiful.*

"You're thinking about your papá," Billy said, seeing the broad-shouldered, mustached man in her mind. "When things are happy, that's when you miss him the most."

Natalia sniffled. "Yeah, but... I mean, at least I have family. I feel so spoiled, complaining about that when... look at you." She turned to Billy, her eyes raw and apologetic. "I don't want you to go into the tank again."

He lifted her chin. "Pain is pain. Tell me about him."

She smiled weakly. "Papá was just here one day and then gone. Poof. I hate that. Even today, some part of me always feels like the guy is just going to walk in here, smile, and say it was all a big joke. Not a funny one, y'know, but..."

"That'd be an *epic* joke, though." Billy grinned.

"Epically bad." Despite her tears, she chuckled. "I'm so scared that you're gonna disappear the same way, Billy. Like, we have this thing, it's so special, but then tomorrow? Who the hell knows? It's so hard to keep *fighting*, all the time, when I just want to lie here with you or run away..."

Billy held her. "I know."

"You do know." They gazed into each other's eyes. Then the fire from Maria's lungs burned through Billy's chest, and he coughed. Natalia examined him. "Hey, what's going on?"

"I absorbed the... the..." He coughed again. "The pain from your mom. Chest hurts like crazy."

"Damn, dude." Natalia smiled, hitting his shoulder. "I mean, that's so cool of you, but whoa, you really know how to hurt yourself all the time." She wiped her eyes again. "You're such a good person. I don't know why the hell you want to spend so much time with a loudmouth like me."

Billy took a deep breath. Butterflies swirled in his stomach. *This is the moment.* "I'll tell you why." He kissed her hand. "Because I love you, Natalia Gonzalez."

Natalia's lower lip quivered. "I... you just said... me?"

"Yeah. I love you." Billy beamed. He kissed her, and they fell sideways against the wall. Their hearts pounded. Her legs wrapped around him.

"I love you too!" she cried, kissing him passionately. They crashed into the wall again, and she laughed. "Okay, this isn't going to work." She jumped out of bed and pulled him into the corridor. "C'mon, you."

"Huh?"

She didn't answer but simply tugged his hand and guided him back through the living room, past all the sleeping bodies. Isabel glared up at them, and Natalia waved. "Going to play in the snow, Abuelita! Be right back."

The old woman nodded, muttering to herself, and Natalia giggled. They tiptoed to the kitchen, put on their coats, and stepped outside onto the snowy walkway, where dozens of other little windows were lit up across the parking lot. Billy started to panic—*I definitely can't leave this complex*—but Natalia dragged him to the next apartment. The lights were off. "Nobody lives here right now," she whispered with a shushing motion. She jiggled the lock until the door opened, and she drew him into the dark room.

Billy's head whirled. *Sometimes I feel like this girl can get away with anything.*

The apartment was pitch-black. Empty. "We don't have much time." She shuffled through her jacket pocket, took out a handful of tealight candles, and placed them on the windowsill. She lit the candles, and the fiery glow instantly reminded Billy of the cabin in the mountains.

Billy ran his hand over the flames and smiled at her. "These are cool."

Natalia winked. "Yeah." She took off her shoes, removed her jacket, and started undoing the buttons of her shirt.

He shivered. "Hold on. What are you doing?"

"You're the psychic." She laughed. "You already *know* what I'm doing."

Billy swallowed. *Holy shit, this is really happening.* She finished unbuttoning her shirt, and she moved closer to him. Their bodies shivered together. Billy ran his hands down her shoulders. "Natalia, are you sure that... uh...?"

"Yeah, I'm sure," she whispered. Her shirt fell behind her shoulders. She took out a small, circular piece of plastic from her pocket. He nervously pulled off his black T-shirt, and she inched up to him, stepping on his toes. She kissed his chest, his shoulders, and his stomach. "*Te amo.*"

Billy took her into his arms. *Did she just say...? Yes, she did.* He smiled. "I love you too."

With the candlelight guiding them, they slowly took off what remained of each other's clothes, trembling with every step, and discovered one another's gangly, inexperienced bodies for the first time. Billy lay on the floor, and as they kissed, she mounted him. Her legs curled around his sides. Memories were unlocked from her muscles, flooding into him. Emotions ran hot between them. Ripples of energy pulsed through their thrusts. Their heartbeats aligned. Their teenage goose bumps gave way to adult sweat, and their naked forms—which moments before had been unfamiliar acquaintances—joined together to become one.

67

Billy could have stayed forever in that candlelit room, with Natalia lying across him. He smiled into the darkness. *This is it. Right here. The best moment of my life.* He lifted her chin and kissed her again. *As long as I hold on to this memory, I'll be okay. I'll get through those nights in the dark tank. I'll find her again on the other side.* His fingers ran down her bare thigh, eliciting a shiver, then played with her belly button.

She laughingly pushed his hand away. "Stop."

"You shouldn't hate it so much." He hugged her. "Nothing weird about it."

"You're just blind apparently. It's a superweird shape." She kissed his neck. "Listen, we should get together for those Jewish holidays too. What's next? Hanukkah?"

Billy grinned. "Sounds good."

She squeezed him. "Hey, how much longer have we got?"

"Oy vey." He sighed. "I guess we should get going."

"That sucks."

They separated, put on their clothes, and walked back into the snowy outside, where frost rose from their breaths. Holding hands, they trudged back down the icy walkway. They stopped in front of Natalia's doorway and gazed out at the shimmering windows across the parking lot. *So many people eating Thanksgiving dinner. So many families. So much love.*

Natalia reached for the door handle, but Billy stopped her. "Wait," he said.

She smiled. "Okay."

She took his hand, flashed her dynamite smile—*I love that smile, so much*—and pulled him down the stairs, beneath the streetlamps, and out into the snowy center of the parking lot. Snowflakes fluttered around them. Breezes blew. The guards stood outside their cars, holding guns, but somehow, none of that mattered. *We're alone in our hearts.*

Natalia raced ahead and twirled between the lights, glowing so radiantly that Billy felt as if he was in a dream. "Come dance with me!" she called out.

Billy joined her, holding her hips. "I don't really know how to dance."

"Music helps, but—"

"Okay. I have an idea." He reached down into the pocket of his coat, took out his dad's dinky old phone, and gave her one of the earbuds. "This is a song that means a lot to me."

"It's going to be another eighties band, isn't it?" She laughed. "Maybe The Police again? Or A-Ha..."

"Yeah. Collective Soul." He grinned. "The song is called 'The World I Know.'"

He and Natalia put in their earbuds and held each other, and as they danced, the song gently reverberated through them, its high notes and its plunging ones beating through their hearts.

Natalia snuggled close to him. "You're beautiful," she whispered into his chest. "I'm never going to let you go, okay?"

They danced between the cars, snow settling on their shoulders. "I love you," he replied, loving how it felt to say those three words. The music weaved through them. The gentle glow of the streetlamps illuminated the spiraling expanse of crystalline fractals cascading around them. *They look like tiny stars.* As they moved to the song, it felt like they were twirling between galaxies, traversing the cosmos.

"Hey, when we go back inside..." Natalia's voice was shaky. "I have a project to show you. I'm almost done, but I've been working on it for so long, and... uh... I just feel like it's important for you to see it today."

"Your drawing." He nodded.

"Hey!" She flashed a big smile and hit his chest. "No peeking in my brain, mister!"

"Okay." He laughed. "But I can't wait to see it."

"It makes me nervous as hell to show you. So for right now, just hold me." She curled back into his arms, and they resumed dancing until the song ended. In the silence, they stared into each other's eyes. "One more kiss," she said, "then we go inside, and I show you my drawing. Deal?"

They kissed again. Though their skin was icy, the space between their mouths was warm. Billy gripped her tightly. *This feels so good. So right.* She clung onto him. He kissed her neck, her cheek, her lips, and—

Click.

Natalia shuddered away from him. "B-Billy..." Her lip trembled.

More clicks reverberated through the night air. Footsteps pounded the asphalt. Engines revved up. All of it took Billy by surprise. *Wait, what...? I don't feel anyone behind me.* He turned around as three armored trucks screeched into the parking lot and opened their doors to reveal dozens of men in body armor, pointing machine guns in his direction. *What the hell?* Glowing red dots appeared on his chest, revealing snipers hidden in the neighboring apartments. The men circled around him, and Natalia nuzzled close. His heart pounded, remembering his family's execution in Beth Shalom. *God, this feels so familiar.* He spun around. *Except...*

"Billy Jakobek!" one of the men shouted. "Surrender yourself!"

I don't feel any of them. No emotions, no thoughts... they're even less human than the bodyguards. Billy couldn't understand it. *How did I not feel this coming?* He and Natalia exchanged confused glances.

She shouted to the men, "What's with the stupid-ass drama, guys? The deal was—"

The back of an armored truck slid open. Caleb Thorne stepped out, aiming a gun at Natalia's face. Thorne smiled, but when Billy tried to pierce into his mind—to feel anything—the void was overwhelming.

"Game over, kids," Thorne said.

68: Natalia

In seconds, the snowy parking lot transformed from a peaceful haven to a beehive of clicking guns, armored men, and laser sights. Natalia spun around, so stunned that she could barely process what was going on around her. The aim of Caleb Thorne's gun—pointed right at her face—was the only thing that anchored her to reality. *Creepy motherfucker.*

"Don't mess with me, Gonzalez." Thorne cocked the hammer. He reeked of alcohol and sweat, had blood running down his collarbone, and looked far from the crisp, clean businessman she knew. "We're taking the subject back in, and if you try to rush me, I'll blow your head off."

Natalia threw her hands up. "Dude, what the fuck are you doing? We had a deal. You were always going to—"

"Change of plans." Thorne smirked. "The subject isn't going back to Kaiser House. Me, him, and that little *Shape* inside him are saying bye-bye to this miserable town, and there's nothing you can do to stop it."

Natalia's heart pounded. "Why are you making such a big scene?" she asked, but the sweaty grin on Thorne's face told her the answer. *He just wants to see me suffer, to dominate me. That's why he's here instead of Linus. Holy shit, this guy is unhinged.* Shuddering at the realization of how much Thorne hated her, Natalia tried to move away from the gun. "You can't do this," she sputtered. "I'll make sure that the workers rally—"

Thorne repointed the gun at her. "I don't need this factory anymore, sweetie. Which makes you, well... quite expendable." He gestured toward his black-suited gunmen, and they closed in on Billy.

"I'm going to demand—" she started.

"You'll never see him again," Thorne said flatly then turned to Billy. "And you, kid? You're going to come with us without complaint, or I'll shoot your little girlfriend right here and follow it up by shooting her entire family. Understood?"

Billy's eyes became slits. A vein bulged in his forehead. The fire inside him grew so hot that Natalia felt as if she was standing beside a furnace. *Oh no.* Billy turned to face Thorne, and Natalia shook him.

"Billy, be—"

"Don't try anything!" Thorne yelled.

Billy marched forward, unwavering and unafraid, his hands clenched into fists. As soldiers closed in around him, guns clicked and laser lights glimmered on his chest. Billy stormed right up to the drunken, sweaty businessman.

"Get away from her," Billy growled, and his ethereal voice sent waves rippling through the asphalt. The streetlamps flickered. Natalia fell to her knees, gasping in pain as spikes dug into her pores. Images of the dark tank—Billy trapped, alone—flashed through her mind. *Pain, pain, pain, loneliness, lost.*

Biting back on it all, she looked up to see Billy addressing Thorne with a demonic scowl. "Put the gun in your mouth," Billy said.

Thorne laughed. "No."

Billy's eyes widened, and he fell backward.

Natalia's heart plunged to her stomach. *Oh, shit.*

Billy turned to face all the men around him. "Drop your guns," he said in a cracked voice.

The men didn't listen. They closed ranks, guns still in the air, totally unaffected. One of them took out a pair of handcuffs. Thorne, still chuckling to himself, brushed past Billy and grabbed Natalia. He choked her in the crook of his arm.

"Don't touch me!" she screamed, and his salty palm closed over her mouth. As she kicked at Thorne's shins, the businessman seemed to feel no pain, as if he were hopped up on drugs.

"Lmmm... mmm... oo!" she cried out, muffled, and then stopped as Thorne pressed his gun into her temple.

"Let her go!" Billy shouted. But as his voice ripped through Natalia's ears, bringing tears to her eyes, ripping up her intestines, Thorne didn't waver. *Oh crap, he's immune.*

The businessman rubbed Natalia's buzz cut, pushed the gun deeper into her temple, and said, "You can't control me, Jakobek. You can't control any of us. We've got your blood coursing through our veins. Now, say goodbye to your girlfriend—forever—and get in the truck like a good little boy." He squeezed her throat, gagging her. "Or give me an excuse to pull the trigger."

Natalia felt Billy's rage cool into mortal terror. The look on her boyfriend's face was unlike anything she'd ever seen before. *Don't give up, Billy!* She squirmed in Thorne's grasp, but his chokehold on her was so tight she could barely breathe. To her horror, the door of her family's apartment swung open. "Mmmfff!" *Oh God, Mamá, Abuelita, Juan, Carlos, don't come outside, don't...*

The door quickly reclosed—to Natalia's immense relief—and Mother's heels came running down the stairs and into the parking lot. "Caleb!" Mother yelled, her tiny blue eyes pointed with anger. "What are you doing? I was going to bring him home—"

"Taking back company property." Thorne's tone softened a bit, though his alcohol-soaked breath cut into Natalia's nostrils. "My apologies for the unexpected change of plans. I had a... shall we say, a revelation." He squeezed Natalia's neck, making her sputter.

"The girl—"

"A casualty if the subject doesn't obey orders."

"You sick fuck." Mother gasped. She spat in Thorne's face. "Your father would be ashamed of you."

Whoa. Natalia was taken aback. So was Thorne, whose body shivered in Mother's presence. *He's totally in love with her. That's fucking weird.*

Thorne wiped the saliva from his face with disgust—momentarily moving the gun from Natalia's head—then quickly choked her again. "Get in your car," he directed Mother. "Now. Drive away. Back off—or don't back off, and see what happens to your little boy, Jamie."

Mother's eyes widened, and she backed away. "I..."

"Go."

Mother opened her mouth—and closed it. She backed away. *She knows he's not kidding.*

The woman then hurried off, jumped in her car, and drove away into the night. As Thorne watched her go, Natalia again tried to free herself from Thorne's grasp. His grip was too tight.

"Get in the truck, Billy," Thorne said as Billy advanced on him again. "Listen, kid, all of my men have direct orders to kill your girlfriend's family. You can't stop them unless I tell them not to. So, either you and I go off together on a new adventure, or the illegals die. Got it?"

Billy stopped, and he stared into Natalia's eyes for a long moment. He looked at the soldiers around him then glanced up at the apartment—where all of Natalia's family were still inside—and back at Natalia. His eyes welled up. "I love you, Natalia." Then he lowered his head. "I surrender."

The gunmen jumped in, closed handcuffs around his wrists, and injected him with a needle. Immediately, Billy's legs wavered. The men caught him, carted him to the truck, and threw his tumbling body into the back. Natalia gasped for air. *No!* She tore free from Thorne's grasp and barreled forward as Thorne scrambled to catch her. She launched right into the crowd of gunmen. "Billy!" she shrieked.

An octopus of arms seized her. Squeezed her. Blocked her path. She kicked. Fought them. *No, no, no. You can't take him!* Billy's crumpled body became a shadow in the truck, and Natalia could no longer see the whites of his eyes. "Billy!" Tears streaked down her face. *I'll never let you go!* Thorne caught Natalia and yanked her back. She turned, swerved out of his grasp, and punched him square in the face. He stumbled back, too shocked to react. She punched him again, splitting his lip. "You're not going to win, asshole!" she shouted. "You'll never—"

"Fucking idiot," Thorne muttered, wiping blood from his chin. Natalia swung for his face again, and—

Bang!

The gun flashed. Pain tore through her back like a lightning bolt. Everything went white. Hot. She spun into the snow, falling flat on her back. She tried to move. She couldn't. Her torso and legs were pinned to the ice-crusted asphalt. Hot blood pooled around her waist, forming puddles around her. Staring into the sky of stars and snow, she heard Billy cry out for her.

"Natalia!"

His voice was distant, hazy—and then it cut off as the metal door of the truck rattled shut. The engine revved, and the vehicle drove away, leaving Natalia alone and wounded in the parking lot. Through blood and tears, she whispered, "Don't go..."

Billy was gone. She tried to move, and the lightning bolt ripped down her spine again. *Can't move... legs. Can't feel... oh god...*

Thorne loomed over her. "Bitch." He stepped onto her chest with his polished shoe, crushing her ribs, and pointed the gun at her face again. "Guess you're not the boss anymore, then." His fake grin had never looked more demonic.

He pushed down with his foot, and her entire spine screeched in agony. "Aaahh!" she screamed.

Blood fizzled around her. *I can't stand up.* Thorne pressed down harder. Her back popped. Her ribs scratched against each other. She screamed again. Her vision went white with pain, and when she could see again, Thorne's smile hovered above her. "Natalia, dear, I want you to know"—his boozy exhalations landed on her face—"this is personal. Very personal. I want you to feel every bit of pain I can give you. And I'm going to make sure your little boyfriend sees it all."

Mr. Linus appeared beside Thorne, holding a camera, and his lens zoomed in on Natalia's bleeding body. She tried to lift herself, grunting, but couldn't budge. Thorne stood up, nudged his foot underneath her back—its leather surface skidding against the raw flesh that the bullet had ripped open—and flipped Natalia onto her stomach like a ragdoll. She screamed, landing hard on her stomach.

"If it helps you find purpose"—Thorne's voice lurked above her—"then please, simply consider your death a sacrifice to your country." Thorne cleared his throat. "Now, gentlemen, finish off the rest of the household. There's a mother, a grandmother in a wheelchair, and two rotten little kids. We want no survivors. And Linus? Film everything."

Natalia moaned in anguish. She lifted her head from the mushy red snow and coughed out blood. She gargled out attempts at words. The men marched past her, ignoring her bloodied body, and stomped their way up to the apartment. Natalia screamed out, "Mamá, run! Abuel—"

Thorne kicked her in the face. Blood sprayed across the snow. Hard pebbles fell onto her tongue, and she realized they were teeth. "Shut up," Thorne muttered.

Fuck you. Natalia spat the bloodied teeth onto his shoe. She tried to lift her body, but pain shot down her spine, and she collapsed back into the snow. *Oh god, I can't feel my legs.* She tried again, but her hands weren't strong enough to support her.

She heard pounding footsteps and looked up to see the gunmen busting down the apartment door. "No!" she shrieked, but her cry was cut off by rattling gunfire. She recognized the sound of her mother's scream, followed by a body dropping to the floor. *No, no, no, Mamá, my family... no!* More gunfire rattled through the air. The lights in every apartment window went off.

A little boy screamed. *Carlos!* Another spray of gunshots shattered the kitchen windows. Suddenly, Juan came running out the front door, a high-pitched wail tearing from his lungs. Natalia lunged forward in the snow—but her body wouldn't follow. "Juan, keep running!" she gargled.

Juan saw her. He paused. "Big sister?" His eyes widened.

"Don't stop!" she cried as a soldier trudged out the front door. Juan turned around—too late—as the soldier shot him. His little body fell to the floor, and Natalia sobbed, remembering how just a few weeks before, she'd held him in the bathroom, telling him about Papá. *Please don't be dead. Please, Juan, please...*

Another scream rattled from the apartment, and a wheelchair went spinning out the front door. "Abuelita..." she groaned. Natalia's vision darkened. *Stay awake.* The gunfire died down, and all she could feel was the cold. Her fingers felt frostbitten. The blood puddle around her had gone icy.

Thorne's polished shoes crunched in the snow before her, and his chuckle reverberated through the darkness. "Stubborn girl. Enjoy your last moments, dear. Good night, and God bless America."

Thorne kicked her in the face again. She barely felt it. Her lips were chapped. Her face was frozen and cut all over. *Can't feel my legs... can't move...* She closed her eyes and collapsed her head into the ice, hearing the cars roll away, leaving her behind.

It's over.

Somewhere in this haze, after what felt like hours, she heard a siren. Sometime after that—after another period of nothingness, blackness, and pain, she felt herself being lifted on a stretcher. *No, I don't want to be alive... let me die...*

The lightning bolt tore through her spine again, and she screamed. An oxygen mask was placed over her mouth. She sobbed, as the faces of her dead family members circled through her mind.

Nothing matters anymore. The shadows closed in on her. *My truth was a lie.*

Part VIII:

Binah

69: Natalia

Natalia Gonzalez was asleep, but she was alive. Somehow, she knew that. Occasionally, she would stir into a strange sort of half consciousness. Whenever this happened, searing agony ripped across her flesh like a whip. The white flash that attacked her pupils blinded her.

They're all dead.

She didn't want to wake up in the world she'd left behind. *I can't feel my legs.*

Tears slid down her cheeks like raindrops. She heard the voices. And whenever she opened her eyes, the dark figure stood before her, blue light flickering from its gaze. Billy's bloodied face sprouted from its chest, and he gasped, "Don't get in the way."

Whenever she saw this, she closed her eyes again. *God, please, let me die. Don't make me wake up.*

70

Cold oxygen rushed down Natalia's lungs. Fluorescent light ripped through her corneas. *Awake.* Everything burned. Perspiration trickled down her sides. Monitors beeped in her ears. Her skull felt like nails had been driven into it with a hammer.

She closed her eyes again. *Can't do it. Just want to go back to sleep... please, back to sleep...* She tried to roll over, but her body was too stiff. Her muscles tensed. *So goddamn dry.* She gasped for air again. *Water.* Her heartbeat monitor beeped beside her, and she squeezed her eyes shut, not wanting to wake up.

"Hey," Felix said. "It's okay."

Felix. She patted around with her hands, using her fingertips to draw conclusions that her eyes weren't yet capable of. She touched a metal side rail, then a long rubber cord. *Hospital bed.* Felix's hand took hers and squeezed. Tears filled her eyes. *Hold me. Don't let go.* She listened to her friend's gentle breathing, and as she opened her eyes, the hazy world came back to life. The square hospital room featured obnoxiously cutesy wallpaper depicting pink flowers. *Like that makes me feel better.* A Thorne-S650 television hung from the wall.

Dried blood was under her fingernails. She choked back vomit. "Felix," she gasped in a crumpled voice on the edge of tears. She shook his arm. "Felix. *Felix.*"

"I'm here, Nat." Felix sat on the bed and hugged her tightly.

She quivered in his embrace. *Great, here come the waterworks.* She drenched his T-shirt with a flood of tears. "Don't you dare let me go," she choked out, and he gripped her even tighter. Wiping her eyes, she mumbled, "Thank you for being here." Her throat was dry.

Carefully, he released her. "Well, yeah." His eyes were damp, and his normally cocky smile looked fragile. "Been here every day, man. You're my best friend. Just waiting for you to wake up—"

"I didn't want to wake up." She coughed.

Felix moved to a little plastic chair beside the bed. "Whatever, dude. C'mon, have a drink." He handed her a Styrofoam cup.

She inspected it. "This is just water, right? Not vodka or..."

He laughed. "You think I'm a psycho?"

Natalia cracked a smile, and she gulped down the most satisfying ice water that she'd ever tasted. Just as she was starting to feel okay, a sad flicker in Felix's expression struck her, and the grave reality of her situation came rushing back. *They're dead.* She teared up again. *Mamá. Abuelita. Juan. Carlos. Papá.* She squeezed Felix's hand. "No..." she whimpered. "No, no, I can't do this."

Felix forced a smile. "I'm here." Then, soberly, he reached beneath his chair and held up a backpack. "Hey, so, I brought some of your things." He sorted through. "Jewelry, tarot cards, clothes... and this." He took out her sketchbook and gave it to her.

She hugged it to her chest. "Oh my god, thank you." Somehow, she'd never even considered the thought of her sketchbook being lost. *Jeez, Felix really does know me. I'm so lucky to have him.*

"I was crazy scared." Felix looked away and exhaled. "This BS was all over social media. Thought you were dead. And then, like, the way Thorne is spinning the news..."

Natalia jolted. "Fuck." *Thorne.* She shuddered, feeling the bruises on her face, the missing teeth. *The way he stood over me.*

Felix continued. "And that stuff about gangs, terrorists—"

"Hold it." Natalia shook the cobwebs from her head. "What the hell are you talking about, Felix?"

"Damn, dude. That's right, you haven't heard yet." He rubbed his eyes. "I mean, I don't know what really happened at your apartment, but I know that Thorne's got the propaganda machine in full swing—"

"Tell me."

"All right." He sighed. "He's using the standard racist lines about Latino gang wars, blah blah, but he's claiming the 'gang' who shot up your fam was connected to this imaginary Middle Eastern terrorist cell he blamed the factory incident on—"

"Holy crap." Natalia reached out for more water, and Felix handed it to her. She drank it with shaking hands. "People don't believe this, do they?"

"Uh..." He collapsed his head into his palms. "I dunno, Nat. Thorne did a whole town hall on TV, with Senator Klein and some other douchebags. He's even claiming that Billy is the one who shot your family for them—"

"Fuck!" She threw the water across the room, and Felix went silent. Natalia's mouth tasted like blood. "Billy, is he...?"

"In confinement again. Rumor is they stuffed him underneath Thorne's base in Johnson City for experiments. I dunno."

Natalia's heart plummeted. *Oh my god, this is so awful.* "The strikes, are they... are they...?"

"People got scared, Nat. They went back to work the day after you got shot up." Felix's voice quivered. "Natalia, what really happened on Thanksgiving? I'm assuming Thorne's goons came in?"

Natalia stared into Felix's tender eyes and saw her battered reflection. *I don't want to tell him. So humiliating.* She remembered what it had felt like to lie in the snow, bleeding out, totally helpless. *Thorne stood over me. Kicked me in the face. Gunshots. Screams. The camera. He killed my family, and I couldn't do anything.*

"We need to change the narrative," she said. "C'mon, Felix. Help me out of bed."

"Nat—"

"Let's go." She tried to swivel her legs out of bed. They wouldn't move. She couldn't feel them. It was like they'd been frozen and stapled to the mattress. She pushed again, and she frowned at Felix. "Hey, what's going on with my legs?"

Felix looked away. "Aw, crap. They're... you don't remember?"

Natalia's heart pounded. She remembered the gunshot. *Oh no, not that. Please, not that.* She heaved outward, trying to spin her legs out of the bed. They collided against the bedrail like pale sticks—but she couldn't feel them. *Oh god.* "Felix." She was shaking. "What the hell is going on with my legs?"

"I'm sorry," he whispered.

"That's not a fucking answer!" She sat upright, collapsed, and sat upright again then touched her bruised knees. Her fingers felt the cold skin of her legs, but the legs themselves felt nothing. She pushed harder. Nothing. "No, no, no..." she whimpered. She tried to wiggle her toes, to bend her ankles, and nothing happened. Tears ran down her cheeks. "No, please, this can't be happening."

"The bullet, uh..." Felix stammered. "Doctors said that your spine, it... below the waist, you..."

"No!" She fell forward, sobbing over the legs she couldn't feel, grabbed her knees, and squeezed the bones. She slapped them. She hit them. She saw the flesh bend in, but only her hands felt the contact. It was like poking wood, rock, something dead. *My legs are dead.* She remembered walking through the hallways of the high school. *Never again.* She thought about racing up the stairs of the fire tower with Billy. *Never again.* Running around the playground when she was a little girl, into the hugging arms of her father. *Never.* Swimming, kicking. *No.* Wrapping her legs around Billy as he kissed her. *All gone.*

"Please be a nightmare." She squeezed her icy toes. "There must be a way to fix this. A surgery. Felix, please tell me something."

Felix said nothing—which, in turn, said everything. Natalia broke down sobbing in Felix's arms. He rocked her back and forth, assuring her that things would be okay, but Natalia knew better. Her family was dead. Billy was gone. The revolution had failed. Thorne had won. Things would never be okay again.

71: Caleb

The outdoor café near the top of the Thorne Century Unlimited Building offered beautiful views but a lonely atmosphere. Caleb wanted to be happy there, but as he sat beside a flaming ambience heater, with the metropolis of Johnson City's financial district spread below him and a one-thousand-dollar cup of coffee in hand, his feelings were mixed. When he'd built that café, he'd planned romantic evenings, social gatherings, and cheerful events he could savor photos of. Instead, the only people around him—from the guards to the waiter—were paid to be there.

Despite the cold, Caleb felt sweaty and feverish. His stomach was knotted up. *I need another shot of psycho blood*, he thought, downing his coffee. *It will help me think straight.* Caleb gestured for the waiter to come over.

"Yes, sir?"

"I think I'll retire to my room." He pushed his drink away with a pinched face. "Inform the barista that my coffee was disappointing."

Caleb took the elevator up to his penthouse apartment. At the door, he stopped to loosen the top button of his collar. His skin was so sweaty it disgusted him. *Feels like I've been dipped in olive oil. It's these goddamn shots. I need to stop, or I'll become addicted.* He opened the door, casting those thoughts aside. *That's foolish. Only weak people like my father get addicted. I know how to stop.*

The apartment was dark. "Lights on," Caleb said, and the lights did as they were told. Spotting the leather sectional, he was hit with a massive wave of fatigue. *Sleep would feel so pleasant.* He'd thought that his insomnia and his hallucinatory terrors would go away when he left Heaven's Hole, but instead, the situation had worsened. He'd also expected Roseanna to follow him to Johnson City, but the twen-ty-carat emerald-cut engagement ring he'd bought for her sat unloved on his coffee table, and it infuriated him. *She could be here with me, and instead, she's still in that pitiful meteor crater, crying her nights away like the fucking woman she is. So goddamn disappointing.*

He lay down on the sectional, reached into his pocket, and re-moved the silver Star of David necklace that he'd stolen from Billy Jakobek's unconscious body. He smiled, twirling the Jewish symbol in the light. *Keepsake.* Everywhere he went, he kept it next to the knife as a reminder of his victory.

"TV on." The TV screen flashed to white, so he said, "Jakobek." Immediately, the television displayed live grainy footage of the boy locked up in the basement of the building. Caleb sat upright. *At least I have my subject.* Sixty-three floors down, in the darkness, Billy was bolted to a table, his veiny limbs pulled into an X. He was strung up with needles, constantly pumping blood and energy into an array of surrounding machines and, most importantly, constantly awake. *That's the key.* Twenty-four hours a day, every day, Billy was kept con-scious with a steady cocktail of drugs and forced to watch an endless stream of violent footage as his emotional energies were sucked out of him. *The more pain he puts out, the more emotion bombs we can de-velop. He has a few years left in him yet.*

"You're doing good, kid." Caleb studied Billy's dead-eyed, drool-ing face. *He's not screaming anymore. I've finally worn him down. Take that, Kaley. I took a boy too powerful for his own good, and I overpow-ered him.* Caleb went to the kitchen and poured himself a glass of Scotch. "To my success." He took a drink.

"It's not enough," a voice inside him said, snickering. His stom-ach squelched.

Sweat ran down his back. He gazed around the room, and the shadows whispered, "Feed us."

He touched the pulsing wound on his neck, which was still not totally healed, and the strange voice whispered, "Put me back inside you."

"Yes, perhaps one more time is adequate." Caleb opened the fridge, flicked a needle, and injected it into his neck.

The door opened. Mr. Linus stepped into the room. "Mr. Thorne, I need to—" Linus's jaw snapped shut at the sight of Thorne shooting up his own neck. "Mr. Thorne, you should have the doctor do... do... ah..."

Caleb finished pushing the plunger. "What the fuck are you doing here, Linus?" The injection site burned. Caleb threw the needle down. "How dare you come here unannounced?"

The world swayed and turned. The shadow voices deepened. *God damn it, Linus is going to give me a bad trip.* Caleb drank more Scotch, looked up at Linus, and tried to ignore the fact that Kaley had appeared behind him, giggling aloud as blood gushed down her engorged stomach.

"Be easy on him." Kaley slithered. "He's loyal."

Caleb sighed. "Sorry, Linus." He poured more Scotch. "What do you want?"

Linus's face became even redder than usual. He adjusted his tie, clearly uncomfortable. "Um." He looked down. "News from the Hole."

Caleb squeezed his glass. "The hospital?"

"Yeah. Talked to the administrator—"

"I see." Caleb's entire body tightened. *I should've injected a double shot.* "So has that little brat died yet?"

"Mr. Thorne, she... woke up." He turned away, as if afraid something might hit his face. "Gonzalez is alive."

The Scotch glass shattered in Caleb's hand. He barely noticed. *That miserable bitch.* Linus jumped back. Shards of glass fell to the floor and embedded themselves into Caleb's palm. Scotch and blood ran down his jacket. *She defied me again.*

"Mr. Thorne," Linus said in a panic. "Are you okay?"

"Make a call for me." Caleb picked the glass fragments from his hand. "An appointment for this evening."

"With whom, sir?"

Caleb looked at Kaley for approval. She nodded, and he faced Linus again. "Billy Jakobek."

72: Natalia

Thorne Hospital was nestled in the highest corner of the crater, and the big windows of the upstairs lobby, right next to the gift shop, overlooked the town. Far away, amid the snow and fog, the light of the fire tower blinked. Natalia rolled her wheelchair closer to the window to get a better look, but the foot pedals of her chair crashed into the wall.

"Terrific." She sighed, tried again, and hit the wall again. "Sucks."

Stealing one last look, she spun her chair around and rolled back to the little corner table she'd placed her stuff on. Her sketchbook was there, untouched. Opening it—with all its pictures of her ruined life—just reminded her of everything she'd lost, so she'd instead been doodling on a less intimidating paper napkin, which was now scrawled with the faces of her dead family. The pen, her hands, and the napkin were slathered with enough black art blood to fill an ocean. Unfortunately, drawing her family had only made her feel worse.

She adjusted herself in the chair with a groan—no matter what she did, her legs always slid forward—and watched the people moving through the gift shop. Most of them, she noted, were surprisingly cheerful for being in a hospital. They traded jokes, flirted, laughed, bought things for their loved ones, and exchanged stories. Natalia glared angrily at their feet step-step-stepping across the linoleum. *They don't know what it feels like. I know I didn't.*

Natalia redirected her attention to the sitting area, where glum families gazed at their phones and didn't talk. *Easier to look at sad people than happy ones, that's for sure.* One family, an old couple and a little boy, sat in silence. She lifted the lid of her sketchbook, started to draw, then slammed her pen down. *Whatever. Nobody cares what I draw.*

She closed her eyes and licked the stitches inside her lips. Her mouth hadn't healed from Thorne's kicks. Everything still tasted like blood, and it constantly reminded her of what it had felt like to lie in the snow at Thorne's feet, helpless. *Don't think about that.* She imagined the looks on Juan and Carlos's faces when the men broke into the apartment with their guns. *I need a joint. A drink. Maybe another bullet—to the head this time.* She squeezed her fingers around her shaved head. *Might as well just burn this sketchbook. Kill off the last bit of my soul that's left. Fuck everything.*

"Hi, miss," said a tiny voice.

Natalia sprang upright. A little girl had approached her, her red shoes twirled together in the iconic pose of shyness. Her enormous brown eyes glistened at Natalia with a look of awe.

"Hi." Natalia cleared her throat.

The girl adorably peeked up at her. "Are you Natalia Gonzalez?" Her cadence lifted. "You look like her."

"Yeah."

"Oh my gosh, that's so cool!" The girl beamed. "You're my hero." She hopped up and down, and Natalia stared at her in confusion. *Whoa, me?* The girl inched closer, leaning against Natalia's wheel, then spoke in a quieter voice. "I'm sorry about your legs. Do they hurt?"

Natalia wanted to collapse back into her pile, to ignore the girl, but she couldn't. Not after seeing the excitement and admiration—the things Natalia had felt for her mother, father, and grandmother—replaying in those big brown eyes. She swiveled her wheelchair to face the girl and forced herself to smile. "What, these stupid things? Nah." Natalia knocked on her icy knee. "They don't hurt. Believe it or not, if you poked 'em right now, I wouldn't even feel it."

"No way." The girl giggled.

Natalia forced another smile. "No?" She pinched both knees. "You'll just have to believe me, then."

"Hmm." The little girl furrowed her brow then shrugged. "Well, I hope you go back on TV soon. My mom and dad always say you're making things better."

Natalia saw herself in those glistening brown eyes. *I would have asked someone, too, if I was her age.* The girl's eyes had no judgment. No prejudice. Natalia choked back tears. "What's your name?"

"Alicia." The girl put her hand out. "Nice to meet you."

"Same here." She shook Alicia's hand.

"Feel better soon!" The little girl twirled away—dancing in her little shoes, like Natalia would never dance again—and returned to the gift shop, which her family was emerging from, seemingly unaware that their girl had been talking to strangers.

Natalia spun her wheelchair around to go back to the window, but her wheel got caught in the legs of the table. *Aw, crap.* She spun backward, and this action pulled the table with her, making it clatter against the floor. Everyone in the room turned to look at her. *Man, this sucks.*

Alicia's father approached to help, and Natalia raised her hand. "I'm okay!" she said, dislodging her wheels from the table. "Everything's okay."

It's not okay. She turned around and rolled back to the window. Her pedals banged against the wall. "Stupid damn things," she muttered, reaching down and disconnecting them. They collapsed to the floor. Her legs hung limply from the seat, dangling in the air, but Natalia didn't care. She wheeled forward, finally able to touch the window. *Much better.* She placed her palm against the cold glass. She stared into the blinking light of the fire tower.

"Can you feel me out there, Billy?" she whispered. "Give me a sign."

She closed her eyes. She waited to feel his warm energies pulse through her, but all she felt were icy pins stabbing into her wrist. She removed her hand from the window.

73: Caleb

As the elevator slid down into the bowels beneath the building, the heat rose in Caleb's stomach. His eyes stung. His neck wound chafed against his collar. *This is so unprofessional*, he thought, counting the floors down. *I've sacrificed so much for this project, and now it's time that the project does something for me.* His stomach squelched, hinting that more diarrhea and vomiting—like he'd suffered for the past month—could be on the way later.

"This is the right choice." Kaley slid beside him, clutching his hand with her cold, dead, imaginary fingers.

"Of course it is," Caleb said, and the metal doors slid open, revealing a long, windowless hallway flanked by security guards. Thorne scooped up his briefcase and walked to the guards, who patted him down.

"Good evening, Mr. Thorne," a guard said.

Caleb cleared his throat. "Evening. I'm going to see the subject. Reasons are classified."

"Right this way." The guard led him past more guards, around the bend, and through a metal detector. They ran his briefcase through twice and opened it, and the mustached man behind the screen flashed Caleb a worried glance. "Mr. Thorne, are you sure you need this... um... you know? Could be risky—"

"Quite sure." Caleb bristled.

The man looked down. "All right. Do you want a blood treatment before you go in?"

Caleb's gut twitched. *You want it. You know you do.* "Probably for the best." He lowered his collar. "Shoot me up."

The mustached man delivered the injection to Caleb's throat. It was weak, watered down—less than half the strength he usually enjoyed—but as his veins pulsed and electricity coursed down his spine, it felt good. "Much appreciated," Caleb grunted.

"Of course, sir. How many guards should come in with you?"

"None. I can handle the subject alone."

The man raised an eyebrow. Sweat dampened Caleb's armpits. *Don't look at me that way, or I'll fire you on the spot.* Caleb walked down the dark hall, past more security guards, and stopped at the end, where a metal vault door was marked with hazard symbols.

The security guard looked back. "Are you sure about this, sir? We are supposed to have two men accompany you."

Caleb slit his eyes. "Are you questioning my judgment?"

"No, sir." The man held up his hands. "We'll be right outside the door."

"Excellent." Caleb scanned his retina. The heavy locks churned within the machinery. The smell of fresh-cut steel wafted out, and the door squealed open. Taking one last look backward—as Kaley waved from behind the men—Caleb stepped into the dark room, and the door closed behind him.

In the shadows, his footsteps echoed through the buzzing ambience of hundreds of screens that hung from the walls and ceiling at every point in the room. Caleb didn't dare look at the footage—he didn't want those nasty visuals in his dreams—but he knew what the screens displayed: snuff films, torture videos, suicide jumpers screaming to their deaths, hospitals being bombed, families being separated, and any other monstrosities his propaganda team had dug up.

Caleb approached the upright table in the room's center, where Billy Jakobek was strapped down. "My god." Caleb covered his mouth. "Seems I did a number on you, boy, didn't I?"

Billy stared ahead with glassy, unfocused eyes. A strand of drool ran down his lips. His bare, hairless chest was covered in bulging veins, and the food deprivation—he'd been fed only via G-tube—had made the boy so skinny that his sweatpants barely clung to his waist. Billy's body was so plugged full of needles, tubes, and wires that he resembled a human porcupine. His blood ran into the room's machines in a steady drip. Though Caleb had watched the cameras every day, he felt sickened by the boy's physical presence and the smell of his teenage sweat. Right in front of Billy's eyes, a giant screen cycled through footage of the Gonzalez family being murdered. Caleb eyed this screen, watching as the old woman in the wheelchair, Isabel, was pumped full of bullets.

Caleb put his briefcase down, and he swerved the screen away from Billy's eyes. "An awful shame."

Billy's hollowed eye sockets peered upward. The boy sucked in his cheeks, which were so gaunt that his cheekbones stuck out like daggers. Caleb stepped closer, and despite the psycho-blood immunities coursing through him, Billy's negative energies sizzled through Caleb's gut, threatening to spill the contents of his bladder.

Caleb smiled. "Can you hear me, Billy?"

"I hear you," the boy said through bloodied lips.

The slight crack in Billy's voice reminded Caleb, just for a moment, that the creature before him was still a child, but he quickly sucked the feelings back inside him. "You ruined that girl's life, you know." He pointed at the screen.

Billy coughed. "Yeah."

"Natalia Gonzalez," Caleb said as the boy shuddered. *There's some life in him yet.* "Her family died because of you. And now, also because of you, she'll never walk again. Your contribution to my emotion bomb project has been wonderful, don't get me wrong, but what you did to that poor family... quite horrendous."

Billy's head dropped. He said nothing.

"I want to offer you a chance at redemption. You can do it for yourself. Do it for me. Do it for your country. But listen carefully,

Billy. I want you to finish the job." He unlatched the briefcase. "I'm going to have Ms. Gonzalez abducted tonight and brought here. I want you to put her out of her misery. Permanently."

The horror in Billy's expression was painfully raw. "I would never—"

"Perhaps *you* wouldn't." Caleb flicked a syringe filled with Billy's blood. "But the Shape will."

The boy recoiled. "No. I won't let... let..." He coughed through dry lips. "Won't..."

"Take a look at this, my boy." Caleb opened the briefcase wide and pointed at the array of vials labeled with different colors. "Each one of these activates a different emotional response in the person injected. Pride, rage, sadness, apathy, you name it. You might control others, Billy"—Caleb squeezed the boy's cold chin—"but I control you."

Billy shook Caleb's hand loose. "Never."

Caleb flicked the needle again—for show, mainly—and then put it down on a metal counter. He reached into his pocket and dangled Billy's Star of David necklace before the boy's gaping jaw.

Billy gasped. "That's mine."

"Not anymore." Caleb reached into the briefcase once more and withdrew the item that had caught the security guard's attention—a blowtorch. Then he hung the necklace from a hook over the table. "This came from your grandmother, didn't it?"

Billy's eyes became panicked. "Give it back." He jerked against his bonds.

Caleb's heart pounded with the energy of the psycho blood and the thrill of power. *I love this.* "Sterling silver." He ignited the blowtorch. "Such a soft, cheap metal. Such a perfect representation of the Jew you are."

"Give it back!"

Caleb pressed the flames to the necklace. The torch squealed. As Billy's screams became a vicious cough, he felt the boy's eyes boring into his skull—trying to peel his hands from the blowtorch—and he pressed onward. Liquid silver dripped off the chain, forming a tiny puddle on the table.

"Well, then." He clapped his hands. Caleb picked up the syringe. He stepped toward Billy, and the boy spat at him. Caleb wiped his face. "Good night, Billy." He injected the needle into Billy's neck and plunged it down. Billy jolted back. Then his head dropped, his eyes closed, and he slumped forward. Caleb tossed the needle aside, stepped away, and watched. *And good morning, Shape.*

Nothing happened. Caleb waited, checking his phone. A minute passed. Two minutes. Billy was still unconscious. *This is taking too long.* Then the hundreds of TV screens around the room flickered on and off.

"Billy?" Caleb looked around.

The screens went dead. The skeletal boy lifted his head. "Not Billy." Blue flames sparked from his eyes. "Not anymore."

Caleb's legs wobbled beneath him. "You're—" He stopped as shadows scuttled around like bats. He looked around. "What's that?" Whispers echoed through the room, bouncing between the steel walls, speaking in a language that sounded ancient, runic, almost alien. Billy bared his teeth in an animalistic grin, and black smoke puffed from his nostrils.

Caleb marched up to the boy. "Listen to me—" Caleb's voice was swallowed into nothingness. *My voice... my...*

The blue flames brightened, and as all the lights died out, Kaley giggled from the darkness. The floor dropped away, and Caleb went toppling into the nothing. Down, down, down...

"Where the fuck am I?" he roared into pitch-blackness.

A whisper crept into his ears. "You're somewhere else."

74: Caleb (Somewhere Else)

Caleb is in the dark. He can't speak anymore. He can barely breathe. All of his accomplishments, money, and power vanish into dust... invisible dust, coursing through his fingers until...

He is in a mansion. No dust. Perfectly clean. Expensive furniture. No people, no distractions. His tiny body—he is only six years old, with a bowl cut and a stained T-shirt—sits on a couch, hearing the maid vacuum upstairs. He's alone, totally alone, except for the buzzing TV in front of him playing his favorite cheesy sitcoms—programs where funny families make jokes, go on picnics, hug each other tightly, and do all the other things his family never does.

He slices a piece of paper across his palm, cutting it open. Blood seeps from the wound. He clenches it. Feels the sting. Something about it entrances him. When the maid whizzes by, rushing to her next task, he hides his hand beneath him. He doesn't want her to see it, bandage it, and take the blood away.

"I like it," he whispers.

"Because you are weak," replies Billy Jakobek.

Caleb tumbles off the couch in fright. Standing before him, invading his childhood memory, is the lanky, shirtless frame of Billy with his flaming blue eyes. But Billy isn't the one talking—not really. Though it's his mouth that moves, the misty blackness puffing from his lungs does not come from a human being. Caleb creeps closer, peering over the boy's shoulder, and sees a horrible spiderlike shadow creep across the wall.

"What the fuck have you done to me?" young Caleb asks.

Billy smirks but says nothing.

Caleb hates, hates, *hates* being shorter than Billy. He stands on the couch, elevating himself, and in his squeaky voice, he says, "You're the Shape now, yes?"

"Not quite." Billy's voice reverberates. "Billy is buried, not destroyed. The Shape is growing inside this body..." The boy stretches his lean, tight, veiny muscles. "But first, we must feed on more pain, more terror, more death... to free the Shape from these shackles. You, Caleb, must set us free."

Caleb feels dizzy. "Pardon?" Holding his hands up, pleading, he says, "That's why I want you to kill Gonzalez—"

"A small goal for a small mind." Billy's guttural voice pounds into Caleb's heart. "We want to go bigger. Deeper. You're going to make it happen. You've been weak, Caleb, but we can show you how to be strong."

"You're just a stupid kid," Caleb says, hating the irony of his statement.

Billy moves forward, and the darkness coils around him. "You still don't believe in the Shape, do you?"

"Of course not. It's just—"

A dark tendril wraps around Caleb's throat, and he can't breathe. The house is gone. Billy is gone. Caleb feels that he is adult again, but a sharp pain cuts through his shoulders and hips—and when he looks down, he is just a torso. No limbs. Helpless. He stares into the darkness, and two glowing blue eyes stare down at him.

"Release me!" Caleb shouts.

Blue flames sparkle from the eyes. Crackling fills the air.

"Let me go!" Caleb cries, and he falls backward. "Please..." He gasps. "No more hallucinations, no more..."

Kaley giggles from the darkness. "I've never been a hallucination, Caleb." Kaley's long fingernails stroke his stubbly cheeks.

"Truth is a lie." Billy's scratchy voice reverberates through the darkness as Caleb drowns. "Nothing has meaning... and nothing *is* the Shape. Apathy is honesty. There's no force for goodness out there in the universe, Caleb—nothing moving us along, watching us, helping us. But there is a darkness, a reality of the void, and that is the Shape—the one you serve, whether you like it or not."

The deep, masculine voice of Caleb's father hammers his skull. "Do the right thing, young man." The darkness peels back, and Caleb finds himself as a teenager in the smoky office of Big Daddy Thorne, as his geeky friends call him. The tall man is drinking a glass of something stiff and dark. He turns to his son, twirls his white mustache with exasperation, and says, "I'm disappointed in you."

Caleb marches forward. "But I love Kaley—I mean, Roseanna... I... wait, what is this?"

Daddy Thorne shakes his head. "This has nothing to do with you knocking up that trailer trash girl, Caleb." He lights a cigar. "Today, young man, you're on the threshold of something big, got it? Bigger than yourself."

"This Shape nonsense?" Caleb tries to storm up to his father but collides with an invisible wall. "Hey!"

"Don't think of the dark figure as a conscious being," Daddy Thorne says. "Think of it as power. True power. The power of giving the pain to something else so you may be above it all, safe and secure. Apathetic."

Caleb slumps down. He doesn't understand. None of this feels like a hallucination anymore. Daddy Thorne's green gaze glistens with love—a love that the old man never showed him in the "real" world—and tears well up in Caleb's eyes.

"Daddy, what is this horrible thing you want me to do?"

"It's time to get out of my shadow, boy. Build yourself up, and be your own man." Daddy Thorne turns to the window, hands clasped behind his back. "Just let the Shape out from inside you, Caleb. Do what he wants, and be the man I raised you to be."

Caleb wipes his eyes, creeps forward—the invisible wall is no longer there—and touches his father's desk. His throne. "Then... you'll be proud of me?"

"Of course I will, son." Daddy Thorne turns around, and his eyes emit blue flames. "We all serve the Shape."

Caleb screams, falls backward, and collapses into the darkness. It spirals beneath him, pulling him deeper into a dizzy, scratching emptiness. Away, away...

75

Caleb woke up in a fetal position on the cement floor. The screens buzzed with white noise. He stood up, groaning, as blood dripped from his neck. *Goddamn wound is open again.*

His vision was blurry, but the hundreds of screens seemed to display a single bit of text over the snow: Truth Is a Lie.

My mind is fucked. Caleb stumbled back, nearly crashing into the mustached armed guards standing there.

He did a double take. "What the hell are you people doing here?" he barked. "I ordered you to stay back."

The guard stood frozen, unblinking, staring into the center of the room. "We serve the Shape."

Caleb stepped away. *Good God in heaven.* As his vision became less hazy, he noticed dozens of guards surrounding him, hands on their guns, fixed in the same steady pose. A chill ran down his spine. *The boy has grown too powerful. The blood injections aren't strong enough.* With great trepidation, he turned to face the table in the room's center. Billy Jakobek was still bolted down to it, but his flaming blue eyes highlighted a sadistic smile.

Caleb swallowed, and he approached the table. *You're Caleb Thorne. Pull yourself together.* "Was... ah..." He rubbed the blood from his neck. "All of that was real?"

Billy nodded. The flames in the teenager's eyes emitted smoke.

"Power. That's what you promised me in the... whatever that was." Caleb dug his heels into the floor. "What do you want me to do?"

"Let us free," Billy rasped. The boy's voice made the screens buzz louder.

The guards raised their guns, pointing them at Caleb. He shivered. *Dear lord.* Black smoke funneled from the creature's lungs.

The annoying mustached guard stepped forward and put his hand on Caleb's shoulder. "The Shape wants us to go to Heaven's Hole, sir."

Caleb turned. "Why?" he snapped.

"You want that Gonzalez girl dead, but the Shape thinks that's small potatoes, sir. He thinks we can do better. He thinks..." The guard looked at Billy then nodded. "He wants us to storm that darn little mountain town, rip up the factory, and blow up the emotion bomb inside it. Get us some trucks, guns, soldiers... we can show those damn immigrants why they never should've messed with Mr. Thorne Century Himself, sir."

Another guard chuckled. "Big boom. Everybody dies."

Caleb turned to Billy, whose grin remained creepily unmoved. "Christ," Throne said. "You want us to murder everyone in that entire town—thousands of people?" He shook his head. "There's no profit in that."

The guard cleared his throat. "This is our great moment, sir. It's for a higher purpose. Heck, sir, it's to clear your name. Make them fear you. Besides, it's what the Shape has called upon us to do."

Caleb stared, slack-jawed, at the blankness of the guard's expression. *He's got no free will anymore, does he?* He looked back at Billy. *I did this. I made him into this. I can either take control of this situation, follow the path, or be the weak person everyone thinks I am.* He swallowed. "So we're going to destroy Heaven's Hole," Caleb whispered.

"To start with!" Kaley crept out of the shadows, dancing between the guards. "Nuke that town with all their nasty-ass emotions, punish 'em for how they treated you... and then, who knows what else we can do? We can go to other shitty towns, nuke them with the same emotions... boom!" She clapped her hands. "It's destiny!"

Caleb felt his body being pulled toward Billy. *Resist. Don't...* He couldn't fight back. His legs followed Billy's orders, as if the puppeteer had yanked on the strings. Soon, he was only a few feet away from Billy. "Roseanna." Caleb swiped his teary eyes. "I don't want her to die there."

Billy's eyes flashed. "We'll spare her. If that's what you want."

"As long as we get her out, everyone else in that goddamn town can die." Caleb gritted his teeth. "I *want* them to die. Every worker, every fucking immigrant... okay." Caleb took a deep breath. "We'll do this together."

This is for you, Daddy. He unplugged all the needles from Billy's body. *Don't think. Don't analyze. Just let the feelings guide you.* Then he went to the touch screen that controlled Billy's locks and pressed his thumb to the scanner. Instantly, the latches holding Billy's shoulders, ankles, and wrists were released.

Billy dropped to the floor. The boy's body was weak, malnourished, and could hardly stand. Cold tingles went down Caleb's spine. "Roseanna lives," Caleb pleaded. "Right?"

Billy stood up, and his blue gaze flickered in the darkness. Caleb stared into his eyes and saw the future. He saw the entire town—an American town—ripping itself apart in a bloody mess of carnage, bloodshed, and slaughter. *Is this truly what I want?* He thought about what Billy had told him. *Truth is a lie. Besides, those aren't real Americans. What do I care what happens to them?* The universe was empty. There was no good, no evil, only winners and losers. *I can't stop the Shape. I can either die for nothing, right here, or walk alongside a god—a living masterpiece—that I created. Me. Caleb Motherfucking Thorne.*

"Okay, kid." Caleb cracked his knuckles. "Let's burn that worthless place to the ground."

76: Roseanna

Roseanna, who was no longer Mother, set her empty glass on the bar. The beer was cheap and watery, but she'd drunk enough that she didn't care anymore. Sitting alone in her dimly lit corner, amid buzzing neon lights, TVs showing football games, and drunken Heaven's Hooligans shouting at penalties, she couldn't remember ever feeling so empty. *My heart's done.* She fingered the glass. *Drowned in alcohol. Christ, have I got a headache.* She hunched over the bar. A strange hand touched her shoulder, and she leapt up with shock.

"Just me." The bartender, Luis, lifted his arms. "Another beer?"

Roseanna groaned. She opened her empty wallet and considered using her Thorne Century employee credit card—*Like the asshole would even notice*—then shook her head. "Sorry, Luis. My paycheck got delayed."

"Hey, it's on the house." Luis refilled her glass from the tap, and he passed it back to her.

"Thanks."

The neon stripper light behind the bar flickered out. As Luis went to fix it, Roseanna sat upright—her head was dizzy—and gulped down the cold beer. *Tastes good.* The football game on the television cut to a commercial break. Around the corner of the bar, Roseanna overheard a drunken old white man mouthing the name Gonzalez.

"Yeah, that Mexican chick got what was coming to her, I say." The man stopped, slurping up a beverage. "Shoulda been more careful."

"C'mon, Joe," the man's friend said. "She meant well."

"That don't matter. Punk kid messed around with something too big for her to handle and got burned. Better to just keep your head down, mind your place, and weather the storm, I say. Like we do. That protest crap never works."

"Guess not. Y'hear she's still at the hospital?"

"Yeah. Don't walk no more, I hear. Heyyy, game's back on!"

Roseanna shook her head in disgust. She wanted to say something, but she didn't feel like she had the right. *I can project superiority all I want, but I'm the only one here who could've stopped what happened.* She sipped her beer. *If I hadn't gotten in my car, that family would be alive.*

Her phone buzzed with a message from Caleb Thorne. Her stomach lurched. *Leave me the hell alone, you despicable human being.* When she opened it, though, her heart constricted in her chest.

Thorne: *Roseanna, get out of Heaven's Hole tonight. IMMEDI-ATELY.*

Roseanna started texting back, but her fingers twitched so much she almost dropped the phone. *What is he talking about?* She hit the call button, and Thorne answered on the first ring.

"Roseanna." He sounded out of breath. "Dead serious. Leave Heaven's Hole tonight. It's a matter of life and death."

"When am I going to see Jamie?" she blurted. "My husband? After all the horrible things you've put me through, you keep pushing this off and pushing—"

"Roseanna, we don't have time for that!" Thorne said.

Roseanna froze. *Good god, he is serious.* "Caleb?"

"You need to leave." A pleading tone entered his voice. "Tomorrow morning, Billy Jakobek and I are... I mean, we have..."

"Billy?" she asked in a hushed tone, eyeing the bar.

"I've already said too much. *Please* get as far away from town as you can. Something is going to happen tomorrow, and I don't want you to be involved with it. Listen, Roseanna, I've arranged for an associate of mine at the hotel to give you a new identity, new passport, airline tickets... new everything. Leave the country ASAP, and in a few weeks, I'll explain in more detail why—"

The line went dead.

77: Caleb

Caleb sputtered in rage as one of his own soldiers, on Thorne Century's payroll, ripped the phone from his hands, threw it to the asphalt, and crumpled it beneath the heel of his combat boot.

"You can't do that!" Caleb cried.

It was already done. The soldier offered no response and simply stared across the parking lot at Billy Jakobek. The pale, shirtless boy stood back like a moonlit extraterrestrial, lighting the night sky with blue flames. More than fifty soldiers surrounded the warehouse, and others were coming in by the truckload.

Caleb picked up the scraps of his broken phone. "Don't you dare do this again," he muttered, but the soldier ignored him.

Billy silently directed the soldiers to carry crates full of machine guns out of the warehouse, across the parking lot, and into the backs of armored trucks. Crate after crate was piled in for the trip. Caleb sighed. *Why the hell am I participating in this horror show? The punk even broke my phone.* He walked past the soldiers and up toward the fence surrounding the property, which overlooked the mountainous wilderness. Far in the distance, the lights of Johnson City lit the skyline only a few miles away. *I could go back. Alert the authorities.*

As Caleb considered this, an ominous snapping filled his ears. *Damn it.* Billy appeared beside him, and his blue fires glared into Caleb's eyes. *So goddamn uncomfortable.* Caleb shuddered, and the boy—*No, not a boy anymore*—turned to stare at same city skyline in the distance with a cheerless grin.

Caleb sputtered, "Perhaps we don't have to kill *every* single person in the town?"

Billy's fiery eyes flickered, and as he turned, Caleb's head exploded in pain. Vomit rushed up his throat and burst from his mouth. He puked all over his suit, his shoes, and the asphalt, then crumpled to the ground.

"Please..." Caleb gasped, and the vomit splashed back up.

Billy pushed his dirty bare foot onto Caleb's head, grinding his face into the rocks, then stepped away.

Caleb wiped his lips. He pulled himself back upright. "Billy!" he roared. He marched forward, intending to bash the boy's head in—but as he got closer, he blinked and felt himself being drawn to the warehouse. Before he knew it, as if he'd fast-forwarded, he found himself picking up a crate of machine guns and carrying it into the back of a truck. He blinked again. *What the hell am I doing?* He was picking up another crate. He hadn't even realized or even thought about it. He had just *been doing* it. Holding on to his moment of consciousness with the tenacity of a dog gripping a chew toy, he looked at the other man holding the crate, his moving partner, and was surprised to see Mr. Linus standing across from him.

"Linus?" Caleb asked, heaving the crate into the truck.

Linus nodded. "We serve the Shape." His eyes were blank.

Caleb shook his head. *This is insanity.* He started to walk away.

Linus's hand clapped onto his shoulder. "Sorry, boss."

Caleb turned around. "Don't touch me, you—" He stopped as dozens of guns were pointed in his face.

Linus nudged Caleb toward the dark inside of the truck they'd been loading guns into. "Gotta go into the truck, Mr. Thorne."

The gunmen all nodded and murmured in tune, "Go in. Go in. Go in."

Caleb's head spun. He stepped back then froze, feeling the blue flames scalding the back of his head. *I can't go.* When he turned to Billy, the pale creature pointed to the back of the truck. All of the men pointed with him. A tight knot twisted in Caleb's chest. *I must go in the back of the truck.* He couldn't breathe. *That's what the Shape wants me to do.*

"I can't go in that... in that truck." Caleb stuck his chin out, choking back tears. "I'm Caleb Thorne."

"Nah, boss. You're the Shape. Just like we are." Linus shrugged. He put his arm around Caleb's shoulder and guided him inside.

Caleb pushed back. "Do you know how long the drive to that filthy town is? I'll be in there all night!" He whispered into Linus's ear, "We must—"

Linus shoved him forward. "Sucks, Mr. Thorne, but you gotta do what you gotta do."

Caleb felt the urge to argue and to fight. But the blue electricity of the demon he'd unleashed, and the dozens of guns surrounding him, made it clear that he had no choice but to follow the orders. "To Heaven's Hole," he whispered as he squeezed between the crates of guns and sat down in the back of the truck and stared out at the crowd of dark silhouettes that had gathered to watch his humiliation. "Will I be alone back here?" The tailgate closed, and he was in darkness.

78: Natalia

The baseboard heaters rattled. The TV played bad reality shows. Pink clouds painted long acrylic streaks across the snowy landscape, the sunlight moving across the hospital room in a way that almost made Natalia want to get out of bed and draw or even try painting. *Almost.* She'd lain in bed for hours, and her pale legs were speckled with ink dots, lines, and bits of blood. She'd stabbed them with her pen, trying to feel something, anything.

"You're not my legs," she said, but the lumps of unfeeling clay before her didn't reply because they were dead. *My real legs used to dance. Run. Stand on top of cars. I don't know what these shitty things are.*

Picking up her pen, she leaned forward as much as she could. She began drawing shapes on the skin of her thighs—nothing advanced, nothing pretty, just a small smiley face and a sentence: *Hi, new legs.*

She shook her head in disgust. "This is fucking stupid." She threw the pen across the room. Tears welled up in her eyes. *Drawing is stupid. My activism was stupid. Mamá, Abuelita, Juan, and Carlos... all dead because of me. Everyone's lives would've been better if Crazy Old Darrell had just shot me up on that mountain.*

Heels clicked down the hallway. Natalia covered herself with the blanket. As the door opened, she readied herself for the social worker or her art teacher. *Somebody who dresses nice.* Instead, a tall white woman with ice-blue eyes entered the room, looking so foreign that for a second, Natalia didn't even recognize her as Mother. *That bitch.*

"Get the fuck out of here!" Natalia screamed.

Mother rushed inside and closed the door behind her. She had a briefcase in her hand. "Listen, Natalia, I—"

"Get out!" Natalia threw a nearby coffee cup at her. Mother dodged, and it splattered against the wall. Natalia scrambled to get up, and her leg spilled off the side of the mattress. *Shit.*

As her body slid off the bed, Mother raced forward and caught her.

"Listen for one second." Mother lifted Natalia back to safety. The woman reeked of alcohol as much as Thorne had on that night. *That bastard.* Natalia flopped back onto the bed, and Mother stood over her. "Listen," Mother repeated, "I know—"

Natalia punched her in the face. Mother reeled back. Natalia swung again, punching her so hard that spit flew out. "Fuck you! You drove away and left us there!"

"I know..." Mother rubbed her jaw. "Listen to me, please. Just five minutes. *Please.* People's lives are at risk—"

Natalia punched her call button. "You're a murderer as much as Thorne is."

Mother sighed. "I know."

This caught Natalia by surprise. *She does know, doesn't she?*

Before she could process this new information, the door opened. The nurse poked her head in. "Hey, is everything okay in here?"

Natalia gnashed her teeth. *Hell no, it isn't.* Just as she was about to have Mother thrown out of the hospital, though, she looked at the pale woman's face and caught something fragile in those blue eyes. *This lady looks desperate. Panicked. She's not here on Thorne's orders.* Natalia eyed Mother again, looked at the nurse, and said, "It's fine for now. Check back in five."

"You sure?" The nurse arched an eyebrow.

"Yeah."

The nurse exited but left the door cracked open.

Mother smiled wanly. "Thanks."

"Fuck you," Natalia reiterated. "You've got five minutes, *Mother.*"

The woman shakily pulled up a chair. Her clothes were rumpled. Her eyes had bags pinned under the bags. Laying the briefcase over her lap, Mother cleared her throat. "I don't blame for you for hating me."

Natalia glanced at the clock. "Four minutes, Mother."

"Please." Her lip quivered. "Listen, I owe you some honesty. My full, real name is Dr. Roseanna Peterson."

Natalia twitched. "So, you have a name." *This asshole sat with my family at Thanksgiving. Drank with Mamá. Then she drove away and let them die. Don't forget that.* "That doesn't mean I'll forgive you."

"I don't expect you to. I don't deserve forgiveness, frankly." Mother brushed a stray curl from her eyes. "But I want you to know that Thorne hurt me too. The reason I've been working for him all these years, he... he has my son and husband. Or so he says. They might be dead. They might be captured. I just... I don't know. I thought this horrendous project would be done years ago and that I'd have them back—"

"So you sold your soul to make weapons for corporate America." Natalia crossed her arms. *Don't show that you feel sorry for her. God, don't let it show.* "You wasted your privilege, telling yourself you couldn't change anything, while a bunch of poor factory workers busted their asses on some nightmare they didn't know about."

"That's not—ah." She sighed. "I suppose. Yes."

"He's never going to give you your family back," Natalia replied. "You know that, right? The dude is totally in love with you. Creepy-ass shit."

"Natalia..." She shook her head. "We don't have time for all this. Last night, I received a call from Thorne, and it was... weird. I've spent all night looking through the database to determine what's going on, but this doesn't fit any of his plans. I think he's gone AWOL, and... and..."

Natalia shuddered. *Okay, trigger the businessman-gone-postal alert.*

"I believe that Thorne's bringing Billy back here." Just as Natalia's heart jumped halfway, Mother—Roseanna—cut her a harsh glance. "But it's not the same Billy. The reports I've read regarding the treatments they've performed on your boyfriend since Thanksgiving… they're awful." She pointed at her briefcase. "Isolation. Sensory deprivation, waterboarding, emotional torture, and exposure to constant brainwashing through violent imagery…"

"Oh my god." Natalia covered her mouth. *My Billy.* She remembered his kisses. His touch. His dark eyes. The sunlight had died down, and the sky had already changed into the wintery, cloudy gray of a December morning. "Why are you telling me this?"

"That phone call…" Roseanna paused, and her voice became quieter. "Natalia, I think that the Shape has taken control of both Billy and Caleb. I think they're coming to make Billy's explosion nightmare come true."

79: Caleb

The hours had never passed so slowly in Caleb's life. Sitting on the hard floor in the pitch-blackness, surrounded by the clattering of weaponry, he'd tried to sleep. It hadn't gone well. Sweaty, miserable, and exhausted, he clutched a loaded machine gun. He'd never used one before, but the second the truck doors opened, he intended to practice it on whoever was unlucky enough to see him first.

Meanwhile, the wooden boards beneath him bumped up and down. The truck rumbled loudly all night, and every time he dozed off for a second, it slammed over a pothole, stopped for gas, or swerved around a turn. It was the most undignified experience of his life, and as the hours droned on, he fantasized about twisting his knife into Billy's ribs or calling the police. *Show that Jew boy why he shouldn't mess with Caleb Thorne.*

But he had no phone, no freedom, and the Shape would certainly force him to drop the knife if he tried to use it. He wasn't Caleb Thorne anymore. He was just an angry little man locked in the back of a truck.

Finally, the truck's brakes squealed to a halt. The engine shut off. Caleb stood up, but the truck jostled forward, knocking him back to the ground. He dropped the gun. *Damn it. Woozy. So dehydrated.* Before he could get ready again, the back of the truck opened, and the bulky silhouette of Linus appeared in the blinding light. The air smelled of pine and gasoline.

"Welcome back, Mr. Thorne."

Caleb stumbled forward, so dazed that he forgot his gun. *Wait, I need to go back... gun...* Linus pulled him out of the truck, into the cold air. The parking lot surrounding them was crowded with trucks, soldiers, and guards, all of whom were dumping guns into a giant pile on the asphalt. Caleb squinted, rubbed his eyes, and reexamined his surroundings. He spotted a playground and a soccer field. The brick building behind them was Heaven's Hole Elementary. *Dear lord.* His stomach lurched. In the windows, first graders pushed their faces against the glass, trying to get a better look at the unholy gun pit.

Caleb nearly fainted, falling into Linus's arms. "We can't do this." To his relief, Linus straightened him up and handed him a can of seltzer.

"Nah, boss." Linus slurped his own can, and he got back to work. "Gotta do what we gotta do. Time to blow up that factory."

Caleb went slack-jawed. "How can you say that so goddamn calmly? There are children here!"

"Young troops." Linus shrugged. "Y'know how many millions of kids your company has killed? C'mon, boss. Don't be naïve." Linus went back to helping the soldiers unload the trucks.

Caleb sipped his seltzer. *Good god.* He ripped his blazer off, panting, and watched the pile of guns grow higher and higher. Just as he was considering making a run for it, a cold tremor ran down his spine. Billy Jakobek stood behind him.

"We can't do this," Caleb said. "Those are children."

The blue-eyed demon smiled.

Caleb jumped at Billy, his fingers reaching for the boy's throat. *Choke him. Kill him!* Suddenly, his legs dropped like wet noodles. He fell to the asphalt, choking on vomit. As blood and stomach acid splashed from his mouth, his skull tightened—and tightened further—until he couldn't see. His vision went dark. *No, god damn it!*

The feeling faded. Caleb looked into the scorching eyes of his master and breathed in the black smoke seeping from Billy's body. *I must do what I must do.* He took a deep breath, nodded, and assisted his allies in unloading the guns. The harder he worked and the more he sweated, the less he thought about the consequences.

"None of these kids are real Americans, anyway," Caleb huffed, dumping guns out of a box.

"True story," Linus affirmed.

A police siren wailed. The children in the windows ducked down. Caleb and Linus looked at each other then turned to face Billy. Three police cars slammed into the parking lot. *Those cars are made by my company.* Caleb gulped. *This is the end of me. Oh my god, I'm going to prison.* Caleb looked around at his soldiers and was horrified that none of them were doing anything except putting more guns onto the pile.

"Move, you buffoons!" Caleb screamed. "Shoot the pigs!"

The blue-eyed monster merely smirked.

The cops busted out of the doors. Their pistols hit the air. The sirens kept wailing and wailing and wailing. "Hands to the sky!" a policewoman yelled.

"Drop the weapons!" another cop shouted.

The soldiers didn't do any such thing. Caleb started to lift his hands then noticed that Billy had walked directly in front of the cops, black smoke trailing in his footsteps. "It's the freak!" a policeman yelled. "Listen, kid, get down on a count of three. One, two—"

Caleb closed his eyes, ducked, and waited. The countdown stopped. There were no gunshots. He stood again, heart pounding, and saw Billy raising his hands to the sky. The officers were frozen. Their eyes rolled to the backs of their skulls, and they lowered their guns. Caleb gazed outward in a combination of horror and amazement as Billy turned around and the cops followed him with big, stupid smiles.

"He did it," Caleb said.

"Sure did," Linus said.

The grinning cops tossed their own guns into the pile then assisted in unloading the trucks.

Caleb turned to Billy with an exasperated laugh. "Kid, you're unbelievable."

Billy nodded. He pointed toward the doors of the school as they clicked open. Scores of elementary schoolers poured out, little boys and girls walking in unison, their skirts and caps and T-shirts in sharp contrast to their grave expressions. Teachers followed them to the parking lot. The two janitors came out in back. Each child walked to the gun pit, took a machine gun, then stepped aside so that the next child could do the same.

Caleb leaned against the truck. For years, he'd pictured the chaos that his emotion bomb could cause. The mad panic. The terror. He'd never imagined it being so calm and collected. *But this gets them to the same place, doesn't it?* Despite the horribleness of what was happening, he smiled. *They're all going to set off the emotion bomb, and then the carnage will begin.*

Billy offered Caleb a machine gun. "Thank you," Caleb said, feeling weirdly honored. Billy—the Shape—smiled and began passing guns to the soldiers. The guns clicked and clattered as the children picked them up. *So many guns. So many kids.* When the children started talking among themselves again, they were giggling. Comparing the sizes of their guns. Tiny little people, heads almost as big as their bodies, with tiny little feet.

"I'm gonna shoot more people than you are," one boy said and laughed.

"No way," said another.

"Bang bang!" a girl cried out.

Billy's hands were outstretched and then closed, as if he were clasping at the heart of every little kid around him. Caleb stepped back, knowing he could do nothing—he was merely an observer. *A participant.* Black smoke seeped from Billy's pores, surrounding him like a cloud from which his blue eyes shimmered. His frail body looked even more skeletal than before.

Caleb looked at the gun in his hands. *I'm part of this. Part of the rebellion.* He glanced at Linus. "We're going to do this." He grinned. "We're making history."

"Damn right."

Caleb looked into the snowy distance. A crowd of adults wandered over the soccer field—a combination of homeless people and low-wage workers from the gas stations, stores, and other nonfactory jobs—and entered the fray.

"Come join us!" Caleb called out to them. "Guns for everyone!"

"Thanks, Mr. Thorne!" an elderly man called back as he took a machine gun into his hands. His bony dog barked, following the same magnetic pull. All of the people in the field grabbed their own guns. The hundreds of people gathered around them giggled, muttered to themselves, and watched the blue-eyed boy in the center of it all.

Caleb turned to Billy. "Where must we go next?" The gun jittered in his hands. *It feels so powerful. God, I can't wait to shoot somebody.*

Billy's lanky body pulsed with dark clouds of energy, veins throbbing, neck stretched out to the sky. He said nothing but nodded at Caleb.

"You..." Caleb hesitated. "Are you asking me to lead the charge?"

The boy grinned.

Caleb shivered and faced the crowd of hundreds. Billy raised his hands, and the people cheered. Caleb smiled, looking at them all—*My people. They're all mine!*—and tears of happiness rolled down his cheeks. "Come to me!" he shouted.

The crowd roared. "Thorne!"

Caleb's grin widened. *These are my family. The family I always wanted. We're all in this together.* He brandished his gun. "Let's go to the factory!"

The crowd shouted again. "All hail Thorne!"

Caleb held his gun to the sky, pulled the trigger, and let it rip, spraying gunfire into the atmosphere. The people followed his lead. They shouted. Cheered. Roared in enthusiasm. Then the march began. Children, adults, policemen, and teachers, rich and poor alike—they were unified. The thunderous footsteps of over three hundred people clapped to the asphalt like a steady drum. *Boom. Boom. Boom. Boom.*

Caleb let the tears flow. He laughed as adrenaline shook through him. "We are together!" he cried.

The crowd bellowed back. "Together with Thorne!" They lifted their guns, sprayed bullets into the sky, and followed his lead. Caleb fired his machine gun at windows, lampposts, and signs. When he ran out of ammo, more was handed to him. His skin was slick with sweat. His pants were soaked with urine. His mouth was dry, his lips chapped. Despite it all, he'd never felt so happy. He ripped off his wet shirt, popping buttons to the ground and exposing his pale whiteness to the cold. *I feel accepted.* He waved his shirt over him like a flag, and the children squealed in excitement. Others copied him, ripping off their own shirts.

Cars spun into ditches. Stray dogs growled then joined their ranks. Entire apartment buildings emptied into the streets, their tenants joining the rebellion. Gas station attendants threw their cash registers into the parking lot. People punched car windows, breaking their hands. Caleb salivated at the thought of what would happen when they set off the emotion bomb. *This will be nothing compared to that. Everyone here, all of us, will finally be free—free to be the animals we are.*

He beat his chest like a gorilla. "I can do anything!"

Despite the chaos, no one had died. Caleb had noticed that. *Not a single fucking person.* He looked at the slender boy in the center of it all, and the reason occurred to him. *Billy's still in there, not letting the demon kill people. That brat is not letting the Shape truly cut loose.* In response, Caleb turned his gunfire to a crowd of teenagers at the side of the mob and watched as they fell to the ground in a blaze of glory. No one panicked. No one fired back. They just kept marching, and he cackled with joy. *Power.* He reloaded and fired again, taking out an elderly woman. She choked on blood and fell into the ditch. Then, screaming with a passion unlike anything he'd ever experienced before—not in control, not in sex, *nothing*—he raced far ahead, feeling the wind rush into his face, hurtling toward the explosion of his dreams. His army sped up to match his pace. *I made this happen. Me. Caleb Thorne. My hard work, my stubbornness.* The gun felt light in his hands as he hollered, "Truth is a lie!"

80: Natalia

Natalia rolled her wheelchair across the hospital. She zoomed past the nurses' station, through the double doors, and into the waiting room—as far away from Roseanna as she could get. She didn't want to face the woman or answer any more questions. She stopped at the window, sucking back tears, and stared at the cloudy sky. Her heart caught in her throat. *I just want to die.* The fire tower blinked in the distance, reminding her of another lifetime, another reality—a period in her life that now felt like a beautiful lie. She kept thinking about Billy's face. His tender little smile. His glistening dark eyes. *Sitting next to him at Thanksgiving, all of us together. It felt so right. This...*

Roseanna caught up to her, huffing. "You left me back there."

"Yeah, that was the idea." She pressed her palms to the glass and closed her eyes. *Are you really out there, Billy?* Chills went down her wrists. She withdrew them, and she turned to Roseanna. "Honestly, Doc? I don't have a clue why you're telling me this. What the hell am I supposed to do?"

Roseanna sighed. "Natalia, dear..." She touched Natalia's shoulder.

Natalia jerked away. "Don't." She crossed her arms. "You don't *know* that Thorne is bringing Billy here. You're just guessing."

"I put the pieces together from his phone call." Roseanna paced the room, eyeing an old man on the other side. "Let's be honest, though. I feel something awful in the air, and that's where I'm getting my conclusions. Normally, that's not exactly a scientific approach, but with these psychic kids... don't you feel it?"

Natalia touched the window again. *Fuck. Yeah, I do feel it. I'm definitely not telling her, though.* "Okay, Miss Expert. What do you think is going to happen?"

"They're going to trip those living corpses in the battery again." Roseanna scratched her chin. "With no Billy to shut off the emotion bomb, that thing will make every person in this town go haywire. I've read the reports. It will be absolute carnage... there's going to be blood running down the streets like rainwater, Natalia. And Billy—" She shook her head. "He's not going to be the same Billy you loved. I'm pretty sure Thorne has carved that good kid out of his skull. All that's left is... you know."

Shudders ran through Natalia. "How the hell are we supposed to stop something like the Shape?"

"Not *us*." Roseanna sighed. "If I get close, he'll take me over and make me kill myself or god knows what. No, I think the only person who can stop him is... well..."

"Me." Natalia swallowed dryly. "Fuck." She heard rustling papers. Roseanna placed a file folder on Natalia's lap. "What's this?"

"All of the documentation on the project. A copy of it. There's also a flash drive in there with the same info, and I've sent you an email with it as well. If I die..." Roseanna inhaled deeply. "If I die, the information I've emailed you needs to be fully exposed to the world. You're the only person I trust to do that."

"Lucky me."

"Lucky you." She flashed a wan smile. "At the back of the folder, you'll find two fake passports I had made this morning and plane tickets."

"Two?"

She started to look, but Roseanna pushed the folder down. "Yes, two. One for you... and one for Billy, you know, just in case, because I can't *not* have hope in a better fate for him. Even if it's impossible. I love that kid." Roseanna wiped her eyes. "If you make it out of this situation alive, Natalia, I want you to leak all this information, take that passport and ticket, and fly the hell out of this country."

Tears tugged at Natalia's eyes. *This is insane.* Her heart pounded against her rib cage. "I can't." Her voice was choked up. "Roseanna, I can't do this. I can't—"

In the distance, many blocks away, machine guns rattled the air. Natalia ducked away, biting back a scream. *No, not again!* A distant hum of chanting—some kind of rally out in the streets—burned into her. *Oh god.* She closed her eyes, trying to escape, and in the darkness, she saw it. *They're marching through the streets.* Thorne, Billy, and a growing crowd of soldiers, children, police officers, teachers, and the homeless were pounding the asphalt, armed to the teeth, making their way to the factory. Within the hospital, she heard panicked voices. Shouts. *People are freaking out.* They were all going to die—everyone in town. Her. Felix. The other kids and families in her housing unit. The guy who ran the gas station. All of her teachers. *There's no way some little person like me can prevent that.*

Roseanna's voice broke through the darkness. "That's him, Natalia! It's happening. We need to move!"

"I can't do anything against some superhuman force of nature, lady." Tears streamed down her cheeks. "I'm just a stupid teenage girl with a big mouth, and I've the bullet wounds to prove how useless I am in a situation like—"

"No." Roseanna grabbed Natalia's shoulders. "You're a tough-as-nails teenage girl who has already proved she can change the world."

Natalia still didn't open her eyes—the darkness was comforting—as the scientist's exhalations landed on her face.

"Listen," Roseanna continued, "I know this isn't fair. You deserved none of this—I honestly believe that. But neither did Billy Jakobek. We both know that he was a damn good kid." Roseanna's voice choked up. "And unless you can stop him, Gonzalez, he's about to kill a lot of people."

Natalia felt something heavy drop into her lap. She opened her eyes. It was a gun. "You can't be serious," she said in a shaky voice.

"He loves you. That's why you're the only one who can get close enough to pull the trigger on him." Roseanna scoffed bitterly. "Billy barely likes me, but you—you're his... his one. And if there's any shred of Billy left in there... Natalia, I know that I'm probably sending you to your death. You probably can't break through to him, but you're the *only* one who has a chance."

Natalia shook her head. In the darkness behind her eyelids, she saw him. "Billy?" she whispered. But the pale, lanky creature before her had the fiery blue eyes of the Shape. Every hair on Natalia's body stiffened. Every scar tingled. Her heart pulsed to the beat. *The Shape.*

But in the shadows, past the dark figure, she saw the tattered outline of a little boy—not the Billy she knew but the one she'd seen in his memory, with a red cape tied around his neck. Little Billy desperately reached out to her and whimpered, "Help me."

Natalia opened her eyes. Roseanna was inches away, every crease in her face lined with sweat. Another machine gun roared in the distance, miles away.

"Natalia?" Roseanne asked. "Can you hear me?"

"I'm here." With a deep breath, Natalia tucked the gun between her thigh and the seat. Then she turned her wheelchair around, and Roseanna followed.

"Hey!" Roseanna called out. "Where are you going?"

"My room." Natalia rushed ahead. "If I'm going to die in such a stupid way, I at least need my sketchbook on me."

81: Natalia

"This isn't Heaven's Hole anymore," Natalia whispered, her face pressed to the car window. "It can't be."

Roseanna drove silently. The town looked deserted. Fire hydrants sprayed water. Trash littered the streets. Shop windows were broken. Brick walls were marred by bullet holes. The closer they got to the factory, the worse the damage became. Over the horizon, at the top of the hill, the smokestacks of the Thorne Century factory loomed ahead. Natalia glanced at Roseanna, sitting in the driver's seat, and was astonished by the woman's bloodshot eyes. *They didn't look like that before.*

"Hey, are you okay?" Natalia nudged her.

Roseanna shook her head. "No." She gripped the steering wheel, white-knuckled. "I'm not... okay."

Natalia squeezed the gun in her pocket. She glanced back at her wheelchair—which had her sketchbook tucked into the side—and exhaled. *This is bad.* Suddenly, Roseanna slammed on the brakes, and the car jolted her forward like a slingshot.

"Holy crap!" Natalia yelled. "What are you—"

Roseanna breathed heavily. "Can't. Can't... can't go..."

Natalia looked ahead. The road was blocked by wrecked cars—a wall of automobile corpses. In front of this, Natalia saw bodies littered with bullet holes. She covered her mouth. *I recognize them. I don't know their names, but...* She squeezed the gun. *This is so stupid. They're dead. Not... not from Billy, though.* Somehow, she knew that. She could feel it. It wasn't Billy—or his powers—that had pulled the trigger on those people. *It was Thorne. That means there's still a chance.*

Roseanna unbuckled her seat belt. "Must. Go." She opened the car door, collapsed out of it, and limped to the passenger side. Natalia squirmed. *God, I feel so helpless.* Roseanna got Natalia's wheelchair out of the back seat and planted it on the sidewalk. Then she opened Natalia's door. "Get in. I'll... help." Her eyes were bloodred.

A buzzing burned through Natalia's head. She gritted her teeth. "This is stupid, Doc. We'll never—"

"Truth is a lie," Roseanna muttered.

"Huh?" Natalia frowned as Roseanna swayed back and forth and her pupils rolled to the back of her skull. "Doc?"

Roseanna tottered backward, pushing Natalia's unlocked wheelchair into the car. "Truth... lies..." The woman stumbled off in the direction of the factory. A vein bulged in her forehead. "Lies... lies..."

"Roseanna!" Natalia screamed. But Roseanna wandered away in a daze, and Natalia was alone. Stranded. Trapped in a car, her wheelchair less than a foot away. "Roseanna, come back!"

But Dr. Peterson tottered up the hill like a zombie, muttering to herself, until she disappeared over the crest amid the roaring laughter, shouts, and gunfire.

Natalia hyperventilated. *Holy fuck, this is bad!* Her lungs seized up. Her heart pounded in her chest. *Calm down! Calm. Calm...*

A car crashed into the wall of automobiles. She jumped. "Oh my god!"

The driver fell out of the car, blood running down his forehead, and glanced back at Natalia. His eyes were red. Then he followed Roseanna up the hill, toward the factory, totally unconcerned with the damage to his car. Over the hill, Thorne's voice rang out.

A shiver ran down her spine. *He's in charge. The Shape is manipulating it so that Thorne leads it all. Exploiting his weaknesses. Man, this is so, so bad.*

Natalia exhaled. *Okay, time to calm down.* She looked down at the open wheelchair beside her. It wasn't locked. *I could throw myself into it. Strategically fall. Right?* She snorted. *Yeah, then I'd splat right on the road and be stuck there while this chaos lights up. Just like I was stuck when Thorne shot me.* Natalia looked at the wheelchair again. She remembered the day that Darrell Jenkins had stuck a gun to her head. She thought back to Thorne standing over her bleeding, broken body in the snow. *Failures, all through. Except...*

Except she'd also rallied a town, broken through the fortress of Thorne Century, and changed things. She stared at the angle of the wheelchair. *I'm not a victim.* She'd faced death. She'd survived it. She adjusted the gun in her pocket, exhaled, and pushed her legs toward the center console. *No, I'm not a victim. I won't give up. I'm Natalia Motherfucking Gonzalez, and if I'm gonna die, it'll be on my terms.* She unbuckled her seat belt. Using the door strap as leverage, she turned her backside to the open car door. She lifted her legs, with a groan, and threw them over the gearshift so they were sticking straight in front of her.

Then she glanced back at the wheelchair. *I've only got one shot at this.* If she landed just right, she would drop right into the chair's lap. If she was off by even an inch, the chair would fly out behind her—and she would hit asphalt. "Okay, you big jerks." She patted her unfeeling legs. "I know you can't do much, but let's get one last win, okay?"

She launched herself backward. For a moment—less than a second, but the time stretched like a rubber band—she felt herself falling. *Game over.* All sound stopped. The air whooshed. *I'm going to die.* Everything—sounds, feelings—slowed to a crawl as her torso buckled and her legs flew above her.

She slammed down into the seat. The wheelchair skated backward. Screaming at the top of her lungs, Natalia grabbed the armrests as her legs flapped down beneath her. The chair crashed back against the curb. It swayed, threatening to topple, then fell back on its own weight. Natalia looked down at herself in amazement. She'd landed.

She patted her knees. "Thanks, guys." Then, using the armrests as leverage, she pushed herself upright. She buckled the wheelchair seat belt, adjusted the sketchbook at her side, and made sure that the gun was still in her pocket. *Check, check.* As the adrenaline from the fall petered out, the smokestacks at the top of the hill glared down like devil's horns. The enormity of her goal became all too evident. The gun took on extra weight, and she cringed at the thought of facing the boy she loved—the gentle, kind soul who she dreamed about every night—and shooting his brains out.

Then a more mundane obstacle became apparent—the hill itself. Grabbing her wheels, she rolled upward. Her chair slid back. She seized the wheels, holding them tight—holding the entire weight of her chair against the flow of gravity—and pushed forward again. "I'm totally fucked," she said through gritted teeth. "Okay."

She pushed the wheelchair ahead again, over a bump. Gravity pulled at her, and she pushed against it, moving up the hill—fighting nature, fighting her emotions, and fighting the throbbing headache that vibrated harder in her skull the closer she got. *I don't want to kill Billy.* She closed her eyes and heard the stomping. The hollering. The cries. She breathed in, and the pain and hatred that surrounded her was absorbed right into her lungs as if she were Billy Jakobek. *He's sending it to me.* Spikes of energy. Razor blades of suffering. Her body folded in on itself, and vomit tried to rush up her throat.

No. Don't give up. I won't give up.

She pushed forward again. Again. Rocks and dirt blocked her wheels. Her hands throbbed. The closer she got to the factory, the weaker she became. The furious presence ahead of her tried to push her back. It blasted at her head. It burned her stomach. She pushed over a protruding rock, nearly flipping her wheelchair over. She gasped, trying not to focus on the near failure. *A fucking rock could have stopped me. There's no way I can do this.*

"I won't give up," she mouthed through anxious tears.

She pushed the wheels forward. The skin of her hands tore loose. Blood spilled down the sides of her chair. *I won't give up.* She pushed fast. Aggressively. Forcefully. The malignant emotions ahead of her screamed out. The marching grew louder. The beat inside her skull amplified, like a knife repeatedly jabbing into her forehead.

She kept pushing. *I won't give up.* She pushed forward then rolled back. She pushed again. The factory grew closer. The head pain spiraled down her shoulders and over her back, tearing apart the discs of her spine. Colors spiraled through the air. She gritted her teeth so hard that she felt chips breaking loose. Natalia reasserted her grip on the wheels. *Push, push!* Agonizing pain and desperate fatigue rippled through every muscle in her arms. The bones were ready to snap. Her palms shredded. Raw tissue became exposed. Every push triggered the nerve endings up her wrists. *I'm coming, Billy.* She lurched ahead, fighting the pull of gravity. *I'm coming, Shape.*

"I won't give up!" she screamed.

82: Caleb

The army thudded into the parking lot. Caleb whooped with excitement. "We're here!" he shrieked at the top of his lungs. He sprayed his machine gun against the front of his beloved factory, shattering the windows, and his heart leapt for joy. Glass blasted across the pavement. His army cheered.

The doors flung open, and the workers spilled out. As the gray sun hit their eyes, their faces went from confusion to shock, horror, happiness—and then, to Caleb's delight, subservience. Caleb marched before the crowd, facing the hundreds of factory workers gathering around him.

"You serve the Shape!" he shouted, thumping his bare chest. "You serve me! And now"—he pointed behind him, at the blue-eyed demon boy—"he will bring light to all of us! To... to..."

Caleb noticed with dismay that Billy was frowning. The lanky boy had stopped in his tracks, and he turned to look at something behind the marchers.

"Billy?" Caleb hurried back. *I can't lose you, son. Stay strong.* Caleb shook the boy's shoulders. "Wake up, son. We're on the precipice of glory."

Billy's skin crackled with electrical sparks. His flaming blue eyes smoked into the sky, and he snarled at the entrance of the parking lot. Suddenly, everyone in the crowd turned in the same direction as Billy. Thousands of people faced backward. Caleb tensely gazed back at the small dark figure in the distance who had caught their attention—a person so weak, so pathetically unthreatening, that Caleb burst out laughing. "Look, the brat is back!"

The tiny girl in the wheelchair stubbornly rolled forward.

83

Natalia's hands were stripped raw. Blood ran down her legs. She panted. She recognized the thousands of faces before her—the entire town of Heaven's Hole, or most of it—but the people normally behind those faces were gone. *This isn't them.* She gasped at the hundreds of people wielding machine guns. Innocent children. Armed soldiers. Policemen. High schoolers—including Felix off in the distance—wielded crowbars, pipes, or anything they could get ahold of.

As she wheeled into the parking lot, a hushed silence befell the crowd. With a quivering voice, she shouted, "Where's Billy?"

"He belongs to us now!" Mr. Thorne Century Himself burst through the crowd, and the people echoed his comment. "He's going to light this place up!"

"Light it up!"

"Light it up!"

"Light it up!"

Thorne was no longer the polite businessmen Natalia remembered. Shirtless, with a machine gun strapped to his chest, he reeked of urine and blood. He was ravenous, cackling, and twitchy. The wound on his neck was so infected that she could barely look at it. "Look how the mighty Gonzalez has fallen." Thorne smirked. "The wannabe hero. I can't wait to sink another bullet into your dirty immigrant ass."

Natalia bristled with tension. She wheeled forward, forcing Thorne to move aside. "I'm not afraid of you." She glanced back. "And listen, asshole. This is a country of immigrants. Hate it all you want, but immigration is America. *I'm* America, more than you'll ever be."

Thorne sputtered with rage, reaching for his trigger, but then a look of fear passed over his face. He lowered his gun. The mob silently shuffled to Natalia's sides, leaving a narrow path between her and...

"Billy?" she whispered.

The pale figure walked toward her, shirtless and barefoot in the snow. It looked like a human. It looked like Billy. It even felt like Billy, inside her heart. Enormous veins wriggled across his anorexic-looking chest and arms like burrowing snakes. *Please, be a nightmare.* Tears welled up in her eyes. *That can't be him. That's not the boy I love.*

Billy strode before her, blue smoke pouring from his eyes, and he smiled. "You're not supposed to be here," he said in a voice that dug into her pores like a thousand needles.

Natalia shivered and looked away from the creature's eyes. "Guess I've never been good at following the rules."

Billy raised his hand to the sky, and suddenly, every child and soldier in the crowd aimed a gun at Natalia. Hundreds of people. Hundreds of guns. Thousands of bullets. Natalia defiantly looked up into the flaming blue eyes that had poisoned the boy she loved, and she wheeled forward.

Suddenly, her hands locked in place. Her movement froze. She choked. *Shit.* Each muscle in her aching, tormented body became completely paralyzed. The guns clicked. Billy walked in a circle around her, his fingers splayed like claws. "Your defiance masks weakness," he whispered with a snakelike tongue. "You think that I love you? You're naïve enough to believe that you can break through me?"

"I... don't..." Natalia grunted through the invisible hand on her lungs. "I don't care what *you* say, shithead."

The slender boy stopped before her.

"You heard me." She gasped. "But yes, I think Billy loves me." Natalia squeezed her fists, fighting against the electricity paralyzing her. "Because you—whatever the hell you might be—are *no* Billy Jakobek. You're just using his body."

The pale figure narrowed his blue eyes. His gaze burned through Natalia's corneas, and she squirmed in pain.

Behind her, Caleb Thorne snickered. "Stupid girl. Jakobek is dead. And soon, you will be too."

The Billy creature smiled. Blood dripped between his teeth. He seized Natalia's throat and clenched. *Can't breathe.* Natalia sputtered and felt her neck muscles crunch inward, and she saw...

Abuelita filled with bullet holes. Juan and Carlos dropping dead. Blood. Gore. Death all around her. Her fault. All of it had been her fault as she sat there in her room, drawing, wasting her time on frivolous little things. She saw Billy rising above a sea of dead bodies, his eyes glowing blue, pointing at her, saying, "It's all your fault. It is—"

"No!" She grabbed Billy's hands. "You're not Billy Jakobek!" She held his fingers, closed her eyes, and focused. *Love.* She thought about the fire tower. *I love you.* The monster's grip on her throat loosened. She forced herself to remember their night together. Dancing in the snow. *I'll never let you go.* Billy released her and jerked back, emitting a monstrous sound so unearthly that the entire crowd screamed in anguish. Natalia's wheelchair skidded back.

Billy made his hand into a pistol and pointed it at himself. Cold metal pressed against Natalia's chin. *Oh, crap.* She looked down. Her hand was holding the gun to her throat. She didn't remember picking it up. She tried to lower it, but her hand wouldn't budge. *He's got me locked in.*

Billy walked toward her with a fiendish grin. Natalia's finger slid to the trigger. *I deserve to die.* She swallowed. *I hurt everyone I love. I want to die.* She looked at Billy's face—a face she no longer recognized but which had once been that of the only person in the world who had ever truly understood her, a person who had seen inside of her, had plunged into her depths, and still found her worth loving.

If he doesn't love me anymore, I deserve to die. A weight pressed down against her chest. A coldness chilled her veins.

"No." She pushed her hand down, fighting the ripples of electricity that pulsed through her arm. "I'm not a victim."

Billy's eyes widened.

Natalia spun her chair sideways, pulled the trigger—and shot Caleb Thorne in the leg.

"You bitch!" he screamed, dropping his gun and falling to the ground. Blood pooled around him. The children with guns clustered around her.

Oh, now I'm dead. Billy approached her, seething with rage. Natalia felt the gun being lifted to her throat again—and she threw it aside. "I'm not going to shoot you."

She turned to face the crowd. She felt each of them, like little fishhooks inside her, and Billy, the *real* Billy, was inside her too. She pointed at the creature behind her. "Listen to me, people!" she shouted, staring into the reddened eyes of everyone around her. "This... this thing back there is not the Billy we know. It's a monster Thorne created. Thorne trapped him, and all of us, in a box. We don't have to stay in it!"

"Fucking—" Thorne started, but he was drowned out by a hubbub of whispers.

"That's not Billy!" Natalia cried, facing the monster again then turning back to the crowd. "Remember who the real Billy Jakobek was? He was compassionate. Kind. He wanted to help people—"

"Silence!" the monster roared, lunging for her.

Natalia whirled. *Think fast.* She reached into the side of her chair and ripped out her sketchbook. She flipped it to *Dark-Eyed Boy* and held the drawing up for the crowd surrounding her. "*This* is Billy!"

The mob went dead silent then began murmuring.

The pale figure ripped Natalia out of her chair, sending it spinning backward. He lifted her into the air, squeezing her throat. Black tendrils whirled around the boy's oily muscles.

Gasping for air, Natalia forced her drawing in front of the creature's glowing blue eyes. "L... look..."

The creature tried to look away. It tried to swat the drawing out of its sight. But Natalia held on to it more tightly than she'd ever held anything in her life and forced Billy to see what she'd done. Hours of painstaking details. Weeks of wrist pain. Months of hard work. All of her energy, poured into the ink, carved into white paper.

The creature's squeeze loosened, and Natalia choked out, "This is the real you, Billy. I love you."

The drawing depicted a tiny curly-haired boy with black eyes, wearing the hulking armor of a medieval knight. The armor was made of sheets of paper falling from the stars and coming together. The boy in knight's armor lifted a glowing sword to the sky, shining a light through the darkness—and that light spread to each of the same stars. He was sharing his light, giving it to others. The armor was too heavy for him, and he was tired, but he stood tall and proud, never giving up.

Natalia kept the drawing mere inches from the creature's face. *Don't let that fucking thing go, girl.* Suddenly, she heard a shuffling in the crowd, and across the parking lot, Felix broke through and raised his fist to the sky.

"She's right!" Felix cried. "That's not Billy! The real Billy is in that drawing!"

Paul stepped up beside Felix and seized his boyfriend's hand. "Free Billy!" he chanted.

Natalia pulled on every hook inside her. She focused on love. *I love you, Billy. You're not this.* She heard clicking and clattering, opened her eyes, and saw the children around them dropping their guns. She felt the heat of passion rising behind her from all of her classmates, the children she'd spent her entire life going to school with.

"Whatever you are, you blue-eyed freak, you're no god-dang Billy Jakobek!" an old man shouted, and his dog barked in agreement.

"Billy would never do this!" Hassan yelled.

Felix's mother stamped her foot. "Bring the real Billy back!"

The monster's eyes flickered dark for a second. "I'm not... not a good... person..." He shook his head, snarled, and the blue flames returned.

"Shut up." Natalia kissed him. He tried to fight her off. She kissed him harder. His mouth tasted of blood, but she held tightly as the creature slumped down to his knees. She collapsed to the ground beside him, her legs knotting beneath her with a loud crack. She couldn't move. Suddenly, she felt a sea of hands lifting her back into a sitting position. She couldn't see. Her head was dizzy.

A hazy shadow emerged before her. Slowly, her vision cleared, and it became the real Billy again. *My Billy.*

His black eyes filled with tears. "Natalia." He was crying. He clutched her. "I'm here."

The hundreds of bystanders, released from their psychic control, huddled together in terror and confusion. Billy held Natalia, and they cried on each other's shoulders.

"Billy."

"I'm here," he repeated, drawing back so she could see him. "I won't—"

Blaring gunfire shredded the air. "This is *not* how it goes!" Thorne roared.

People screamed. Bodies dropped. Thorne limped through the crowd, trekking blood, gunning down anyone in his path. He sprayed the front of the factory with bullets. Flames gushed from the windows. The crowd screamed. People ran. Thorne charged forward, and his gunfire sprayed all the nearby cars, lighting them up into glowing orange flowers, spilling smoke into the sky.

Billy's eyes flashed blue.

"Billy!" Natalia grabbed him, but Billy stood up. She seized his leg, pulling him back—and his eyes went dark again. "Stay with me!" she cried. "Make him drop the gun!"

Billy winced. Veins throbbed on his neck. He turned to Thorne with dark eyes and said, "Drop the gun, Caleb."

Thorne sneered. "Not so powerful when the Shape isn't around, are you?" He swerved to butt the gun against Billy's face and froze in midair. His hands slowly pried themselves loose from the weapon, and he released it to the ground.

Billy collapsed in exhaustion. Thorne grunted, crawled forward, and tried to grab the gun again, but Billy kicked it away. Fire spiraled around them. The front of the factory collapsed, bursting into flaming pieces in the parking lot. Suddenly, Thorne broke into a seizure, shaking and twisting as he desperately tried to reach for the gun again.

Another burst of flames shot into the air. Sweat poured down Natalia's skin. A piece of metal flew from the burning factory and missed her ear by less than an inch. "We need to get out of here!" she called out then choked on the fumes.

In the reddened flames, a dark shadow appeared behind Billy. It was the darkest thing Natalia had ever seen, a cutout in time and space. Total blackness. Two glowing blue eyes lit up on the Shape's face, and snakelike tendrils jutted out from its sides.

Billy, totally unaware of the menace growing behind him, crawled back toward Natalia. "Hey, we need to get you—"

"Watch out!" Natalia shrieked.

Billy turned—too late. The Shape seized him in its claws. Its eight-foot frame towered over Billy's body, and it dragged Billy away, right through the flames.

Natalia tried to pull herself forward. "Bring him back!" she called out.

The Shape turned around, and for the briefest of moments, it gazed upon Natalia. Despite the flaming catastrophe, shivers ran through her as if she'd stepped into a freezer. A sense of loss ripped through her heart. *It's over. It's all meaningless. Life is... nothing... nothing...*

Then the Shape looked away, and the heat returned. The fire crackled. Thorne limped off, spilling blood, and as smoke cascaded into Natalia's lungs, she felt herself slipping into unconsciousness. Staring into the distance, she was relieved to see that the thousands of bystanders had mostly run far away. *I saved them.* Flames scorched her flesh. *But Billy...*

"Come back..." she groaned.

The Shape cut through the air with its claws, carving another black hole in the fabric of reality. Shadows screamed from the fissure. Flames were sucked inside. The Shape stepped into its cosmic gateway, dragging Billy along with it, and the portal closed. "Come back here, Billy!" Natalia screamed. "I love you—come back!"

A hunk of debris exploded into Natalia's head, and she went unconscious.

Part IX:

Chokhmah

84: Billy

Billy's senses faded. Sight disappeared first. Taste became a dry feeling on his tongue, and then he had no tongue at all. Smell went from bitter pungency to nothingness. For what seemed like an eternity, he was imprisoned in a state of blackness. Nothing existed, but flashes of memory struck him like lightning. *Torture. The TV screens.* He twisted in the ether. *The factory. They followed me...* He twisted back. *Me. I was their master. Guns. Carnage.*

He gasped, bursting through a cloud of darkness. "That wasn't me." He barely remembered it. *It doesn't feel like me.*

He woke up on his back, sprawled out upon hard rocks. The scarlet clouds of the Shadow Place loomed above him. He rolled over and coughed. Somewhere far away, flames snapped. *That's from the real world. I'm not there anymore.*

"Oy vey," he groaned, shakily rising to his feet.

Machinery clattered around him. Deformed pistons of flesh towered over him, a factory powered by muscles and charged by tubes of blood and electricity. Crackling noises cut into his ears, and smoke burned into the sky, feeding the Feeders. He shaded his eyes, staring into the redness, and caught a glimpse of a Feeder's wormlike body twisting through the clouds. *Disgusting.* He stepped away from the flesh factory. *The Shadow Place feels different this time. It's not a dream anymore. This time, it's...*

"It's real," said Natalia.

Billy jumped. "Natalia?" His voice echoed through the factory, and he spun in a circle. "Where are you?"

He walked into a darkened tunnel, calling her name. To his side, on a blackened brick wall hung millions of hooks, and upon each was suspended a groaning, squirming human skeleton. The bony creatures helplessly reached out to him. Billy dodged their fingers as one pulled on his hair. "I can't. I'm sorry." He danced away, shivering, and then bolted through the tunnel, back outside the factory, where he nearly collided with a barbed wire fence. Beyond the fence awaited a black-sand beach surrounded by an ocean of blood.

"Natalia!" he cried out. "Are you out there?" The bloody ocean rustled in the wind. *She's somewhere in there. I feel it.* Billy seized the fence, and the barbs sliced into his hands. He gritted his teeth. *Fight through it. Don't give up.* He pulled himself higher. "Natalia!" he shouted.

Her voice flittered through the air. "We can be together, baby."

Billy's wrist tore open. He fell backward. He climbed back to his feet. Across the fence, Natalia emerged from the ocean, stepping out of it like a blood-soaked mermaid. Every inch of her body was coated with red.

Steam rose from her as she tiptoed along the water's surface, finally approaching the fence with a beaming smile. "Hey, you."

Billy's heart lurched. "Why are you here? This is the place of nightmares—"

"This is reality, man." Natalia's slender arm snaked through the barbed links. Her skin was impervious to the spikes. She squeezed Billy's hand, and he sighed at the electrical tingles. *It feels just like her.* Blood dripped down the sides of her shaven head. "Billy, you need to join me so we can be free."

"Free from what?"

"From caring about others." Her eyes glowed vulnerably. "Free from spending all our time trying to care, trying to help, instead of just selfishly focusing on our own needs. That's what we need to do, Billy. That's what *you* need to do."

Billy frowned. He squeezed her hand. "Natalia, what are you talking about?"

"Salvation." She pursed her lips. "Freedom in apathy."

Billy turned back to the pumping machinery behind him. He listened to the rattling of the skeletons. "I don't understand."

"You need to stop caring about others all the time." Natalia smiled at him, running her bloody fingers across his neck. "Let the world be chaotic, baby. Let pain happen. Let people suffer. You can't fix it, so why waste time caring?"

"But people... we're all in this together."

"No, Billy. You're better than them." Her eyes narrowed. "You're a *special* person. That's what you've never understood. The Shape showed me that."

Billy jerked away. "No." He released her hand. "Stop it."

"It's time for you to take the next step." The blood-soaked Natalia stood across the fence with hooked fingers. "Then we can be together. Forever. *Forever*, Billy, with no messy human bullshit to tear us apart ever again."

Behind her, as the red ocean rustled, more familiar faces swam onto the shore. Eli lunged onto the black sands, giggling like the little boy he was. Billy's parents came next, holding hands, offering Billy warm smiles. "Join us!" they called out. Natalia's two little brothers followed, running around in circles as blood dripped from their bodies. The reddened crowd stepped up to the barbed wire fence, and they all reached through the rungs, trying to grab Billy.

"Hold my hand, son," Dad called out.

"The Shape will lead the way," Natalia said.

Caleb Thorne, limping from the water, cast his eyes downward. "I was always jealous of your power." He looked up. "You're better than all of us. Above us. You deserve to be free from our shit."

Mother emerged next. "You were always the best of us."

"You're the coolest, Billy!" Red-stained Eli hopped up and down, splashing blood at Juan and Carlos. "Stop wasting your time on other people!"

"Yeah!" Juan cried.

Billy backed farther away. The distant squirming sounds of the Feeders tightened his jaw. *Maybe they're right.* He shook his head. *No, no, I can't think that way. I can't. Unless...* He faced the demonic factory—the Shadow Place he had feared his whole life—and stared into its hideousness. *I've had nightmares about this place so many times. But it's not scary anymore. It's not any worse than the world I know.* He carefully examined the tubes pouring smoke into the sky. At the base of each tube, screams of pain, sadness, and heartbreak pumped from the earth. *It's my world that feeds this place.* He closed his eyes and shuddered at the memory of an entire town following his command. *It wasn't me. Something else was commanding my body. But the moments I remember, they feel... it felt so... so...*

"He has come!" Billy's mother yelled, and all of the bloody people kneeled. A look of adoration overcame their faces.

Oh, man. Here it comes. Don't panic. Tension sizzled the air. Smoke ran across the ground. Machinery squealed. *Stay cool, Billy. Stay cool.* Rusty gears pierced the musculature that powered them. The hot air churned with white noise. *Don't look into its eyes.*

Billy turned around to find the Shape hovering before him.

"Truth is a lie!" the crowd screamed in unison.

The dark figure lowered to the ground. Its incandescent-blue eyes cast light across the desert. Billy crashed backward into the fence. Its barbs sliced open his back. "Ah!" he cried, jumping away.

The Shape moved closer. *Don't panic, Billy.* There was nowhere to hide. The expressionless shadow emitted the coldness of a freezer door left open. Billy stood before it, his heart pounding harder and harder, and he coughed out words. "You're the Shape." His voice was weak, tiny. "You were controlling me. You... used me."

The Shape examined him up and down, but it didn't speak. *It doesn't do that.* Its black shoulders heaved in and out as if it were breathing, and wisps of smoke streamed from its sides.

"He is the answer!" Caleb Thorne yelled from behind, and Billy's father sobbed tears of joy as he shouted, "The Shape is freedom!"

Billy's stomach rushed up his throat. *This is the end.* "You've always tortured me," he said, lowering his gaze. Anxious tears stung his eyes. "You've been manipulating me. Trying to poison me. Poisoning everything I care about. The world—you're the one destroying the world."

The Shape reached downward. The ground rumbled. Rocks and stones warped upward in its magnetic grasp, forming massive rifts within the earth, each one emitting an ethereal glow. The Shape turned away and walked back to the factory, ripping new holes in the ground as it went.

"Follow him, big bro!" Eli yelled.

Billy turned to face Natalia. She looked sad. "Please follow him," she pleaded.

Billy's heart thudded. "Okay," he whispered. He followed the Shape's path, looking down into the interdimensional rifts, and saw portals into the real world. Inside the first crack were scenes from the Nazi concentration camps. He jumped back, horrified and angry. "Why are you showing me this?"

The Shape kept walking toward the factory. Billy looked back at the Nazi camps, caught a glimpse of his grandmother's face, and walked onward. *It's awful.* In the next fissure, he saw human slavery. Men and women were forced onto boats, shipped to another country, and sold like objects. Whipped, chained, tortured. The fissure rushed through time, showing generations of Jim Crow laws, mass incarceration, and police brutality.

He shook his head. *I can't look at this.* In another crack, he saw Japanese internment camps. Another one showed the atom bomb—millions of people destroyed by death, disfigurement, and cancer.

He looked back at the red ocean, and the crowd of blood-soaked people cheered him on. "Keep walking!" they cried. "Don't stop looking!"

I won't stop. He looked in another fissure and saw children in cages, separated from their families. He saw Nazi rallies on US soil, where hate-filled faces shouted, "Jews will not replace us!" and he kept walking. Latin America was torn apart before his eyes, violence begetting more violence. The destruction of Aleppo rang through his ears. People were shot. Torn apart. Beheaded. Shrapnel explosions in Laos tore off a farmer's face. Children in the Congo were turned into child soldiers. Billy looked at all of it, following the Shape into the darkness, and his heart felt sicker and sicker.

"Stop!" Billy shouted.

The interdimensional rifts instantly sealed up. The Shape turned around. Its blue flames flickered.

"I know that all this horrible stuff happens in the world." Billy quivered. "Why are you showing it to me?"

A little boy stepped out of the Shape's darkness, and Billy instantly recognized it as himself, the child he'd once been, wearing a red superhero cape. "Because these things aren't caused by the Shape, Billy," the child said.

Billy shuddered. "Stop it."

"It's true." The boy had teary eyes. "All the bad stuff is caused by humans, you know."

"Yeah." Billy hated looking at his younger self. *Get that thing away from me.* "Manipulated by the Shape to—"

"That's not an excuse." The little boy looked up, now possessing the dark figure's glowing blue eyes. "It was people who *did* all of this. The hatred, all that crap. Please, Billy"—the little boy crept forward—"stop caring. Stop hurting yourself over other humans. Humans are evil. You're better than them. Let them hurt each other.

Please, please..." The boy's voice warped to a deep drone. "Give in to the Shape."

The Shape's eyes burned hotter. Black tendrils shot out of the figure's abdomen, seized Billy, and slithered down his throat. He gagged. The tendrils tasted of iron. They filled his mouth, crept into his eyes, and constricted around his limbs.

"Mmfff!" Billy tried to breathe.

"You're above them all!" Natalia's voice cried out in the distance. "Billy, you are the power! You can be free. You are the Shape!"

"The Shape!" they all chanted. "The Shape! The Shape!"

Billy gasped for air. He grabbed at the tendrils, trying to rip them from his throat. He stared into the glowing blue eyes of the Shape—and those of his childhood self—and screamed against the hot slime pouring down his lungs. "Gnnnghh!"

"You're better than them," the little Billy said in the same horrible warped voice. "You know that... and you love the power. The privilege. The strength."

Billy struggled against the tendrils. *No, I don't want of this!*

"Yes, you do!" little Billy pleaded. "Stop lying, Billy! Every time you've killed people... hurt people... fed from them... you've loved it! I'm you, so I know. *We* loved it."

Caleb Thorne rattled the barbed wire fence. "I wish I could be you, Billy!"

"When you absorb their pain, you make yourself weaker." The little boy stepped closer, holding Billy's hand. "You give them strength, but you hurt yourself. Stop hurting yourself. Be free. Let the Shape do what it's gotta do, and you... feed off them, like the Shape does." The boy looked up, his eyes glowing hotter. "Let the world burn. You can't fix it. Otherwise... the Shadow Place will always be inside you."

Billy struggled to breathe. The Shape's tendrils were wriggling inside his skull. *I want to be free. I don't want to be in the Shadow Place.*

"I want to be free!" he wheezed then coughed out slime. "Please... please!"

The little boy stepped back into the Shape's darkness and faded away. The tendrils slithered from Billy's throat. He buckled forward, coughing out acid. His eyes stung. His head felt congested. *Breathe... breathe...* The Shape stood over him, waiting and watching. "I don't... want... to be in the Shadow Place." Billy gagged again. "Free... want to be free..."

The blood-soaked crowd roared in approval. Little Eli's voice rose above the rest, screaming, "You're special, Billy!"

Billy nodded. *Maybe I am special. Different. Maybe I do deserve to not give a shit. I sure as hell can't fix the world's problems.* An icy sensation struck his chest. He stopped breathing. *Wait. I can't feel my heartbeat.* There was no pain. No emotions. No electricity. *Oh no.* He felt his neck and couldn't detect a pulse. His heart had stopped.

The dark figure's feet stepped before him. Billy lifted his gaze. The Shape held out a dripping, bloody lump of flesh, which was beating frenetically. *The Shape's heart. To replace mine if I...* He shook his head. *Why the hell do I suddenly want to eat it? That's gross. But... I do?* He stood up, and the dark figure extended the heart closer. It dripped with wet, slippery redness. Black veins stretched across its surface. Billy looked closer.

Wait. That's not a heart. It was a fruit. An apple.

Billy's reflection stared back from the apple's liquid surface. *I look so young.* The word *apathy* was carved into its stem in tiny letters.

"Eat it!" cried Dad.

Mom joined in. "Eat it now! This is the final step!"

Billy looked up at the Shape's smoky eyes. He looked back at the apple that had been wrenched from his chest. *Eat it?* Despite the bloody grotesqueness of the fruit, his mouth watered. *Hell. I actually want it.* Tears stung his eyes. *Freedom, that is.* He could already imagine the satisfying crunch of his teeth biting into it. He imagined the sweet taste of it in his mouth, its glistening juices running down his chin. *This is what I was meant to do. This is who I am meant to be. I can feel it now.*

"If I eat this..." Billy looked up. "I'll be free from all the pain?"

The Shape nodded, and Billy was oddly reminded of himself—the silent, nodding boy he had been for most of his life, unable to speak normally. *The Shape is just like me.* He reached for the apple then hesitated.

He looked up at the Shape. "This is my only chance at happiness, isn't it?"

Again, the Shape nodded. *This is it.* He breathed in deeply. *Last call for a happy life. No more pain. No more losing everything.* He took the apple into his hands. It was cool, wet, and succulent. He ran his finger down the stem then stared up into the scarlet sky, past the Feeders, and into space. *Bubbe*, he thought, *is this right?*

He closed his eyes, and the colors disappeared into a cascade of blinding lights.

85

He is somewhere else. Not in the reality of the Shadow Place. Not in the world he knows. A rainbow kaleidoscope of lights blinds him, and the glowing outlines of other people cast fractal shadows upon his eyes. He can't see, but he can feel the energy of his grandmother, and suddenly, the heart-apple feels heavy in his hands. "Bubbe, I don't know what to do."

Bubbe sighs. Her heavy frame stands before him, and her silhouette sparkles with all the colors. In the distinctly Eastern European accent that lines all his childhood memories, she says, "Not up to me. It is your decision to make."

"I'm afraid of being hurt even more." He looks down in shame. "And I... did like the power. God. Even though it wasn't really me. After everything I've been through. It felt so good to..." He grits his teeth. "It *feels* so good to be angry."

"Yes."

He tries to hug Bubbe, but he cannot touch her. She is in the mist in the rainbow lights. He shakes the apple in his hands. "Bubbe, am I... special?"

"No," she says.

Billy looks up in surprise. "But you always said I have a light—"

"Inside you, yes." She chuckles. "But you, yourself? You are not the light, little one. The light is in all of us, as human beings. You? You just have the power to see that light, to help us all bring it together, yes?"

Another darkened figure appears alongside Bubbe, an old woman in a wheelchair—Isabel, Natalia's abuelita, sitting alongside his own grandmother. "It's not about you," Isabel says. "It's about all of us."

To Billy's amazement, dozens of fractalized people appear in the mist. Hundreds. Thousands. He can't see their faces, but he feels their energies. They are his real family—the people he has met in his life. Inside all of their chests, Billy sees lights, thousands of little rainbow refractions reaching out to him. Within each of these lights, he sees acts of kindness. Compassion. A man teaches his daughter how to ride a bike. A nurse lifts an old man off the ground. People line up at a blood drive, getting no payment but the reward of helping others. Volunteers help the people in a drowning village, building new houses for them on dry land. Each person has light inside them. Each person shares that light with others. Everyone—people helping others. Two boys run through a field, laughing, with little capes tied around their shoulders.

"Kids in capes..." Billy swallows, remembering. Each of the pulsing hearts emanates love. In the light, people hug each other. Nurses heal the sick. Bullies are brought down. People feel. They connect. They stand up to tyrants. The thread unifying the lights grows stronger. "I see it," he says. He looks down at himself and sees how his light is linked to all the others by glowing threads of energy.

"Yes." Bubbe nods. "But it goes deeper. We are all on the same path. We all connect. There are no individuals, Billy. Everything is one."

In the sky above it all, shining brilliantly like a series of suns, are ten glowing spheres. All of these spheres are connected, and pathways move between them. Malkuth. Yesod. Hod. Netzach. Tiferet. Chesed. Gevurah. Binah. Chokhmah. Keter. A tree of life. Billy sees that the lights inside him, inside everyone, are connected to these spheres. "That's the path," he whispers. He looks down at the apple in his hands. "I understand."

"Do what you must," Isabel says.

"Yeah," Eli whispers. "Do it for all of us."

Something soft wraps around Billy. He feels the arms of Natalia gripping him tightly as she kisses his cheek. "Remember who you are, baby," she whispers. "Remember where you come from."

The light fades. Billy opens his eyes.

86

The polluted air crackled. The Feeders squirmed through the clouds. Billy stood in the Shadow Place, across from the Shape. The apple glistened in his hands. "I'm ready," Billy whispered. "Ready to do the thing I was always meant to do."

The Shape's eyes flickered. It nodded in approval.

Billy smelled the apple's sweet aroma. He turned it around, letting the cold blood flow over his fingers. His mouth craved it. Taking one last glance at the Shape's penetrating blue gaze, Billy closed his eyes, cleared his throat, and recited, "*Baruch ata Adonai Eloheinu*"—as he spoke, the light ignited inside him—"*melekh ha'olam po'ke'ah ivrim.*"

The light was joined by a cascade of more lights. He opened his eyes. The Shape backed away in shock as its blue eyes widened. The Shadow Place shuddered. The blood-soaked imitations of everyone he knew melted into the ground.

"I believe in humanity." Billy dropped the apple. "I don't believe in you."

Billy crushed the bruised fruit beneath his heel and kicked away the remains. The Shape's electric presence screeched in horror. Lights burst through the darkness, shining like lasers into Billy's heart. He opened himself to them. *It's not about me.* He felt heat rising into his fingertips. *It's about us.* The lights of the stars bathed him in energy.

Smoke swirled around the Shape. It grew taller. Deeper. Tendrils spiraled from its sides. Billy ran toward it. He ran faster, faster, feeling the rainbow of lights swim around his body and form segmented shapes over his skin—iridescent fractals—becoming like a second skin. A Star of David glowed from his chest, and a glowing armor spread around him—a thin, breakable one, no thicker than paper, but an armor that gave him strength, powerful because it was fragile and formed of so many pieces. *I'm not the light. All of us are.* He thought back to Natalia's drawing as that very image came to life around him. *Thanks, Natalia.*

He leapt over an explosion, continuing his battle charge toward the Shape. With every step, the knight expanded around him. He saw the faces of his loved ones running beside him—inside the knight, part of the knight—and he smiled at his mom and dad. Bubbe was there. Eli leapt on his shoulders. Suddenly, he heard a myriad of voices speaking in other languages—from Russian to Spanish to Yiddish—and he saw the faces of his ancestors all running alongside him inside the armor. A tall dark man strode to the front, wearing his own armor, and he had the same black eyes as Billy. *It's the ancestor who shares my middle name. Heh.* He smiled. *Isaac, the Spanish knight.*

Everyone raced forward, charged into the collapsing factory, and collided with the dark figure. The Shape's shadowy claws wrapped around the giant knight's throat. The armor protected them, but they shuddered at the monster's blows. Billy's lungs seized up. *Think fast.* Remembering Natalia's drawing, he reached to the sky. The light of the stars raced toward him, shimmering up the length of his arm with ripples of electricity. A glowing broadsword appeared in his hand.

Billy brought the sword down upon the Shape. Its shimmering blade sliced right through the dark figure. The powerful being split in half. A reverberating scream echoed through the city, bringing down the remains of the factory. Blood ripped from the sky like rain.

Billy fell to the floor. The knight disappeared, but Billy still held the glowing sword, and in the place where he had cut the Shape hovered an illuminated hole in space. Inside it, he saw the flames of the Thorne Century Factory. Heaven's Hole. He saw Natalia—the real Natalia—trapped on the ground, crying out for him.

The sky crackled. The Feeders groaned. Billy looked behind him. The dark figure was rapidly pulling itself back together. *I need to go back.* He leapt into the portal—but before he could vanish inside it, the Shape seized his legs.

"No!" Billy cried.

Natalia reached through the glowing rift and grabbed his hand. "Come back here, Billy!" She held on tight, but her grip slipped on his sweaty fingers.

The portal was rapidly fading. *I don't have much time.* The Shape seized Billy's arm, pulling it back, ripping open the tendons and snapping the bones. Billy screamed in pain.

"I love you! Come back!" Natalia tried to yank Billy through the glowing portal while the Shape pulled him to the shadows. His shoulders snapped back and forth. The Shape's glowing blue eyes raged at him with relentless intensity.

A chunk of debris slammed into Natalia's head. She went unconscious. Her fingers slipped free, and she disappeared into the glowing whirlpool. The Shape's claws cracked the bones in Billy's right hand, shattering his wrist. His shoulder popped out of its socket.

The portal was almost closed. Billy pulled and heaved, but he wasn't strong enough. He swung his sword at the dark figure, but it dodged every slash.

Billy glared into the Shape's furious blue eyes. *I can't go to the future without losing something of the past. I knew that. I always knew it.* Screaming at the top of his lungs, he brought the shimmering blade down upon his own right arm. It slashed right through his muscle and bone, lopping off everything beneath the shoulder. His nerves screeched in pain. Blood gushed from the wound—but the Shape flew backward, clutching the severed limb.

Billy dropped the sword. "I'll never give up."

Billy leapt into the glowing portal. Light embraced him. The Shape disappeared, locked away in its Shadow Place, as Billy was flung into somewhere new—a place of light and darkness mixed together. *It's all together. We're all together.* He saw nothing, but he felt Natalia's hand grasping his, drawing him deeper into the glowing energy and deeper into the world that the Shape had thought so unsolvable. Warmth filled Billy's chest.

He faded into the light.

87

Lightness. Darkness. All of it intermingled. Billy stands in a colorless landscape, seeing time and space spread before him like a map. He's holding Natalia's hand. She smiles at him. They're on the fire tower again, with the universe beneath them.

"Can we stay like this forever?" Natalia asks.

"I don't think we can stay here yet." Billy holds her tightly. He never wants to let go. "It wouldn't be right. This here, what we have... I think this is what comes after."

"After what?"

"After we die." He shrugs and looks at her. "You're not going to die today. I don't want to lose you—"

"What if I lose you first?" Natalia asks worriedly. She is staring to fade. He knows that the moment is ending. She knows. Neither of them knows what comes next.

"I'll wait for you no matter where I am. Here. There. Wherever." Billy feels himself fading away then gaining weight, heaviness, mass. "But if we meet again someday, I'd like to hold your hand, while the world—"

88

Tiny droplets of water speckled Billy's face. *It's raining.* He opened his eyes and saw snowflakes melting in orange plumes of smoke. *No, not rain.* His body was soaked in perspiration. Flames snapped around him. *Oy vey.*

"Natalia..." he groaned.

The air felt like an oven. *I have to get up. Natalia needs me.* A distant scream rushed through him. He rolled over, rose to his knees, and coughed out the smoke in his lungs. *So thick.* Sweat dripped over his face. He tried to lift himself up on the weight of his right arm, but nothing happened. *It's asleep.* He pushed up again, but he wasn't strong enough. He wriggled his fingers, felt them move—then saw that his right arm was a stump. No wound, no lacerations. It was just gone, as if it had never existed. *Holy shit.*

His horror was tamped down by a sense of urgency. *I don't have time to deal with that. Natalia is—*

Fire burst from the factory. Pieces of shrapnel spewed outward. Billy got up, using his still-existent left arm for leverage, and stood. He crashed back down, choking on the fumes. The front wall of the factory was a mess of molten metal and glass. Most of the crowd had run far away. *I feel them. They're safe.* But the remains of a wheelchair were melted before him, and near that, trapped under a piece of burning wall, was Natalia.

"I'm coming!" he shouted.

Billy rushed forward, keeping his head low. When he coughed, his lungs felt blackened. A siren hollered in the distance. *Too far away. Keep going.* Fire licked his skin off. The pungent odor of burning oil nearly caused him to pass out, but he pushed forward. Onward. *Keep fighting.* Natalia was unconscious. A section of burning wall had pinned her to the ground.

"I'm here!" he cried then broke down coughing.

He seized the debris. It scalded his one hand, and he jumped back. "Damn it!" He grabbed the wall again, screaming as it burned his hand again, and fell back. Amid the crackling flames, Natalia breathed weakly. Her cheek was flayed, as was the back of her neck. Horrific burns had torn blackened holes into her shoulders and back.

"Shit!" He kicked at the debris. It fragmented. He kicked harder, and the collapsed wall broke into chunks, clearing a path for Natalia's body. Billy broke down coughing. *Move. Move!* Crouching down, he grabbed her and pulled with the strength of his only arm. *Damn it, if I ever needed the other one...* He kicked at the wall again and yanked with all his might. Natalia slid free. "Yes!" he cried.

With a deep heave, he lifted her over his shoulders. *God, for a tiny girl, she feels so heavy.* Her beloved sketchbook had been pinned beneath her body, uninjured by the flames. Billy tucked it under his arm—swaying, with Natalia on his back—and pulled her through the flames like a train with too much weight on it.

An explosion rocked the building behind him. He trudged through the smoke. He couldn't see. All he felt were flames, sweat, and heaviness. The sirens amplified.

A blast of water broke through the flames. *A fire hose.* Others followed. *They made it.* Billy broke through the wall of smoke into the clearing past the flames and crashed into the asphalt. He rolled Natalia off of his body, dropped the sketchbook, and coughed. Fire trucks surrounded him. Firemen sprayed water onto the factory. Another ambulance screeched into the parking lot. *So dizzy.* He started to collapse then roused himself. *Keep pushing on.* He kicked the sketchbook ahead of him, grabbed Natalia's collar, and pulled her toward the ambulance. Ashes fell from the sky, mixing with the snow. The doors of the vehicle slammed open.

"Hey!" Billy called.

In the haze of smoke and fire, two EMTs lunged through and grabbed them. Billy shook them away, pointing at Natalia. "Get her!" He coughed. As they lifted her onto a stretcher, Billy went back and tucked the sketchbook under his arm.

Despite his pleas, another EMT ran up and put an oxygen mask on his face. "Breathe, son."

The cool crispness in his lungs had never felt so relieving. He inhaled. *Wow. That feels good.* The man wrapped a blanket around Billy's shoulders.

As his senses returned to him, he looked back at the factory. The firemen were winning the battle. The flames were dying down.

Billy felt a series of heartbeats pitter-patter in his chest, and he listened.

"We're free," a sea of voices whispered from within the factory.

He quietly lowered his oxygen mask. "You're free," he repeated as one last burst of flame emerged from the factory's bowels. The battery—and any scraps of life within it—burned away, their torment finally ended.

Natalia groaned behind him. "Billy... can you hear... Billy..."

The paramedics carried her stretcher into the ambulance. She had an oxygen mask strapped to her face. Just as they were about to close the doors, Billy lunged into the back of the vehicle. "I'm going with her."

The paramedic in the back nodded. "Fine, then sit down, and let's move!"

Billy did so, and the paramedic handed him a new oxygen mask. The ambulance hollered down the streets of Heaven's Hole. Billy looked back at the smoky inferno. Most of the factory was still standing, but the battery was dead. *That's what matters.* He shuffled next to Natalia's stretcher.

She smiled at him, revealing eyes so engorged with blood that their whites were dark red. "Hey, you." She coughed.

"Hey." Billy smiled back. "I brought this." He showed her the sketchbook.

She closed her eyes. "Turn... to the back page."

The ambulance shuddered over a pothole. Billy almost dropped the sketchbook. Leafing through it—it took longer than expected, due to his missing hand—he came upon two passports tucked into the back with a wad of cash. "What's this?"

"Passport..." The ambulance went over a bump, and she cried out in pain. "You... you need to go..." She broke into another cough, and the holes in her flesh cut into Billy like knives. "They'll... blame this on you..."

"I don't understand." He glanced at the paramedic, but the man was too preoccupied with equipment to listen.

Bloody tears streaked down Natalia's reddened face. "Passport..." Her voice was scratchy. "Look." With her charred, blackened hand, she thumped the passports. "You need to go. Please go."

Billy looked. The passports contained his and Natalia's pictures but different identities—Samuel Miller and Cynthia Rogers. He shook his head. "We, you mean." His eyes welled up. "Together."

"No, *you*." Her lip quivered. "You have to go alone, Sam."

The ambulance rushed down empty streets, past a crowd of confused onlookers. Billy looked out the window. The pillar of smoke from the factory filled the skyline. "I can't leave you," he said.

"You have to go." She sobbed. "Promise me you'll go." Her damaged eyes were so red he could barely look at them. "Sam Miller, fucking promise me that you'll take that passport to the nearest airport and get the hell out of this country. Do it. Go places. Help people. Do some good in the world. Be safe. Don't let them lock you up again."

Billy shivered and glanced back at the paramedic. *He can't hear us.* The ambulance zoomed down the road.

"Almost there!" the man shouted.

Billy leaned close to her. "But Thorne Century will—"

"I have to stay here. I have to take that company down. I'm the one who has to do it." Natalia ground her teeth. "Mother emailed me everything. All the dirt. I'll..." She winced. "What's coming ahead... that's my battle to fight, not yours. Please go. Don't let them take you again. Take my sketchbook too. Take the drawing, and look at it whenever... whenever..." More bloody tears ran down her neck. "God, this sucks."

Billy shook his head. "But—"

"Promise me."

He stared into her eyes. "I promise." He pressed his hand to her bloodied forehead. "I love you, Natalia." He closed his eyes, and his own flesh absorbed the pain in hers. His vision blackened. Psychic holes tore through his skin and muscles in the places of her burns, white-hot pain, hotter than anything he'd ever felt. The pains inside her rushed into him.

"Billy, don't do that..." She was crying. "Don't—"

"Shh." He closed her eyes. "I can take it." He touched the burns on her arms and legs, and her heartbeat slowed. Her breathing steadied. The pain scorched his insides, and he exhaled it out. "Sleep," he whispered through pained tears.

"Dark-eyed boy..." she mumbled, half-conscious. "I feel okay..."

"No pain," he said.

"No... pain..."

He clasped her hand. *Sleep, Natalia. Rest.* Her eyes fluttered closed. The ambulance pulled into the hospital parking lot. "Natalia..." He kissed her lips as the ambulance shuddered to a stop. "If we ever meet again someday, I'd like to hold your hand as the world explodes around us."

The back doors popped open. The paramedics unloaded Natalia's stretcher from the back of the truck. Her fingers slipped from Billy's hand as the paramedics hurried her into the emergency department and away from Billy's life. He looked down sadly and was startled when another paramedic appeared before him.

"Hey, kid! Let's get you in here too."

Billy shook his head. "Forget I'm here." The paramedic frowned, stepped back, then wandered into the hospital, looking disoriented.

Billy crept from the ambulance and looked at the passport in his hands. *Sam Miller, huh?* He clutched the sketchbook, feeling every bit of love that Natalia had poured inside every page. *All those nights staying up late, pressing her pen to the paper.* He kissed it. *I'll never let this go.*

He took one look back at the hospital, and despite his fears, his heart knew that Natalia was going to be okay. *Even if I never see her again.* He brushed the tears from his eyes and walked away.

89: Caleb

Caleb Thorne limped into the forest, tracking blood behind him. His pants were drenched with so much blood, sweat, and urine that he could smell it. He pushed through the hills, fighting the pain, occasionally stealing proud glances back at the smoldering fire he had started. *That was me. Not Billy. Nobody owns me. Nobody.* He pushed onward, trying to make as much space as possible between him and the scene. *Eyewitness reports from a bunch of illegals mean nothing. I can blame this on Jakobek. Easy. I just need to get far away from the scene.*

He stopped, leaned against a tree, and panted. *Of course I made it. The strong always survive.* He pushed up the crest of the hill then turned around and looked down at the burning skeleton that remained of his factory. The fire trucks were putting out the blaze. He grinned. *Only I could destroy my own masterpiece.* He exhaled. *Once I return to the city, the real project can get underway. Emotion bombs will be constructed around the country with the power I harnessed here.*

Another fire truck rolled into the parking lot. He looked between the flames, trying to spot corpses. "If you're not dead, Gonzalez," he said, "I'll go to your hospital bed and shoot you myself." He took the pistol out of his pocket, the same gun she'd fired at him, and twirled it. *Irony is beautiful.* "I'll make you watch as emotion bombs ripple across the world. I'll track down every family member you have, distant cousins, anything, and shoot them too. I'll rip your heart out of your chest and make you eat it, Gonzalez, you loser—"

Something snapped behind him.

He flipped around, waving his gun in the air. The trees were too thick to see through. As the heat roared behind him, snowflakes bit his flesh like little ice monsters. He crept forward. A stray branch whipped against his bleeding leg. "Aw, motherf—" He bit his lip.

"That's right," a female voice said. A loud pop went off. A searing pain jolted through his abdomen. Blood spurted onto the snow. Caleb felt the bullet wound in his stomach, gasped, and dropped to the ground. He crumpled, coughing out blood, as heavy footsteps crunched into the snow beside him.

"Asshole." Roseanna kicked him.

Caleb looked up at her face. *She's still so beautiful. Why is she doing this to me?* He coughed out blood. "Roseanna." Tears stung his eyes. "I... took care of you... why...?" He lifted his hand to touch her.

"You ruined my life." She shot his hand, splitting the tendons open.

"Ahh!" he screamed. He dropped his gun and cradled the broken hand. Blood spurted up his throat and down his wrist, and the bullet holes burned hotter than the flames had. "You ungrateful cunt!" He gazed up.

Roseanna smirked. "You don't know the half of it, Caleb, I just emailed every bit of classified information about the project. Your name is all over it. Human rights abuses that you'll never recover from. Your dad's company is going down."

"Emailed..." he groaned. "Who?"

"Natalia Gonzalez." Roseanna leaned down and blew a sweaty lock of hair from her eyes. "She's going to live through this, Caleb. And she's going to be interviewed by every major publication in the country. That child is going to destroy you."

Fucking bitch. Caleb reached for Roseanna's throat, but she stepped back. He coughed out blood. "I can... can just make calls, cover up the—"

"It's too late, Caleb." Roseanna tapped her gun against his head dismissively, and his heart burned with hatred.

He crawled toward her, sputtering out gore. *Traitor.* His heart pounded. "You'll never see your son and husband again," he growled. "I'll have them murdered—"

"Not if you're dead." Roseanna sighed and looked out at the flames. "Listen, Caleb, I know..."

As she gazed out upon the destruction, Caleb seized the moment. He slid the knife from his pocket and stabbed her ankle. She jumped back in shock. Caleb seized his gun, fired it, and pumped three bullets into Roseanna's chest.

She looked down in horror. "Christ."

She collapsed on top of him, gasping out blood, and Caleb wriggled out from beneath her. She tried to hold him down. He kicked her in the face, breaking her nose. *Dizzy. Stay steady.* He pointed his gun between her eyes. "You're the one who dies today, Peterson."

He listened to the ambulances below. *Need to get there fast. They'll treat my wounds.*

Roseanna looked up—shaking, blood pouring from her gut—and through her tears, she grinned. "No." She brought her gun to the center of Caleb's forehead. "We both die."

She pulled the trigger just as he pulled his—two gunshots in the forest, simultaneous, heard by no one. Roseanna Peterson died smiling, and Caleb Thorne slumped down into a muddy ditch, cast into the blackness, never to breathe again.

90

A few nights later, Natalia sat upright in her hospital bed. The room was dark except for the glow of the laptop—borrowed from Ms. Stevens—and the lamppost outside her window. It was two in the morning. The bandages on her body felt stiff. The burns ached. The IV still weirded her out. She felt tired but didn't want to go to sleep because every night since the incident had only brought nightmares.

An ambulance hollered outside, and she shuddered. *God, I don't want to remember.* She rubbed her eyes, wondering if it was time to call in more pain medication. She hated having to ask. *That crap makes the nightmares worse.* When the ambulance finally roared away, she felt relieved. *I wonder if I'll ever be able to hear that sound again without freaking out.* In her discomfort, she'd sunk into the bed, so she propped herself upright as best she could, fighting against the weight of her paralyzed legs. As she thrust upward, her bandages pulled hard against the raw wounds on her back. She cried out in pain. *Man, this blows.*

She cursed under her breath and flicked her screen back to life. She scrolled through the eight hundred fifteen unread emails she'd received from an endless wave of journalists, news stations, and Hollywood producers wanting to interview her, photograph her, or even adapt her story to a TV movie. *They don't waste any time—that's for sure.* So far, she hadn't replied to anyone—she'd barely been conscious until that night—and the news world was still desperately trying to find a narrative for the Heaven's Hole disaster. It didn't make sense to them. No one knew about the psychic part of the story—the key element. No one realized how corrupt Thorne had been. *All they know is some Guatemalan girl in a wheelchair stood up to Caleb Thorne and stopped a whole town from burning. I guess that's totally insane when you think about it. Hope you're proud, Abuelita. Your granddaughter is a lunatic.*

She scrolled farther down into her inbox—down, down, down—until she found the email from Dr. Roseanna Peterson with the subject Classified. She opened it. Three hundred documents were attached in a zip file. She hovered over the forward button, getting ready to blast it to every journalist who had emailed her... then stopped.

Natalia turned off her screen. She was tired. The pain was heating up again. *I just want a goddamn break.* She needed more pain medicine. *Or maybe just the healing touch of...* She shook her head. *No, he's gone. It's good. He needs to be gone, even if it rips my heart to pieces every time I remember his voice. Billy, can you hear me thinking about you?*

Billy. That was one element that all the confused news stories had commented on—that the test subject, a teenage boy, had vanished into thin air. He'd become a wanted fugitive, so she knew she would never see him again. Caleb Thorne had been found dead on the scene. *Best motherfucking surprise of my life.* The authorities were investigating his company. Still, analysts were already talking about who the new CEO would be. Thorne Century would live on. *Unless...* She touched the mouse pad. *Unless I can stop it.*

The screen flicked back to life. Dr. Peterson's email stared into Natalia's face. *Forget about my personal safety. This is about something bigger.* Natalia downloaded the files, went through her hundreds of emails, and sent the classified documents to every single person who had emailed her. She wrote up a press release, which she then copied and pasted, clearing the names of Billy Jakobek and everyone Thorne had framed. Then, just to make sure, she went on social media and uploaded the same batch of files to the public.

"It's done." She closed the laptop. "Hope you're enjoying hell, Thorne."

Natalia pushed the tray table aside, lowered the head of the bed, and nestled into her pillow. She closed her eyes. *I did it, Billy. Can you hear me?* She reached into the air, trying to feel him, trying to grasp at the spark of light that had once never felt far away, but he was gone. *Really gone this time. I'll never see him again. It's better for him if he stays disappeared. Besides, I have work to do.* She swallowed a choking sob.

"Goodbye, dark-eyed boy," she whispered.

Part X:

Keter

91: Sam Miller

The desert heat burned through Sam Miller's skin like the blades of a warmongering sun. His pack, filled with canned food, medicine, and toiletries, slid down his sweaty shoulder. As he walked down the muddy potholed road, surrounded by craggy rocks and sand, his limbs felt so dry he expected sawdust to seep out of them. He stopped, took a drink of water, then shook out his legs and arms. *Arm*, he reminded himself. *Just one.* Even though he was in his late twenties and had lived an entire decade without that long-lost appendage, he still felt the pressure of the phantom limb trying to feign its existence.

The tents of the refugee camp poked out over the horizon. Sam felt a pinch in his gut. *They're hurting again today. Like always.* He closed his eyes for a moment. *Some more deaths last night. Flood damage. More people sick. I feel it.* Though the refugee camp had many volunteers, there still weren't nearly enough people on hand to take care of the fifty thousand displaced persons who struggled to survive inside the camp's borders.

Grimacing, Sam walked around to the back of the camp. He wasn't an *official* volunteer. His name wasn't on any rolls. He didn't get photographed. His fugitive status forced him to keep a low profile, and he used his psychic abilities to ensure that as few people as possible noticed his comings and goings. He'd been volunteering at this particular refugee camp for three years, but it wasn't the first, and it wouldn't be the last. In all of Sam's travels, from country to country, war zone to war zone, he'd seen the way that capitalist greed reached far and wide with its skeletal fingers, always leaving a trail of bodies among the world's most vulnerable populations.

I'll have to pack my bags soon, though. People are starting to recognize me too much. He sighed. *I can't stay much longer. Never can.* Sam walked in the muddy paths between rows of tents, keeping his head low and the bag over his shoulder. A young boy walked by, pushing a wheelbarrow, and looked at Sam with darkened eye sockets. A younger child, whose ribs poked from his chest, lay on his back and played with a broken action figure. A preteen girl on a crutch, missing a leg, looked after a toddler while her mother boiled a pot of water over a campfire. Most of the people he passed were children, and their crowded tents were dirtied and damaged by the recent flooding. The puddles had mostly dried up, leaving baked mud, but the damage was still present. After these people had survived airstrikes, bombs, the murders of their families, the loss of their homes, a flu outbreak, and the paranoid hysteria of governments across the world, the floods had taken away their meager remaining possessions, and still, they had to keep pressing on.

Sam kept walking, waving at those who knew him and handing out cans of food to those whose insatiable hunger throbbed the deepest within him. As he passed by a blue tent, a young nurse named Doto—another volunteer—waved him over.

She exhaustedly wiped the perspiration from her brow with her forearm, avoiding the blood and pus on her glove. "Hi, Sam." She ripped her gloves off.

"Hey, Doto. How's it going?"

"Same shit, different day."

"I hear you." Sam nodded. "Last night, that one kid... Ibrahim. Is he still...?"

Doto shook her head. "No, man. He's done. Awful night."

Sam swallowed bitterly. "And Qamar?"

"So far, she's okay. Dunno about later. Tim's gone too. And Omar isn't doing well either. He's suffering, man. Might die today. His mother asked me to send you his way, to do that... thing you do."

Sam lowered his head, remembering Omar's smile just a few days before. He felt the sting of tears in his eyes, but he didn't cry. Not yet. He still hadn't started his rounds, and there would be plenty of time for crying later.

"Okay, I'll go do that." He put down the bag of food and supplies. "My friend Moussa, a neighbor back at the place I'm staying, asked me to pass these out—"

"I got it." Doto nodded. "Thanks, Sam."

Sam weaved back through the tents, through a mud pit, and stopped at a tent where a skeletal old woman named Aya sat out front, rocking a crying infant. She offered Sam a wan smile as he approached.

"Hey." He crouched beside her and nodded at the tent. "How is Omar?"

Though neither Sam nor the woman spoke a shared language, the woman clasped Sam's hand and, through his psychic gift, understood the meaning of his words. She shook her head.

His health is not good. Sam sighed. "Okay. Let me know if I can bring anything, okay? Food. Medicine. Books or toys, even. Anything I can do." Aya squeezed his hand in appreciation. Then the baby cried, so she returned to rocking her.

Sam crawled inside the tent, which was dark, musty, and smelled of disease. As soon as he entered, a little girl—Ranim—raced up and gave him a huge hug. "Hey, kiddo." Sam hugged her back. "You okay?"

Ranim cried. She pointed to the back, where a bundle of blankets held her skeletal, shivering brother. Sam held her, pushing feelings of comfort and understanding out from within him. *Stay strong, Ranim.*

Once Ranim's heartbeat steadied, Sam proceeded to the back of the tent, where young Omar lay crumpled in a ball, his face and body riddled with cancerous tumors.

Sam sat beside the boy and patted his leg. *Hey, man*, he thought. *I'm here.*

Omar looked up at him with pink infected eyes. Scared eyes. He reached toward Sam, and Sam squeezed his hand. *I'm here.* The pain coursed into him. Sam's flesh burned in the same spots as the boy's tumors. Black spots appeared in his eyes, and sweat ran down his face. The physical pain was worsened by the emotional trauma—the memories of gunfire, bombs, and blood that tore through Omar's childhood—and though Sam felt helpless, he held on to the boy's hand. He never let go. Omar squeezed hard, absorbing Sam's healing electricity for two hours, and finally drifted off to sleep.

92

When the sun went down, Sam caught the next bus back to the village. To his right, the desert sailed past like a silent ocean. Once he'd walked away from the bus stop, the village itself possessed no streetlamps, making the streets pitch-black, so when he looked at the sky, millions of stars lit his way. Dark as it was, he enjoyed this nightly walk. Being alone in the shadows gave him time to release all the aches, pains, and emotional traumas he absorbed every day at the refugee camp, and the stars themselves reminded him of a cascade of rainbow lights he'd once seen in a dream long ago. *Another life.*

As soon as he reached the rickety gates of the apartment he'd been renting, though, a queasy vibe entered his stomach. *Something feels off.*

A shiny black car was parked outside the gate. It was the sort of car that rarely came into the village, and when it did, bad things happened. *I don't like this.* Sam looked around, but no one could be seen or heard other than the distant light and laughter of a bonfire gathering a ways out in the desert. Sam took a deep breath, locked the gate behind him, and crept slowly between the buildings until his apartment came into view.

A man was knocking on Sam's door. Illuminated only by the lights glowing from the neighboring apartment's windows, the man was little more than a black silhouette. Sam cringed. *I hate when people become dark figures.* He focused on the strange man's energies. *Wait, I know him. He's...*

Sam froze. "Not again," he whispered. Beads of sweat ran down his forehead. *I can't let him hurt anyone here. Not my neighbors. No-*

body in the village. No one. The fancy black car suddenly made sense. *All those years of hiding. Running. None of it matters anymore.*

The man knocked on Sam's door again. Sam rushed toward him, and as the shadowed man turned to look, Sam shot a glance through his body. "Don't move!" he shouted.

The man froze in place and gasped for air. "Can't..." He coughed. "Breeeathe..."

The man shakily clutched at his own throat. Sam punched him in the face, knocking him to the dirt. The man slid back, raising his hands in surrender—and sure enough, it was Father. Fake Father. *The one who treated me like a science experiment.*

"Wait!" Father scuttled backward like a beaten puppy. After ten years, his hair had grayed, and his face had become even craggier.

"Why the hell are you here?" Sam squeezed his fists—one real, one phantom—and stood over the cringing man. "You tortured me, held me captive. I was just a kid!"

Through the hazy glow of the neighbor's window, Father squinted in amazement. "My god," he whispered. "It's really you."

Heat spread through Sam's chest. He considered making Father clench his own throat. But the panic in the man's eyes—and in his heart—threw Sam's balance off. *He feels different than he did before.*

"Not here to hurt you," Father choked out, struggling back onto his feet. "Or anyone." Then Father took off his glasses, wiped them, and sighed. His hands were shaking. "I came here to say that I'm sorry, Billy. For everything."

Billy.

Sam trembled. He hadn't heard that name in so long that it felt like a cut being torn open. He tried to respond, but his mouth felt locked shut—*like Billy's mouth used to be*—and he glared instead.

"Billy," Father said, breaking eye contact.

He's terrified of me.

"I owe you an explanation. My actual name is Glenn Watkins. I regret what I did to you. It was wrong. I know that, and I can't fix it. But I can... well, explain."

"Explain." Sam stepped back. His head felt dizzy as distant memories blazed back to life. *I'm not ready for this. Billy. He called me...*

"Back when I was... Father," Glenn said, "I was afraid for my family. Thorne had murdered one of my sons and held the other two captive. If I didn't finish the project, I'd never get to see them again." He looked down. "Or so he said. Truth is, Thorne had killed them, too, without telling me. I didn't know. I'm sorry. All those horrible things I did to you, Billy... they were for nothing."

Sam exhaled. "Why are you here?"

Glenn's mouth opened. He fidgeted with his briefcase. "You're wanted back in the states."

"As a fugitive."

Glenn's brow furrowed. "Are you not on the internet? The news from the US?"

"I don't want to be tracked." Sam shook his head. "Don't want to know. What are you talking about?"

"Good god, son." Glenn laughed in astonishment. "A lot has changed since you disappeared. Your charges were cleared years ago. On the official books, you're dead. But eyewitness accounts about you have popped up for years. Stories about some strange wizard who goes from place to place, healing people's pain. You're an internet hero, even if most of the world thinks you're dead."

Sam's head whirled. *Well, I didn't expect that.* "Ah." *I can't believe this. I'm not a criminal?* "Thorne—he must've—"

"Thorne died in that factory disaster, son. His entire company folded. Criminal charges up the wazoo. Once all the classified documents got out, the emotion bomb project went kaput. Dead. Thorne Century... it's gone, Billy."

Sam snorted. He stared into the flames. *It's gone.* He exhaled deeply. "So... you want me because...?"

Glenn stepped forward, suddenly beaming with confidence. "To be frank? For me, I came here to repent. The person who sent me, though..." He unzipped his briefcase, revealing a stack of papers. "There are still problems in the US, Billy, and because of the experiences you went through—back there, and now around the world—we think you can help." Glenn's eyes softened. "You have no reason to trust me. I get it. But I think you'll want to hear me out."

For a long, tense moment, Sam stared at the man who had once held so much power over him. *He's not that man anymore, though. Maybe he never was.* Sam had grown taller than him. Stronger. *And he's telling the truth. I can feel that in his heart.*

Twitching with nervousness, Sam unlocked the door to his apartment. "Come on. We'll talk over some coffee."

Sam flicked on the lights. Glenn followed nervously then peeked around at Sam's sparsely decorated studio with its cracked walls, rusty plumbing, and lack of air conditioning. The whole place was a single room with very little furniture—just a wobbly computer desk, a stool, and a thin, ratty mattress without a bed frame. Sam gestured Glenn toward the faded cushions on the floor. "Take a seat."

Sam went to the sink, boiled some hot water, and prepared a French press. As he did so, he watched Glenn's reflection in the window and was dismayed to see that the man was staring at the one single picture hung up on the wall—a charred, yellowed drawing of a Medieval knight—that was Sam's most cherished possession. Sam tensed up, feeling protective of the drawing, briefly entertaining the ludicrous fear that Glenn might try to steal it. *That's dumb. Whether he knows the history or not, he wouldn't do that.* Sam pumped the French press, and a coffee-scented waft of steam escaped. Then he poured coffee into two clay mugs, clutched both of their handles in his single shaky hand, and passed one to Glenn. The man nodded appreciatively.

Sam sat across from him. "Cream? Sugar?"

"Sugar's fine, thanks."

Sam pushed the jar over. "So you're telling me"—he swished his mug—"that I got cleared of all charges. That Thorne Century was wiped out. I'm assuming the world knows about my abilities, then?"

"Yep." Glenn took a sip. "Good coffee. Yeah, everyone knows what you are, but there's a lot of skepticism and debate about whether you were the last psychic or if more might be hiding out there. Lots of phonies too. You can imagine. But yes, like I said, all the classified docs got out."

Sam smiled. *It must've been... her.* He was tempted to ask, but even mentioning her name felt dangerous. *Besides, if something bad happened to her because of that, I don't want to know.* "What else has changed?"

Glenn scoffed. "Heck of a lot."

Sam took a drink. *Hmm. I should let it cool down.* He switched on the lamp he used for reading at night. "Tell me."

"Well, you'll be happy to know that whole anti-Jewish law got shut down. Big hubbub. It's now perfectly legal for Jewish people like you to live wherever they want in the US, work wherever they want... they even got a couple Jews in the Senate again."

Glenn looked at him for approval, and Sam nodded. *I've heard about that, at least.*

Then Glenn continued, "Many changes afoot. A new wave of young people getting into politics. This new blood is changing everything, Billy. They're trying to take down some of the megacorporations that popped up in Thorne Century's wake. Managed to get new infrastructure, high-speed rails, and universal healthcare passed. There are still a lot of fights going on, though, especially with immigration." He shook his head. "It's not easy, with the massive corporations fighting back, but these new kids are making progress. Congress sent me to find you. They want your help."

"Congress." *Jeez.*

"Well..." He seesawed his hand. "One particular congressperson, anyhow. I think... hmm." Glenn had another drink and pinched his lips. "Sorry, this is more bitter than I'm used to." He stared into Sam's eyes for a long, pensive moment. "It's so strange to see you... y'know, alive. An adult. All those scars on your face are new, right?"

Sam felt his forehead. "Burns." He touched his cheek. "This one is shrapnel. Nearly died." He displayed the bullet scars on his forearm. "Three years ago, from a war zone." He lifted his shirt, showing even deeper scars on his stomach. "These ones, six years ago. Trying to rescue people from the earthquakes."

Glenn shook his head. "I must say, son, you've been doing some really good things with your abilities."

"Yeah, well, I damn well should be." Sam fidgeted with his hand. "You know, I always liked comics. And there was a writer in the sixties. Jewish guy, like me. Wrote this great line about how with great power comes great responsibility." He shrugged. "I believe that."

"Well, you're definitely making a difference for all those people out there. The eyewitness accounts say—"

"Not enough of a difference," Sam said, shaking his head. "And don't start with that *those people* thing. Don't other them. They're just people. It could've been you or me out there if the wrong bomb dropped. And when I'm out there, I'm sure as hell not fixing the world's problems. Those issues are bigger. Institutional problems. Corruption problems. Capitalism problems. This refugee camp doesn't need me healing people—it needs proper funding. It needs wars to end... it needs countries to let these people come in safely. I'm just putting Band-Aids over gaping wounds inflicted by the world's governments..." He bit his lip, shaking his head. "People are good, Glenn. Deep down. But the world is broken."

"That's why we need you back home, son." Glenn nodded. "To use what you've learned to make bigger institutional changes."

"What can I do?" Sam tapped his cup. "Mind control, sure. But how unethical would that be?"

"Be an advocate and speak up. That's what. I believe there are other psychic kids out there, Billy, and God knows what other corporations might be doing with them. Those same companies are still committing human rights abuses around the world with countless marginalized populations, as you've certainly seen..."

"Yes." He sighed. "I've seen."

"You have firsthand experience. You can be a powerful voice. I'm no psychologist, but I truly believe you'd want to come back if you knew the difference you could make."

"I really doubt I'd *want* to go back." *Sure. My head sure doesn't want to. But my heart does, much as I hate it.*

"Listen." Glenn sipped, pursing his lips at the bitterness. "Can I ask you something, Billy?"

"Sam." *That's what I want to be called.* But talking to this man, he already felt like Billy Jakobek again. All the scars associated with that name had never really left. They'd just been hidden. *Maybe I am Billy.*

"Sam, then," Glenn said. "After all the horrific things you've seen out there, why is it that you still have hope in the human race?"

No, I'm still Billy. Might as well face it. Billy looked down into his clay mug of coffee. He swished it around, and he smiled. "Glenn, have you ever noticed that a cup of coffee is never really perfect?"

Glenn frowned. "Okay."

Billy continued, "Seriously. Think about it. We try to mix it just right. Hot water. Fine ground, coarse ground, maybe cream and sugar. But something's always a little bit off. Too bitter. Too bland. Too weak, strong, whatever."

"Sure," Glenn said, "but, um..."

"Hear me out," Billy said calmly. "Fundamentally, the coffee is always wrong. It always fails. But let me ask you—does this really say anything about the coffee itself? Or does it say something about us?"

Glenn scoffed. "Means we're stupid creatures. Never satisfied."

"Maybe." Billy smelled his coffee. "Maybe our nature dooms us to some eternity of hopelessness, sure. But think about this. Even though every cup of coffee we ever make will be a failure, we keep trying. We never give up."

"Okay."

"Seriously. We fail. Again and again. But we keep trying, keep fighting to create something perfect, whether it's a personal dream or an equal society—all this, even though we know perfection is impossible. As a species, we try to accomplish dreams that we'll never quite see realized, at least, not quite the way we originally imagined them. It's like..."

"Like what, Sam?"

"Call me Billy." He sighed. "And what I mean is, well... achievement comes from failure. From trying, knowing we can't succeed, and trying again." He stirred his coffee. "So yes, I have hope in people. Because even though humanity is flawed, it never stops trying to be better. Every generation is one step closer than the last. There's always a forward thrust. And..." He finally took a drink. "That's why I'm going to spend the rest of my life trying to make a perfect cup of coffee, no matter how impossible my dream might be."

Glenn raised an eyebrow. "What are you trying to explain?"

"The beauty of human failure." Billy grinned. "Isn't that what this is all about?"

93

As Glenn was leaving, he handed Billy a flash drive. "Listen to the audio file on here," Glenn said. "It will explain further."

Billy's stomach lurched. *I feel like I already know what's on there.* He sensed it, and it made his heart chew itself to pieces. When Glenn dropped the flash drive into his hand, it landed like an iron weight.

"Just listen," Glenn said, "and if you still don't want to come back home, well, your choice. But by giving you this, I did my part. You have my number. I've got a plane ticket for you, whenever you're ready. Give me a call."

Billy shrugged. "We'll see."

To his surprise, Glenn's craggy face pulled into a smile. "It's good to see you, Billy." Then Glenn got in his fancy black car and rolled away into the night.

Billy retired to his apartment, but these living quarters felt different now. *Like they belong to someone else. Someone named Sam Miller.* Still revved up from the late-night coffee, he sat down at the desk and took out his laptop.

He studied the flash drive in his palm. "Oh boy," he muttered and plugged it in. The computer beeped. His heart pounded. *No going back now.* The flash drive contained a single audio file, titled BILLY_1.mp3.

Billy rubbed his scruffy chin. *Jeez, this is scary.* After a few moments, the screen flicked off. He touched the mouse, relighting the screen, but still didn't click the audio file. His hand shook, and his phantom stump twitched, trying to reach out and do what the living hand wouldn't. Finally, he right-clicked the file and examined its properties. It was forty-five minutes long. *Oy vey.* He turned up the volume, swallowed, and clicked. The media player popped up. *Here we go...*

The speakers buzzed, and a female voice—*her* voice—broke through the noise. She sounded older, more weathered than he remembered, but instantly recognizable. Tears stung his eyes.

"Hey, you," Natalia said. "So, I guess I've never let you go."

94: Billy Jakobek

The airplane slammed to the ground. The wings shuddered. Billy's sleeping head bumped into the window. As the plane slowly wrapped around the runway like a steel serpent, a scratchy voice blared from the intercom. "Hello, passengers! Temperature in Johnson City, Olakhota, is a cool forty-two degrees, with rain and fog. Wear a jacket! We hope you've had a nice flight, and—oh, before I forget, welcome to the United States!"

Billy rubbed his stinging eyes and cleared his throat of the mucus that had settled there. *Welcome back, buddy.* The air conditioner blasted down at him, matting his hair to his forehead. As the other passengers turned on their phones, stood up, and gathered their bags from the overhead compartments, their emotions flew into Billy's chest. *Americans are always in such a rush. Their thoughts, emotions, everything. Jeez.*

Billy, though, took his time, trying to process the weirdness of returning to the place that had banished him and feeling like a stranger. The climate outside looked every bit as dreary as the pilot's announcement. *Johnson City. The United States. Home. Like that means anything to me anymore.* Of all the places he'd been in the last ten years, this already felt the least comfortable. However, the more he thought about it, the more he realized that his increasing nervousness had nothing to do with his location.

I'm not ready to see Natalia again. That's the problem.

He fidgeted with his seat belt. Hearing her voice had been strange enough. Learning that his first girlfriend had grown to become a celebrated congresswoman—a political activist who regularly made headlines for her blunt style and her human-centric proposals—only made things more surreal. The thing that truly weirded him out, though, was the emotion in her audio message. *She missed me as much as I missed her.* He shook his head. *It's like we've been up on that fire tower all these years.*

The other passengers shuffled off the plane. He remained seated. *Procrastinating.* He brushed off his shirt—he wore a plain black T-shirt, just like he used to as a teenager—and looked at the empty seat next to him. The image of Bubbe, alive in his mind if not in reality, smiled at him. "Hello, little one."

"Hey, Bubbe," he said. It wasn't the real Tzeitel Shulz, of course. *Or maybe it is—I don't know.* But she came to him from time to time, and he didn't care if the other passengers thought he was talking to a hallucination or not.

The old woman frowned. "You're scared."

"Yes." He shrugged.

"This girl." She poked him in the chest. "She asked you to come, yes?"

He stared out at the other passengers and sighed. "I know." He unbuckled his seat belt. "But what if it goes badly? I mean, I never... you know..."

"You never stopped loving her. Right. Of course." Bubbe grinned. "Well, perhaps it will go nicely, meeting again?" She raised an eyebrow. "That also scares you, yes? Having someone you care about on that level, someone who knows you, the real you, like no one else does."

Billy looked down. "Guess so. I'm afraid of putting down roots. I feel like that might happen. She could get hurt by everything inside me—"

"She's an independent woman, Billy. She makes her own choices, and she's taking a chance by reaching out to you. Because she wants to," Bubbe said, rubbing the numbers tattooed on her wrist. "Don't forget that."

Billy smiled tentatively. His stomach fluttered. He was still hours away from seeing her. Even after he got off the plane, he would have to catch a shuttle ride to Heaven's Hole, and that terribly winding road stood out vividly in his memory. *But the moment's getting closer. However it goes, it'll happen soon.*

He stared into Bubbe's kind dark eyes. "They say you can't go home again."

"You can't, no, never." She hugged him. "But if you keep your mind open, you can always find a new home inside the old one."

95

After hours of riding a cramped shuttle bus through cold white mountains, Billy saw the crater of Heaven's Hole glowing from below like a golden beacon. The fire tower blinked above it all, steady and unchanged. Despite himself, Billy smiled. *Weird. Thought I'd be having a panic attack. Instead, I'm feeling nostalgic.* As the shuttle dipped down roads that were no longer potholed, Billy was startled by how different everything looked—and by his own growing excitement. While the overall landscape of concrete housing remained unchanged, broken windows no longer dotted the streets. The buildings, walls, and sidewalks were lined with breathtaking rainbow-colored graffiti displays. Bus stops had become centerpieces for abstract, surrealistic sculptures that—to Billy's amazement—commemorated the town's rebellion against Thorne Century. Everything was colorful.

The shuttle stopped in downtown. Billy hiked his bag over his shoulder, stepped out into the cold mountain air, and took a deep breath. "Thanks for the ride," he called to the driver, who smiled back. *The vibe is so good here. People are happy in this place.* As his fellow passengers met with their families, he checked the clock. *An hour early. Cool. I have time to walk around.* He rounded the street corner, where a bearded teenager in a dusty coat and fedora played a five-string banjo in front of a small Tupperware bowl. Billy dropped some money into it. "Keep it up, man."

The teen bowed flamboyantly and tipped his hat. His T-shirt displayed Congresswoman Natalia Gonzalez's face in bright colors with the caption Badass.

Billy did a double take. "Wow, is that...?"

The teenager pointed at his shirt. "This?" He grinned. "C'mon, dude, that chick is awesome. Fights for us." He revealed a Vote Gonzalez button on his jacket as well. "She's the one who brought this town back to life, y'know?"

"I believe it." Billy shook his head, laughing to himself, and walked away. *You're telling me, kid. I always knew she was a badass.* He strolled through the neighborhood, increasingly astounded by everything he saw. The blighted industrial town of the past had become a vibrant arts community with graffiti displays worthy of a museum. Far from the town being gentrified, culture was everywhere. Walking through the small downtown area alone, he passed restaurants advertising Guatemalan, Honduran, Cambodian, Eritrean, and Venezuelan dishes. *So many options.* There were local gift shops. Local food stores. Art galleries. Hostels. Coffee shops. Farther from the center of town were an assisted-living facility and a homeless shelter. The high school was totally renovated. *Not a Thorne Century logo in sight. Love it.*

He stopped at a newspaper stand, where a headline proclaimed: *MAYOR NAZARI ANNOUNCES NEW AFFORDABLE HOUSING ON THE WAY.* From the front page, a bearded Mr. Nazari—now with deepened crow's-feet and white hair—smiled back at him. In the article, the teacher-turned-mayor thanked Congresswoman Gonzalez for her assistance.

Hey, that's great! Billy gleefully flipped through the paper, and a smaller story announced the opening of the Best Grinds Café, a third-wave coffee shop managed by—he read it twice to let it sink in—Felix Kabongo and Paul Vieux. *That's awesome, guys.*

Light rainfall washed the streets. As Billy progressed to the more rural part of town, he came upon the familiar brick structure that had previously been Thorne Century Groceries. His legs shuddered beneath him. *I remember this.* He walked into the parking lot, recalling the horrible visions he'd experienced there. *The shooting. Crazy*

Old Darrell. The Shape. The scars on his body—both physical and emotional—stung anew, and he considered turning away. *This place is a graveyard. I... wait.*

He looked again. The windows were lit up. "Huh," he muttered.

He approached the building. Warm energies emanated from its brick walls. *This isn't Thorne Century Groceries anymore.* He kept pushing closer then broke into a run, past the cars in the parking lot and right to the heavy wooden front doors. Music hummed from inside. Chanting. A song he recognized. *Please be real.*

The Thorne Century logos were gone. Instead, the wooden doors were emblazed with a Star of David. Hebrew lettering identified the synagogue as Temple Beth Shalom.

"No way," he whispered as a smile spread across face. He closed his eyes, listened to the music—*I feel it. It's in my blood*—and touched the door handle. In that brass fixture, he felt the energies of all the Jews who now called Temple Beth Shalom their spiritual home. Children. Parents. The elderly. "This place is alive again."

"Yeah." A female voice laughed behind him. "Had a feeling I'd find you here."

He grinned so hard his cheeks hurt. *Oh, man.* His heart raced in his chest.

"A bunch of the former Beth Shalom population moved here," the unseen woman continued, coming closer. "Inspired by your story, I guess. They have a plaque in there, honoring you. They've been writing me for years to try to get you back." Her voice softened. "Not that I wasn't trying like hell to find you, anyway."

Billy's grin stretched even tighter. *That's her.* Billy opened his eyes, and slowly—shivering so much he barely could stand—he turned around to stare into the equally nerve-racked grin of Natalia Gonzalez Rodriguez, Olakhota congresswoman, sitting in her wheelchair behind him. Her gray dress coat and short, professional hair were speckled with rain. She had more crinkles around her eyes than he remembered, much like he did, but her smile hadn't changed whatsoever.

"Hey." She rolled forward. "There's my dark-eyed boy."

Billy looked down then nervously peeked up again. His legs were shaking. "Well." He laughed. "There's Congresswoman Gonzalez."

Rain pitter-pattered onto them. Billy stepped toward her, panic clenching his lungs—echoing the fear he'd felt that first time she'd sat across from him in the high school cafeteria—and to his amazement, he saw their history etched in every line of her face. *The fire tower.* Her eyes flickered. *The cabin. Dancing in the parking lot.*

"I thought I'd never see you again," she said, blinking back tears.

Billy dropped to his knees before the wheelchair. "Natalia." He beamed. "Natalia! I can't believe you're real."

She laughed. "Yeah, I'm real." She wiped her eyes then wiped them again. "Seriously, man. It took me so ridiculously long to find your ass. I tried not to. I tried to let you go. But you were always in the back of my mind, and once you were cleared of charges, I kept hoping that one day, I'd... you'd... whatever." She again brushed tears from her eyes. "God, I'm a crying mess. Great."

"Mess? You're a legend, Natalia. I mean—" He stood up, pointing back at the town. "Wow! Look at what this place has become! It's like you took the same attitude that people like Thorne complained about and brought it to Washington, where you just make spectacular things happen—"

"Oh, stop." She waved a hand. "Do you know how many policy battles I've got coming up later this week? This Washington stuff is painful, man. But yeah, me and the other newbies have done some good." She ran a finger down her wheel. "Still a long way to go, though. Immigration issues, human rights... your help would really be appreciated. Your voice could be so influential in—"

"I'm down," Billy said. "I want to be involved."

She flicked the hair from her brown eyes. "I hoped you'd feel that way." More tears emerged. "God, Billy. I've missed you. I've kept so busy I don't usually have time to even think about it, but..."

"I've missed you too." Billy knelt beside her. Her feelings rushed into him. *I never stopped thinking about you either.* She smiled, and he smiled back. *Never. Not even once.* "There's a lot of work to do with this refugee situation, for one," Billy said. "The place I just came from needs massive funding. That's a priority. People here don't understand what it's like out there. Media attention would help—"

"I agree, and we'll do that, but let's talk about this stuff later today, okay? I haven't seen you in ten years, Billy, and I've got something to show you." She swerved her wheelchair forward, rolling past the synagogue, and called back, "Follow me!"

Billy scratched his head, but as she whizzed away into the rain, he followed. *Still the same girl.* He rushed to catch up—stopping for just a moment to listen to the singing inside the synagogue again—and followed her to the forested landing behind the building, lit by streetlamps. The wide, crystalline expanse of Solitaire Lake opened up before them. Natalia hit the brakes—right next to the oaken bench they had sat together on all those years before—and parked. She looked back at him with a sly expression. "Remember this place?"

Billy sat beside her, dazed by his surroundings. *This feels like a dream.* He touched the wet bench, feeling all the new carvings. *New memories. New kids. Another new generation.* Then he looked up and was crestfallen to see the skeletal remains of the Thorne Century factory still standing there, burned, blackened, but not demolished. Billy shivered. "I hate that it's still there."

"Me too. How about we change that?" She reached into her jacket and handed him a smartphone. "One for you." She took out another phone. "One for me."

He took the phone, confused. It had a red slider button displayed on the screen, labeled Detonate. "I don't get it."

"See that hellhole out there?" She gestured toward the shattered remains of the Thorne Century factory. *Ghosts.* "Billy, there are explosives strapped all over that place. Big project underway. It's finally coming down." She smiled—far more shyly than he was used to from her—and pointed at the buttons on both of their screens. "The plan is to replace it with affordable housing. Mr. Nazari wants to call it the Jakobek Center if you're okay with that."

"I mean... ah." He looked at the factory, and a shiver ran down his spine. He imagined a new building standing in its place. *Wow, they want to name it after me?* "Can you give it a different name?"

"Nope." She leaned close. "Okay, truth is, the Jakobek Center has been under contract for a while, and the name... honestly, everybody thought you were dead. Not me. I always had hope. And y'know, after all those nightmares you had about exploding this place and everything Thorne did to you..." She shrugged. "I always hoped that it could be both of us who finally blew this place up someday. The fact that you finally turned up right when it's time to legitimately blow it up, well..."

Billy reeled. "Destiny." A smile came to his face. "Fulfilling those old visions. Heh."

"Nah, more like giving those visions the finger, if you ask me." She pointed at the screen again then looked up at the darkening clouds. "Everyone is ready on your mark, but the weather isn't looking so awesome, so we'd better move fast, or we'll have to reschedule. The question is, are you ready?"

He gazed upon the wrecked factory. He thought back to the nights in the dark tank. The blood that had been harvested from his body. The experiments. The children who had been turned into batteries. The pain that Thorne's work had inflicted on so many around the world. *I love that they're turning it into affordable housing. Thorne would loathe that.*

"I'm ready," he said.

She grinned. "Go."

They pressed their buttons.

Boom! Explosions rocked the factory. The middle sections came down first. *Big boom.* Windows shattered. Billy held his breath as a cloud of dust and debris rose from the wreckage. The smokestacks toppled. Far away, the sound of distant cheering from an audience surrounding the factory broke into the air.

"And the crowd goes wild!" Natalia cried with tears of joy in her eyes. Another blast rocked the highest tower. *Crash!* The last smokestack tumbled inward. The distant crowd roared.

Billy squeezed his fist with excitement. *I'm free. It's finally done.*

Natalia reached for him. "Hold me?"

He clasped her hand. "Always," he said as electricity surged between them. *Warmth. Passion. Strength. God, Natalia, I've missed you.* As the factory toppled, they weaved into each other's souls. The outside world faded. Their memories came alive. Natalia hurtled through Billy's recollections of the refugee camps and war zones while Billy zoomed in on everything she'd been through. He saw her sitting at a desk, writing a proposal. *Long nights. Loneliness. Constant media scrutiny. But you never gave up, did you? You always kept fighting.* He watched her giving speeches to Congress, doing interviews, visiting detention centers and prisons, raising funds for families in need, and fighting back against those in power every time she could. *You're going to keep doing that. Even as you get tired. Even when you lose battles. You'll never stop fighting because that's who you are. And I love that person. I want to fight with that person.*

They raced back in time. The years receded. It was like they were kids again, standing on that fire tower, the whole world before them.

"I never let you go either," Billy whispered, putting his arm around her. The Thorne Century factory was gone. Only dust remained.

"Billy, I have to admit something. My feelings, they still... um..." She looked down. "I still—"

The sky cracked with lightning. The clouds tore apart, spilling buckets of rain upon Solitaire Lake. Billy leaned back, opening himself to the sky, and as he laughed, Natalia laughed with him. Rain washed over them, drenching their clothes. The water washed away their pains, their tragedies, and their losses, like a mikvah from the sky, and they were reborn. Thunder rumbled. Lightning struck again.

Natalia laughed with Billy, wiped her hair out of her eyes, and shouted over the weather, "Billy Jakobek, I love you! Okay? I love you!"

He leaned over her chair, and her eyes softened. He smiled. "I love you too." He kissed her.

She grabbed his head and pulled him closer. Hot energy raced between them. Their heartbeats connected. A cascade of lights—the cheering populace of the town around them—rushed into their bodies as their souls tied together. *It's like we never stopped kissing all those years ago. Like we've always been here. Right here. Right now.*

Her wet hands wrapped around his ears. "Don't you ever leave again, mister. You got that? You're with me now." Her lips tightened. "Promise?"

Billy beamed at Natalia, memorizing every curve of her face. "Promise." His heart pounded. "Listen, Natalia, I think this is it. The time we always talked about."

Lightning ruptured the sky again. She wiped her eyes. "What?"

"We've met again." He seesawed his head. "The world, well, it looks awfully explosive—"

"Yes!" Her eyes lit up. "Absolutely."

Billy reached toward her, past the falling rain, past the lost years, and into the future. Their fingers interlaced. Applause roared in the distance. Music played in the streets. Everyone in the city rejoiced, not letting the rain hold them back.

Billy and Natalia never looked away from each other. *We're here again. Tomorrow. The next day.* Their mouths met, they kissed, and they didn't let go.

They held hands as the world exploded around them.

Acknowledgements

No story is written in a void. No writer truly works alone. While I've been developing *Knight in Paper Armor* for years, and it's as close to my heart as a book could be, I can't forget to mention the many people who helped me along the way to the finish line.

First, being Jewish myself and the descendant of both Ashkenazic refugees from Russia and Sephardic refugees who fled from the Spanish Inquisition, I want to acknowledge my ancestors, their struggles against prejudice, and their history, which lives so deeply in every line of this book and in every day of my life. Without them, I would not exist. I also want to acknowledge the small number of Holocaust survivors whom I have been lucky enough to meet, listen to, and learn from.

Next, I want to thank my cultural sensitivity beta readers, particularly Alejandra Prego and Carolina Blackman, who were an amazing help in regard to establishing Natalia's cultural background, making the book more accurate, and catching my errors (which, of course, included correcting my Spanish!). I also want to thank Lynn and everyone at Red Adept Publishing, my favorite publishing company, for giving me the opportunity to bring this book to the world. An extra thanks to my editors, Jessica Anderegg and Sarah Carleton, for their outstanding insight, suggestions, and fine-tuning. You guys are amazing.

I can't forget to thank everyone in my family—both by blood and by friendship, the living ones and the departed—for always supporting my dreams. That additionally goes for my daughter, Zaharina, who certainly wasn't yet born when I first started working on this book but was just as certainly grinning at me and watching with those little dark eyes of hers by the time I finished. Finally, a special shout-out to my wife, Veronica. From my earliest conceptual notes about *Knight in Paper Armor* until these final drafts finally became solidified, she has been there for me—with her trademark brand of enthusiasm, brilliance, and passion—through every stage of the book's creation.

A final note: we all share the same world. We're all in this together. No matter what, we should do the best we can to take care of each other.

- Nicholas Conley

Also by Nicholas Conley

Pale Highway
Intraterrestrial
Knight in Paper Armor

Watch for more at www.nicholasconley.com/main/.

About the Author

Originally from California, Nicholas Conley has currently made his home in the colder temperatures of New Hampshire. He considers himself to be a uniquely alien creature with mysterious literary ambitions, a passion for fiction, and a whole slew of terrific stories he'd like to share with others.

When not busy writing, Nicholas is an obsessive reader, a truth seeker, a sarcastic idealist, a traveler, and — like many writers — a coffee addict.

Read more at www.nicholasconley.com/main/.

About the Publisher

Dear Reader,

We hope you enjoyed this book. Please consider leaving a review on your favorite book site.

Visit https://RedAdeptPublishing.com to see our entire catalogue.

Don't forget to subscribe to our monthly newsletter to be notified of future releases and special sales.